MARTIN A

THE REICHENBACH PROBLEM

A NOVEL

LION FICTION

Published by Lion Fiction
an imprint of
Lion Hudson plc
Wilkinson House, Jordan Hill Road,
Oxford OX2 8DR, England
www.lionhudson.com/fiction

ISBN 978 1 78264 016 5
e-ISBN 978 1 78264 017 2

First edition 2013

A catalogue record for this book is available from the British Library

Printed and bound in the UK, February 2013, LH26

To Maggie, Emma and James with love

Author note: This is a work of fiction. While it uses certain facts about Conan Doyle's background, it does not purport to be an accurate historical record of all the events occurring in his life at the time this story is set.

ACKNOWLEDGMENTS

I am very grateful to:

The estimable Ali Hull for her help, support, enthusiasm and expertise. I am so glad we have finally found a project we can work together on. Sorry for the split infinitive. Sheila Jacobs and Jessica Tinker for their encouragement and invaluable editing skills. Ken Baldry, for guiding me, A. C. D. and Father Vernon safely over the Eigerjoch. Surrey County Cricket Club, for their indispensable assistance and excellent archive.

And finally, I am most particularly grateful to Arthur Conan Doyle, for the years of delight he has given me and countless others. Although this book is a work of fiction, I have attempted to include as many aspects of his life and work as possible. In doing so, I hope I have been faithful to the spirit and genius of the man, even if I have been forced to take liberties with the facts once in a while. Making the facts fit the case? I can hear Sherlock harrumph over my shoulder even now!

"Off abroad again, are we, doctor?"

"Yes, I'm visiting some friends in Vienna, then on Saturday I shall be travelling overnight to Zürich and on to a village near Interlaken."

"Oh, very nice. Switzerland. I've heard it's most invigorating."

"So I understand. I have never been there before."

"Nice little holiday for you, then, doctor. I'll just pop the valise and the trunks on the four-wheeler and we'll be off. Waterloo, is it, sir?"

"Waterloo, please, yes."

ONE

I was still not quite sure when, exactly, my disinclination towards people began. I know, though, that it had a great deal to do with the bane of my life – the great Mr Sherlock Holmes.

I suppose, at mid-morning on a Sunday, if I had wanted to get away from people, Zürich Station was not the ideal place. It was teeming with humanity. The only good thing about it was that it was summer, so everybody was bustling about with less luggage and lighter clothing. A small benefit, but nevertheless evident, as it made my journey through this human torrent marginally less difficult.

I had spent the first three days in Vienna with the friends Touie and I had met when I was studying ophthalmology there. My family was unable to accompany me. Mary, our daughter, was still very young; it was Touie, though, who insisted I go. We were expecting our second child, and Touie herself was not in the best of health. Gentle, sweet, kind Touie, who endured my restlessness, coped with my bouts of depression, and watched me struggle with my preoccupations. Now I was on the way to reconnoitre Switzerland. It was our hope that we may come here for the summer next year. I had heard good things about the country, not least from our friends, yet was determined to ensure everything was satisfactory before I risked my very young family's health and well-being on a sojourn abroad.

I had other motives as well, however.

I waded the stream of humankind and followed the porter with his barrow, wheeling my trunks, onto the platform where the train for Interlaken stood steaming quietly to itself.

It was an indulgence, I know, but I had decided to travel First Class; after all, I had begun to harvest a semblance of an income from my stories. My need to avoid as much of humanity as possible on this occasion necessitated it. Rarely would the carriages I would travel in be full. In addition, even if there were other occupants, we, as a class, would keep ourselves to ourselves. In the frame of mind I had, this was very much a mercy, and one I would jealously guard.

I was well aware that Sherlock Holmes had already brought me a degree of fame and fiscal comfort. It would be churlish of me to begrudge him the beneficial effect he'd had on my, and my family's, life. However, with that fame or, I would prefer, notoriety, I had lost any privacy I had ever had. I was no longer able to walk along the street in Norwood without one wag or other nudging his or her companion and crying out, "Ho – Conan Doyle! Elementary, my dear Watson!" or some such witticism. Of course, not everybody in the world recognized me. However, Norwood was a small suburban community and, even thus removed from London, people had seen my picture in the press, or on a fly-poster, or in a bookshop window.

It had been suggested to me that my splendid moustache was the primary identifying feature and that perhaps, if I were that concerned, I might shave it off. However, I resented the notion that public pressure of any sort might force me to change any aspect of my personality or appearance.

It would be rare, therefore, for me not to be accosted by someone or other at least twice a day, every day of the week – on the street, in a restaurant, on the train. This had gone on for a number of months. It was starting to affect Touie, too. After nearly a year of being pointed at, leered over and laughed behind, the novelty of celebrity had begun to pall in the Conan Doyle household.

Switzerland, at least, offered me respite. I didn't know it and, more importantly, it didn't know me. I pushed my valise up onto the leather webbing luggage rack above my head, and settled back onto the seat cushions. I turned off the lamp beside my left ear and, with a long, lingering sigh, closed my eyes. Less than five minutes later, I sensed that activity had increased outside. There was a sound of people bustling, one or two were running, and others were calling to one another. I opened my eyes. A porter hurried past, followed by a large lady in a large hat in which appeared to nestle a complete pheasant. Then came the sound I was waiting to hear, the guard's whistle. Looking out of my compartment window across the corridor on the platform side, I was startled a moment later to discover a pair of grey eyes looking straight back in at me. These were lodged beneath a bowler hat and set in a lean, lightly tanned face that had a few days' stubble on the chin. It was a young man who, apparently, had been jogging along the platform and had hesitated for a moment outside my window. Just as quickly as our eyes had met, they separated; he had averted his, and had recommenced his pressing trot along the platform.

The guard blew his whistle again, this time with a degree more urgency, and the action of slamming doors and calling out became general. This was immediately followed by a familiar sequence. A long loud blast on the train's whistle, a great huff of pent-up energy being expressed by the locomotive, and a series of judders and clanks. About thirty yards ahead of me, great pistons were bearing down on huge wheels, forcing them to obtain purchase on the iron rails and overcome the inertia created by ton upon ton of, up until that moment, lifeless metal and wood; hopefully thereby dragging me and this whole miracle of man's ingenuity on towards Interlaken.

Good, I remember thinking, *I have the carriage to myself*. I looked again out onto the platform, only to discover my view interrupted by a charcoal grey woollen waistcoat. A man was standing in the corridor, blocking my view, lurching as the train lurched and gathered speed. Then he leaned back, clasped the handle of the compartment door and drew it open. I barely managed to conceal my irritation that, at the last moment, my splendid isolation was going to be ruined by a companion for at least part of the journey.

The man, who was the same as the one who had looked in at me, flung his travelling bag onto the luggage rack. He then flung himself onto the seat diagonally across from mine. He let out a long whistle, followed by a whoosh of air, suggesting that he was pleased with himself and that he wanted me, for some reason, to know this. I had closed my eyes the moment I had realized the intruder was intent on settling in my compartment. The noises he made, which practically echoed the locomotive's on coming to life, caused me to open one eye and look across at him.

He was looking at me.

"Full," he said, and jerked his grizzled chin in the general direction of the rest of the train.

"First Class," I replied, and jerked my head at the golden numeral 1, painted on the window beside me.

"I know." He grinned and shrugged. "I'll have to pay extra, I imagine. Oh well, I suppose it will be worth it." There was a pause, and then, "English?"

"Irish," I growled, just to be difficult. It seemed to hold him. I could have said Scots if I'd preferred. I had spent most of my life in England, but was of Irish stock, and had been born in Edinburgh.

We sat in silence for a while, watching central Zürich pirouette away from us through our respective windows while drawing into view row upon row of the terraced cottages which comprised the city's immediate suburbs. I can think of no better experience than sitting on a comfortable train watching a grimy city loosen its grip on me, and allow its huddled suburbs usher me into the lush countryside.

I swam up and out of my thoughts and, once again, noticed those keen grey eyes contemplating me. I knew what was coming next.

"You're Doyle, aren't you? Sherlock Holmes and all that."

I tried to bluff it out.

"That's what a lot of people think," I replied.

He laughed. It was a nervous laugh. "Oh, very good. Yes. I wouldn't imagine you're very fond of people accosting you all the time. That's a very clever answer you have worked out there. To people who aren't sure, it can mean 'no – I'm not' and they back away; to those who are sure, and persist, well – you haven't lied to them, have you?" He paused and gave me a grin, which I supposed he intended to suggest complicity; to sympathize with what we celebrities had to put up with; to let me know that he wasn't any common-or-garden member of the public. To reassure me that I could, even, rely on him to be a species of intimate. A friend, perhaps.

They were the worst type.

"I don't blame you for being coy," he continued. "It must be an awful bore to have people recognizing you wherever you go and making a fuss..."

"Yes, it is," I responded.

He didn't take the hint. He looked out across the row upon row of low roofs curling past the window and continued, "... no – I don't blame you. Utter wretches they must be." He considered my plight a moment longer and then spat out his conclusion: "Why don't they just leave you alone?"

There was, I felt, no answer to that.

A further silence held us, for which I was grateful. Eventually, assuming the conversation – if one could call it that – had ended, I reached down my newspaper from my valise, shook it into a readable shape, and began to scan the inside pages. It was a five-day-old *London Times*. I had bought it at Newhaven just before boarding the steamer to Dieppe, and had dipped into it ever since; savouring every paragraph as if it were my last. It would be some time before my Swiss hotel may supply me with an English newspaper – if they were able to – and, even then, it would most probably be a week out of date at the very least.

I found I was unable to concentrate on the words, however. Generally, I am a traveller who likes best of all just to sit and stare out of the window. Many hours can pass by satisfactorily in this way, I have found. I have even come to the conclusion that time itself takes on a different form when travelling. It is as though the faster one travels, the quicker it seems to pass. The main reason, though, for my sitting and staring at the scenery is that it allows me space to think. In the hurly-burly of my London and literary existence, I rarely get the opportunity to think. I imagine it is the reason I try to get away so often.

The newspaper, on this occasion, therefore, was simply a screen. I found, though, that it wasn't working. My companion's presence was distracting, and it was very galling. After a few minutes of trying to read and failing miserably, I lowered the broadsheet and laid it on the seat cushion beside me. Inadvertently, by doing so, I found myself glancing across at the young man again. He was observing me. How long he had been doing so, I could not estimate. There was one occasion, among many such incidents, in one of the dining rooms at the Langham, when a young woman at another table found that she could not take her eyes off me. I am not that fascinating. It was most disturbing to be scrutinized while eating, as though I were an exhibit. She at least had the courtesy to apologize on her way out at the end of her meal. I put it down, therefore, to the fascination of celebrity, which it was, of course. I wondered then, as I did now, whether I would not have been the same, as a younger man, should I have chanced across Stevenson or James or Poe in a restaurant. The thought of that young woman, and her flustered apology, to an extent gave me pause. I had hardened my heart towards someone I didn't even know. In truth, I had hardened it towards the general public as a whole of late. Yet it was not their fault. It was not his fault. It was Sherlock Holmes's fault.

"Beautiful day," I ventured, but not with any real warmth.

"Beautiful." He continued to look out of the window. I could see, even from the angle at which I was sitting, that he had allowed himself a smile. As if he were bucked that I had spoken to him of my own volition.

"Have you visited Switzerland before?"

"No, never." He turned to face me.

"Neither have I. Although I am led to understand it is all beautiful – once you get out of the cities."

He looked again out of the window. We were starting to break out and into a stretch of scenery that featured rising land, meadows and the occasional meandering burn. "Charming," he breathed.

This little exchange had enabled me to observe my travelling companion more closely. He was about ten years younger than me, in his early twenties, and reasonably presentable. His tan was new, like mine, and he was unshaven. He had an underlying nervous energy about him that reminded me of when I was his age; that fidgety, driving will to get on in the world, frustrated by lack of experience and opportunities for preferment. Most interesting, to my mind, were his clothes. The bowler hat, now perched on the cushion beside him, the waistcoat, the city boots and the grey worsted suit all spoke to me of a bank clerk or an office worker rather than a gentleman tourist. Young men of limited means rarely have sufficient funds for a truly comprehensive travelling wardrobe, but there was that in his whole aspect which told me that he was not in Switzerland for his health. Grudgingly, for I wished it were otherwise, I allowed my curiosity to get the better of me.

"Are you travelling far?" I asked.

"Don't know," he replied. His conversation had descended into the familiar rather too precipitously for my liking.

"Don't know?" I echoed, despite myself. I had not intended to interrogate the fellow.

"Haven't decided yet," he explained. "Sort of spur of the moment thing, really."

"Ah," I responded.

Not married, then, perhaps. Certainly his outer clothes and his shirt were crumpled; his collar unstarched. What wife would allow a husband to journey in such a state? Not that that was any proof, either way, but it did not, at least, disprove my view.

"Where are you going?" he enquired.

I told him.

"Where's that?"

"High in the mountains. In the middle of nowhere, really. The air is cleaner, the sun is brighter and the world is quieter. Fresh, green meadows all around, yet just a short march away, the snow

13

line and then the Eiger, the Mönch and the Jungfrau – among the highest peaks in Europe."

He was impressed, possibly by the fact that I had been so expansive after having been so taciturn; some may say brusque. For my part, I was perturbed at my own talkativeness. It was not my habit to wax lyrical in the company of strangers. Yet there was an aspect about the man that had drawn it out of me.

I think it was loneliness.

Either his or mine, I couldn't be sure.

After a few moments he nodded, slapped his hands firmly down on his knees, as if he had just won an argument, and declared, "That's decided, then. That's where I'm going, too."

I was appalled. To have this chap accompany me all the way, and then to have him bumping into me at every turn, to bore into me with his grey eyes across every restaurant, was too much. The village I was going to was tiny; we couldn't fail to encounter one another every day.

"You haven't the right clothing…" I blurted out. It was all I could think of.

"No, you're right. Thanks," he replied gratefully, as if I had given him a traveller's exclusive insight. "I'll buy some when I get there."

"So, what have you got in your luggage?" I asked, or rather demanded to know.

"Not much. Just a few bits. Thrown together. Left in a rush." He shrugged and looked up at the luggage rack above his head. I glared up there as well, as if it were the bag's fault. The case appeared brand new and it wasn't English. Swiss, perhaps; possibly French. I couldn't quite establish the maker's name, embossed on the leather strap, from across the compartment, but there was a *de* or a *de la* in it.

This man was a conundrum. Was he running away from someone? If so, whom? And, more importantly, why?

"You do have a passport, don't you?" Again, I was unable to prevent my curiosity from getting the better of me. Or maybe I was

14

hoping he didn't have one, and would have to get off at the next station to return from whence he had come, and retrieve it.

"Oh yes," he replied, patting his breast pocket, "and money."

At least he wasn't going to try to touch me for a few francs. And that wasn't an idle concern of mine. Famous authors are not immune from the occasional begging letter.

At that moment, the guard arrived to examine our travel documents. I showed him mine and was saluted for my trouble. Negotiations were then entered into between the official and the young man, regarding his potentially unauthorized occupation of a First Class seat. Much to my further disappointment, a deal was struck. Monies changed hands, and a contract of travel or *billet de voyage* was written out and handed across.

The guard, a gaunt fellow with a bristling moustache, straight back and crisp, sharp creases to his uniform, advised us of the time at which lunch may be taken in the dining car. He spoke German, which I understood as I had spent two years in Austria, studying medicine and, a few years prior to that, at school in Vienna. He touched the peak of his claret and gold *käppi* with the tips of his fingers once more, backed out of the compartment, like a cuckoo returning into its clock, and slid the door shut.

A few moments passed as we both sat and listened to the steel wheels clattering on the rails. Then the young man began to fidget. He was building up to a further remark, I was sure of it.

"Do you mind if I smoke?" he ventured at last.

"Not at all," I replied. "In fact, I think I'll join you."

He had started to pat at his pockets, presumably looking for his smoking materials. "I suppose you enjoy the occasional pipe?" he said, while continuing to rummage.

"I do, yes," I returned, producing the item in question, followed by my sealskin tobacco pouch, a Vesta case and my pipe knife. "How did you guess?"

"I just imagined that since Holmes did, you did," he replied, eventually producing a packet of Three Castles.

"Ah – Holmes," I remarked; primarily to myself.

The satisfaction on his face at having discovered the whereabouts of his cigarettes soon reverted to a frown as he revisited his pockets and, one by one, began to turn them inside out.

I embarked on the complex, painstaking, yet ultimately satisfying procedure of the cleaning, rubbing, filling and tamping that is an essential element in the pipe smoker's ritual. Halfway through this process, filling the bowl with a mixture of Virginia, Burley and Black Cavendish in a medium loose cut, I noticed that he was just watching me with a rather forlorn look on his face. A moment later, I realized why. I tossed him the Vesta case.

"Thanks." He popped a cigarette in his mouth, took out a match and scratched it along the red sandpaper glued to the side of the box. The little stick of wood fizzed and flared and, hidden momentarily behind a cloud of sulphur, he lit up.

He tossed the box back to me, which I was glad to catch neatly with my right hand. There is nothing more undignified than an allegedly proficient cricketer and goalkeeper scrabbling down on the carpet for a spilled box of Vestas.

Soon we were both puffing away in, for me, welcome silence; he edgily on his Three Castles, I leisurely on my Kapp & Peterson.

We journeyed in this fashion for some while, rattling across the immaculate Swiss countryside. In doing so, my travelling companion and I would occasionally exchange the odd remark. We took it in turns to comment upon any items of interest which hove into view through our respective windows, pointing; he with his finger, I with the glistening stem of my pipe.

"Sheep."

"Burn."

"Flowers."

"Glen."

"Trees. Pine trees."

"Mountains."

"Snow."

The train tipped over the brow of this particular stretch of rolling Swiss upland, threaded its way through a long, steep embankment, and began its steady descent towards the valley; beyond it lay the chalky, turquoise waters of the Brienzersee, or Lake Brienz.

It was lunchtime.

I knocked my pipe out and replaced it, with its accompanying articles, in my pocket. I stood up, stretched, stifled a yawn and made a move for the door. For a fleeting instant, I considered whether I should take my valise with me. I didn't know this fellow. There was, plainly, a degree of mystery surrounding his presence on this train. There was no one else in the compartment to protect my belongings or, at the very least, to shout "Hoi!" were this fellow to make a move towards my possessions. Reluctantly, I concluded that there was no other option. Until I had established my young acquaintance's credentials, I was obliged to keep him in sight for a while longer.

"Would you care to join me for lunch?" I asked, through gritted teeth.

"Rather!"

I was not at all comfortable with the next generation's mode of speech. And now I would have to endure it for another hour at least. I cursed my mistrust of human nature, and began to wonder whether the loss of a few nick-nacks from my valise were not a small price to pay for a few minutes of independence and a modicum of solitude over lunch.

As we staggered along to the dining car along the jolting corridors like sailors on shore leave, I reflected on what had actually grown this suspicious nature of mine. I hadn't always been like this. When I was a few years younger, I was carefree, always laughing and joking, and eager to grasp any opportunity to chat with each and every person I encountered. The thought that they were in any way possessed of a darker nature never even crossed my mind. It was only after I had begun to write the Holmes and Watson stories, only after I had begun to explore the underworld with which they were obsessed, that my own gloomy outlook on human nature had begun to form itself. Once again, I was moved to acknowledge that there was much for which I had to be grateful to those two. However, whatever I had gained had come at a price.

There was a species or sub–genus of veal cutlet for lunch, with beans, accompanied by a full red wine from the Vaud region of Switzerland. I had been told about Swiss wine before. It was one of the world's best-kept secrets. Row upon row of lush vines, reaching up in terraces on the sunny slopes beside Lake Léman, produced a most agreeable wine. The Swiss do not export it, however; they keep it for themselves. Some may say that is uncommonly selfish but, having sampled a glass and begun to embark upon my second, I understood how wise they were. A return visit to introduce Touie to it was plainly to be considered.

Early on in our meal, I discovered what name my guest went by. I say "went by" as, apart from demanding to see his passport, I had no means of ascertaining that what he told me was actually the truth. Not that he should necessarily be gallivanting around Switzerland under an assumed name, of course. This was just my suspicious nature rising to the surface once more.

He called himself Richard Holloway but, he informed me, I may call him "Dick". I replied that, while I was honoured, naturally, that I should be allowed such a degree of intimacy, I would prefer to call him "Holloway". This seemed to gratify him. He had claimed, shortly before, that he was an Old Alleynian, from Dulwich College. So he was familiar with the courtesies and social niceties created by the juvenile hierarchies of the English public school system. When a senior chap wishes, through magnanimous condescension, to be on familiar terms with a junior chap, then the former will call the latter by his surname alone. It elicits a surprising degree of intimacy between the two, without the need for actual friendship, although this can follow. No matter how the relationship developed after this, the practice itself usually created a powerful bond between them that would last all their lives. To call Holloway this, therefore, to him, probably appeared tantamount to me slapping him on the back, calling him "old boy", introducing him to my gentleman's club, and offering him my daughter's hand in marriage.

The adverse side-effect of my gesture, on the other hand, was less satisfactory. He began to call me "Doyle". I tried to correct him twice and suggest that "Conan Doyle" would be more acceptable. However, he, purposely or unconsciously, singularly failed to implement my suggestion. Doyle he had dubbed me, Doyle I remained.

I asked what few questions courtesy demanded of me about his background, but received very little specific in reply. He lived in south London (somewhere) in rooms. He was not married and disliked his landlady who, it appears, was far too pernickety about his social life, which was virtually non-existent, according to him. His personal cleanliness and living habits were also a subject for discussion between the two of them and were, Holloway insisted, none of her dashed business. I discovered that he was a sportsman and indeed played centre three-quarter for Blackheath Rugby Football Club. When I reminded him that my creation Watson had played for that illustrious team, he looked disappointed. Maybe he treasured playing for the world's first open rugby club, and did not care to think of an old fuddy-duddy like Watson (albeit fictitious) having a prior claim on the club. Or maybe he felt he had given away more about himself than he had wished to.

Looking at him across the dining car table, I became aware of certain things about him I had not previously noted. While tanned, I could see that underneath his skin was pale, sallow. Although not exactly haggard, his features were drawn and those grey eyes were set so deep into their sockets, he had a haunted air about him. His nervousness had become more pronounced since we had sat down. Facing each other, I felt that he believed I was monitoring his every move, as if I were liable at any moment to criticize him. I have known people to twitch and to proffer a sweaty, tremulous hand for me to shake upon first encounter, as if I were a lofty potentate or great historical figure. Perhaps I had a similar effect on my restive guest, though I suspected a more complicated reason for his demeanour. In fact, the doctor in me suspected an ailment or, perhaps, abuse. Alcohol or another substance. It was not, I felt, a nicotine addiction, as he had only had one cigarette all the time we had been associated. Unless, of course, his abstinence was enforced – due to a singular lack of matches. However, being a smoker myself, I knew that this was no great obstacle. If it were an important part of one's psyche, an addiction on that scale was liable to mean you made sure you were always able to pander to it.

Luncheon completed, and I having paid the bill – an act for which he was unctuously grateful – Holloway and I returned to our compartment. Once back in our, by now, customary places, I explained that I always made a habit of taking a catnap after lunch and, if he would excuse me, I was not proposing to amend that habit that afternoon. He quite understood. In fact, I believe he was probably just as relieved not to have to struggle to make further conversation for the time being. I made myself comfortable underneath where my valise lay in the rack, so that anyone wishing to access it would have to clamber over me first. I put my handkerchief over my face and settled down to forty winks.

My plan was to remain incommunicado under my handkerchief for the most part of the remainder of the journey to Interlaken. When I awoke, consequently I remained concealed there for quite a while, until I realized how absurdly and curmudgeonly I was behaving. I pulled the linen square from my face and sat up.

He was gone.

My first action was to look above my head. My valise was still there. My second action – which I later realized should have been my first – was to look to see whether his bag was still there.

It was not.

All of a sudden, the entire train juddered, the brakes squealed and the locomotive let out a great expiring "whoosh" of steam. Close to panic, I leapt up. What was happening?

In an instant, the answer came. Not much. We had simply arrived at our destination. I could see the terminus sign and heard a basso-profundo intoning: "*Interlaken Ost!*"

I had slept longer than I had anticipated. To one extent, I could not have asked for more. To another extent, however, I remained concerned. Where was Holloway? Not that I was interested in his welfare. I simply wished to establish his whereabouts, since we were both destined, apparently, to continue on our journey together. I was particularly keen, also, on discovering why he had left me.

Still disconcerted, I prepared to leave the compartment. Folding my handkerchief so that I may replace it in my pocket, I began to take a more balanced view of the situation. A moment later, and a further sensation was sluicing the feelings of concern from my system. I was relieved. The young fellow had grown tired of me. Maybe the sound of my snoring had put him off. I always maintained that I did not snore, but Touie insisted that I did, and that it had the resonance and timbre of a highland stag calling to its mate across a misty glen. Whatever the reason for Holloway's departure, however, he had gone. To me, that was, naturally, the best outcome for the journey so far.

With optimism beginning to burgeon within me, I brought my valise down from the rack, and stepped out into the corridor. The door onto the platform was already open. I climbed down the steps and onto the cobbles.

"Ah, Doyle!" a voice called from behind me. I turned to see Holloway approaching with a porter. "I was coming to wake you – if you hadn't woken by now. You really should get your sinuses seen to, by the way. Thought you may like one of these." He gestured to the porter as if he were a mechanical implement like his barrow, rather than flesh and blood. "They can be the very devil to get hold of sometimes, and I'm sure you have luggage."

My heart returned to its customary place, lying disconsolate upon the diaphragm.

"I do; a couple of trunks. Thank you," I said, and we walked down to the baggage car.

Holloway was remarkably cheerful and seemed more relaxed, less self-conscious, as we three proceeded across the station towards the platform from which our little mountain train was due to depart.

"Sleep well?" he asked.

"Thank you," I replied. My manner was growing surly again. This was my trip. These were my trunks. This was my Switzerland. Yet this young fellow had practically commandeered all of it. I resented being "looked after" in this manner, as if I were an elderly colonel. I was perfectly capable of looking after myself. In fact, I wanted more than ever at that moment to be allowed to continue my journey alone again. Had I not two cumbersome brass-studded and leather-bound travelling trunks to take into account, I'm not sure I would not at that point have clamped my hat to my head, taken to my heels and fled this limpet of a man.

But, of course, such behaviour would have been unthinkable for a self-respecting, albeit tetchy, doctor–novelist.

Two

The journey along the valley was as agreeable as the train, with its industrious little locomotive and its clatter of carriages, was charming. The deal-clad compartments' slatted birch-wood seats and the small guttering gas jets, which passed for lighting, created an overall cosy effect. The views grew even more appealing with every gentle sweep of the track. The grass was as lush and as emerald green as any I had seen on my honeymoon in Ireland. The wooden cottages scattered among the fields had pictorial motifs and edifying words of Scripture, or other similar encouragements, painted or engraved on them. Every *chalet* – for that was their name – had orderly rows of logs and kindling. They were stacked along the walls and reached up to the broad eaves. In this way, the wood could be kept dry in most weathers, and would enable the occupants to have a cheering, crackling fire all through the dark, snowbound winter months.

The verdant valley we were rolling through seemed as though it had been completely cut off from the rest of civilization. I began to feel as if it were a lost world, and that I was the first oafish heathen of a corrupt race to have chanced upon it in a thousand years. I resolved to allow this magical place to refresh me, and allow its simple pleasures to work their purifying charms upon me. I did not want to bring the turpitude of my own world here, and so be the one responsible for sullying its timeless integrity.

The whole soothing effect of the journey along the valley gave one the impression of a homecoming. It softened my unease where my persistent travelling companion was concerned.

On the way up, Holloway and I played the same desultory game of tourist "snap" that we had shared on the journey to Interlaken, pointing out everyday landmarks that had taken on new life and vibrancy in this setting.

"Stream."

"Cattle."

"Waterfall."

"Pine trees."

Disembarking at the small valley terminus, we engaged a waiting dog cart to haul us up into the high Alps. Holloway carried his bag; my luggage would follow later, I was assured.

It had been raining quite recently; the brows of the lower mountains were garlanded with misty clouds and we could see no peaks. There were many streams, too. They hurled themselves down the slopes and on, pell-mell, into the valley. Oftentimes they would convulse into waterfalls and other cascades in their eagerness to comply with the demands of their mistress, Gravity.

The lower mountains were a deep, ivy green. They were covered above the timberline, where we could discern it, with a thick carpet of alpine plants and grasses. Beyond them lay the great peaks that we could not yet see; the noble mountains that lent the Oberland their majesty.

Nature's phenomenal alchemy of mountain vegetation and summer rain meant that as we toiled upwards in the rickety cart, we found ourselves soon enshrouded in heavy mist – or cloud, as Holloway, enthralled, pointed out. A lofty eeriness descended on the place. The silence was all-embracing. Nothing, it would seem, dared make a noise in such stillness, save our brave little cart with its steady rattle and creak. It was as if we were in the castle of a giant king who, although out of sight, nevertheless commanded utmost respect and awestruck whispers.

After a while, we passed through the occlusion and, it felt to me, entered another dimension; a place where reality took on a different aspect. The mist, which I noticed had gathered only in patches across the valley slopes, had been left behind. Visibility was still restricted, though, as we remained immersed in the serried ranks of proud pines.

The climb took an hour. Thanks to the cart's hard seats, its sturdy iron-rimmed wheels and singular lack of any perceivable suspension,

I found that I had bruises in places I did not even know I had. But it was all worth it. We turned the final corner of the mountain track, pulled away from the forest, and presently came upon the main thoroughfare of the tiny Alpine village that was to be our home for the next few days.

It is hard to describe my precise emotions as the village in the mountains unfolded before me. I had last experienced a similar sense of a cleansing breeze blowing away the cobwebs – and timeless peace descending – when, on a walking holiday in the highlands in my student days, I crested the brow of a hill and was treated to the breath-taking vista of a superb plain sweeping away into violet infinity before me.

The Alpine village sat nestled on a ledge with an area about the size of a dozen rugby football pitches. It was perched on the edge of a sheer drop down into the valley on one side, and had its back braced against a sharp mountain wall which climbed into further cloud on the other.

The watery early evening sun, only just beginning to burn through the mist, was nevertheless sufficient to give the whole vicinity a cheerful aspect. The terrace was essentially meadow, studded with individual wooden chalets of a type I had noticed on the mountain train. There was a slight rise in the centre, which seemed to contain common land and one or two small barns with haylofts. Everywhere there were balconies – designed to allow the inhabitants of the chalets to sit on the upper levels of their homes and glory in the summer sunshine, or marvel at the winter snows. Each balcony was decorated with plants and flowers in pots and window boxes; geraniums, pink, gold and red, predominantly.

The main street was barely 150 yards long. There was human activity but it was sedate. It was as if everyone here had all day to get from one end of the village to the other, and nobody was pressing them to behave otherwise – which was very likely the case. On first inspection, I could make out one or two more commercial enterprises, such as a hotel and a bakery. No doubt there were other

25

shops, many of them in what appeared to be private homes, but by far the predominating impression was that of residence. A place of close community, settled and content with its enviable lot.

The cart added its gentle creaking and rumbling to the discreet hubbub of the village. Again the combination of the flowers, light and colour gave the new arrival the distinct impression that they had just chanced upon an Eden. As we entered the main street, I started to wonder if I shouldn't simply wire my family and have them come and join me here immediately, never to return to England again.

Just as my thoughts were starting to warm to this particular theme, an item – very large and very heavy – plummeted past my right ear and landed on the street beside me with a mighty crash.

Startled, I leapt out of my seat and stood, clutching onto the wrought iron cart rail for balance. This was exceedingly difficult. Although the cart had momentarily stopped, it was now juddering and rocking back and forth on its wheels. The horse was agitated and threatening to bolt. The driver was wrestling with the reins. So I sat down again and clung on. From my seat I looked down onto the road and what it was that had just missed braining me. It was a terracotta flowerpot. Mangled geraniums lay among spilled loam and shards of pottery. I became aware of noises around me. There was some shouting or disturbance going on. The driver, having managed to settle his horse, was now standing, holding the reins and gesticulating at something or someone somewhere above us. He was giving vent to his feelings in no uncertain terms. The possible loss of income, had I been rendered unconscious – or worse – by the missile, no doubt being the motivation. Holloway, too, was looking up and shouting. I raised my own eyes to the apparent source of the descending crockery and saw a woman, with swags of jet black hair, teetering over her balcony, yelling and gesturing in our direction.

I recognized that she wasn't gesticulating at us, however. Just to the left and behind the cart was a muscular, stocky fellow, with a broad forehead and heavy jowls. Wearing just a vest, braces, fustian trousers and stout boots, he was bellowing back at the woman. Some of the villagers stopped to observe this altercation for a moment or two, but I noticed that others simply passed by without even concerning themselves. Could this be an everyday occurrence, I wondered?

Eventually, the woman gave a parting shot, and withdrew. She slammed her shutters, ensuring everyone understood that proceedings for the day had concluded. The aggrieved fellow, whom I assumed was the lady's husband, stalked off; I imagine to seek solace in something liquid and consoling.

Our disgusted driver perched himself back on his seat, as did Holloway and I on ours, and we clipped along at a brisk pace, covering the remaining few yards to my hotel in double-quick time.

Stepping down off the cart, and still somewhat shaken from my close encounter with the flowerpot, I paid the driver in full; an act for which Holloway was again excessively grateful. Holloway followed me into the hotel.

"Have you booked?" I asked, knowing full well he had made no plans.

"I'm sure there'll be a room for me," he returned.

"It's a very small village and a very busy season." I tried to sound as though I cared for his welfare.

Before he could respond, a bright young fellow with a milk-and-apples complexion appeared from the back room. He came out from behind the hotel counter, and beamed a welcome.

"Herr Doctor," he said, "you have arrived. I am Anton." He spoke good English and his pleasure at seeing me seemed entirely genuine. We shook hands and then he looked at Holloway. "Oh, I am so sorry," he said. "I did not realize you were bringing a friend."

I winced at the description, but ignored it for propriety's sake. "It's quite all right…" I began.

"No, no, if you have written to us that there were going to be two of you…" Anton left the self-reproachful sentence unfinished, went back behind the counter, and started to leaf through his ledger.

"That's quite all right," I began again. "Mr Holloway was not intending to come until the last moment. We met on the train. I'm sure that since you have no rooms available, Mr Holloway would be more than happy to seek accommodation elsewhere..."

"No, no, we have rooms, Herr Doctor, do not worry."

He turned to a second ledger and ran his fingers down the availability column. I, for my part, silently clenched and re-clenched my fists.

"Here we are," he continued. "Will it be two weeks also?" He looked at Holloway.

"For now, yes," replied Holloway. "I'm not sure exactly what my plans are yet, to be honest."

"Good." The obliging eyes returned to engage mine. "Will you and your friend be sharing the room, Herr Doctor?"

"No." I shuddered, pitched forward and muttered at the young man, "A different floor would be entirely acceptable." I could not stop myself adding, "And he is not my friend."

"As you wish." He returned to his ledger and, with a few deft flicks of a pencil, assigned us our respective rooms. Mine on the third floor, with balcony, as requested, Holloway's on the first, at the back.

"When the cart comes up from the valley with your luggage, I shall ensure it is brought to your rooms."

"That's all right," Holloway assured him, raising his bag. "This is all I've got at the moment, actually."

"Then may I show you both to your rooms?"

At the top of the first set of stairs, he drew Holloway off to inspect his accommodation.

And away from me.

At last.

I extricated my smoking materials from my pocket and filled my pipe. I hung the lighted Vesta over the bowl and sucked on the stem. For the first time since earlier that morning, I began to feel that fate was at last treating me with the respect I deserved.

My luggage arrived soon after I had been settled into my room, which was comfortable and spacious and had a fine outlook, south-east across the village meadow towards the mountains. Dusk had settled by the time I had unpacked, washed and changed for dinner.

The dining room, lit by oil lamps and replete with crystal and silverware, was intimate and welcoming. The food was honest and plentiful. Perhaps it was the mountain air, perhaps the exertions and stresses of an eventful day – nevertheless, I did not hold back. I even had a second portion of a dish the Swiss called *rösti* – shredded and fried potatoes in a marinade – accompanied by some thumb-thick rustic sausages. The wine, again, surprised and delighted.

Over dinner, I surveyed my fellow guests. There was Holloway, of course, looking about him in the manner of a fox engaged in eating its prey; anxious and alert for predators. Next to him, a Bavarian, Günther Werner, here for the hunting. Apart from exchanging the occasional sentence with Holloway, he tended to keep himself to himself and hummed his way through all four courses. Having said that, I noticed, at one point, the Bavarian's eyes leap from his plate to look up and across directly at me. I could only guess what it was Holloway had told him. There was a French couple, Monsieur and Madame Marcus Plantin, who appeared to be oblivious of the fact that there was anyone else in the room save each other. It was a while later that I noticed Plantin was in fact confined to a rolling chair. There was a morose middle-aged Dutch couple, the van Engelses. They, it seemed, would rather the others were not there at all. Then there were the two Croats, Tomas and Anna Pivcevic. They had greeted me warmly when I entered the dining room, and insisted I sit between them throughout the meal. They hailed from the Balkans but, owing to the confused situation in that region, currently resided in Bosnia. Being both teachers, they were much-travelled and well educated. We were able to exchange views on a large number of different topics.

There was one final member of this present company of hotel visitors, I learned, who was not at table that evening. He was an Englishman: Peter Brown. A distant, highbrow fellow, I came to understand, reading between the lines of my fellow guests' comments. A keen walker, he barely exchanged a word with anyone else and was always striding off with his alpenstock somewhere or other. He had indeed wandered off earlier that afternoon and had not yet returned. The general consensus was that he had walked too far, found that he was unable to return before dark without risking becoming lost, and had sought temporary lodgings in another village for the night. This was not regretted by anyone present. No doubt, the view went, I would encounter him on the morrow and form my own opinion of his evident incivility.

Providentially, none present, saving Holloway, had ever read any of my stories – or at least, if they had they either didn't like them or didn't make the connection. Whatever the reason, we did not discuss them at all. Holloway did attempt to introduce the subject at one point but I managed to deflect him and bring the discussion round to the apparent dearth of internationally renowned Swiss novelists, and why this was the case.

At the end of the meal, the ladies retired to the hotel withdrawing room, while we gentlemen took to the smoking room, which doubled as the hotel's library. If, indeed, four shelves of well-thumbed novels in different languages, half a dozen half-baked reference books in Swiss- Deutsch relating to the typography, flora and fauna of the region, plus one shabby Holy Bible in English could be dignified with the term library. The Bavarian, Werner, brought Plantin through in his rolling chair.

We had all consumed a significant amount of wine at the table, so we were all considerably more relaxed and easy in each other's company by this time – despite the fact that some of us had only met barely an hour or so earlier. Some of us smoked and some did not. The young Swiss, Anton, who had met us on our arrival, came in and asked if there were anything further we required. We ordered our nightcaps. Werner, eschewing anything so *bourgeois* as cognac or port, ordered up copious amounts of Swiss beer, and contented himself with that for the rest of the evening.

Plantin, despite clearly missing his beloved, made a noble attempt to appear content in our company and brought the conversation round, in his faltering English, which was the common tongue for the assembled, to Günther's beer. He wondered if we realized that the Swiss word for light beer was *hell*. He found this amusing, he told us, because, of course, hell was the last thing one would associate with "light" unless, of course, it was something to do with fiery furnaces. He looked particularly pleased with himself that he had essayed a joke in English and had plainly managed to carry it off admirably.

"Is there such a thing as hell, Herr Doctor?" Werner looked at me. "You know – evil, the devil?"

There was that element in his attitude which I found, alas, all too familiar. I felt sure I was about to discover that my optimism in there being no one who knew of my stories was sadly misplaced.

"Why ask me?" I replied. "Doctors don't study evil – they study medicine."

"Ah yes," came the reply, "but you are no ordinary doctor, are you?"

"Am I not?" I responded, now sure that the inevitable was about to arrive, like watching a train crash.

"No – you are the author of the Sherlock Holmes stories, are you not?"

I looked across at Holloway, who appeared delighted that my secret was out, once again. This was possibly because he could now claim an association with me. Reflected glory, to a fellow like him, would be preferable to no glory at all. I also put two and two together and came to the conclusion that he had been instrumental in this whole new development. It was this which he had shared with the Bavarian and had made the other look across at me so sharply earlier. However the subject had raised itself, I now knew that my stock response of "some people think that" would not be employable on this occasion. Doubtless Holloway would only interject and scotch any defensive gambit I may have played.

"I have written a great deal more than the Holmes stories, you know," I decided to reply.

"Sherlock Holmes?" Plantin looked at me in surprise. "I have been to England three times these last two years. You are very famous M'sieu," he said.

"I wouldn't say that," I replied, not entirely self-deprecatingly; I wasn't *that* famous, for goodness' sake.

It transpired that the Dutchman, Professor van Engels, had apparently not heard of me and, judging by his behaviour – which involved attempting to lose himself in repeated sips of cognac – he had no wish to rectify this. Tomas Pivcevic admitted that he had seen my name in a bookshop on a rare visit to London, but had not, he apologized, managed yet to read any of my work.

"So, Herr Doctor," Werner pursued his question. "Do you believe in evil?"

"I have come to the conclusion," I reflected, "that individual humans are capable of being evil. 'Evil' as a force other than that which can be brought about by some humans' deeds *may* exist. It may be an abyss that lies somewhere beyond our five senses, beyond our comprehension, but you can be sure that by far the greatest amount of ill that befalls the human race is as a result of its own behaviour. Or, I should say, misbehaviour."

"Do you believe, though, in the paranormal?" Holloway asked.

"I believe that there is much which is beyond our understanding. But you should be clear – I also believe that there are vast tracts of unexplored territory in the mind. We have not even begun to have the faintest inkling as to what the human brain is capable of helping us to believe. Much of 'reality' is based upon perception and experience – and these things are notoriously subjective. I am sure that it would be fascinating to explore that uncharted territory, while also venturing out into the unknown beyond our everyday preconceptions and sensual experiences."

"The supernatural?" Plantin asked.

"Perhaps 'psychic' would be a better word. It has a meaning related to the human mind, yet also related to matters beyond the present realm."

"Are you considering undertaking such an exploration, doctor?" Pivcevic enquired.

"I have visited large parts of the world. The space inside a man's imagination is far greater and far more fascinating even than those wonderful far-flung places. I like to think of myself – perhaps a conceit, I'll grant you – as an explorer. An adventurer, a pioneer. What better place to start than right here?" I tapped Holloway's head. It was an unconscious act – or perhaps it wasn't. However, he received it as if a bee had stung him and he cast me a most baleful look.

"What are you suggesting?" he demanded.

"Nothing, Holloway. You were simply closest to hand. I didn't mean to offend…"

"What's wrong with your own head?"

"I've often wondered that myself." The remark achieved the laugh from some of the others that I had intended. But it failed to placate Holloway, who sat brooding in silence for quite a few minutes afterwards.

"I am a writer, too." Werner threw the fact at me as if he were slapping my face with a kid glove and inviting me to cross épées at dawn. "Plays. Perhaps you could read them. They are in my room."

"Are they in German?" I asked.

"Of course." Werner looked astonished, as if any language other than Schiller's and Goethe's could produce such fine literary craftsmanship.

"I'm afraid I may find that rather difficult, then…" I began.

"I have heard you speaking German," Werner interrupted.

"I am hardly fluent," I retorted, taken aback. "But," I retreated before that formidable stare, "I'll gladly have a look."

"Good."

Werner was one of those fellows who believed that the deepness of one's speaking voice has a direct correlation with maturity. The deeper the voice, the greater the wisdom. I had just decided that the roundness of his booming tones was becoming, frankly, offensive.

"I am a writer, too."

We all looked around. Van Engels had emerged from his glass and was addressing no one in particular. *Oh no*, I thought, *I am attracting them like moths.*

"I have come to Switzerland for inspiration."

"The mountains, you mean?" Werner interjected and then, with a shrug, as if by way of explanation, "The Netherlands are very flat."

Van Engels fixed me with an unsteady gaze. "Where do you get your inspiration from?"

I was tempted to say from a left luggage locker at Paddington station, but resisted. "I just look at my experiences and knit pieces together from here and there, really," I said.

"Oh," van Engels replied, returning to his cognac.

"I am still not clear, Herr Doctor," Werner continued. "Are you a spiritualist?"

"Whatever gave you that idea?"

"You are not, then."

"I didn't say either way. I just wondered what gave you that idea."

"People say," Holloway piped up, sullenly.

"Which people?"

"I don't know – maybe I read it somewhere."

"Read what?"

"That you have embraced spiritualism."

"Ah," offered Werner, sagely, "and did you not write a book… ah… was it something like… *The Mystery of… Cooper…*?"

"Coomber. Yes, that was mine. And yes, it did explore the idea of the concept of life beyond this one."

"Are you, then?" Plantin asked. "Are you a spiritualist?"

"I don't know."

34

"That's no answer," Holloway grumbled.

"What kind of answer is that?" Werner agreed.

"The truth. In my Holmes stories, the detective wrestles with the supernatural as he sees it. On my behalf, perhaps. Now I'm doing so myself; Holmes cannot do all my wrestling for me."

"So you do believe in spiritualism?" Tomas sounded disappointed; as if he had discovered a failing in a pupil he had entertained high hopes for.

"I don't know. I believe in the possibility of life after death." I began to feel as if I were in the dock.

"So you have turned to spiritualism?" Plantin asked.

"I have not. At least, not in the way you mean."

"But they say..." insisted Holloway.

I interrupted him. "These *they* that you have such faith in seem to be very certain of their facts – despite never having spoken to me." I paused. The gathering could see that I was becoming vexed by the subject. I began again, patiently, "Holmes would tell you that the only true way to discover the thinking of the criminal mind is to think like a criminal. To all intents and purposes *become* one, if necessary."

"So spiritualists are criminals?" Plantin asked.

"I do not propose, for one moment, that they are – although there are undoubtedly charlatans and abusers, just as you may find in any walk of life where there is profit to be gained or power to be had over another. Human beings are constantly drawn towards justifying themselves by seeming to have something special that another does not have. But I am talking of the principle of assimilation, rather than any direct comparison with the criminal mind."

"I do not understand," Werner interjected. "You are talking nonsense. You believe in spiritualism, yet you do not. You believe in the power of the imagination, but you do not think that imagination is all..."

"All I am saying," I sighed, "is that a doctor is taught, while learning his profession, to examine himself, experiment upon himself if need be. To use himself, if you will, as a guinea pig. Rather than come at spiritualism with any preconceptions, I keep an open mind. The true open mind, if it is to explore a phenomenon properly, must expose itself in as full a way as possible to that phenomenon – with all the attendant risks – if it is to examine its effects methodically."

Holloway, who had been picking at the fraying braid on the cushion cover of his armchair, perked up.

"Do you believe Sherlock Holmes has a spirit?"

"In what way?" I asked, confused.

"In the way that I asked," he replied, archly. "Do you believe that the spirit of Sherlock Holmes exists?"

"That is a different question. However, it is one I find easier to answer. Yes. I believe that there is such a thing as the spirit of Holmes, and that it could quite likely live on, even after I have long left this earth."

"Like a ghost?" asked Plantin.

"No... I do not know exactly what I mean. Undoubtedly there is happy alchemy in the values with which I imbued Holmes. These, taken together over a number of stories, one may acceptably define as a spirit. Goodness, integrity, intellect, wisdom, patience – and impatience – resourcefulness, stoicism, courage… and fallibility."

I listed all these attributes as if I had planned them. In fact, this was the first time I had ever discussed the character of Holmes in such depth with anyone; including myself. Holmes had been and always would be secondary to my other interests. Running through my list, I realized why so many people had taken to him. I marvelled at the fact that, yes, he had come to life; under my hand perhaps, but a life that was growing independent of its creator. He embodied values that people esteemed highly. Values, I daresay, as a race we have rarely managed to achieve with any consistency.

If he were so noble, however, why had I begun to dislike him?

Would I like to spend an evening with him at my club? I am sure I would find his analytical processes and the hair-raising tales of his escapades wholly absorbing. The likelihood, however, of his expressing himself in that way in my company would be highly improbable. I was sure, were I to meet him, I would find him distant and cool; possibly even insufferable. Polite, yes. But arrogant, aloof and pompous, too. I am sure he would have very little time for my bumbling approach to life. Others may consider me methodical and intuitive. I know better. I don't doubt Holmes would see through me in an instant.

I suddenly realized, at that moment, that this was what I disliked in him; the fact that there was a possibility that he would not care much for me at all – his creator. I wondered if that was why I had invented my alter ego, Watson. To deflect any criticism Holmes might otherwise have directed towards me…

I paused in my internal musings. I noticed everyone had stopped talking. They were looking at me.

"Well?" Holloway repeated with studied patience. "What do you think, Doyle?"

"I – I'm sorry," I replied. "I didn't catch that last bit…"

Holloway raised an imperious eyebrow; Werner snorted into his beer glass. Conan Doyle, in the flesh, was a disappointment. An overrated booby, gently losing his faculties as he meandered towards middle age.

"We were wondering," Plantin explained, more considerately, "whether you would join us in an experiment?"

"What kind of experiment?"

"To raise the spirit of Sherlock Holmes."

I looked at them all looking at me. They were serious.

"I beg your pardon?"

"Doyle, listen," Holloway began to gabble. "If it is possible – beyond tangible creation – for spirits to exist, then why isn't it possible for a man's intellect and imagination to create spirits that also exist on a different temporal and spatial plane?"

"Because it is self-evidently preposterous," I frowned. Judging by the blank expressions on the faces before me, I had obviously not made myself clear enough. "Nonsense, gobbledegook, hocus-pocus,"

I elucidated. My mind flitted to an image of every author's and playwright's creation inhabiting a literary purgatory; condemned to roam the nether regions by their creators' fevered imaginations. Hamlet hobnobbing with Little Miss Muffet? Absurd.

"I thought you approached spiritualism with an open mind," Werner sneered.

"Now you are twisting my words."

"No – we're only exercising our imaginations, Doyle," Holloway pressed. "Don't worry, you won't have to do anything. Just be there as his creator. You are merely the catalyst."

Merely? Forsooth!

"Be *where*, exactly?" I scrutinized the room, confounded.

"There is a medium in the village," Plantin explained. "We have agreed I would try and arrange a… how do you say *séance* in English?"

"Séance," I obliged.

"So," Plantin nodded approvingly. His language had once again proved a proud infiltrator of that clumsy and ugly hybrid, Anglo-Saxon. "We shall arrange a – séance. And you shall be there to bring the psychic energy."

"The what?"

"… and I will be the vessel Holmes can inhabit," added Holloway.

"You'll be what?"

"I will make myself available to the spirit of Sherlock Holmes. He will surely need a human form in which to manifest himself."

"Or the psychic will, of course," Pivcevic suggested, playfully.

"Yes, we will need a vessel," Werner agreed, perhaps jealous he had not thought of this exciting possibility for himself; the great Sherlock Holmes's host human.

"Or the psychic," muttered Holloway.

I sat in stunned silence. No doubt we had all had a very long day and had drunk and smoked and talked ourselves into a stupor. No doubt it was very late at night, when men's imaginations traditionally slip loose their moorings and venture upon voyages they would never have undertaken in the cold light of day. No doubt, too, that whatever inhabited Holloway, it was not Holmes. Nor was it nicotine or alcohol alone.

"Well?" he said. "What do you say?"

The project was unlikely to go ahead unless I agreed. Furthermore, I didn't want the Conan Doyle who sadly disappoints in the flesh to be their abiding image. A vanity, I freely admit. Yet, like most people, I preferred folk to think well of me. I sucked on my pipe, which had long since expired. The project was the epitome of balderdash. Yet the notion did appeal to my sense of whimsy. A voice, in the fundament of my being, cajoled: *Go on, what harm could it do…?* I took a last pull on my dead pipe, expelled a wraith of non-existent smoke, and surveyed the expectant faces.

"Why not?" I declared. "We will do it."

THREE

I rose later than I had intended. It had been a long day and an even longer night. I performed my ablutions and dressed. Returning from the *salle de bain*, I discovered the hotel proprietors had left my breakfast tray on the wicker table on my balcony.

The sun was well on its way in its journey across the clear blue sky, girding its loins for giving the day the full effect of its power. However, the sight that took both my attention and my breath was the view I had been unable to enjoy the previous day because of the clouds and the mist. It was the whole Jungfrau mountain range, dazzling white and momentous, like a vast army in full battle array. If I were a composer, a Mascagni or a Mendelssohn, I would have brought the whole orchestra to a swooping of strings, climaxing as my eyes rose and encountered that glorious view. They stood, those peaks, like giants or gods; with folded arms they pitied us poor wee timorous beasties.

I sat in my basket chair beside my table and marvelled.

To breakfast in such illustrious and majestic company was a delight. The food was excellent: bread, cured meats, mountain cheese and rich, acidic, wine-dark coffee.

Refreshed and relaxed, I reluctantly left my companions and prepared to venture beyond my sanctuary.

Presently, I was stepping out of the hotel and exploring the locale that was to be my home for the next fortnight. I sported my mottled green and grey hunting hat with its wild boar brush and embroidered edelweiss motif. I had acquired it in Austria when I was studying medicine in Vienna. The sun and the mountains had passed their agreeable temperament on to the locals. To a man and woman, I was welcomed with a *Grüss Gott* and a warm smile. *Here is our village, of which we are justifiably proud. Enjoy it!* The spirit of

Christian hospitality had been ingrained in just about everyone. Although no longer religious myself, I recognized that the moral principles enshrined in Scripture were everyday practice for these modest folk. *Greet everyone as a friend, for many have entertained angels without knowing it.*

I was just starting to suspect that I had, in fact, died in my sleep and been transported to paradise, when I was roused from my reverie by a single word. A name, in fact. It was said in a most pleasant and charming tone. Yet it nonetheless swamped my whole being, like a storm-tossed whaler broached by a great wave, rounding the Horn.

"Doyle!"

I was filled with dread.

Holloway.

I thought about affecting not to have heard him, and marching on in the opposite direction.

"Ho! I say… Doyle!"

My choice was clear. One: I could carry on ignoring him and risk his continuing to raise his voice. My name would grow louder and shriller until it caused an avalanche. Two: I could acknowledge my tormentor.

"Morning, Holloway." I touched the brim of my hat. "I trust you slept well?" I had little interest in the response, and continued on my way without turning to look at him.

"Like a top, old boy. You?" I fought the shudder that threatened through being addressed in the middle of the street as his "old boy".

"Well, thanks," I said. "Well, won't keep you. I'm sure you have a lot to…"

I had turned to address my final remarks to his face. The sight that greeted me finally brought that latent shudder to the fore. It was a fearsome sight, as vulgar as the mountains in the morning had been sublime.

Holloway was dressed in a short-sleeved check shirt and purple braces. Lime green corduroy knickerbockers were set off by bright red socks. They featured, I believe, an assortment of creatures from the Alpine region. Possibly ibex and chamois, though it was hard to say for sure since the needlework was not of the highest standard. The whole ensemble was completed by a black, high-pointed Swiss mountain felt hat and a pair of calf-length leather boots with Swiss motif pokerwork. He looked like a cross between an Italian cowboy and a warlock.

"You appear to be half-dressed."

"Not a bit," he replied. "It'll be hot all day. The peasants round here dress like this all the time."

I didn't doubt Switzers in the fields stripped down to shirtsleeves on occasions. However, I felt sure they would never go so far as knickerbockers and calf-length boots; with or without pokerwork.

"You have just purchased these items?" I tried to keep the disbelief out of my voice, but rather fancy I failed.

He jerked his head along the street. "Outfitters – 'for the walking and climbing gentleman'. All sorts of climbing equipment, too. And some strange planks of wood that the shopkeeper insisted I could put on my feet."

"Skis."

"What?"

"Worn in the winter-time. Helps one walk along when there's snow and ice."

"Like ice skates, you mean?"

"A little."

"So – why don't they wear ice skates, then?"

"They need them for their mountain tracks. It is called ski-running. They carry the wearers on a horizontal plane for miles in relative comfort, speed and safety. These are hardy people, but their winter livelihoods mean that they have to get about as much in the winter as in the summer. Did he show you any poles?"

"What?"

"Walking sticks with a small spider's web of leather straps at the bottom?"

"Oh yes, they had spiked tips. I thought they were some kind of harpoon."

"They walk on the skis and propel themselves along with the poles. It also gives them purchase and balance. It helps them avoid side-slipping and plummeting pell-mell down a mountain slope. Although," I continued, remembering the trip to Norway I was proposing later that summer, "there is a Norwegian writer fellow who wrote a tale about his exploits in Greenland. He suggests that one may actually plummet downhill in that manner out of choice. For one's amusement."

"Oh no, I don't think I hold with that at all."

"On the contrary, I rather suspect it may be diverting. Now, as I say, I am sure that you have much with which you would care to be getting on with, so I shall detain you no longer. Goodbye, Holloway." I pinched my hat brim courteously and turned.

"Hoi, Doyle," he said amiably, and tugged at my jacket sleeve. "Got any ideas where I could go?"

I considered telling him exactly, but manners prevented me. "Sadly not."

"Never mind," he shrugged. "Tell you what, we could explore this place together."

"I really don't think…"

"Yes, definitely," he said. He looked speculatively up at the inviting mountains above the village. "Just a couple of hours' stroll before lunch. A meander up into the hills, eh? What do you say?"

"I am not sure…"

"Do, please," he entreated. "I've not done anything like this. Ever."

I relented. "I'll meet you outside the hotel in one hour." It would have been boorish to refuse him.

"Righto! Thanks. Thanks awfully!"

"Oh, and Holloway…"

"Yes?"

"Put a jacket on – there's a good fellow."

"Right you are, Doyle."

I reconnoitred the village, to get an idea of the facilities on offer. They were limited but by no means Spartan. I then returned to my hotel. There a young boy met me. He spoke a little broken English. He handed me a calling card. The name embossed on it was *Frau Ruth von Denecker.*

"Frau von Denecker," he began, reciting, "invites that you take tea with her this four o'clock at the afternoon. Hotel Jungfrau." He paused and narrowed his eyes in an attempt to recollect a postscript to this message. "Please to bring your friend also. Hollow… Hollow-way."

I was again irked by this "friendship" assumption. Was this the impression of the whole community? Before long, if I was not careful, we would be invited everywhere together, like husband and wife.

"Holloway is not my friend." The youngster smiled but did not comprehend. I dropped a couple of coins into the palm of his grubby hand and growled: "*Doch ohne* Holloway. Not Holloway." He grinned, pocketed the money and skipped away.

I entered my hotel and headed for the stairs. Here I passed our young Swiss host whose parents, I had discovered, owned the establishment.

"Ah, Anton…"

"Good morning, Herr Doctor," he smiled. "How may I help?"

"Is there anyone you know who may accompany me and my…" I stopped myself in mid-sentence. I refused to allow the word "friend" to pass my lips. "Anyone who may accompany myself and my *acquaintance* Mr Holloway on a short walk this morning?"

"Where would you like to go?"

"Not far. My legs are not up to a long march so early on in my stay. Two hours should be ample."

"There and back?"

"Two hours in total."

"Good. You shall meet with my sister…"

"Your sister?" I was not sure as to the appropriateness of a young woman accompanying two men into the mountains. However,

Anton had offered her and, therefore, I supposed it was both acceptable and common practice.

Anton misunderstood my hesitation. "Oh, don't worry, Herr Doctor, she is very strong." He flexed a bicep. "Stronger than me. And she knows all the ways. Very well. She is a... um... a tom."

I puzzled over the word for a moment. "Oh – you mean 'tomboy'?"

"*Ja*. Exactly. She can run faster, swim further, climb higher than anyone else in the village. She is the best guide."

"Splendid!" I clapped Anton on the shoulder. "I shall look forward very much to meeting her. Shall we say in twenty minutes? Here?"

"Twenty minutes. Good."

He moved off in search of his sister, and I went to my room. I returned a few minutes later in my trusty tweeds, brogues and puttees with the hat and an ice axe I had acquired in Austria. Holloway was already waiting. He had found himself a dark green jacket, which marginally toned down the garish effect of his costume. He hovered on the street.

Anton arrived immediately and brought with him someone who could only be described as a walking summer's day. Eva, his sister, was barely twenty. Tall, slim; her blonde hair short and her healthy, tanned features the perfect setting for a pair of shining green eyes. I fell in love with her immediately. Platonically, naturally. My heart warmed to her as an uncle's towards a favourite niece. Holloway, though, was evidently smitten in a much more powerful and serious way. Having been shifting expectantly from one foot to the other, he now stood stock still. An English setter on point. His hands hung limply at his sides, as though the nerves and sinews had been severed. His eyes were set unblinking beneath his conical black hat.

Eva, who spoke excellent English like her brother, shook our hands. She wore trousers, boots and a shirt with the cuffs rolled back. She carried a knapsack and an ice axe with its pointed ferrule and the leather wrist strap that kept the owner from losing it down a hillside, should they stumble. While deferential, it was readily understood that she was queen and we were mere courtiers.

I was still not entirely comfortable for Holloway and me to be alone in the company of a single woman. Anton, however, appeared just as unconcerned as when he had first suggested his sister. Surely he would not have suggested such an arrangement had he not trusted us. I detected, though, perhaps an erosion of that trust in the way that he looked at Holloway and his outlandish garb. But if he had developed any reservations at that point, he did not voice them. Instead he bade us farewell, safe return.

We set off, three abreast, Eva between Holloway and me. Her *joie de vivre* soon had all three of us chattering excitedly about the walk, where we should go, what we may see. Schoolchildren on an outing. To any observers, we may just as easily have been long-standing friends, reunited after a period of separation and intent on revisiting the haunts and joyful experiences of our lost youth. A few moments later, I even started to sense, for the first time, a thawing in my attitude towards Holloway. The influence of Eva's personality, I don't doubt, creating an atmosphere of unity and conviviality. Despite myself, though, somewhere buried in my psyche I begrudged him his present happiness.

Within a quarter of an hour, we had scaled a considerable portion of the slopes that provided the backdrop to the village, dwindling to a bauble beneath us. The track was wide enough for us to remain three abreast. The forest, coniferous boreal, had become more dense meanwhile. The smells and sensations were an invigorating experience. Eva explained that the word "alp" actually referred to the high summer pasture and not the peaks themselves. We could feel the heat of the sun drumming down on the pine canopy many yards above our heads. However, beneath, in our secret fairy tale landscape, it was cool, pleasant and intimate. A chough, disturbed, broke cover and flew twisting and twittering into the trees. Everywhere, streams still carried yesterday's rains switching down through ragged gullies. Occasionally, Holloway and

I would miss our footing and skitter unceremoniously on the path. Eva never missed a step and, I am sure, would have comfortably pressed on at twice the pace, had she not diligently remained in our company.

In due course, the path narrowed and the party split up into two sections, Eva and Holloway in front and me bringing up the rear. Not that I was finding the going difficult. I believe I was more capable of sustaining a brisk pace than Holloway. It was simply courtesy that had brought about this particular succession. I was married, and happily. Eva and Holloway were not, and they had plainly found much in common in such a short space of time. Acting as an impromptu chaperon, I had decided to take the honourable option and haul off to allow the two of them time on their own. Knowing what little I did of Holloway and his erratic character, many may feel that this was irresponsible of me. My brief but entrancing experience of Eva, so far, had already shown me, though, that she was more than capable of looking after herself.

We were nearing the furthest point in our excursion and were close to turning for home again when we broke free of forest. We stepped out into some Elysian fields; Alpine meadows basking in crisp, clear mountain air and sunshine. Here grew wild blueberries and strawberries, orchid and gentian. Beyond this idyll, presently out of reach but, one hoped, soon to be ventured upon, gratifyingly craggy mountains with tempting crisp linen napkins of snow. Eva pointed out one peak in particular, which she called a widowmaker. The Eiger. Then, all at once, with an exclamation, she fell to her knees. She beckoned to us. We stooped, and then kneeled, to look. It was edelweiss; grey and furry like a moth, or a roebuck's newly grown antlers. The velvety bracts that served as petals resembled paint splashes; a young child's first attempts at drawing a sunburst. Within this lay a cluster of a dozen or so tiny bee-yellow pincushions. These constituted the pollen-bearing element of the plant.

Holloway let out a low whistle and reached his left hand towards the stems. He plucked one.

"Do not pick them!" Eva cried. "I like them to stay on the mountains. Not to be kept indoors like... prisoners. Not to be torn from the earth to die."

Holloway looked flustered and, significantly, sharply hurt that he could have disappointed her.

"I – I'm sorry... I didn't..." He tailed off, looking as cowed and guilty as a beaten puppy.

Eva laid a cool hand on his forearm.

"Don't worry, you were not to know. Keep it now." She pressed Holloway's hand back towards him. Taking it as an absolution, and the newly picked flower as its symbol, he inserted it into his lapel.

The incident over, Eva leaned forward and placed her nose close to the little huddled plants. She inhaled deeply, held her breath a moment, and then let it out again.

"Smell," she motioned to us.

I leaned in and sniffed. Holloway followed suit.

"What does it smell of?"

"I don't know," replied Holloway. "Flowers?"

Eva laughed and turned to me. "Herr Doctor...?"

"Honey," I said.

"*Ja!*" she cried, and beamed at me. I felt the way I had when I was seven years old and had just won first prize in a school spelling competition.

It was indeed a subtle scent of honey. I was reminded of the gentle downland, on the south side of the London plain, with its sweeping lavender fields on a dusty summer's day; bee-loud, and rich with a sea of gently undulating purple rolling away into the distance.

A fleeting thought drifted across my mind like a cloud's shadow across a field. Maybe I could retire Holmes. Put him out to pasture? He could keep bees? Then, just as quickly as the thought came, it had gone.

I looked up and saw that Eva and Holloway had already moved on. They were climbing up the ever-rising path that crossed the meadow towards the Alpine peaks. I set off at a brisk pace to catch them up.

As I closed in, I saw movement beyond them. It appeared to be a group of walkers approaching from the other direction, away from the peaks. They were a good distance from us. But there was an element not quite right about them. It took me a moment to work out what it was. They were huddled together as they approached. It was hard to understand exactly why this scene was not consonant with the idyll that had been mine to date. Something was definitely amiss.

Eva had seen the group, too. I could tell by the way she hesitated and tensed that she did not like the look of the approaching group, either. She lengthened her stride, leaving Holloway and me behind. We kept up with her as best we could. As we closed, we began to make out details. There were four people in the group, and between them they carried abaft their shoulders what appeared to be long staves. Between these was a blanket or a tarpaulin. There was a person at each corner. They were carrying something. An animal, perhaps? Were they hunters? Was this their trophy? As they drew closer, we could tell that this was not the case. They did not have the jaunty air of a group of friends who had had fine sport that morning and were now swinging proudly down the mountain track. This group walked with measured step, as if they were mourners; as if what hung between them suspended from the staves was a coffin.

Soon it became clear that my speculation was not far off the mark. It was, indeed, a funeral procession. But there was no burial at the end of this particular journey. That would come later. At the end of this procession could only lie, to begin with, questions. Between the four men bearing the staves swung, wrapped in a blanket, what could only be the body of a human being.

As we reached them, they acknowledged Eva, whom they had plainly recognized from some distance away. They set their burden down so that we could inspect the contents of the blanket. These were simple Switzers who worked the high pastures in the summer months. They did not speak English, but Eva translated for us. The body belonged to a man. He had been found at the bottom of a rocky drop near a great cataract. They thought that his neck had been broken.

Eva, her brow furrowed, took a closer look; we joined her. He was a man about my age, small and wiry. He lay on the coarse blanket, which had been fixed onto the staves by strong hemp cord. It only took her a moment to recognize the face.

"This is Herr Brown!" she cried. "From my parents' hotel!"

So, I thought: Brown, the solitary. Brown, lying there like a dead fledgling on an avenue pavement. Brown looking even lonelier now than I had imagined.

Someone had retrieved his cloth cap from the vicinity of where he had fallen, and had placed it reverently on his chest.

"Why did you move him?" squeaked Holloway. His features had grown pallid under his thin tan. "Who told you to move him?"

Eva translated, but threw him a sidelong glance as she did so. The Switzers looked at each other and shrugged.

"It is the foremost principle of any suspicious death," Holloway continued. "You must not disturb the scene until the authorities have inspected it."

Eva obligingly translated again, and further unresponsive looks resulted from the bearer-party.

"You tell them," Holloway urged me. I must have looked as blank as the Switzers, so he repeated, "You tell them!" Then, seeing that I had no intention of doing any such thing, he addressed the gathering. "This," he said, waving a wild hand in my general direction, "is the creator of Sherlock Holmes. He is also a brilliant doctor. He will investigate the catastrophe."

"Catastrophe? What do you mean?" asked Eva.

"Yes," I added my ha'penn'orth. "What do you mean?"

"Doyle, listen, this may be nothing. It may be exactly what it appears to be. An unfortunate accident. Or it may be something far more sinister…"

He had no need to complete his thesis. I could quite follow where he was taking this. I, apparently, with my uncanny powers of detection and superb medical skills – as witnessed by my Holmes stories – would leap into action, explore every aspect of this mystery and, no doubt, come up with some startling revelation, to gasps of amazement and admiration from a grateful community. For him it was a natural equation: Here was I, to all intents and purposes a detective. There was a body. Ergo, a mystery had occurred. *Quod Erat Demonstrandum*.

On the other hand, my own concern at that precise moment was for the poor unfortunate who lay on that blanket. He was a thousand miles away from his home and his family on some foreign brae. The question was not whether he should have been disturbed from the place at which he had been discovered, but rather, how could we get him down to the village with something resembling dignity?

Ignoring Holloway, who continued to twitch, I asked Eva if there were anywhere that villagers took people who had had similar unfortunate accidents in the mountains.

"Yes, we usually bring them to lie in the church. Father Vernon looks after them until they can be brought down into the hospital in the valley."

"Father Vernon?"

"He is the priest of the church. Catholic." She crossed herself by way of further explanation. The others, not understanding what had been said, but noting the gesture and thinking that a holy exchange had taken place, copied her.

"Ah," I replied, "and then…?"

"And then the body is examined, if it is a sudden death, and when it is time the family can collect the poor man for the funeral. It is very sad."

"It is."

We both looked down at poor, lonely Brown. "Then that is what must happen next," I said. "Tell your people that we shall accompany them."

"Aren't you going to examine the scene?" blurted Holloway.

"Why should I?"

"In case there's been a…"

"A… what… exactly?"

"An incident. Suspicious. You know…"

"My dear Holloway, not every untimely death is suspicious. And even if I were concerned, it is frankly no business of mine. The doctors in the valley – whose training, I am sure, was every bit as excellent and thorough, if not more so, than my own – will be more than capable of establishing the cause of death. If they have any reason to take the matter further, I am positive that the Swiss police are similarly more than capable of pursuing any line of enquiry necessary."

"Yes, but…" Holloway's squall of enthusiasm for the world of the detective was blowing itself out against my implacable resolution.

"I do understand, Holloway," I sought to reassure him. "However, we cannot go gallivanting around a foreign country misappropriating every unfathomable incident just on the basis of the fact that I happen to have authored a number of popular mystery tales."

Eva laid her gentle hand on his arm.

"Richard, come…" she said. "It is best if we carry on this discussion at the village. It is not… good… that this poor man lies here. And my friends need to get back to their work."

"All right." Holloway allowed himself to be drawn down the slopes by Eva. Like an errant pony being led to the stables.

But then, no man could have resisted Eva.

Four

We accompanied the makeshift bier back down the slope, assisting where necessary when the going became treacherous underfoot. It was a sombre, dispiriting return in stark contrast to the light and joy that had attended the outward leg. When we reached the line of the village's outlying chalets, we set our burden down, to catch our breath and regain our strength. Holloway was not interested in the whole affair. He had fallen back upon simmering resentment. Eva had attempted to lift his spirits, but this served only to drive him further within himself. Interestingly, however, Eva neither took offence nor rejected his bad humour outright. Sympathy was her watchword. She walked beside him, casting him the occasional solicitous glance. If I were Eva, I thought, I would mark this chap down as a bad lot and find some other fellow. Someone who would more readily respond to her, as a flower opens its petals in the presence of sunshine.

As soon as he was able, Holloway left our little group with its poignant burden, and struck out into the village. I, too, took my leave. "*Requiescat in pace,*" I murmured instinctively. The bearer party and Eva began to wend their way towards the spire, on the far side of the community. I turned onto my path back to the hotel. In my room, I rested my ice axe against the little escritoire and hung my hat on the hook at the back of the door. Having changed and washed, I decided that I was hungry. It was well past midday, so this was not an unreasonable conclusion.

I wandered into the dining room to discover a cold collation and Madame Plantin completing her meal. We nodded hello, I collected my own selection from the sideboard, and sat down across from her. She took a sip from a glass of water and smiled at me. I returned the smile, took a forkful of salami, chewed and swallowed.

With the two of us in that large room, and with just plates laden with sliced cheese and cured meats for company, the silence became unbearable. I chose to break it.

"Monsieur Plantin did not join you for lunch?" I did not mean to pry, but it was an unavoidable question; they had appeared to be inseparable.

"*Ah. Oui!* He was here earlier but now he has gone out."

"By himself?" I enquired, wondering how, considering he was confined to a rolling chair.

"*Non.* Herr Werner has accompanied him."

"Splendid…" I was somewhat abashed that I had misjudged the Bavarian for no reason other than personal antipathy. "Have they gone for a walk? It is very beautiful around here."

"Yes, it is very beautiful. They have gone for a walk, but only to try and find the psychic."

The evening before crowded in on me. I had hoped that the previous night's conversation had been dismissed as so much nonsense and badinage and forgotten. I reflected again upon a day that had started out so gloriously, but in which cloud upon cloud had now banked upon it. If this trend continued, I may find myself stalking morosely around the town staring just a yard ahead of my boots, like Holloway.

"Concerning this psychic…" I began, then fell silent. I surveyed my companion across the dining table. I was not convinced that she would be able to respond intelligently to my confidences. Not that she wasn't intelligent. Not because she was French. Because she was young. I estimated her to be about half Plantin's age. She was pretty, too, possessing a very pleasant temperament and plainly adept at choosing clothes that set off her colour and vivacious disposition admirably. She was wearing an electric blue chenille dress, which complemented her olive skin and tight blonde curls.

"I wonder if such an experiment is wholly ethical?" I asked.

"Ethical, Monsieur?"

"Do you think it is proper, this séance?"

"But of course," she shrugged.

My dealings with the French people had almost always been of the most amicable and constructive nature. Also, despite his obvious failings, I was a great admirer of Napoleon, and his outrageously flamboyant *Grande Armée*. However, on this occasion, I found the matter of fact way she dismissed my reservations, before I had even had the chance to form the reason, as somewhat trying.

"It is sad about Monsieur Brown, *n'est-ce pas?*"

It took me a moment to recollect about whom she was speaking.

"Oh yes. The Englishman." I suspected Holloway of spreading the news the moment he had returned.

"*Oui*. I mean to say, Plantin did not like him one little bit, but it is sad all the same."

Two questions popped into my head. I chose to address only one of them.

"Why didn't Plantin like him?"

She looked at me quietly for a moment and pursed her lips. She decided, on balance, to confide in me. "You are a doctor, *non?*"

"I am."

"Marcus, he has not the use of his legs."

"Yes. I am sorry."

"Why should you be?"

I had no idea. It was just something people tended to say in these circumstances.

"He was in the war as a young man. It was a *bouf! – canon*."

He was about forty, so I assumed the war to which she referred was the Franco–Prussian conflict.

"A shell exploded?"

"Exploded. *Oui*. It had cut his… how do you say…? His wires… from his head to his body…"

"His nerves?"

"*Oui*. It cut them and *bouf!* He could use his legs no more."

"Tragic."

"*Tragique*. I did not know him, then."

This much I suspected.

"But when we married two weeks ago, I had known him for many months. In all this time I did never know him to be angry or unhappy. We have a good marriage."

"I am sure you do."

"But since he has come here, he does not seem to be so happy. Oh yes, we are in love and spend many happy hours with each other. But still he is cross, he is not content. He has been so content in Paris. And then this Mr Brown, he makes Marcus so unhappy. Even when he walks into the room, so Marcus becomes cross. I can tell. It makes me nervous, doctor." With this last, she leaned across and laid a hand on my wrist.

"You have talked about this with him?" I asked.

She started, and sat back in her chair. "Do married people talk about such things? Is a wife supposed to? What about her husband's dignity? What if he does not wish to discuss this? Or even wish to think he was behaving so? Would he not be angry with me?"

"You should hope to discuss everything together in private, with one another. There should be no secrets. My wife and I have no secrets. If I am sad or angry or frustrated, then she will come to me. When we are quiet and alone together. And she will say 'Is something the matter?' and then we will talk about it."

She had watched me with her blue eyes growing wider by the second. A true newly-wed. A true naivety about their husband and wife relationship. However, her manner and approach to her marriage did answer the second question. The one that had leapt into my mind when I heard that Plantin did not like Brown at all. The question was whether she had any opinion of her own. Perhaps it was one of which she was ashamed? Or was her husband's opinion in all things sufficient for the both of them? "I will speak to him," she resolved. "It is a wife's duty to ask her husband if there is anything the matter." She stood up, looked across at me and bobbed her head. I felt as if she were my daughter and I had given her permission to buy a new dress. "Thank you, doctor. *Vous êtes trop gentil.*"

"*Je vous en prie.*"

She giggled, and left me to the rest of my luncheon. I conversed briefly with Anton, who had come to tidy the dining room, and complimented him upon his sister, which seemed to gratify him. I then retired to the library for a pipe, and after, sauntered upstairs.

I awoke, startled. In my bedroom, I had closed the shutters. This had rendered the room so dark that I was initially disorientated. My heart hammered at my rib cage and my breath came in gasps. And then I recalled. I had gone for a nap knowing that I couldn't lie there for too long. I had an appointment to keep with Frau von Denecker. I leapt from my bed like a disturbed grouse, and felt my way across to the shutters. Flinging them open, I was dazzled by bright sunlight and gleaming mountains. If the sun was still high in the sky, I could not be that late, I reasoned. I jerked my watch out of my waistcoat on the back of one of the chairs, and brought it to the window. It was three fifty. I had ten minutes to present myself at Frau von Denecker's door. I had never met the lady, but something about her embossed calling card and the way she directed little messenger boys suggested it would not do to be either a minute late or a minute early. I smoothed my clothes as best I might, wet my hair, brushed it, swept a comb through my moustache and, donning my best city boots, left for my appointment.

Walking along the main street at a businesslike but not overly hasty pace, I happened to glance up at the Hotel Jungfrau. On the second floor balcony, which seemed to stretch the breadth of the building, a woman stood looking down at me. She was in her late fifties, I estimated. Her grey hair was tied tightly to the back of her head and held in place by a black lace toque. She wore a black satin dress, buttoned to the neck. She did not flinch when she noticed I was looking up at her. In fact, all she did was nod slightly then turn and withdraw into her room, supported by a silver-topped ebony cane.

I presented myself at the door and knocked. The little Swiss boy opened it and beamed a grin at me.

"Herr Doctor, Conan Doyle," he announced to nobody in particular and, pushing me in the small of the back, mischievously pressed me inside.

"You may go, Dieter. Thank you," said a voice from the next room, in high German.

He gave me another grin and a large wink and closed the door behind him. There was silence. I was not sure at first whether to stand there until I was permitted into the presence, or to take the liberty of entering unbidden. I chose the latter; I was on holiday. At such times, certain protocols may perforce be set in abeyance.

I entered the room to meet with a pair of steel blue eyes. Although she had grey hair and wore widow's weeds, these eyes, while grave, were by turns sprightly and commanding. I presented myself and she gave me her hand. I held the tips of her fingers in mine for a moment and let my head bob towards them courteously.

"Frau von Denecker. A pleasure to meet you," I said.

"The pleasure is mine," she said, in her elegant German. I have seen eyes gain a radiance when a new idea, or a piece of mischief, or a moment of humour occurs to the owner. Frau von Denecker's did so now. The question was, which of the three stimuli had occurred to her?

She indicated a Windsor chair on the far side of an occasional table. She sat, formally, uprightly, upon a *chaise longue*. The silver-topped cane leant against the arm, ready for use whenever it was called into service, like a footman.

The table supported plates and knives, a rich glazed apple *torte* and a chocolate marble cake. The latter was formed in an O and was dusted with icing sugar. There was a jug of milk, a jug of cream, some tall, thin glasses with handles, and a large teapot. A bowl of large, amber sugar crystals, like rough cut agate, completed the display.

"It has been a beautiful day, has it not?" Frau von Denecker remarked.

"Indeed. And I have marvelled at the mountains in such a light."

"Would you care for some tea, doctor?"

She lifted the bowl of sugar, with its silver spoon. Why did she offer me tea, but hold up the sugar? I did not dare suggest that it was the pot which contained the tea.

"I have been coming here for eighteen years. First with my husband and then, when he died, on my own…" She spoke while preparing tea. The reason she held the sugar bowl became apparent a moment later. "You may not know, doctor," she continued, as she gathered up a few tawny crystals onto the spoon and dropped them into the first glass, "and there is no reason why you should, that my family comes from East Prussia." I felt I could say or do nothing other than nod. She resumed, "This means that we have inherited some of the customs of our neighbours, the Russians. Which is why…" She paused, a spoonful of sugar crystals suspended motionless above the second glass, "I like my tea in this manner." The crystals fell into the bottom of the glass with a jingle. "Now," she said, lifting the teapot, prior to pouring, "listen…" With that, she poured piping hot tea upon the crystals. They crackled like kindling; thorns in a flame. She moved the pot across to the second glass and repeated the procedure. "Like ice breaking, is it not?" She smiled at me. The smile had a similar effect on me.

She returned with the teapot to completely fill both glasses. She then slid a slice of lemon in each.

"I understand that in England one prefers milk in one's tea? And it is a matter of protocol which goes into a cup first – the milk or the tea?"

"That is correct. It is to do with the quality of one's porcelain. Whether it can withstand the boiling water, or needs the milk to temper it."

"So, it is to do with class."

"Is not everything?"

"Everything," she agreed.

I accepted a plate with cake. I presumed to sample both varieties, one after the other, and found them equally quite exquisite. No doubt Frau von Denecker had them made in the village especially to her explicit recipes.

While I was sampling both cakes, we discussed my Sherlock Holmes stories, many of which, to my surprise and gratification, she had read. She had spent her early years in England and had Come Out at St James's. She had consequently taken a great interest in English literature. She had once even been privileged enough to meet Mr Charles Dickens. A fact, I assured her, that made me most envious indeed. She often had Austrian embassy staff bring her the latest reading matter from London on their frequent visits home, which was how she had been introduced to my stories.

"Do you think, doctor, that your central character is a little too scientific for his own good?"

"In what way?"

"I am concerned that he cares little for people and more for results. In my experience, it is not good for a person with great talent or great position in society to remain aloof from others, to the extent that they treat them as objects existing solely for observation, or their personal benefit."

"I assure you, Frau von Denecker, that my intention in creating Holmes was to invest him with warm red blood and a heart of flesh. If he did not come across in this way, then I shall make it my business to ensure his humanity be more evident in future. *If* I write any more, that is."

"I am exercised, doctor, by the possibility that your excellent creation's future could be in any doubt. In my opinion, it would be a sad loss to literature."

"Regrettably, Frau von Denecker, I am currently unable to reassure you in this regard. However, if it is of any consolation, your views chime entirely with those of my own dear mother."

"I am glad at least that your mother and I see eye to eye, doctor," she smiled. "On further consideration, I imagine that he is probably neither aloof nor immune to human sensitivities; his own or others. In my opinion, perhaps he concerns himself more with a person's motive and the product of that motive, rather than with the person, but not at the expense of that person, rather to their benefit. This gives me some comfort, particularly because Holmes's creator is clearly devoted to humanity and its care thereof."

"You are very kind, madame. However, I fear your view greatly overestimates my character."

"The correct response. A true gentleman is always humble. Now," she moved on to another topic, "it is terrible news to hear about your countryman, Mr Brown."

"Terrible," I agreed.

She fixed me with a glittering eye. "Did you know him?"

"No, in fact we had not even met. I arrived after he had left for his, as it turned out, final, fateful walk."

"Ah… So…" I hoped I wasn't hiding anything, because the gaze that now held me made me feel as though she could see into my very soul. "Are you staying with us long, doctor?"

"Two weeks," I replied.

"Exactly?"

"Well, in fact… ah… you are quite right, it is only twelve days now, as I leave this Saturday week."

This answer appeared to satisfy, and the conversation moved on. She told me how she was still just about mobile, but nowadays she found it hard to venture much beyond her hotel, since her hips and knees were stiffening with age. I did not do her the disservice of seeking to flatter her in this regard by telling her she did not appear old to me, or some such nonsense. I merely nodded my doctor's understanding of her trying circumstances. She said that everyone was so kind and considerate in the village, and brought her every last whim to her very door. Even the local priest was good enough to bring her communion once a week. I could quite believe that her manner commanded such attentiveness. She continued by telling me a little more of her provenance. She had been married to an

61

Austrian gentleman. They had lived most of their married life just outside Salzburg. We discussed that city's most famous son, Mozart. She was then interested to learn that I myself had spent two separate periods of my life studying in Vienna.

The discussion then shifted onto the political situation in Europe and beyond; the Austro-German alliance and the three emperors' alliance of Austria, Germany and Russia, which had collapsed five years previously. I could not help but think that she was involved in the intricacies of these diplomatic treaties. She was plainly well versed in their political subtleties. We considered the French government's rapprochement with the Tsar and the fall from grace of Bismarck, which had led to the *détente* between the German and Russian royal houses. Not only an intelligent, but also a well-informed woman.

She asked me, naturally, how the British government viewed this "elegant gavotte", as she called it. I responded as best I might, not being absolutely clear on my government's policies in this regard myself. I knew there was great concern that the wrong alliance could threaten the Balkans and the near east and, consequently, our trade routes to the subcontinent and beyond. I also knew that there was a growing rift between any number of Queen Victoria's grandchildren who seemed, presently, to occupy half the thrones of Europe.

Then, just as I was about to launch into a long and complicated theory regarding the relationship between the Austro-Hungarian Empire and the Turks, she stood up. "Well, doctor," she smiled, "I must detain you no longer." A command. My mouth closed. I quite understood, and did not wish to outstay my welcome. Listening to a British ophthalmologist's views on high international politics was not, perhaps, the most enthralling way of spending an afternoon.

Taking my leave, I offered my thanks and took the hand she held out. I bussed it with the gentlest of touches from my lips, and made my exit.

I stepped out of the hotel just as the church bells began to ring. They sent their peals echoing across the village and the valley beyond. I fumbled for my smoking implements. Having filled my pipe, I strolled down the high street, puffing away like a Swiss valley locomotive, and reflected on the day.

I recalled Madame Plantin and her concerns for her husband. I also remembered both her and Frau von Denecker's sympathy expressed to me of Brown's tragic demise. Why to me? Because I was his countryman? Frau von Denecker had asked if I had known him. *Was* I expected to do so? Or was it just a simple expression of sympathy, which I had started to take personally and to complicate? And why had I had such a fitful sleep and a reawakening in such disorientation? It cannot have been that I was unnerved by all of this. I am a doctor. I have seen many a corpse. Indeed, I have dissected them. I have been witness to the personal outcomes of many tragic cases in the past. Yet, I *was* disturbed. Why didn't all of this make sense? Why was I beset by such a sequence of unconnected yet individually unsettling events and unwarranted conversations?

I had an overwhelming urge to be at home, in the bosom of my family; with Touie and Mary and my new child-to-be. Safe and secure in normality and predictability; a safe haven in an inconstant sea.

A walker strode by, supported by a thick, gnarled alpenstock. I stopped. This reminded me of something I had not realized I actually knew. Something I had not even fully understood that I could know. A secret knowledge, secret even to me. As I wrestled with whatever it was in my mind that was so keen to bring itself to my attention, I took a long pull on my pipe. Then the cloud of unknowing dissolved. Brown was an ardent and accomplished walker. His hat had been found and returned to him as he lay upon the blanket. Where, though, was his alpenstock? An alpenstock without which an experienced fellow like he would not have ventured out upon mountain tracks; treacherous after rain. An alpenstock, moreover, with, I supposed, the ubiquitous leather strap. A strap designed to prevent it leaping from the owner's presence, should they stumble and lose their grip on it.

I looked across at the spire. The bells were summoning people to mass on this Sunday evening. I searched my memory: how long was evening mass? Under an hour? I resolved to cross to the church after the service had finished. I would discreetly ask to see the body before it was claimed by the officials from the valley hospital, which could be as soon as tomorrow morning for all I knew. Moreover, I decided that nobody must know that I had just taken an interest in the affair. I did not know why, but I knew that this was most important.

I filled the intervening time by strolling around the village and inspecting the architecture. It was varied and had been understandably subjected to a number of different influences: Swiss, French, German, Italian. I had at length reached the grounds of the church when I encountered the congregation leaving. There were just a few of them, as this was not the principal service of the day.

To my surprise, I discovered Holloway among them. He nodded and weaved through the small exodus towards me.

"Going to see any body?" he asked, slyly.

"Have you been to see it just now?"

"I got here right at the end of the service and had a word with the padre." He shrugged. "Our Mr Brown, it would seem, is not receiving visitors today. Though it eludes me what holy reverends are doing denying people access to anything. Especially in a place of worship." He paused, and looked me up and down. "You going to give it a try?"

Whatever answer I gave, my principal concern was that he did not accompany me. The nuisance of it all was that he had already received the answer that I was seeking. Yet I could not bring myself to return to the hotel.

"Are you going back to the hotel now?" I asked. He made a non-committal gesture, which was becoming difficult to see in the gathering dusk. So I continued, "Have you eaten since you returned?"

"I had something in a café."

"Then perhaps you would be best advised to have something a little more substantial. Long mountain walks take it out of one, and if you wish to maintain your stamina throughout your stay, then I would advise you to keep up your strength."

He looked at me critically. A smirk stole into his eyes. "You're the doctor." He began to move away. "Besides… Eva may be at the hotel…"

The congregation had dissolved as the morning dew during the course of our exchange, so I was able to step into the church unnoticed. I removed my hat out of deference to the institution and tradition. When in Rome…

Once inside, the space had a familiarity bred from years of common practice and concerns by clergy and churchgoers the world over. I had been schooled by Jesuits and brought up a good Catholic. As my scientific and medical research had developed, and my library had grown, my opinions and beliefs had gradually altered. I did not discount, by any means, certain possibilities these days. But I rejected absolutism, institutionalism, and exclusiveness in religions. I had naturally been to church on numerous occasions for a variety of purposes since my exploration of faith had begun to widen its scope. I still trusted its comforts while rejecting its dogmas. I abhorred its threats and applauded its struggles. Nevertheless, this church felt strangely welcoming, and I entered with neither trepidation nor antipathy.

The gas jets had, in the majority, been extinguished. All the old standards that I remembered well from my youth were there: the oak pews, the dog-eared service books, the rose-coloured light flickering in front of the reserve sacrament, and the candlesticks and cross almost glowing in the residual light.

I sat down at the back to consider this place and review my feelings about it all. If only it were all true, I thought, life would be so much simpler. But if it were true, why did people continue to murder one another? I heard a rustle and looked up. Coming from the vestry in the simple, rough, donkey-brown habit of a Franciscan friar was the priest.

"Father Vernon?" I guessed. My voice, coming as it did from the shadows of the church, made him jump.

"Yes? May I help you?" He spoke German, as had I.

"My name is Doctor Conan Doyle." I emphasized the "Doctor". "I was with the party on the mountain that brought Herr Brown down this morning."

"Another Englishman?" I was not happy with the assumption as to my nationality, but I let it go. "There seems to be a great deal of English interest in this gentleman's sad demise," he continued. I was not sure, but as he approached me, I believed I could begin to smell a hint of alcohol on his breath.

"Am I not," I responded, "as a doctor and fellow national, duty bound to spend a moment in vigil with him?" Needs must, I told myself. It wasn't exactly a lie but, I confess, it wasn't completely true either.

"You may, of course, observe your vigil," Father Vernon replied, graciously. "Here." He pointed to where I was already sitting.

I wondered whether Holloway had used my name in vain with this priest, once he had found access to Brown wasn't going to be granted him. In which case Sherlock Holmes's name might well have entered the conversation, too. Father Vernon had that all-too-familiar look about him. That look which said, "*I know who you are, but I'm blessed if I am going to demean myself by showing you that I know it.*"

"I may not sit with him, though?"

"You may not."

"May I ask why?"

"Apart from the fact that the sanctity of the human being should be preserved in death as in life, and that I do not consider your picking about around him to be appropriate, you mean?"

"I was not proposing to 'pick about around him' as you put it," I bridled. "I merely…"

He broke in, "I do not doubt that your request is presented with the highest motives. It is simply my duty to ensure that the body is not touched until the correct authority has taken responsibility for it." He looked at me pointedly at his phrase "correct authority".

"In which case, I bid you a good evening, Father." I replaced my hat.

"And I you… but…"

I stopped. Had the priest relented?

"Are you not going to stay and pray for him?"

I would hesitate to suggest that a respectable man of the cloth might actually gloat. However, few if any other words would suffice to describe how he looked at me at that moment.

"Thank you, no. Since I may not sit with him, I may just as easily pray for him at my hotel." At which non-conformist remark, I bowed from the collar upwards and withdrew into the evening.

My rebuff at the hands of the priest was just beginning to rankle to the point of self-righteousness, when my swarming thoughts were interrupted by a low voice addressing me.

"Hoi! Doyle! No luck, either?"

FIVE

"Holloway?" I peered into the gloaming.

"Over here."

He was sitting on a low wall, drumming his heels against the brickwork. The glow of a cigarette grew and faded. He had found some Vestas of his own, then.

"What do you mean 'No luck, either'?"

"You know. Brown."

"I thought that you were going back to the hotel."

"So did I. Then I realized I wanted to see how it all came out. You and the Pope, there. Not a sack of laughs, is he?"

"He is only doing his job."

"Telling folk to push off? I thought they were supposed to welcome us?"

"I did not care to press him. I sought to respect his office."

"But you are suspicious, all the same?"

"How do you mean?"

"What do you mean 'How do you mean?' Seems to me that's just a delaying tactic while you gather your thoughts. Seems to me you would rather I wasn't around asking awkward questions and stirring things up. But seems to me I have hit upon something where Brown's concerned and you are just too big and famous to admit it."

"All right, Holloway, it did occur to me that there had been more to Brown's tragic death than meets the eye. And I do not think myself too big and famous to admit it."

He gave one of his long low whistles, like a pigeon's wings as it settles.

"But it was not thanks to your coaxing or any such consideration," I added. "I had given it up until barely an hour ago, when the church bells began to ring."

He took another pull on his cigarette and exhaled some smoke in my direction. "Well, then, Watson, what have you deduced from all this?"

"Where," I paused, perhaps overdramatically, "was his alpenstock?"

"I don't know. Where was it?"

He really was a most irritating fellow.

"That is precisely the point. A walker, yet where was that stick? It could not have gone far, because of the wrist strap."

"Maybe they just didn't pick it up?"

"They had collected his hat for him."

"Yes – but a stick's a stick. Could have got mixed up with any number of other branches just lying around there. It is a forest, after all, Doyle."

"Listen, I thought you were the one who wanted to establish some kind of evidence of mischief-making?"

"Yes. But *real* evidence. Not all of this namby-pamby stuff."

Namby-pamby? Forsooth!

"Well, since you are plainly the expert in such cases, perhaps you could tell me what evidence you have amassed?"

"None."

"None. So why are you so dismissive of my opinions?"

"I am not. I'm just exploring the case from every angle. Seeing if it all fits together."

"So, how would you propose to explore this further?"

"Do some more investigating."

"Return to the scene, and see if we can unearth the alpenstock?"

"Oh no, I am not going all the way up there again. Not unless I have to."

"So – what do you suggest?"

"We take a peek at Brown."

"But... well... we are not permitted..."

"Who said anything about permission?"

The silent dusk grew deeper and darker.

"How do you mean?"

"Churches are always open, aren't they? Priests have got to go to bed some time or other, don't they?"

I gaped at Holloway. Unfortunately, it was dark and he was unable to note my disbelief.

"Well?" he said. "Do you believe in Justice, Liberty and Truth? Or is Mr Sherlock Holmes going to slink away with his tail between his legs?"

The cigarette glowed again.

"All right,' I said, much against my better judgment. "We will do it."

We set off towards the hotel together. It was decided that we would lie low there until we could be sure that the priest was asleep. I recollected the smell of alcohol on his breath, which I felt was fresh; possibly occasioned by red wine. Someone who drinks like that would, I felt sure, fall into the arms of Morpheus in an hour or so.

At the hotel, rather than come in, Holloway left me and went off mumbling something about having something else to do, which I didn't catch.

I returned to my room, changed quickly for dinner, and presented myself at my chair a few minutes later. It was a sombre meal. The fact that one chair in particular was empty – Brown's – was a reminder to the rest of us. Events high up on a dark, lonely brae, while we were safe and warm enjoying our food and wine.

Holloway was also missing. Though I doubt any of us regretted that unduly. Having said that, of course, no one regretted Brown's absence either, and look what had happened to him.

There was another reason for the maundering tone to our supper. Plantin was undoubtedly markedly discomfited. His countenance clouded over with dark introspection. I looked across at Madame Plantin, who had noticed my concern. She gave a weak smile and a shrug. I wondered whether this change in Plantin's disposition were due to my conversation with her. I felt obliged to try to broach the subject. "Monsieur Plantin," I began, "how did you find today? It was an excellent and invigorating day, did you not think?"

He glared at me for an instant. *Le Roi ne s'amuse, point.* Then out of, I suspect, sheer politeness, since there were others present, he confirmed that it had indeed been an excellent day. Then fell to his dark thoughts again. I considered returning to the fray, but his glower became even more pronounced. I looked to Madame Plantin, who raised her eyes heavenwards and jammed a fork into an innocent cut of meat.

Having failed to navigate the waters of Plantin's black lagoon, I turned my attention to Werner. He was shovelling his meal into his mouth like the fireman on a London to Edinburgh express. He paused only to wash down a mouthful with beer. Not having Holloway for company that evening, he spent even less time in conversation. Hunting does that for an appetite, I surmised.

In contrast to the Plantins, the van Engelses seemed relatively buoyant. While not exactly sparkling like champagne, there was definitely a lighter mood about them. They even exchanged a word or two in Dutch with one another. They conversed in low tones, as if confiding, or perhaps plotting, some carefully constructed plan. She it was who appeared to be leading the discussion. I would not say that it was returned by a reluctance on his part. It was more something he wanted to do, too, but for one reason or another he had reservations.

For fear of snapping the delicate gossamer thread that currently joined them, I made my small talk with the Pivcevics. We discussed the weather, the mountains, the meadows and forests. I told them about the edelweiss, which enthralled them. They had not yet encountered the plant in its wild state, so decided to venture out the very next morning.

The meal concluded, we separated as before. I found myself ensconced, once again, in the library, puffing on my pipe and savouring a small, assertive cognac. Both van Engels and Pivcevic beat me to the departure. The former made no excuse but just swept off peremptorily, the latter pleading other business. I was consequently left alone with Werner and his beer, and Plantin and his funk.

We sat in unfathomable silence for some while. A silence broken only by the occasional sipping noises perpetrated by Werner. I was just finishing my pipe and had begun making the kinds of moves one makes when one is on the verge of leaving company when Werner spoke up.

"Ah. Doctor, we have arranged your séance."

I knocked my pipe out on the hearth.

"Had you forgotten?"

"No."

"It will be tomorrow evening. We shall all go after supper."

"All?"

"*Ja*, of course. Everybody in the hotel wants to come."

"Everybody?" To have to endure this folly at all was an awful prospect as it was. But to have the event turned into a sideshow or a music hall revue was too ghastly by half. "Surely these matters are better conducted in an atmosphere of intimacy…?"

"*Ach, nein!* The more the merrier, as you English say…"

"I'm Irish."

"Irish say…"

"I am not sure that *merry* is quite the appropriate adjective to employ in the same breath as *séance*, but I will let it lie."

Throughout, Plantin had been staring gloomily at the bookshelf, his chin in his hand. Without changing his posture, he announced mournfully, "I do not know that my wife and I shall be attending."

Did this imply that his presence and mine at the same occasion were incompatible? "Monsieur Plantin?" He didn't look at me. "Marcus – may I speak freely?"

"Don't you always?"

"If I have offended in any way…?"

"What did you tell my wife?"

"How do you mean?"

"You discussed matters of a highly personal nature to me. What did she say?"

"Well, first, Marcus... I am a doctor and it is not uncommon for wives who are worried about their husbands to –"

He waved a dismissive hand, "I do not care what is not uncommon. What did Marie say about me to *you*?" He jabbed an index finger towards me: *j'accuse*.

"She said nothing improper, I can assure you. We simply discussed, well, her concerns for you…"

"What concerns for me? Do I have anything that she has to be concerned about? *Non*." He tapped the arm of his rolling chair with the fingers of one hand. "Of course, I am sitting in this. But that is a long time past and we have talked about this openly. Before, during and after we are married. So… *non*… there is nothing to discuss." He sat back and folded his arms Napoleonically.

"She was wondering whether anything was upsetting you," I persisted.

"Nothing. Absolutely. We are having a splendid time. Until you arrived."

"I do hope that I have not in any way upset your holiday."

"You have not upset this. But you must not make personal enquiries about me with Marie any more."

"I can assure you that that would be the last thing I should wish to do."

Werner had been watching this exchange, swivelling his head this way and that, as if at a tennis match. His beer glass remained suspended between thigh and lips throughout. He finally took a sip and replaced the glass on his thigh. There it joined a succession of wet rings, created by the condensation running down the outside of the glass and collecting on the bottom.

"Since you have organized this séance," I returned my attention to Plantin, "I would deem it a pleasure if you and your wife would join us after all."

"We will consider this."

The interview ended and, my pipe once again knocked out, I finally made my own exit.

"I bid you both goodnight."

As I lay upon my bed, waiting for Holloway's and my covert expedition, I could not help but reflect on Plantin and his wife further. I had a vague theory that he was in some way frustrated by being unable to fully enjoy these beautiful slopes. However, I was sure that there was transport available to take him and his wife as high up into the mountains as practicable. I wondered whether, perhaps, there was an even more personal problem than that. It was hard to tell on such a glancing encounter. If I wished to get to the bottom of this, then I would have to explore further. Or, then again, I could just leave them to their own devices. As far as Plantin was concerned, the case was closed. I recognized that unless it was reopened voluntarily by one or other of them, I would not concern myself with it a moment longer.

I had just reached this satisfactory conclusion when there came a firm rap upon my door. I clambered off the bed and, yawning, opened it. I fully expected to see Holloway, bright and early for our expedition. I did not expect to see Professor van Engels.

"Do come in."

The Dutchman shuffled in and closed the door behind him. I could detect an invisible curl of cognac fumes. He was clutching something close to his chest. It was tied with red ribbon like a legal brief.

"Do please sit."

He settled on the room's only armchair. I took the ladder-back seat, situated before the escritoire.

"I am afraid I am unable to offer you anything by way of liquid refreshment," I said. This was true, but it was also a relief. I did not feel much like entertaining a man apparently devoted to alcohol by supplying him further.

"It is no matter. I have come to see you to discuss a subject of some importance…'

I let him gather his thoughts.

"Do you see…? I am very keen to write myself. I have done this for many years. Since a boy, in fact. In my job I became too busy for such trivia." He waved the dossier, then replaced it against his chest. "So, I let it slip. But now, I have begun again to write. Stories. Intricate, artistic stories. Complex. About complex people. I try to write stories that make people add up. Like equations."

"What is it that you do for a living?"

"I am professor, mathematics. Utrecht."

As I suspected.

"I try to give the people in my stories characteristics. So, for example, character number one has characteristics A plus B plus C. Then my character number two has characteristics X plus Y plus Z. So…"

I nodded to indicate that I followed him.

"Then I create circumstances and situations and, depending upon these, I multiply or divide or add or subtract. It is very simple formulae. But it works."

"And you believe that all human life can be explained by, for example, quadratic equation?"

"You should read my stories."

"I should like to."

"They are not like ordinary stories."

"I am sure that they are not."

"They are original and revealing."

"Absolutely."

"Of course – they do not read as other stories do."

"I surmised as much through your explanation. Professor van Engels…?"

"Yes?"

"Is there love and hate, pain and joy in your stories?"

"The reader may interpret the various outcomes in this manner, *ja*."

"But it is for the reader to interpret?"

"It is for the reader to feel. The writer is merely the instrument, surely?" He looked at me as if I were unable to grasp some basic tenet of literature. He gave the impression he was amazed that I had come so far as a writer without knowing such a simple fundamental fact.

"Dickens wept as he wrote," I said.

"*Nej*, Dickens was imprecise. He would start in the morning, not knowing what he would put down on paper, and write until dark, following his instincts. He was all passion and emotion, like van Beethoven."

"And you have no emotion?"

"*Ja*, of course. I am only human. I have every emotion. Including, though I think that you do not suspect this, a sense of humour. But literature demands precision. Objectivity. No emotion, only technique."

"I have heard music which is all technique. Music which is applauded to the rafters in conservatoires. Applauded by those cognoscenti who understand music theory, all across the world. But I prefer my music to be born of emotion."

"*Ja*, so, well… I would put overemotional down for you as characteristic A."

"Really? How intriguing. What other characteristics would you give me?"

"Do you really wish to know?"

"Of course. For purely scientific reasons, you understand?"

"Then I would say… characteristic B – indiscipline."

I looked at him closely. He was not displaying the slightest indication of the sense of humour he professed to possess. "And characteristic C…?"

"Anger." He looked pleased with himself. It was as if he had just resolved Euclid's fifth proposition. Was I really just an equation? A sum of parts that could be dissected and itemized? Can a human being's personality be compartmentalized and explored in purely scientific terms? There was work going on when I was in Vienna to that purpose, I knew. Furthermore, William James had published his excellent principles of psychology recently. But I was unsure as to whether a person could be simply entered into a ledger and then minutely analysed. I did not doubt that it would have a value in the most extreme circumstances; with profoundly mentally ill patients, for example. It may even be that it would work upon more superficial levels; for people who, perhaps, needed a little clearer direction as to who they were and where they may go in their lives. But to have such a clinical analysis as a be-all and end-all? Would that not lead to a situation where those who had characteristics A plus B plus C were despised by those who had characteristics X, Y and Z? Or at least lead unavoidably to relationships being terminated because such-and-such a type was scientifically proven to be incompatible with so-and-so type? It left no room for chance, this formula. And chance, although it brings pain and confusion, also brings joy and beauty and that inspiring happenstance that is the fundamental alchemy of all humankind's existence.

Yet, I wondered, was that what I had made Holmes do? Reduce personality into component parts? No. Frau von Denecker had put her finger upon it. Holmes analysed motive, and the product of that motive. He allowed human beings the dignity of self-expression; even if that meant that this was manifested sometimes in murder. Not that he condoned it. But he allowed that the freedom for it to occur existed, since without that freedom, we would all be automatons. Or formulae as expressed by Dutch professors of mathematics.

"I should be glad to read your stories, Professor van Engels," I said.

With only the slightest hesitation, he gave his precious brainchild into my safe keeping. "You know, my wife said you should read these. I was not so sure." He departed, and I left the dossier on my escritoire to be examined at leisure later. I looked at my pocket watch. It was ten minutes after Holloway's and my appointed rendezvous. We had not discussed how we should convene, so I assumed that as he had not come to find me, it was my task to go and find him. I picked up my hat and left my room.

His own room was empty; or rather he did not answer when I knocked. Nor when I knocked more firmly a second and a third time, assuming that he had fallen asleep. This lack of Holloway left me uneasy. Not that I was pining for his company. I just had, like van Engels, put two and two together and the product left me equating Holloway's absence with that of Brown's the night before. That is to say, half a notion lurked in the back of my mind that they had dealt with him the way they had dealt with Brown.

Whoever "they" were. Even if "they" existed.

Then again, if Brown's death were not an accident…?

I pulled myself up short. It was clear to me that I was beginning to formulate hard and fast theories before I had fully established all the facts. And worse, I was beginning to incorporate Holloway's lack of response, simple and ultimately explicable though it probably was, into these wild suppositions.

Another consideration occurred to me. Was I secretly hoping Holloway had been disposed of, like Brown? I did not know. I was unable to peer that deep into my consciousness. Even if I were hopeful – why? Surely I couldn't want Holloway murdered? Or anyone for that matter. I was a doctor, and a writer of moral stories to boot…

I shook all these morbid and ultimately futile thoughts off, and brought myself round to considering what was to be done next. I tried to think analytically. Was Holloway dead, asleep or even just not in his room? I could not resolve the first two questions immediately, unless I could see inside the room, which I could not. Therefore, I needed to get in there to find out.

I made my way downstairs. It was by now very late and I had not intended that anyone should know I was still up and about. I did not want difficult questions about churches and bodies later. There was no other sign of habitation, not even in the back office, behind the reception desk, which was in darkness. Dare I reconnoitre the office in the hope that Holloway's bedroom key was there?

I stole into the room behind the desk and looked around for a gas jet or an oil lamp. There was one of the latter on the writing desk, covered by a damask cloth. I lifted off the glass and put it down on the blotter. I then fumbled in my pockets for my Vesta case.

I had just produced a stick and was pressing it against the sandpaper when I heard a curious, metallic scratching noise. It was coming from the far end of the lobby. I immediately ducked beneath the desk and held my breath. The noise became more distinct, and I realized with a mixture of relief and anxiety that it was the front door latch. A key had been trying inexpertly to find its way into the lock, had now done so, and was in the process of being turned.

I remained concealed behind the desk for a few moments more, until I heard a whispered exchange. One voice was Eva's, it would seem. The other voice came in a gruff whisper; the increasingly familiar tones of the current bane of my life. I stood up and walked out from the darkness of the office into the light of the reception area. My sudden appearance produced in Holloway a most gratifyingly shocked expression.

"Doyle!" He clutched at his pocket. "What are you doing here?"

"Waiting for you."

"Good evening, doctor."

"Eva... good... good evening."

"Why are you waiting for Richard?" she asked.

I looked at Holloway.

"I asked him to," Holloway said, taking his cue. "We had agreed to meet up at this hour…"

I glared at him. Was he about to let Eva in on our proposed expedition?

"… for a stroll and a smoke and a chat before bed."

Eva was not wholly convinced. I noticed that she had seen the Vesta case in my hand. Her eyes roved about to see what else was possibly amiss. I watched her eyes dart past me, into the office and back to me again. I realized that although dark, the uncovered oil lamp, the cloth and its glass may still be visible.

"Come along, Doyle." Holloway took my arm and pulled me towards the front door. "I'm eager for that cigarette. Eva doesn't approve – so I shall have to smoke it out of view. See you've got your Vestas." He laughed and Eva smiled in return.

"Goodnight, Richard," she said, with warmth. She turned to me. "Goodnight, doctor," she said, rather more coolly.

Outside the hotel, Holloway lit his cigarette.

"Where were you?" I hissed.

"None of your business. Come on – let's get this over with…" He sighed.

"There's no need to sound so world-weary, Holloway. After all, it was your idea to do this."

I let the argument tail off. It would get us nowhere and, besides, the need for silence was paramount. Even a hissed exchange of views could carry a long way at night in the still mountain air. We arrived at the church to discover that it was agreeably quiet and dark. Tiptoeing around to the west door, we both steadied ourselves for the trespass we were about to commit. At that point I suddenly received a pang of conscience, as sharp as a barb in my stomach. I am not afraid of much, and I have often had the resolve to approach difficulties with sanguinity. But to enter consecrated ground in the dead of night in order to paw over a corpse – an action for which we did not have permission – was that not desecration? If Touie could see me now, what would she say? And as for my devoted readers… Such a gentleman. Such a moral champion and a fine upstanding pillar of the community. A beacon of light in the sinful darkness of humanity. Pish. And, indeed, tush.

"Come on, Doyle. Let's get on with it." Holloway grabbed at the door.

"No!" I seized his wrist, fearful that his little burst of temper would result in him wrenching the door open unceremoniously and causing the most awful row, which would wake everyone within earshot. The priest's house was only a short path distant.

Having stayed his hand, I stepped forward myself and gently, painstakingly, curled my fingers around the doorknob. Gripping it firmly, I began to manipulate it. I turned it to the left, but it refused to give. I twisted it to the right and, similarly, the door did not respond. I turned towards Holloway.

"It is locked," I announced.

SIX

"Now what do we do?"

Trespass is bad enough and unforgivable. Trespass in a place that many consider most holy and revere above all earthly things, is doubly so. Trespass in order to conduct an investigation of a dead stranger's body trebly so. On the other hand, what if it did transpire that something was not as it should be concerning Brown's death? What then? To be found here, doing what I proposed to do, what would that say about my innocence? I was not Sherlock Holmes. I did not have his reputation and respect as a guardian of truth and justice. This was the real world and, all too often, the real world was far more complex than anything an author's mind could contrive. My stories were all very well but they still conformed to a reasoned-out structure in my mind. Real-life mysteries may well have a reasoned-out structure as well – cause and effect – but what the participants may propose does not necessarily equate to what fate may eventually dispose.

And why was the door locked? I speculated further. Were we being watched, perhaps? I could quite understand Father Vernon being suspicious. An Englishman dead. Two fellow countrymen appearing in quick succession to plead that they may be given permission to inspect the corpse. It would be enough kindling for anyone's suspicions. Would I lock the door, too? I considered that, yes, I most probably would. Of course, it could be more innocent than that. It could simply be an act of courtesy; to allow the body of a departed soul to rest undisturbed through the watches of the night. To rest in peace, secure in this place of worship, this house of God. Again, it could be that the priest was under instructions to keep the place where his charge lay locked until the body could be recovered and both the medical people and the police in the valley could investigate the whole affair themselves.

"Doyle!" Holloway had been scouting around the side of the church. His hoarse whisper summoned me to his side. He was standing at an open door.

"You didn't force it?"

"Naturally. But it was easy. You didn't hear anything, did you? There you are, then. Well… what are you waiting for? Get inside…"

I edged along a passage leading into the body of the church. Holloway drew the door closed behind him, leaving us in utter darkness. He struck a match and lit a dark-lantern. "Did you bring one?"

"A lantern? No… I didn't expect…"

"Lot of use you are."

We skulked to a door behind the sanctuary, next to the vestry. Holloway tried the handle; it didn't move.

"Hang on, there's a key in the lock." It gave way with a well-oiled click.

An odour met us. There was also the reek of wet wool. The lantern showed us a trestle table, laid with a white linen cloth. There was a second linen cloth on top of this which, with its peaks and troughs, resembled the mountains that loomed over the village outside. They were also the contours of a human being. At the end where the head rested were two solemn oil lamps, lit. The priest had reverenced the mortal remains of the departed soul, and had then ensured that the lights would keep Brown company through the long watches of the night.

"Excellent!" Holloway set his lantern on a free-standing bookcase of missals. He pointed its lens towards the body. "You had better get straight on with whatever it is that you do. The quicker you're done with it, the quicker we can be out of here."

He stepped aside and lodged himself against the bookshelf like a spectator at a game of billiards.

I stepped forward and turned up the oil lamps. I then folded back the cloth from the deceased's face. It looked much as it had looked when last I saw him, on his blanket upon the brae. The eyes had been closed then, as they were closed now. Just as my old tutor Dr Bell had always taught, I contented myself with simply observing in the first instance. As I looked, I drew back the sheet further and further, noting every detail. I discovered the source of the wet wool smell: his tweeds were still damp. I studied every blemish, lesion and abrasion on the skin, wherever it was exposed. They were on the face, the neck, the hands. They were all consistent with a fall down a rocky slope. It was evident that this slope also contained shrubs, as one or two of the lesions were long and jagged tears. There were also occasional places where a branch had simply jabbed straight at the flesh. One hand, the left, was of particular interest. The fingers as far as the second joint were covered in dried mud.

Reaching the feet, I noticed particularly the shoes: the scuff marks and the residue of soil and vegetation. It was moss and grass mainly, along the edge of the sole and upon the sole itself. I noted the condition of both soles, which were leather. By their wear, I should have said that they were at least a month old. More used to the scuffing that came from city streets than an alpine village with its preponderance of grass and earth tracks. They were worn pretty evenly on both balls of the feet and both outsides at the heels.

I completed my initial observation and decided that the next thing was to search the pockets. I did not believe that this would have been done to date, since no one who had so far encountered the body, with the possible exception of Father Vernon, would have had cause to do so. The sum total of my inspection was a watch; some local currency; a wallet containing banknotes and other documentation; a fountain pen; a pipe; a tobacco pouch containing, according to the sweet aroma, Virginia tobacco; some matches and a striking case. In his trouser pockets I found just a handkerchief. Having showed them, one by one, to Holloway, I replaced them all and stood back.

"Well?" he asked.

"Well what?"

"What next? Strip him down, I suppose. Do you want a hand?"

I looked at Brown and considered. I was not squeamish. I had helped undress any number of bodies in my time; one or two in an advanced state of decomposition. Yet there was something about the sanctity of the environment, the violence of his end, and the fact that he was being honoured by this gentle laying-out, that stayed my hand. I could not bring myself to unbutton a single item of the unfortunate fellow's clothing.

Instead, I leaned forward and started to sniff. All those years ago at medical school I had had it drummed into me. When examining a patient, use all of the senses. I had looked. I had rummaged in his pockets but had found nothing that warranted tasting. Now it was smell. Apart from the first odours of corruption and the wet-wool smell, there was little else as my nose travelled along his body a few inches above the surface. Then, when I reached Brown's face, I caught a whiff of something abnormal. Something herbal on his lips? Peppermint? What? I inhaled again and tried to place it. I beckoned Holloway over.

"What is that smell on the lips, do you think?"

Holloway bent to Brown's mouth and breathed in. He looked up and exhaled. "Don't know – liquorice?"

"Yes. Bravo! But not liquorice. Anise-seed."

"Anise-seed? What does that mean?"

"I don't know, yet."

I continued my examination. Having finished with smell, it remained only for me to feel and to listen. I palpated the body through the clothes, twisting the limbs this way and that, gently turning the head first onto its left temple, and then onto its right. It was not easy – rigor mortis had set in. All the time I was listening for any unusual clicks, crackling or moist, even liquid, sounds. Noises that would indicate, for example, the presence of broken bones and the formation of any fluids under the skin.

It was a long, laborious process. At last, I stood up and eased my aching back. I then declared myself to be satisfied that I had gleaned as much information from the body as was possible, considering the circumstances.

"Finished? How can you be finished?"

"I have all the information that I need from the cadaver."

"That's nonsense. You have to examine the whole body – you haven't even taken the jacket off."

"I have no need to…"

"What do you mean, you have no need to? Of course you have need to. There could be stab marks, a gunshot wound, anything…"

"They would have left a mark where they penetrated the clothing. You saw me roll the body over, first on one side and then the other. There were no such entry marks."

"But how can you tell if he'd been struck, or something, before he died?"

I started to turn down the first oil lamp in the manner of a professor who had just successfully concluded another illuminating and engrossing lecture. "My purpose was not to determine the cause of death, but –"

"Hang your purpose! Your squeamishness means that you have most probably missed vital evidence and, further, you have rendered all the risks we have taken here farcical and a waste of time."

"I can assure you, I am missing nothing that –"

At that point, Holloway leapt from his observation point and knocked my hand away from the second lamp.

"Don't turn them down!"

Too late, we both noticed that in the knocking away of my hand, the oil lamp had been overset and cast onto the flagged floor. The glass shattered, the oil spilled and the flame that had lain practically dormant burst from the wick. It began devouring the oil hungrily. A bright and, considering the small space, large and hungry flame resulted.

"Run!" said Holloway, and bolted for the door.

The flames were large, and the prospect of them growing larger was increasing by the second. Yet, while everything within me urged me to emulate Holloway and make good my escape, I could not leave the chapel, or Brown, to be consumed by the blaze.

Pulling the top sheet away from Brown's body, with a flourish of which a magician or a matador with his cape might be proud, I folded it in half two or three times and then dropped the wad on top of the flames. The rectangle was agreeably large enough and thick enough to cover the spreading fire, enclose it, deprive it of oxygen and, thankfully, within just a few seconds, extinguish it.

I began to collect everything back up off the floor and restore what I might back in its rightful place; the lamp without its glass, the sheet, singed and crumpled, over Brown's body, when Holloway hissed at me from outside the building.

"Psst! Doyle!"

"Yes?" I was haughty; I had stood upon the burning deck whence all but I had fled.

"Quick! Get out of there. The padre's coming."

The priest had been roused from the dreamless sleep of the innocent by the noises of the excitements of the past few minutes. I dropped everything and scuttled out of the building. Outside, Holloway was waiting for me, hopping from one foot to the other. Grabbing me roughly by the elbow, he bundled me off into the darkness.

"Forgive us our trespasses, eh, Holloway?"

We reconvened in my room at ten o'clock the next morning. The sun was high, but the morning's lingering freshness hindered its sturdy heat. The sky was clear and the gleaming mountains sang their silent Gloria. I had been making some notes, so I set them aside when Holloway came in. I was interested to establish what impressions he had acquired of last evening's escapade.

"Never mind all that. The whole village is in a ferment. Eva told me. They're clucking away like chickens with a fox in the coop. A person or persons unknown invaded the sanctity of the church at midnight and tried to cremate Brown's earthly remains."

"By Jove! Is that what they are saying?"

"Rumours and counter rumours abound, according to Eva. But the main contention is that it is either some form of devil worship or possibly a pagan funeral."

I could not resist a smile. "So, no one suspects us directly, nor what we were really there for?" Relief was starting to grow within me. Last night's exploits had left me tense and strained and I had not slept at all well.

"Who knows what they suspect, or whom? We were the two who asked to see him; we were the two who were refused. It would not take too long for someone to establish that with the vicar and reach his or her own conclusions. It is early days yet in the rumour-machine."

"Thank you, Holloway. Most reassuring. We can only hope that we were not seen, and that there was nothing left behind to connect us directly with the event."

"So, what did you get?" He took an apple from my breakfast table and sank his fangs into it.

I cast a glance at my notebook, which was still on the table where I had been working on it, and then looked back at Holloway. "Before I say anything, I would be interested to hear what you feel you found out last night."

Holloway snorted and shrugged. "Never mind me. You're the doctor." His eyes fell on my notebook and, before I could stop him, he had picked it up and had begun to read. After a moment or two he lowered it to his lap.

"Is that it?"

"How do you mean?" I responded, indignantly.

"There you go again with your 'how do you means'!" Then, referring to my notebook, he read aloud a few selected words and phrases: "'Broken bones… lesions and abrasions… consistent with a fall down a rocky slope… alive… shoes… pipe knife… anise-seed…' What is all this, Doyle?"

"Well," I replied, bristling, "if you would let me explain, rather than misappropriating my personal effects without so much as a by-your-leave, then we would progress this conversation more efficiently."

He looked at me, startled. In all the length of our – albeit brief but intense – association, this was the first time that he had actually noticed how disgruntled I was. There was no apology. I could not read contrition in his eyes. But he was compliant at last – which was a start.

"Let me take you through all of this step by step," I began, like the patient yet authoritative professor I had once had in Edinburgh – Dr Bell, upon whom I had based, at least in part, the character and methods of Sherlock Holmes. As I spoke, I began, most extraordinarily, to feel as though I were growing in stature and assurance. As if there may be something to this notional "spirit of Holmes" after all. Although I knew that, patently, it could not truly be the case. But suddenly, beyond stories and into the real world itself, all the concepts I had grappled with in *Scarlet* and *Four* and the other stories started to take shape. To coalesce. To gather into solid form and invest in me a degree of knowledge, wisdom and insight that, hitherto, I had not realized I possessed.

The vague concept of the science of detection no longer seemed to me quite as fanciful as I had thought while composing my tales. To me, they were a good device and an excellent, original approach to mystery writing. But that was it. I no more believed that they were actually physically possible than to have a man with a wooden leg scale a mountain in real life. Although in literature, if wrought carefully and crafted dextrously, he would be able to attempt the climb, and every reader would cheer as he stood upon the summit and believe that if it were possible for him, then it could be possible for them. Wish that it were. Urge it to be so.

There is a glass divide between fiction and reality. Although it would seem as if one might be part of the other, there is an impassable and invisible obstacle between the two. The art is to help readers – who are complicit in this – to suspend their disbelief. To start to want to accept that such-and-such a thing were possible even though they knew that it was patently impossible. Yet, as I related to Holloway my findings and my propositions, I began to think that, after all, there was indeed something very real about this science of deduction. And also, may I be forgiven my undisputed vanity, that I was actually really rather good at it.

"First – broken bones, lesions, abrasions. From what I could feel and hear and see of them led me to the conclusion that he was still alive when he pitched – or was pitched – down the gorge or rock face on that fateful evening. I had no need to undress the gentleman since there was more than enough evidence on the surface for me to reach this conclusion. Moreover, I propose to wire the hospital in the valley and ask them, in my official capacity as a doctor, if they would be so good as to allow me sight of their post-mortem report, when they have completed it."

Understanding, and something which I was vain enough to believe was respect, began to dawn in Holloway's ever-widening eyes. I continued.

"In addition, you may recall in my tale *A Study in Scarlet*, Holmes's character is introduced early on by description. This is given by an acquaintance of Watson's called Stamford, who says that Holmes had been conducting dubious experiments upon cadavers by beating them, to analyse the extent that injuries manifest themselves after death. This is no mere fantasy, but was in fact testament to the genius of one of my tutors at Edinburgh, Dr Bell. It was a subject upon which he was most expansive and illuminating, and from which I learned a very great deal. I can assure you, therefore, that I discovered more than enough evidence in what I could see and feel to guarantee that Brown was still a living, breathing, sentient being as he fell. May God rest his soul."

Holloway shuddered. The horror of such a dread misfortune as to be fully conscious as you began the terrifying and grisly plummet to extinction, was too unbearable to contemplate.

"Second, shoes. First, we note that the heels are worn down at the outside edge. This denotes a male; men tend as a sex to wear this part down rather than the inner. It is not significant – although it might be if another part of the heel were worn."

"Why?"

"Because although Brown dressed like a man, he might possibly have been a woman, which would have explained his taciturn behaviour. But as he was not, the observation of the heels is of no further use to us. The smooth but worn leather on the soles, however, told me a completely different tale."

"What?"

"That they were his daily wear in town; consistent with paving and cobbles, not country paths and mountain tracks. They were not walking shoes. There was no support for the ankles and, scuffed and bruised though they were, they were not damaged by continual use on mountains. More likely the damage was new and therefore consistent with a fall down a gorge. This proves very little in practical terms, other than that they were most probably the shoes he wore when he tumbled. The alpine grasses clinging to them bears this out. However, the significance of these shoes lies in the question: *why* was he wearing them? He was an experienced walker. He would know that to go up a slope after rain in town shoes with smooth leather soles would be sheer folly."

"Fair enough."

"Third, I mention that there is no pipe knife in the list of his personal effects. Do you not consider this strange, Holloway? You know my own list of smoking implements: pipe, pouch, matches and… disembowelling tool. The tool which scrapes out the clinker welded on the inside of the bowl, tamps the newly rubbed tobacco firmly in place, and loosens it with the spike if it is too firm? It is indispensable. So, where is Brown's?

"Finally, the smell of anise-seed upon his lips and which, when I parted his jaw, was present within his mouth also… Strongly present, along with an odour which, if I dare leap to any conclusions at this desperately early stage, could only be alcohol."

"What do you mean?"

"My dear Holloway, why do you ask, 'What do you mean?' Do you not have any thoughts of your own?"

"He had been drinking."

"It is one possibility. Nevertheless, again I should rather receive the post-mortem report from the valley hospital before any further conjecture of this nature."

"And the anise-seed?"

"There, I would dare to venture, lies the key to this whole mystery. In terms of simple facts, although one might also fairly place what I am about to say in the realm of conjecture also, the herb is a quite common additive in a number of strong alcoholic liquors. The French, and by close association the Swiss, and the Germans are particularly partial to this flavouring as they complete the distilling process."

"So, what should we do now?"

I deliberated. It was hard to know exactly what to do with all this information. We, or rather I, had established some anomalies that begged further investigation at the very least. Should I, perhaps, bring my findings to the police? Well, no, I couldn't, because they would like to know, with justifiable reason, how I had come by such evidence. This, therefore, left me outside the law, yet working to uphold it. I have to say that I found the thought quite diverting.

But only for a moment. A greater realization was hard on its heels. I had, after all, broken into a church. I had also caused criminal damage. It wasn't serious and I doubted I would have more than a fine to discharge my obligations to society, if ever I found myself before a magistrate. But the concern was how any information of this nature would be received at home if it became public. Touie would understand; she always does. But my "public" and my publishers? The gentlemen of the press? I wished, above and beyond Holmes, to be taken seriously as an historian and literate novelist. How would such mischief advance my ambitions? And as for my being a medical man… To all intents and purposes, it could easily be interpreted as a macabre act equal to the worst excesses of

Messrs Burke and Hare. A doctor practising on a corpse of someone who wasn't even his patient? I could be struck off.

The thought was too awful to dwell upon. It made it all the more clear to me that I needs must try to discover whomever, if anyone, killed Brown. Once that person, or persons, were discovered by me, my minor unorthodoxy could be forgiven in the light of the greater good. The thought that I might have to see the whole business through to its bitter conclusion provided cold comfort. All I had wanted to do was to come for two weeks and clear away the cobwebs. What if everything I undertook from here on did not resolve before the end of my stay? What if I were identified as the chapel invader before I had a chance to advance my theories? What if something worse happened to me?

I shivered again and decided that such speculation served little purpose save to create a sense of dread and undermine confidence. I had a great deal of confidence. If only I would take a moment and employ it. Had I not expertly read all the signs upon Brown's body as if reading a textbook? Had I not established, beyond reasonable doubt, that something untoward had happened upon that mountain two nights ago? Had I not revealed that Holmes's methods were, indeed, practicable in the real world beyond the pages? I should have more faith in myself.

"Well, what do you think?" Holloway was waiting for an answer to a question I had not heard. I vaguely remembered him saying something about the scene of the fall.

"We should, as you say, visit the scene," I said, and watched Holloway carefully to see whether that reply met with approval or confusion. It appeared to hit the spot.

"Good. So you agree, this afternoon, then?"

"This afternoon?"

"That's what I said – weren't you listening?"

"This afternoon. But first, I must wire the hospital in the valley – to ask them for the results of the post-mortem, when they have them. I should also wire an old friend in Whitehall. We were at college together. He will be able to advise me on the protocols in such matters."

"Fair enough." Holloway took to his feet and moved towards the door. "I shall see if Eva is able to escort us to where they found Brown."

"As you wish."

"What we need, though, Doyle, is a Sherlock Holmes moment."

"A what?"

"You know – like in your stories… a leap of imagination, a sudden inspiration. Try to have one of those, would you? I feel sure that's the sort of thing that will bring us our culprit…"

"I shall work on it," I laughed. Although I was not sure that humour was Holloway's intention.

A felicitous moment in a story? But when it comes to seeking just such a moment in real life…? One cannot conjure elegant leaps of thought and reasoning out of thin air just like that.

Having smoked, enjoyed the scenery, read and reflected a little, I discerned that it was time for lunch.

At the table were the Plantins and the Pivcevics. Werner had been there earlier, but the others told me he had left to prepare for an afternoon's hunting. The Plantins appeared to be in a more settled mood. Plantin had rolled over to the buffet to collect a second helping of breads and Swiss country cheese. Madame Plantin leaned across to me and said, conspiratorially, that she and her husband had begun to speak about certain matters. Although not much had been actually discussed, it was Marie's impression that progress had been made.

Anna Pivcevic witnessed this conversation and expressed her curiosity by raising an eyebrow. Marie, thinking, as young married women often do, that she was unjustly being suspected of flirting with someone other than her husband, smiled. She said quickly, for Plantin was returning, that whatever impression Mrs Pivcevic was under, it was erroneous. I, she told her, had been good enough to consult with her on a matter of a delicate nature in my official capacity as a doctor. My wisdom had been much appreciated. She spoke in a low tone, since her husband had now reached the table. Finally, she commended my counsel to Mrs Pivcevic most highly. She then turned with that frisson of feminine energy which all new brides possess, and directed every last ounce of her attention towards her beloved husband.

At the close of the meal, as Holloway and I rose to leave for the next task, Mrs Pivcevic plucked at my sleeve gently. She whispered that she should also like to consult with me. She released me, and I left with Holloway, overhearing Mr Pivcevic asking his wife what it was that she had said to me. She replied that she had not said anything of any interest.

I returned to my room and Holloway to his. I collected my hat and took up my ice axe, which was leaning at the side of the escritoire.

At the side of the escritoire?

The last time I had handled my ice axe, I had left it against the escritoire at the front. Now it was at the side. Of course, it could easily have been moved by one of the hotel staff. But was there a more sinister reason? Putting my things down, I made a thorough search of my room. I could not find anything missing. Nor was there any evidence of anything having been disturbed. I was imagining things, surely? Alternatively I was, conceivably, slowly going out of my mind. I shrugged to myself. If my room had received a burglar in my absence, it was a very neat and tidy one. They had no need for anything of mine. Perhaps I should be offended that my possessions were of so little value that they were considered not worth a sou in a Swiss flea market.

I turned suddenly and cast one final glance around my room. As if I might be able to catch out whatever was amiss. Like a child playing "What's the Time, Mr Wolf?". I discovered nothing, collected my things and left.

SEVEN

Holloway and I met in the lobby, ready for both a visit to the telegraph office and a walk up the hill. However, a curious sight met our eyes. Eva was talking intently with Anton, who appeared quite distressed. The moment we appeared, however, they took pains to compose themselves.

We bid them both good-day.

"Are you ready for our walk, Eva?" asked Holloway, ever tactless.

"I am afraid I must stay here awhile. I am sorry." She cast a concerned glance towards her brother.

"We quite understand," I replied. "Please do not worry."

"But..."

"Perhaps, Holloway, we should postpone our walk until a time more convenient to Eva."

"Very well."

"Oh no," Eva interjected, "I would not prevent you from making your walk. It is a very simple route. I can draw you a map. All you will need is some water to drink and a compass, to be sure that you are safe."

"Do you think we shall be able to navigate for ourselves?"

"It is not hard, doctor," she said. She grabbed a pencil and notepaper from the reception desk and began to sketch out a rough map for us. As she was preparing this, a middle-aged couple appeared from a downstairs room in the private quarters. I had not met them before. I imagined them to be the hotel's owners and, therefore, Anton and Eva's parents. They were dressed to go out. The father looked very severe and there was no doubt that the mother had been crying. A sharp frost descended upon the lobby. Anton and Eva stiffened, and the parents, while acknowledging their existence and ours, said nary a word to any of us. I identified no anger; just, perhaps, disappointment – profound sadness, even.

The parents left the building and Holloway looked across at Eva, who returned his gaze.

"Do not worry," she said. "It is a family matter. No more. All will be well."

"Are you sure?" I had not known Holloway to possess a tender tone to his voice. But here was evidence that he did.

"Sure." It was Anton who replied and forced a smile.

In a few moments, our map and directions were completed and we were ready to set off.

"A compass!" I cried, remembering Eva's cautionary words.

"I have one," Holloway said, and patted his jacket pocket. "I purchased it from the outfitters yesterday."

"Then all is well."

"Hardly that..."

We headed for the telegraph office which, we had been told by Eva, was just off the same street. We found it quite easily, set back a little from the main thoroughfare. I entered and Holloway followed. I found a writing stall, a pencil and a form and began to compose a message to the hospital in the valley. Of course, the moment I started, I realized I did not know to whom I should address it. Although I may quite easily secure the address of the establishment from the telegraph office clerk, a general message would not be treated with sufficient care and attention.

"Why have you stopped writing, Doyle?"

"I realize, Holloway, that I have no authority, other than a British doctor's credentials, to demand to see confidential medical records."

"Well, that's that, then."

"Although..."

"What?"

"The gentleman to whom I propose writing in Whitehall may very well know which strings to pull in order that we may gain access to the post-mortem examination record."

"Which gentleman is this, again, exactly?"

"His name is Robert Ignatius Steen. As I said, we were at college together. He was studying politics and law. Found himself a very excellent berth in the corridors of power. We meet up occasionally at his or my club. He is something of an enigma and a voluptuary. He is also a great cynic, but we have developed a firm friendship. I have no doubt that he is due eventually to find himself a most influential post within the labyrinthine workings of government."

"Then wire him. And stop prevaricating."

I took up the pencil stub and the form and began to compose.

My dear Steen. Urgent.

Peter Brown British citizen deceased.

Accident or otherwise.

Any information or advice.

Need access to post—mortem report.

I added the name of the hospital in the valley, then addressed the message to Steen's office in Whitehall. I handed the form in to the clerk, paid the fee, and left with Holloway for our walk. By the time we returned, I felt sure, we would have a response from my friend.

As we left the office, Holloway nudged me sharply in the ribs and pointed. In the distance, coming away from the church and heading down the valley road, was a cart bearing the unmistakable burden of a human body wrapped in canvas. I removed my hat in a gesture of respect.

The climb, such as it was, had not the same gaiety about it as the one we had made in Eva's company the day before. We trudged most of the first hour in silence, pausing only to look back down at the village and to take a drink of water. The walk seemed much harder this time and, when we passed the edelweiss in the meadows, just a little poignant.

The map was clear and we made the vicinity where Brown's body had been found quite easily. It was on an escarpment across a coomb from the mountain in whose shadow our village sheltered. The area was very green and dank. Ivy and other climbers with heavy oppressive growth clung to the slopes and mingled with the ash, the pine and the sycamore; like a jungle.

We could hear a continual drumming, throaty noise as we approached the exact spot that Eva had marked on the map. There was a waterfall somewhere near and, judging by the noise, the force was substantial. The trail led through the undergrowth and over another steep slope. We picked and scrambled our way up this further obstacle, and began to follow the most explicit instructions that had been jotted down on the hotel notepaper. I asked Holloway for a glimpse at it – he had cherished it since Eva had presented it to him. He opened it up and showed me. It told us to go over the ridge, follow the path down, at a large rock on our left turn right, follow the path and go down the slope until the path stopped at an open space. It was there that Brown had been found. The note ended with the ominous expression: *Take great care.* This last she had double underlined. Since it was Holloway who had taken the map, and I had not seen it until that moment, the stark, explicit instruction had great impact.

"What does it mean?"

"I don't know, Doyle. Come on. This way…"

The going became harder and we sweated and puffed and struggled our way onwards over the crest. With some relief, we began our descent and drew nearer to the fearsome drumming sound. It was becoming more and more intense by the minute. In my fancy, we were not walking a Swiss mountain path, but forcing our way through the jungles of the African interior.

We followed the trail for a few paces more, turned a corner around a rocky outcrop, and forced our way through some overhanging vegetation. At that moment, the reason for Eva's cautionary note and the source of the fearsome noise became clear. Rounding the outcrop, it was as if the scenery had burst. Directly before us was the most powerful waterfall I had ever seen. It was not the largest by volume. It was not the broadest. It was not the highest. What made this particular force so spectacular and fearsome was the fact that an incalculable amount of water was being pressed through a very narrow aperture at the top of its fall. This unyielding pressure created an incredible, formidable jet of water, which shot out and then down, spearing into a boiling pool a hundred or more yards below. There were further falls beyond that. The water energetically leapt, in fits and starts, down a great gash of sheer and glistening gorge. Stamping and shouting and hurling itself all the way to the foot of the cliff, about half a mile below us. But the main force, the primary fall, upon which we had stumbled in such surprise, was the most spectacular. A stallion's tail of water that arched towards its destruction through the gap and down into the pool, throwing up cloud after rolling cloud of mist and spray.

"The Reichenbach Fall!" Holloway had to shout above the water's clamour to be heard, indicating where Eva had written its name down upon our map.

"Magnificent!" I cried, and ventured as near to the edge of the cliff as I dared. The rocks and the undergrowth were particularly greasy and treacherous here. I did not feel secure enough to go too far. I clung on to my ice axe for further comfort, and ensured its spiked ferrule had sufficient purchase upon the slimy mud that clung doggedly to the rocks at the edge.

"Come on, Doyle. We haven't reached the exact spot yet."

I withdrew as carefully as I had ventured out, and rejoined my companion on the path. We set off again, in what I might only describe as a slithering totter. The track led straight down the cliff side, keeping the savage plume of the fall company.

After ten minutes of sweating and striving to keep our foothold, we reached a small plateau or shelf among the rocks.

"Here!" Holloway waved a hand about him to show the place where Eva's map indicated Brown had ended his life's journey.

The roar of the fall drummed all around me and dulled my senses. My very bones vibrated. I began to pick my way carefully over the scene, looking for any scrap of information I might uncover.

"What are we looking for, Doyle?"

"Anything! The pipe knife, the alpenstock. Anything!" I soon arrived at a part of the rock shelf where the mud had been churned up more than somewhat. "Here!"

Holloway joined me immediately. The telltale signs of little gobbets of blood from Brown's wounds, as his battered body lay waiting to be discovered, were all around this spot. They had been kept moist and glistening by the constant mist and spray and the close atmosphere in that oppressive gorge. The mud had been churned up, I was sure, by the boots of the men who had come to bring the body back to the village. I looked up from the position and inspected the impossibly steep path we had just negotiated, at great risk to life and limb. I was gripped by what an extraordinary and heroic feat it must have been for those men to have manhandled a dead weight back up that almost vertical cliff face. They must have been as sure-footed as chamois and as courageous as bears. I sat back on my haunches, imagining every perilous step and stumble, blew out my cheeks and marvelled.

"Can't see anything!" cried Holloway.

I shook my head and shrugged. There did not seem to be anything there other than the signs denoting where Brown had lain and where he had been gathered in. This, though, was at least something rather than nothing: no pipe knife, no alpenstock. What could we infer from their absence, I wondered? I stepped gingerly towards the rim of the shelf. The pool, although closer, was still a terrifying drop below us. It slewed and bubbled and convulsed with every hammer blow of the force above it.

The turmoil of the waters notwithstanding, there was an infusion of a milky white colour, with a hint of turquoise, indicating the presence of some mineral, perhaps copper. Whatever the reason, the water was cloudy as well as disturbed, which made spotting anything lying at the bottom of the pool next to impossible.

I resolved, however, to explore one further avenue before I could complete my initial investigation. I would need to look for the pipe tool and stick in Brown's bedroom. I felt sure that Eva could accommodate me as far as access was concerned. That is, if his effects had not already been collected together. Perhaps they were, even now, trundling their way through the valley upon the cart with their late owner?

"Nothing here at all, Holloway."

"No!" He had been rummaging around in the shrubbery.

It had not unduly surprised me – this singular lack of anything significant to show for our endeavours. I had always known that the main area for our search would be back up at the top of the fall where, as it were, Brown had commenced his descent. "Come on," I urged Holloway. "Back we go!" I pointed cheerfully up the cliff with the tip of my ice axe. Holloway surveyed the return journey and, with a heavy sigh, put one pokerworked boot in front of the other to begin the long ascent.

Fatigued and heaving for breath, we arrived back at the top of the cliff. We drank some water and sat down to regain our strength.

"Waste of time that was, Doyle."

"Not a bit of it. Having found nothing down there is not a negative result; it simply means that there is nothing there to find and that therefore the absence of both the pipe knife and the alpenstock remains a significant factor."

"If I may say so, Doyle, what a load of gobbledegook."

"You are entitled to your opinion, Holloway. However, we should now be seeking evidence of a fight or some other event that would have preceded and even precipitated Brown's downfall." I got to my feet and started to scout the immediate vicinity. Holloway listlessly followed suit.

After about ten minutes of searching in vain, my companion started to mutter to himself. I could not hear what it was he was

102

saying, but I had no doubt that it was about me and that it was both highly personal and indelicate.

"What *exactly* is it that we are looking for now, Doyle?"

"Well, again the knife and again the alpenstock. But also: crushed foliage, spilled blood, broken twigs, footprints, pressed grass."

"Pressed grass! What on earth for?"

"Well, my dear Holloway, while the theory is that violence has taken place – if the fall was not an accident – one must not leave any stone unturned, literally, in seeking evidence of *any* event."

"Like what?"

"Well, like, for example, perhaps there was a slip following a passionate embrace."

"A what?"

"Might Brown have attended a tryst here? They embrace, they kiss, they share a joke, they chase one another, he misses his footing… and tragedy."

Holloway considered this proposed scenario for a moment, and then pronounced: "I have never heard such rubbish in all my life."

I was aggrieved. "It is possible."

"Nonsense. What on earth would two people be doing having a tryst up here, perched on the edge of a precipice? If they were both from the village, why didn't they meet in the woods, or one of the meadows where they would not be disturbed? If they wanted not to be disturbed, that is, because the relationship was illicit for some reason."

"You are right to consider the illicit, or otherwise, nature of such a hypothetical relationship. However, if it were not frowned upon or restricted in some way, it is entirely possible that they might have met here simply because Brown was a stranger in the area, and had not seen this landmark before. In fact, they might even have *chosen* to make their way here, whatever the legality of their relationship. Indeed, it might even be that the second party came from another direction entirely, and this was an easily identifiable place for them to arrange to meet."

"But why meet?"

"I do not know... but... if you were making love, where would you choose to do it? Why not somewhere as wild, and exciting, and desperately romantic – yet dangerous – as this?"

"Doyle! Never in all your stories have you ever given any indication of this lurid side to your nature."

"I am not averse to exploring such matters, provided it is done responsibly, tastefully and for the right reasons." I fell silent and gazed at him steadily, until I could discern that he had settled a little. I also hoped that my silence might unnerve him. I was becoming increasingly irritated by this gentleman's preconceptions and assumptions as to my nature and character. Why did everybody, I wondered, imagine that through my stories they could come to know me in the slightest? I would never allow any impropriety into my stories, and abhor those writers who venture there. Nevertheless, this was the real world and I a doctor. Such unspoken matters do exist between people, and it would be folly, when one needed to explore every possible avenue in a case, to ignore them.

"But if they arranged to meet, or came here on purpose," Holloway broke my studied silence, "then why did Brown come with town shoes and without his alpenstock?"

"Because it was a spur of the moment matter. Brown, perhaps, was just out around the town when he received the opportunity to come here. Or... perhaps he was not thinking straight for one reason or another."

"What reason?"

"I don't know. I don't have all the answers. If I did, we wouldn't be standing here arguing. We'd be back in the village resolving matters directly."

"No, precisely, you *don't* have all the answers, Sherlock. You make yourself out to be the great detective. But you stumble and bumble about these bizarre locations, pretending you know what you are doing; yet it is evident you do not have the first idea of what it is you are about."

"I disagree. I…"

Holloway held up a hand. "No. Do not give me any more of your buffoonery. I have had my fill of all your absurd hypotheses. I am going to return to the village and have done with all of this."

"I beg your pardon. It was your fault. You engineered this whole affair in the first place. If you had not inveigled me into assisting in your crazed schemes I would, doubtless, right now be engaged on a gentle stroll through some Alpine meadow with a lit pipe and uplifting thoughts."

"My fault? You are the great detective with all the preposterous theories. I have had my fill of all this. I am going. You may do what you will."

"But – we need to continue our inspection of the location…"

"Then you had better get on with it. Before darkness falls, and you end up not being able to see anything. Not that there is anything to see, anyway."

And with that, he departed.

I stood stock still for some considerable while, dumbfounded and infuriated by the gall of the man. I had a sneaking suspicion that much of the dissent he had just displayed was premeditated. To my mind, he had grown weary and flummoxed by the clambering up and down of cliff faces and, being flighty by nature, had no stomach for the task. So he had latched on to the first opportunity to withdraw his services. If he could, at the same time, make me the villain of the piece to justify himself, then all to the good. I sat down on a moss-covered rock and filled a pipe. I lit it, and considered what my next move should be.

It did not take me long to decide that I had come there to do a job, and do that job I most decidedly would. Holloway or no Holloway. I got up from my seat and began, again, to systematically search the area.

I divided into quadrants that part of the track and surroundings which I believed offered the most likely starting point for Brown's struggle. I then searched each one thoroughly. It took almost a whole half-hour and returned nothing of significance. I sat down again on my rock and had another think.

Obviously, if there were no story to tell from the landscape, then there was no story to be told. No scuffle, no fight, not even any evidence of a courting couple having pressed down a soft part of the surrounding vegetation by their intimacy. I set my chin in my hand and my elbow upon my knee. I was aching all over from my exertions and I was growing weary. Yet the stubborn part of the Conan Doyle in me refused to admit defeat. I had walked all the way here, walked all the way down to the shelf on the cliff, and struggled all the way back up again. I was blessed if I would go back to the hotel with absolutely nothing to show for it.

Above all, though, I refused to allow Holloway to have the last laugh. If I came back with absolutely nothing, he would, I was certain of it, set about whispering into the ears of everybody who would care to listen, and even those who would not: *Doyle's a booby. Doyle's a pretentious bumpkin with asinine theories that simply do not hold water.* I could hear him saying it even now. And I hated him for it. For contorting my whole visit here into a fantasy of monstrous proportions.

I rose again from my seat. I had been scanning the immediate vicinity while cogitating, and had seen the cliff edge near the force. Of course, if there had been any struggle at all, it would not have necessarily started until his life was seriously under threat. If a person had grabbed him without revealing his or her ultimate intention of thrusting him over the edge of the cliff, Brown would have simply walked backwards with the pressure to begin with. If he were anything like me, he would have tried to persuade his persecutor that whatever violence that person had in mind would not solve anything. So he would back away and back away, all the time talking in a soothing, hopefully disarming voice. And then, when he realized that he was now near the edge of the cliff and his life was very much in danger, that he was barely a foot from extinction, *then* he would struggle. Then he would dig his heels in. Then he would twist and squirm. Then he would try with all his might to wrestle himself out of the grip of his oppressor. And then, with fear clutching at his heart and the force roaring like some terrible ravenous dragon in his ear, he would try to wrench himself free. And he would yell... Yell for dear life that someone may, please, please, come to his rescue! Yet the yell would not have been heard. How could it, with such a din going on all around him, as it was even now? Would that be why he had been invited up to this fearsome, isolated precipice? So that no one could hear him scream?

There was nothing for it. I would have to creep towards the edge of the cliff and examine the ground there. If Holloway had been here, I might have taken comfort in the fact that he could have held me as I explored the area. But on my own...?

The thought filled me with a plunging dread.

Then I told myself to just get on with it.

I laid my ice axe down alongside my jacket and my hat, and crept forward.

The rocky outcrop, which formed the lip and created the overhang which led to the plummet, was greasy and covered in moss and mud. The spray from the cataract at the top of the fall created a mist, which set everything nearby glistening. I held my breath and edged even closer, like an explorer peering into a volcano that was liable to erupt at any moment. I still could not see the edge clearly enough, so with great trepidation, I shuffled forward a little more and stooped, so that I might more clearly see if any marks had left their impression in the surface. I started to feel quite dizzy and unsteady on my feet. I did not think I was prone to vertigo, yet the proximity of the force and its incessant downward rush was compelling. It was as if I were drawn to it, and in thrall to it. *Come! Fall with me! It will be the most exhilarating time of your life! Come! Fall! Fall with me!*

Suddenly, I started to sway involuntarily; my knees began to buckle and my legs shook. I looked for something to cling on to.

But there was nothing. Did Brown look in vain like this? I sank onto my haunches. My centre of gravity having been lowered, I was able for a moment to steady myself and feel just a little more secure. Like a duck, I waddled even closer to the edge. My toes were a few negligible inches from the precipice and still the cataract sang its siren's song: *Come! Fall!*

And then I saw something. A scuff mark. Two. In the mud. Right on the edge. Undoubtedly, they were the marks of shoes as the wearer slid backwards. I could tell because whoever it was, and I suspected that it was Brown, had tried to right himself before he had lost his balance and skewed over backwards. He had, perhaps, leaned forward and dug his toes into the mud; possibly even whirling his arms forward as one does when trying to keep one's balance.

And then he must have lost the struggle – his town shoes unable to offer him any purchase. I looked to left and right of that fearful evidence. Were there any other signs, I wondered?

And then, O piteous sight. I saw it.

The mark of a hand, Brown's left hand, imprinted into the mud.

As he toppled, he must have made one last despairing lunge and caught hold of the edge for an instant. Then his hand was dragged backwards over the precipice as the weight of his body, combined with gravity, pulled him inexorably to his doom.

I huddled there, just at the edge of the gorge for a moment, and ran through the whole scene in my mind's eye. A stroll, perhaps. Some kind of initial struggle, whereby Brown began to be forced backwards. A greater struggle as he realized how close he was to destruction. A final push, which set the poor man tottering and whirling his arms in empty space. The loss of balance, the fall, the final despairing clutch at terra firma and then his scream: lost in the roar of the force.

Gone.

I could imagine him turning and tumbling, then cracking his head and his bones on the unforgiving rocks of the perpendicular gorge; his flesh being torn on the shrubs and branches.

I shuddered. It was as if I had been the one falling myself. And that image produced another terrible thought. The person who had pushed him, if indeed that is what had happened, would have been standing immediately behind where I was even now squatting and peering over the abyss. That notion created in me an irrational fear; a sense that perhaps that person, that agent of evil, was right this minute behind me. Perhaps they had crept up on me and were even now bracing themselves for one simple shove abaft my shoulder blades. One little push and I, too, would be sent hurtling into the chasm to my death.

The mind plays the most desperate tricks on one. Yet, before I could rationalize my way out of this morbid notion, I found that the idea had me in its grip. I stood, suddenly. I was compelled by the urge to turn and face this imagined foe. As I stood, I realized I had stood up too quickly. I was immediately overcome by an uncontrollable dizziness.

I reeled.

My left foot caught one of the slimy patches and shot out from beneath me, backwards into space. In an instant my other foot followed and I knew that I was now helpless and unable to preserve myself.

I toppled.

The fearsome chasm began reaching out for me with its terrifying, grasping fingers, hauling me down into my own private Charybdis.

Come! Fall!

I screamed.

Nobody could hear me.

EIGHT

There is an interesting phenomenon associated with rugby football, and rugby players in particular, that those who have never played this remarkable game might not really begin to appreciate. It is this.

When a player is being tackled, it is usually around the legs. This means that he is restricted in how he moves. After many seasons of dashing about a muddy field with merry shouts, the good player begins to adopt a technique which enables him to still have some degree of control over his body as it is being felled in the tackle. It is an adjustment of weight. A turning of the torso, definitely. But it is also, more subtly, an expression of will.

One of the places a player is quite often tackled on the field of play is within a yard or so of the scoring, or *try,* line. If he has the ball in his hands, it is absolutely imperative that he makes it his most earnest intention to ensure that as he loses the purchase on his feet and topples, the ball is placed on the right side of that line. Notwithstanding in which direction his body is presently travelling. He wants to score. It is a matter of life or death that he does score. And he has no intention of allowing such a minor inconvenience as having his legs swept away from under him by a burly sixteen-stone full-back prevent him from achieving that aim. So he *wills* himself to fall in the right direction, shifts his weight as he falls, twists if necessary, and sends as much of his body as is practicable pitching forward towards the try line.

So it was with me. Something ingrained through my school and college years of playing rugby football instinctively came into its own as I toppled and lurched on the edge of the precipice. As my legs disappeared from under me, and I twisted to regain my balance, something within me willed myself to send my body lurching forwards towards level ground and away from the abyss. A wing three-quarter scoring the winning try for England in the dying moments of a match at Rectory Field could not have performed the feat any better.

I landed with a thud and bounced my head unceremoniously on a low, mossy rock. Although my feet dangled almost comically in space over the edge of the cliff, nevertheless I was safe. I dragged myself forward and brought my feet inboard. Slowly, still on my stomach, I inched myself further inland until I was sure that this time, if I stood up, not only would I do it slowly, but I would also do it without any possibility of putting myself at risk again.

It was then that I saw the second set of footprints. They were not town shoes but studded boots. I stood up unsteadily, and transfixed by these new marks began to follow their story in the damp earth atop the cliff. Here and there they brought me to other marks, which were undoubtedly town shoes. Brown's. It was the prints of the boots that were on top. This told me that they had been put there after Brown's. The boots were worn at the outside of the heel, so they belonged to a man. They were also about the same size as Brown's feet. So, one must imagine that, whomever it was, was of a similar height and possibly a similar build. Brown, by estimation, was just below average height and was slightly built. He did not have very big feet. Could they, perhaps, have been owned by one of the body-bearers who had brought the poor fellow back to the village? Possibly. Although as far as I could recall, there were only burly fellows, above average in height. Moreover there was no evidence of any of them having been at this particular spot.

I followed the trail of footprints back towards the edge of the precipice and noted my heartbeat rising proportionately. Fear returned, but I forced myself to press on. Now that I had a clear view of these tracks, it was important to pursue them to the conclusion of their story. There was a point at which there seemed to be a lot going on. Feet were being placed down in quick succession, without taking full-sized steps. And then I saw, now that I had this trail to follow, that Brown had taken two or three paces towards the precipice. The others never ventured closer than about five feet; wise fellow. Then the footprint story ended. Grass, moss, rocks, rain, everything had conspired to stop the tale before I could glean everything possible out of it.

Having explored as much as was evident, I sat down once again on my trusty rock. Then, finally, nervous reaction set in. Feeling now both nauseous and shaken, I placed my head in my hands and sat there shaking.

In due course, I managed to settle my nerves and light my pipe. Soon afterwards, having restored my equilibrium, I gathered up my accoutrements and began my return to the village. Although it was well into the afternoon, I began to make haste as I intended to be back as soon as possible after the draining of the westering light. I did not wish to overnight at some wayfarer's lodgings.

As I walked, I meditated upon the scant evidence that I had collected up on that fateful cliff top. I decided to omit the second set of footprints for the moment. I speculated upon whether it were possible for a walker to chance upon the edge of a precipice and accidentally tumble over. Of course it was. It was also true that Brown had fallen at night. At least, that had to remain a supposition until the post-mortem revealed the actual time of death. A report I hoped I would ultimately be able to see.

So Brown walks near the precipice in the dark. Only, too late, he realizes his proximity to destruction, turns around and, trying to regain his equilibrium, falls off backwards. This never happens – you come to the edge, you rear backwards in terror. It could be, of course, that he did exactly as I had done: crept forward for some reason, then spun around and slipped at the same time. I was investigating the edge, though, in a crouch, and the blood had rushed from my head. Why would he have crouched? Dropped something over? His pipe knife? His alpenstock? Would he have looked over to try and see whatever it was? In the dark? Accident seemed an unlikely theory. There were too many elements that would stop him doing what I did. The roar of the force was enough warning for any sane person. Unless, like me, they had a very pressing reason for approaching the rim. I could not believe Brown had a reason, apart from folly. But, by all accounts, he seemed a particularly serious, introspective fellow.

The second possibility was suicide, of course. He was said to be a morose chap. There were no signs of actual struggle that I could detect. It may explain why he did not care to take his usual walking equipment. In my limited experience, however, of the suicide's emotional frame of mind, I believe they rarely ended their lives without leaving behind some indication of why they had felt bound to take such a terrible and desperate step. In that case, an inspection of Brown's belongings became additionally important. Having said that, if it had been suicide, a note might well have already been found, and a small village's rumour factory would have done the rest. It was also highly unlikely that a suicide would choose to leap off a cliff backwards. In addition, if I were to kill myself at that place, why would I choose to land on a ledge? I would most probably leap off into the force itself, believing that if the crashing against the rocks of the waterfall didn't kill me, submersion in the pool beneath, while helpless and probably unconscious, would.

This left the third possibility, to which I could not but return: that a person or persons unknown forced him off the edge. Which returned me, naturally, to the boot-wearer. Whether this person's prints indicated elements of duress, misfortune or, indeed, complete innocence, remained to be seen. The evidence, though, so far fitted the facts. Brown had fallen off the cliff backwards. An unlikely event in terms of accident, but highly likely if he were talking to someone, pleading for his life or trying to prevent them from achieving their aims. He had attempted, at the last gasp, to cling on to the edge for dear life. He was dressed inappropriately for such an expedition.

Why, though, would anyone wish to kill him? It remained meaningless to speculate at this stage. I wondered whether Holmes would have speculated.

No. Theories, to him, clouded the precise, clinical analysis of the situation. I resolved, therefore, not to speculate for the time being, either. As for Holloway? I further resolved not to tell him about the second set of footprints. Or, indeed, anything.

I continued for some considerable time, relishing the peace and quiet of this splendid district. Presently I began to recognize the features of my own village's locality, the conjunction of the mountains to the south adopting a familiar aspect.

The sun, although very low now, was still giving off a bronze light. The sky directly above had grown profoundly blue. The mountains gleamed proprietorially while, from the east, a cumulus mass was marching in, in splendorous rank upon rank, like Napoleon's *Grande Armée*.

I crested the last ridge and wearily began my final descent through the forest to my hotel. A hot bath and a hearty meal was what I desired most now. Why should I let this sorry business ruin my holiday? I had come to rest and enjoy myself – so rest and enjoy myself I would. With that happy thought, I stopped on my downward trudge to fumble through my pockets and refill my pipe.

At that exact moment, a brief but sudden noise, a foot or so from my right ear, startled me. It was like the heavy hum of a stag beetle in flight. But it did not approach, arrive and pass in that preposterously aimless, indolent way stag beetles have. This noise was faster, busier, more purposeful. It came and went in an instant. I then heard a smack or slap, like a butcher dropping a steak onto his chopping board from a height. The hum had come from somewhere off my starboard quarter, down the slope. The slap had been some yards ahead, on the rise off my port bow. Immediately afterwards, I became conscious that there had been simultaneously an increase in atmospheric pressure and a brief rise in temperature, which I had sensed on my cheek. The conclusion that I drew from all this evidence was as unbelievable as it was shocking.

I had just escaped being shot.

Had I not stopped to feel for my smoking materials, I might well have walked into the bullet, for bullet it was. All of this went hurtling through my mind as, instinct taking command, I flung myself onto the ground, scrabbling along on my belly for the second time that day. I found shelter behind a fallen trunk.

I lay there for an indeterminate period, drawing in copious breaths full of air, yet trying to remain as silent as possible. The hardest thing was to try to suppress the surge of adrenaline that was flooding my system and creating the most agitated and anxious state within me. I longed to take to my feet and run as far and as fast as my legs could carry me. Yet I knew to rise from my position of relative safety was the last thing I should do. I lay there consciously trying to calm myself. My nerve ends were making my whole body tremble. My heart was drumming erratically, like a pebble being shaken in a balloon.

Regaining some degree of equilibrium, I started to take stock. There were no noises that I could discern above and beyond the usual woodland rustlings. I waited a further minute or so, listening. No indication of anyone trying to make their way stealthily through the undergrowth. No twigs snapping, or creatures disturbed by an alien presence in their territory. I took my ice axe and placed my hat upon its iron ferrule. I then raised it just above the log.

Nothing happened. No movement. No unusual noise. Either this was a very patient hunter, or the person who had loosed off the round had moved on.

After a further interval, I decided to move. I crawled back a little along the way I had just come, but also deeper into the woods. I chose to go this way in case whoever it was expected me to head in the more likely direction, back to the village. Finding a broad enough tree, I then stood up behind it. It was good to be back on my feet. A sense of something approaching normality enveloped me. I peered as cautiously as I might around the trunk to inspect the surrounding forest.

No movement. No unusual noises.

Having established, as best I could, that I was alone, I looked around over my shoulder in the direction in which the bullet's trajectory had taken it. According to my best estimation, it had lodged in one of three possible trees. Steeling myself for a move, I took a deep breath and crashed across open space to the relative safety of another, marginally thinner tree. I waited a further moment and then peered around behind me to try to inspect the other trees I had marked out. After a long perusal from a distance, I saw a glimmer of arboreal flesh. This was where the bark had been chipped away by the impact of the bullet.

There was nothing for it but to take another chance. Once again, holding my breath, I leapt across the intervening space and stuck myself behind a further tree. From there I could more clearly see the place where the projectile, which had so very nearly separated me from my loved ones, had struck.

In all, I was about two yards away from this location. I could now see the dull gleam of the bullet perfectly clearly. It was buried up to the last quarter of an inch in the tree. Since I could still see it, it must have been nearly spent. It had already travelled a significant distance before it had reached me and the tree. If it had not done so, it would have embedded itself right inside the tree and the flesh would have closed over it. Indeed, if it were from a high-powered hunter's rifle, loosed from just a few hundred feet away, it would have most probably passed right through the trunk; such was the velocity generated by such technically proficient weapons.

This information was, for me, curiously comforting. I could have every reason to believe that I was not actually being shot at deliberately. A stray shot loosed at some unsuspecting creature had missed its target. It had continued on its trajectory and ended its humming journey just a few feet from me. Astonishing that it had not encountered another trunk in all that distance. Yet, I imagine, that is why hunting in woodland, while observing strict protocols, is possible. Stray bullets, if they miss their mark, are unlikely to travel too far, and not beyond the vision of the hunter.

I thanked all that was merciful in creation. Then, tentatively at first but with growing confidence, I stepped out from behind my protection and began to walk downhill. I started looking for the path I had left some while ago. The only question was, in which precise direction should I look? I knew that it was downhill and to my left somewhere. The problem was that, my attention having been otherwise occupied, I had lost my bearings. Moreover, rain had started to fall. Heavy drops like blood were breaking through the tree canopy. Along with the rain the mist had descended, making visibility difficult. Meanwhile, I realized both the sketch map and the compass resided currently in Holloway's jacket pocket.

I scouted around tentatively through the trees, trying to find a path, any path. After a fruitless few minutes, I remembered the bullet tree. If I could find that, I could take a back-bearing on its trajectory and find my original path.

All very logical and practical, no doubt. And, if I had chosen to do this from the outset, I would already have been on my way back to my warm, dry bedroom. As it was, bumbling about the woods in vain had served only to disorient me further. In short, I had absolutely no idea in which direction to commence my search for the bullet tree.

There was nothing for it. I would have to use gravity for my guide. So I began my descent. It was exhausting, uncomfortable, laborious and painful. Not only was the slope uncommonly steep and uneven, it was laced with tree roots, hillocks, hummocks and sudden hidden holes. These were designed, as far as I could tell, for the express purpose of trapping the foot and breaking the ankle of unsuspecting blunderers. I barked my shins on fallen branches. I became caught up in all manner of shrubs, brambles and other forest vegetation.

After twenty minutes of this arduous process, I began to wonder: what if I tripped now and broke my leg, or hit my head? Deep in the forest and without sustenance, I began to become apprehensive. Notwithstanding the mist, night had come. The darkness of the forest had consequently deepened. Meanwhile, another thought occurred. If the hunter's bullet had not been directed at me, what had it been directed at? Deer or chamois, perhaps? Yes. But what about boar or bear or wolf?

By way of emphasis, at that moment I heard a throaty, creaturely growl. Not too far away, in my estimation. I began sincerely to regret leaving the bosom of my family in South Norwood. I had selfishly sought isolation; I had acquired it to excess.

Resolutely casting aside my rising self-pity, I set my face to recommence my descent. No doubt, at some point, even if I missed the village or any further tracks or habitation, I would ultimately find myself in the valley. Even if it took all night. Or a day and a night. However long it took, there would be a conclusion to this difficulty. It was simply my task to keep myself gainfully employed and, by doing so, to ensure that the conclusion came sooner rather than later. I filled and lit my pipe.

Giving vent to a great cloud of pipe smoke, I watched it mingle with the fog that now clung to everything. I then puffed off into the night like a locomotive. I set my sights on the happy homecoming I was intent on enjoying. Thus lifted, I believe I even began to sing. I seem to recall it was "Through the Night of Doubt and Sorrow", but I could not guarantee that it was.

"Doyle!"

The voice was distant and muffled by forest and fog. I cupped my hands to my mouth and hallooed back.

"Holloway?"

"Over here!"

"Where's here?"

His voice was coming to me as if from out of the grave. It echoed around me, with no substance and seemingly from no specific direction. There was a further silence, then: "Stand still, be quiet and listen!"

I did as instructed. A moment later there came a short, shrill blast on a whistle. There were further echoes, as the mountainside threw the noise from one surface to another, like children in a ring with a ball. However, the initial sound had definitely come from my left and slightly below me. I estimated about five hundred yards on a level march but dropping a yard or two every so often.

"Coming!"

After a few moments, I heard Holloway again: "Stand still! Listen!"

I waited. Then came the whistle again. This time it was definitely clearer, definitely closer, and more on the same latitude as I.

"Coming again!" I revised my course.

We repeated this procedure for about five minutes and then: "Doyle?"

"Yes?"

"We have a lantern. Don't know if the fog's too dense. Can you see it?"

I peered through the darkness.

"Nothing!"

"Keep coming!" Holloway's voice was now very close and almost echo-free.

I had barely stumbled another ten paces when, indistinctly, through the dense dark foggy forest, I could see the vestiges of a yellow glow.

"I can see you!"

And, presently, I was with my rescuers.

I never thought I would say it, but I was actually pleased to see Holloway.

Eva and Anton were with him. They appeared to be in better spirits than the last time I had seen them. We set off together towards the village. Holloway seemed to have improved where his temperament was concerned. Whether this was because he was with Eva again, or whether his raised spirits had been artificially enhanced, it was difficult to say.

"I got back to the hotel and found my compass and the map in my pocket. I was in such a stew. I didn't think straight," Holloway explained. I waited for the apology – but it did not appear.

"And when we saw the clouds roll in and knew that it would soon be dusk," Eva said, "we thought that we had better come to look for you."

"I am very glad that you did. I am afraid that I became rather lost."

"You were not so far from the path," Anton informed me. "Why did you leave it?"

"Well, actually, I left it some distance further up the mountain. You called out to me when I was employed in the task of trying to re-establish my connection with it…"

"You left the path?" asked Eva. "Why?"

"Do people usually come hunting in these woods?"

"Of course," replied Anton. "Although they know to keep away from this path. To hunt more to the north and the west."

"If they know what they are doing."

"Was there some kind of difficulty, Doyle?"

"Only a little, Holloway."

I then proceeded to tell them the story of the stray bullet. I have to say that they made an excellent audience, emitting low whistles and short gasps at all the appropriate moments.

"It has been known for this to happen," said Anton, "although I do not remember if anyone has ever been killed or injured by this stray bullet accident before."

"As you say," Eva added, "it would seem that it had travelled a long way and had been fired for some other reason."

"Still, nevertheless, Doyle… you never know."

"Thank you for your contribution, Holloway."

"A – how you say – narrow squeak?"

"A narrow squeak indeed, Eva." I did not tell them of the other narrow squeak I had experienced atop the force. It seemed to me that they had endured quite enough excitement for one day; as had I. There was also the sense in which to have told them I had nearly foolishly flung myself accidentally from a precipice would have meant changing again the increasingly good-natured aspect of the party. We had, after a long day, reclaimed some of the bonhomie we had experienced at the outset of my stay. I did not wish to sully that with tales of my own ineptitude. Not to mention Holloway's probable sententious reaction to my folly. His approbation I could take or leave alone ordinarily. But I had felt wholly isolated during the past four hours, and his association, if not actual companionship, I recognized I would still need, as we continued our pursuit of whatever and whomever it was that we were pursuing.

We sauntered into the village; the Four Musketeers returned from a successful sortie against the cardinal's men. Arriving at the hotel, Anton and Eva bade us farewell. As we made our way upstairs, Holloway informed me that, back at the hotel earlier, he had managed to persuade Eva to allow him access to Brown's bedroom. He had made a thorough investigation of it, he told me. I did not point out that it would have been better if we had made this thorough investigation jointly. Nor did I feel it was appropriate at that moment to remind him of the reason why he had found himself back at the hotel, and therefore able to pursue such a course in the first place. I merely asked him what it was, if anything, he had discovered. He told me.

"Nothing."

"Nothing?"

"No. Brown's effects had been gathered together and taken down to the valley on the cart with his body."

As I had thought. It was most galling and frustrating. I wished I had had the wit to think about exploring Brown's room first, rather than delay until after I had inspected the body. Now it was too late. I supposed I might still be able to assess his personal effects at a later date, should I get to see the paperwork from the valley hospital. But it was a long shot, and a pretty rum thing to boot. I would rather have had that evidence now to assist with my deductions.

"That's a bit of a blow."

"Absolutely. However, all is not lost…"

"Is it not?"

"Because it was Anton who collected up Brown's things and, for propriety's sake, he wrote down an inventory of everything he put into Brown's trunk to be sent down into the valley. Eva let me have a look at it."

"Well, bless young Anton! And bless young Eva, too. And, while I'm at it, bless you as well, Holloway."

"Thanks, Doyle."

"So… what was the outcome?"

"Pipe knife absent. Alpenstock present."

"Alpenstock present, eh?"

"Nothing of any import beyond that, regrettably. Just the usual collection of clothing and other junk that folk are prone to take away on holiday with them."

"Any bottles? Liquor, alcohol, that sort of thing?"

"None. Why?"

"Just a theory. Anise-seed, you know…"

"Ah. Yes. No – nothing of that sort."

"Papers, letters, *billets-doux*? Lavender-scented notepaper from an amour?"

"Nil."

"Oh, well. Well done anyway, Holloway, and thanks. Perhaps I might get a glimpse of this inventory sometime if I need to."

"If you would like. Though I doubt you will extract any more information from it than I have."

"You may well be right."

On the first floor landing, I informed Holloway that I did not feel able to join the others in the dining room that evening and that, once changed out of my soggy attire, I would arrange for a light supper to be brought to me.

"Quite understand, old man. See you after that, then."

"After that? Why? What is going on?"

"The séance. Meet in the reception area at eight-thirty."

With the details of that dread appointment ringing ominously in my ears, I stumped up to my room.

I entered it and discovered on the floor, slid under the door, two telegram envelopes. Good old Steen, he'd reacted as efficiently and thoroughly as I had expected. But who was the second message from? I washed and changed and sat down on the corner of my bed to read the missives. They were both, according to the datelines, from London SW.

The first was, indeed, from Steen.

> MY DEAR OLD THING.
>
> GOOD TO HEAR FROM YOU.
>
> RE BROWN I HAVE NO IDEA.
>
> NOT MY TERRITORY I AM AFRAID.
>
> HAVE GIVEN MESSAGE TO EXCELLENT
> YOUNG FELLOW FLEMYNG.
>
> CAPITAL OPENING BAT.
>
> HE WILL WIRE YOU WITH A VIEW.
>
> HOSPITAL BUSINESS IN HAND,
> WILL WIRE SOONEST.
>
> BESTEST. STEEN

Well, I said to myself, it was a start.

The second was from the young chap, Flemyng, on to whom Steen had passed my enquiry about what to do regarding Brown's demise. It was short and to the point and read:

> DEAR CONAN DOYLE.
>
> LEAVE IT TO THE SWISS.
>
> HOLMES IS SUPERB.
>
> KINDEST REGARDS.
>
> FLEMYNG
>
> P.S. WILL ASSIST FURTHER IF REQUIRED.

I cast the forms and envelopes aside onto the bed. One step forward, two steps back. Further news from Steen might change the situation in due course, and I hoped I could rely on the sincerity of Flemyng's postscript, but for the present I felt that all the hard work I had put in had led absolutely nowhere. I looked down again at those next-to-useless missives with distaste and regret. And noticed something most peculiar.

I picked up one of the envelopes, and then the other. I inspected them both closely. I could not believe my eyes, so I inspected them both again. There was no doubt about it. They had been tampered with. Along the bottom edge of both envelopes there was a thin slit, which had been glued closed again. An opening had been made in the paper, by a razor perhaps, just large enough to extricate the message inside. Then, once read, it had been replaced and the aperture resealed.

Someone had read my wires.

The question was – who?

NINE

We departed, all together, for the séance after dinner. It was a short walk from the hotel; held in one of the village houses. As we walked, I caught up with Werner and engaged him in conversation.

"Did you have any luck up on the mountains?"

"No. I did not manage to shoot anything."

"I am sorry to hear it. Where did you try?"

"Oh, just up there…" He indicated with his chin towards the ridge over which Holloway and I had strolled after lunch, and down which I had struggled late that afternoon.

"Was it up that way, or that way?"

He jerked his head again. From what I could tell, he was indeed in the same area as I had been, although by the lack of precision that is the consequence of pointing with one's chin, he might have been a mile or two further north than the path down which I had come.

"Did you actually see any creatures?"

"One or two. Boar. Deer."

"How exciting. I would have been interested to see that. Perhaps I may accompany you on one of your next shoots?"

"Perhaps."

"I have been grouse hunting on the moors. Pretty good shot, if I say so myself. But I have never hunted in forest. Don't all those trees get in the way?"

"Sometimes. It depends on the forest."

I tried to picture the forest where I had become lost, in my mind's eye. It was busy with trees, but they did not stand shoulder to shoulder. Three, maybe five yards apart at times, by and large. It would be possible, at some quite considerable distance, to lie in wait, and to pick a target some distance away at which to fire a round. Not easy. Far from easy. But possible. Especially if the target were slow-moving, proceeding at an even pace, and one knows in which direction it is travelling. Possible. Particularly with a telescope sight.

"Do you have a good rifle?"

"The best."

"What sort of sights does it have?"

"The best."

"Telescope?"

"Of course."

"I should very much like to see it some day."

"Perhaps."

We trudged a little further in silence. He was a most uncommunicative gentleman. There might be, I considered, many reasons for that, of course.

"Did you fire your rifle at all this afternoon?"

"Three or four times."

"Really? But you did not hit anything?"

"Too fast. Too far away."

"Are you not worried that the bullets might fly off and hit something you can't see?"

"No."

"Why not?"

"Because if I cannot see it, it means there are trees in the way. They stop the bullets."

"Every time?"

"Naturally."

"Can you be sure of that? Can you be sure that you see everything in your line of fire for as far as the eye can see? Can you really be sure?"

He looked at me with a fierce, defiant light in his eyes that could have been kindled by either guilt or anger.

"It is my job as a hunter to be sure. It is why I am allowed to be a hunter. Because I am sure all the time."

I decided I would call his whole hunting brotherhood into question, since he thought it was so perfect.

"A bullet from a hunter's gun just missed my head by this much." I spread thumb and forefinger apart. "Up on the mountain this afternoon. Was it you?"

"*Nein.*" He didn't look at me, but continued his trudge.

"Well, it must have been someone. How many hunters were there on the hill? Do you know?"

"It was not me. It was not anybody I was with. It could not have been a hunter."

"How can you tell?"

"A hunter does not miss."

"You missed."

"Not like that."

He was, by now, positively seething again under that bluff Bavarian exterior. Wiser counsel prevailed and I decided to desist in my questioning. We were nearly at our destination anyway.

It was an old Italianate thickset house with shutters, like those I had seen on the Ligurian coast. It was not a chalet, since it was in the centre of the village. Whatever it was once, it now did not seem to have any community function other than as a residence. I imagined in the past it might have been an artisan's dwelling or, perhaps, some kind of shop. It did not occur to me immediately that it was the house from which had fallen, or had been flung, a terracotta flowerpot on the day of my arrival. I only recognized the sullen, well-built and gruff man from that incident when the door was opened. He stood there eyeing us all with suspicion. If this was our medium, we were in for a very melancholy evening indeed. Plantin introduced himself and the purpose of our visit. The fellow stood grudgingly aside to let us pass. We all gathered in the hall and, as we did so, were met by his wife.

The hall lights were dim and this, perhaps, added to her mystery and charm. She was not porcelain pretty, rather very attractive. Not tall, but neither was she petite. Not slim, but not large. Her attractiveness lay in her being of average build and average height. But to employ the word "average" did not do her justice. The words "perfectly proportioned" might have been closer to the truth. I had never met a woman that had been perfectly proportioned. Not in the way a Michelangelo or a daVinci might have portrayed perfection. But this certainly was the nearest example in real life I had ever encountered. Tangled raven black hair framed her oval face and her almond eyes, and contoured itself decorously over her bare shoulders.

She seemed genuinely pleased to see us, and her eyes shone with excitement and promise. She introduced herself as Francesca, and her husband as Hugo. She spoke in a faltering, lilting English that hinted at Mediterranean sunshine and olive groves. I could not decide if the accent was French or Italian. Latinate, definitely.

She was one of those women in whose company every male delights, and whose intimacy they covet. She was someone who was well aware of her charms but did not abuse them; at least, not deliberately. Her femininity was something that came naturally to her. At risk of willingly or unwillingly becoming infatuated with her on the spot, as I am sure men had done for many years, I reminded myself of the fiery temper that she also possessed. The one which had been evidenced by the terracotta pot incident.

She said that she was nearly ready to commence, and asked Hugo to take us through into the room she had prepared for us. This her husband did with diffidence. She, meanwhile, repaired upstairs to complete whatever it was she had started before we arrived.

We were brought through into a back room, just off a kitchen hung with pots and pans, cured meats, fowl, herbs and onions. The room was spare and dark. It had only one window, which was redundant as it looked out onto a dingy back yard. It was night time anyway.

There were thick velvet curtains which, once upon a time, would have graced a larger, more opulent house. Dried flowers were placed decorously in front of the blacked iron fireplace. There were no coals or logs, although some ash lay beneath the grate. There was a table. Disappointingly, it was neither round nor steeped in mystic mystery. It was deal, and plain and scratched. Vessels of hot and cold liquids had been placed upon this surface over many years and had left their blanched, circular autographs upon the stained wood. I imagined that it had been wiped for the occasion. Nevertheless, flecks of ancient varnish gave the table a rough, uncomfortable feel. It looked, for all the world, as though it had some untreatable and contagious skin complaint. When one rested one's hands and wrists upon it, one developed an overwhelming urge to scratch.

Hugo, in the desultory manner he had apparently adopted for the evening, motioned for us to settle around the table. He then left us to our own devices. We took our places around this curious item of furniture and sat, expectant.

Francesca had not reappeared. She was presumably still preparing herself. Having said that, from what little I knew of these events, preparation was not wholly necessary. If one had the gift, the gift came unbidden. It was the gift's choice and not the medium's. No amount of preparation could summon it.

Presently we heard raised voices, in Italian. The words were muffled by at least one closed door: ours. The strength of the argument swiftly increased, as did its volume, if not its clarity. I began to wonder whether this had anything to do with our presence in the back room. I rather suspected that it had.

Eventually, there was a loud thud, which was the slamming of a distant door. There followed an uncomfortable silence and a long wait. At length, our door opened and Hugo presented himself with a face like fury and a thunderous brow. There was a simple pine armchair with turned legs tucked away in the corner of the room. He stalked straight across to it and threw himself into it. He then folded his arms in a perfect portrayal of an immoveable object and stared, unseeing, directly before him.

Having observed his arrival, attention turned back to the table. Sitting with my back to him, knowing he was quietly stewing there, was most intimidating.

Again we waited. I began to wonder if, even at this eleventh hour, the whole event might be called off. The whole concept had been pure folly from the start. I really could not see how there would be anything of value to be gained from it all. I looked around to see if there were any others with corresponding thoughts working through their minds.

The Pivcevics, I could see, were sitting patiently with blank features. Assuming, from our conversation in the hotel when discussing this event, that they were dyed-in-the-wool sceptics, I supposed this was a form of politeness. They did not wish to simply sit and scoff, and they could not feign interest, so they resorted to indifference.

Holloway twitched with nervous anticipation. But of course, he was hoping to become the vessel into which the spirit of Sherlock Holmes was to be poured. If it were possible for a human body to hum like a telegraph wire, then that was what he was doing. I felt sure that if I touched him on the arm, he would leap ten feet into the air and lodge his head into the ceiling.

Both van Engelses sat patiently. They appeared to have the capacity to switch themselves off at any time. If they were capable of switching themselves on again at any time during the proceedings remained to be seen.

Werner sat looking about the room in his solid way, as if he were waiting for a tram. He passed the time by wheezing a Bavarian folk tune to himself under his beery breath. He perhaps thought no one could hear him. Or perhaps he didn't care.

Even Monsieur and Madame Plantin had been moved to cease their lovers' whispers. She sat with her hands lightly resting on his arm, which in turn rested upon the arm of his rolling chair. Occasionally they would look at one another and raise an eyebrow or allow the flicker of a conspiratorial smile to pass between them.

My companions duly surveyed, my thoughts moved to other occupations. I began to assess the wait. Why was it happening?

What was it for? I did not mean to disparage Francesca and her kind, but was it all part of the performance? I had witnessed a few séances before, when living in Southsea, and had noticed that every medium had their own particularities. Might I describe these as methods? Was this leaving us in silence, bringing us to the verge of indolence, part of her routine? Was Hugo and the row all part of it? There were, I knew, countless charlatans masquerading as psychics. They all had their little stage acts. One or two that I had encountered, in my limited investigations, had even led me to guffaw at their flummery. Capes covered in mystical signs draped across the forearm and held in front of the bridge of the nose. Eye-rolling and strangulated voices. I suppose they imagined these tricks gave them the appearance of being other-worldly. In truth, they were simply risible.

The idea that this evening might end up as being just such another elaborate hoax or confidence trick began to exercise me. I had had an uncommonly tiring and emotionally draining day. I had traipsed up hill and down dale, been soaked by a waterfall and a rainstorm and been insulted by someone for whom I had little or no respect. I had nearly disappeared over the edge of an abyss. I had nearly had a stray bullet, if it was stray, gouge a channel through my brain. I was therefore in no mood to be trifled with. The image of my own bed began to rise before my eyes and, although I pushed it aside, it returned.

And then Francesca entered.

We all stirred and settled again in that "at last" way people have when they have sat still for a particularly long time − before the overture begins, or in a doctor's waiting room. It was clear by the puffiness around her eyes that she had been crying, and had been waiting until she had stopped before attempting to make her face as presentable as possible for visitors. It was also clear by the way she fired a baleful glower across at her husband, ensconced in his armchair in the corner, who was the reason for the tears.

"We shall begin," she announced.

She sat in her chair. It was the usual medium's property: high back, arms.

"Do you require 'tyraps'?" I asked, using a word which I imagined was English but which I thought might have been universal in the world of the medium. She looked at me quizzically.

"The bonds to secure your arms to the chair."

"No, that won't be necessary. I do not feel that I am under scrutiny. I have no need to prove my truth. I am also not proposing that I am a physical medium."

"What's that?" asked Holloway.

"A physical medium sometimes has manifestations of a physical nature," I explained, like the scientist and rational human being that I believed myself to be. "Things moving about the room, strange noises, ectoplasm, that sort of thing…"

"Ah," said Holloway, seemingly disappointed.

"Usually séances are conducted in the dark, and the medium does not wish to be accused of getting up from his or her chair to perform these so-called manifestations personally, if you see what I mean?"

Francesca was looking at me again. Was that curiosity in her eyes? Or was it concern that I knew this much?

"So, we are not going to do this in the dark?" asked Marie, also expressing disappointment. I suspected that this was for a different reason. Perhaps, for her, everything must conform to the stereotype or it would not be the full authentic experience.

"Yes, we will have it dark," said Francesca, "but I do not need to be secured to my chair. I am merely going to report what it is that I hear."

"And what is it that you do hear?" asked Pivcevic, disarmingly.

"This I cannot say."

"Because you do not want to, or you cannot because there is nothing there?" This time is was Anna who spoke, more challenging than her husband.

"No, I cannot say because it is difficult to describe. It is like *knowing* something you did not know. *Hearing* something you have not heard. *Understanding* something no one has ever explained to you."

"And what is it that you don't know, don't hear and don't understand?" Pivcevic asked, playfully.

"We shall find out, I hope," said Francesca and turned the oil lamp, which had been standing patiently in the middle of the table all this time, right down.

Hugo coughed, perhaps to remind his wife that he was still there. If we had been able to see clearly, I suspect the furious look she might have returned would have melted steel.

"Let us begin," was all she said, but the anger was evident in her voice.

We sat in silence for a moment.

"Do we hold hands?" asked Marie, from out of the darkness.

"You can hold mine," said Plantin, and they giggled together like the lovers they were.

"Shhh!" said mevrouw van Engels who, despite having said nothing or moved one inch since she had entered the room, was evidently a believer.

"Is there a John?" Francesca asked suddenly. "I can sense a John…"

I was immediately disappointed. John is one of the most common names in Britain. She knew that she was trying to accommodate Holloway and me in this séance and, I supposed, she thought that we might respond. I refused to do so. She may not feel that she was under scrutiny this evening, but I had not promised to refrain from examining and testing everything she said and did.

Marie spoke up: "Could it be… *Jean?*"

"He is an old man – a grey beard."

"My uncle!" Marie said.

"Has he passed over to the other side? This… Jean… is on the other side."

"*Oui!* He died six years ago."

"He says to tell you that all will be well."

"What will be well?"

"This thing that concerns you most deeply at this time. The thing that you do not feel you can talk about. The secret thing. I do not know if it is secret to all or secret only because you should not talk about it in this company. But this thing… all will be well. Do you understand?"

There was an expectant silence.

"She understands," Plantin answered for her.

"*Oui*. I understand very well. Thank Uncle Jean for me…"

I was very disappointed. These were all generalities. *Jean* or John. Common names in any language. And this "all will be well" platitude. Everybody has secrets. I thought of mine. "All will be well" would fit that just as effectively. I admired the woman. I was enjoying just sitting in her company and listening to her warm voice. Nevertheless, she would have to do better than that.

"Someone broke something before they came here. Very precious. Given by a special person."

Generalities again, I told myself.

Van Engels spoke, "My spectacles?"

"No… no… it is… porcelain. Or glass."

"My spectacles," insisted van Engels. "I have lost them," he explained, somewhat unnecessarily.

"Shhh!" admonished his wife.

"No… no… a container. Flowers?"

"A vase!" Werner erupted. "I gave my wife a vase for her birthday, two years ago. I broke it before I came. I have told her to replace it. I gave her money."

"Is it blue?"

"Blue?" Werner thought for a moment. "It has blue in it. Or it had blue… now it is broken."

"Then your wife has bought a new vase and this is blue."

"Nonsense!" Pivcevic laughed. It would seem he could restrain his cynicism no longer.

"Tomas, please…" Anna scolded in the darkness.

"Well – she is just saying anything that could apply to anyone. If there are enough people here, you can choose anything to have happened and, in all the thousands of things that happen to people every day, you will *always* find a match."

"Tomas, please…"

There was an uncomfortable silence. My eyes had started to become adjusted to the profound darkness in the room. Although I could not quite make out shapes, I could at least detect a difference in the degrees of darkness if somebody moved. Francesca sat stock still while others, I could see, were more animated. Eventually, Francesca broke the silence.

"I can only say what I am given to understand. The new vase is blue. He will find it when he gets home. And when he finds it, he will know that I am right and did speak true."

I admired her dignity. She was a very strong, as well as magnetic, woman.

Holloway, through all of this sideshow, had understandably become increasingly impatient with these exchanges, and wanted to get on to the main event on the playbill.

"What about Holmes? We came here to see if Holmes's spirit would come."

"*Ja!*" agreed Werner.

"Did you not see anything about my spectacles?" asked van Engels, sounding disappointed. It would seem, however, that even the world beyond was not as interested in him.

"Forget about your stupid spectacles!" exclaimed mevrouw van Engels, displaying an animation none of us around that table could have guessed that she possessed. "The spirits cannot talk about anything they would like, or what you tell them to talk about; it comes when it comes. Please proceed, Francesca."

The room, I noticed suddenly, was filled with a fragrance. Lily of the valley. It was not, though, a psychic manifestation. It was the fragrance that Francesca wore. I had noticed it as I had entered the house, and as she had entered this room. Why I should suddenly smell the scent at that point, I did not know. It just seemed to waft across to me. Perhaps, in the darkness, although I could not confirm it, she had leaned closer to me across the table for a moment. Whether she had or not, in the end did not concern me. What did concern me was that I then began to wish that she had. In fact I began to wish that she were sitting right next to me, rather than across the table from me. I wanted her to be closer, so that I might enjoy her warmth and her fragrance and her personality…

I shook myself out of this absurd reverie. It was impossible. She could not possibly captivate me. No other woman has captivated me apart from my beloved Touie, who favoured, I reminded myself, lavender water.

But that lily of the valley was an entrancing fragrance. Fresh, young. Vital. Full of promise and spring and meadows and young love. The early days of love, before familiarity and the daily round set in.

What was happening to me? What was beguiling me…?

"I do not know if I can discover whether there is a spirit of Sherlock Holmes," Francesca said. "Yesterday, I wondered if it might be possible. Today… now… I am not so sure… I cannot make things happen."

"You must!" cried Holloway. "You take our money and then you give nothing in return. I like your business, madam. Would that I could share in it. I daresay I could. Just turn out the lights and repeat: 'The spirits tell me they have nothing to say today. That will be one guinea, thank you. Close the door as you leave.' Oh yes, a most convenient method of procuring an income, I must say."

"If you are not satisfied, I will not take your money. But I say again, I cannot make things happen."

"My friends," Plantin said, "I suggest that this is *inutile* and that we should close the meeting for tonight. Are we all in agreement?"

Some agreed, some did not. Some mumbled non-committally. It was hard to tell who was who. I said nothing.

"Doyle?"

"Holloway?"

"Concentrate."

"What?"

"Think about Holmes. Picture him in your mind. Summon him into your thoughts. Bring him alive in your imagination. Like Shelley's Frankenstein, summon life into your creation."

I considered objecting, but realized that this was the precise reason for our presence around this table. There were also Francesca's feelings to take into account.

"Very well," I said. Not that I was in any way taken with the woman. I was happily married. Dear Touie. "Happy to oblige."

"Are you thinking about him?"

"Just about to."

We sat in strained silence for a short while. All at once, Francesca gave a sharp gasp.

"Is it Holmes?" asked Holloway.

"Sounds like she has a headache," said Pivcevic.

"Shhh!" said Anna and mevrouw van Engels.

Francesca cried out again; this time her voice was deeper.

I carried on concentrating on Holmes. I was imagining him in *Scarlet* when we first encountered him, bending over a bench, conducting a chemical experiment. Lean, intense, intelligent and absorbed in the science of deduction. Arrogant. Powerful yet flawed; greatly flawed. A musician, a pipe smoker, a lover of orderliness and propriety. A seeker of truth and justice. Outside the law. Tenacious. Heroic. Quick tempered. Easily bored when not occupied in matters of the greatest moment. Alone. Lonely. Misunderstood.

"Oh!" cried Francesca once more.

"What is it…?" a number of the assembled asked, concerned for any number of different reasons. Worried for her health, worried for theirs. Frightened of the unknown, or eager to learn more and experience a hitherto unimagined journey into the mystical and the psychic planes.

"He is falling!" Francesca wailed.

"Who is?" we asked.

All of a sudden the table began to vibrate. The legs rattled on the flagged floor and there were both gasps of surprise and whimpers of concern.

"Falling… falling!" Her voice was strange, trembling, agitated. "He turns… Once, twice…"

The table was now lifting and bucking as if it were alive and trying to shake us off. Marie moaned in fear and mevrouw van Engels sniffed. Werner rumbled uncontrollably.

"Ahhhh!" Francesca screamed.

I was practically thrown off my seat as the table convulsed and flung itself halfway across the room. Judging by the exclamations, others, too, were similarly affected. There were also cries of pain as people perhaps caught glancing blows. The table landed with a crash upside down somewhere outside our circle. The oil lamp, which had been set in the middle of the table, followed it an instant later, with a resounding clang and a smashing of its glass lens.

Those of us who had leapt to our feet in the confusion blundered about the room in the darkness, seeking to calm one another and regain a sense of perspective. This went on for a few moments until someone, I think it was Pivcevic, had the presence of mind to go to the door and open it. The light from the hallway flooded in and we all winced at the unaccustomed brightness after the gloom of the room.

Francesca sat in her seat, head bowed, her chin resting on her sternum. She looked exhausted. Holloway was still sitting also, staring in a dazed, unseeing way.

It took us some further few moments to calm down and regain our dignity and equilibrium.

"I think…" suggested Pivcevic, wisely, "that is quite enough for one evening. Perhaps we should all go straightaway back to the hotel."

We all agreed. Holloway started to stand up, and Werner helped him to his feet. They followed Monsieur and Madame Plantin and the van Engelses out of the room. Hugo, Francesca's husband, was only too eager to see them to the door. The Pivcevics thanked Francesca, who had also recovered herself sufficiently to stand, for a splendid evening's entertainment, and paid the bill. Francesca made a play of refusing the money, but Pivcevic insisted and, to be honest, she didn't try too hard to object the second time.

The Pivcevics having left, only I remained with our hostess. She looked at me and smiled.

"Was that what you were seeking?" she asked.

"I was seeking nothing. But I think the desired effect was achieved."

"Sherlock Holmes came?"

"I am not so sure of that. I'm not so sure what it was I witnessed tonight, to be frank. However, the effect was that we all were shaken and some even frightened out of our wits. I do not know what occurred, but everybody has probably gone away from here taking with them whatever they desire to take with them. Be it belief or scepticism."

"And you?"

"Me…?"

"Why did you agree to this?"

"Like you, I expect. One can never discover new territory from the comfort of one's own home. You have to get out there in your little coracle, paddle for all you're worth and hope you do not get swamped and drown."

"Coracle?"

"Boat."

"We are both explorers. We have just caught sight of a great map. An indication of a dark continent that we feel we might some day investigate further. It excites you, yes?"

"It intrigues me. But as far as this evening is concerned… I shall say no more."

Hugo returned and stood with folded arms in the doorway. I took the hint. I nodded my goodbye to Francesca, sidled past her husband, who filled most of the doorway, and allowed him to accompany me off the premises.

"Goodnight." I stepped out into the street. "We must do this again sometime," I added, not entirely seriously.

I heard the door close firmly behind me. I set off to join my companions on their stroll back to the hotel through the fresh, starlit night.

Up ahead, Holloway seemed to be engaged in an argument with the Pivcevics. It was not hard to discover its nature. The young hothead was convinced something spectacular had happened at the house they had just left. The Pivcevics, for their part, were more sanguine about the whole experience. There is nothing so annoying for a new convert than to have ice water flung on recently kindled passions. With a final expression of exasperation, he dropped away from them, fulminating. He slowed to allow me to draw alongside him.

"It's obvious, isn't it?" he said, as if I had been privy to the whole preceding conversation, which I had not.

"What is?"

"They don't want Holmes, do they? They can't afford him to be around."

"Can't they?"

"Because they are concealing something and, if Holmes had appeared, they would be found out."

"Ah."

I left it at that. I had relit my pipe and was, to be frank, more rapt in my own musings. I did not have much time for my companion's rants just then, really. This was a state of mind that quickly became clear to him. With another expression of impatience, he veered away to find some other poor soul among our company upon whom he might lay his wild imaginings.

I was neither concerned nor unconcerned about the events we had just witnessed, despite Holloway's obvious conviction. For my part, I doubted very much that Holmes had put in an appearance.

Nevertheless, if there were anything at all to this humbug... well then, might it not have been the spirit of Brown? After all, Holmes had never fallen off anything in my stories. At least not as far as I could recall. Nor had I planned any such adventure for him. Although, I supposed, that was not entirely out of the question.

TEN

I tracked Holloway down to the library the next morning after breakfast. I discovered him sitting in a wing-back staring intensely at nothing at all. I presumed he was thinking hard.

"There you are, Holloway. I believe that we really should attempt to gain access to Brown's belongings. It is most probably too late, but it needs must be done."

He turned and looked at me. His face wore a curious expression. Benign but superior. As if he were indulging me. He tented his fingertips. "I shall ask Eva. She has already informed me that she will help me in any way she is able."

"You have not told her?"

"Of course not." He wafted his hands in the air.

"It is imperative that we keep the nature of our enquiries strictly between ourselves."

"But of course."

"So – what did you mean by saying Eva is willing to help us?"

"Simply that… I told her that we were concerned for our countryman, and that you wanted to make sure that he was repatriated with dignity. You are a doctor."

I was not convinced. Nevertheless, as Eva was involved now, it could not be helped. She could even be useful, among other things, in gaining access to the deceased's belongings. That was, if they were still at the valley hospital and not already packed and making their way back to England. I drew the line at breaking and entering again.

"When do you see her again?"

"We have an arrangement to meet this morning."

"Then please ask her this. Which way was Brown lying, where was he found precisely, and who found him? I would like to know

142

the exact details. Perhaps she might elicit a description from one of the fellows who discovered him?"

"There goes your wretched vanity again, my dear Doyle."

"My vanity!?"

"You have, for some reason, decided that you are in charge of this case. Yet, try as I may, I can find no significant evidence upon which you might justifiably base such an assumption."

"Now, look here, Holloway…"

"We have attempted to follow your methods to the letter these past few days, and where has it brought us? I respectfully suggest, nowhere. By your own admission," he continued suavely, "there was nothing at the fall. You have some half-baked theory about a missing smoker's knife and…"

"Just a minute…"

"… and an alpenstock that was immaterial. It was left behind in his room. Forgotten. Not needed. Who knows? Who cares? What does it prove? Unless we had found it in the murderer's grasp. Even then, I doubt it would prove anything. We need real clues, Doyle. Specific and unambiguous. Undeniable and empirical." He had the impudence to raise one eyebrow in my direction. "No, my dear Doyle, I suggest that you put your vanity to one side with good grace and allow me, if I may, to pursue your interests on your behalf."

I had never heard such impertinence in all my life. Was it not he who had harried and cajoled me into exerting my influence upon this sorry business? Was it not he who had engineered the investigation of Brown's body? Was it not he who had forced the pace and driven all the interests before him? I had merely been gulled into complying with his bidding. And now, here he was, tantamount to accusing me of manipulating the whole affair to my own ends. It really was beyond the pale, and I told him so.

He just smiled sardonically to himself and, in a manner which suggested affectation, tented the tips of his fingers together again, and rested them thoughtfully against his lips.

"I fear, my dear Doyle, that the facts speak for themselves."

"You just said that there were no facts."

"The facts, Doyle," he sat forward in his chair to stare directly into my eyes, "and forgive me if I hurt your feelings at this point – the facts are that you have made a bit of a botch of the whole affair to date. To the extent that you even found yourself hopelessly lost on a mountainside at night in the fog. Which, if nothing else, serves as a very significant metaphor." He held up a thin white hand to stay my objections. "We hear some, frankly, implausible tale about your being shot at by hunters. Hunters who, according to reliable reports, were not within at least two miles of you. In my opinion, you concocted the whole fairytale simply in order to try to save face in the light of your ineptitude..."

"Now, look here, Holloway…"

"But if we allow fate to be the judge between us, then further facts present themselves. It was I who rescued you. It is therefore evident that my star is in the ascendant, while yours is in sharp decline. The gods, as it were, have judged between us and have ordained me as their representative, if you like. I know that this appears to you to be fanciful, and I am aware of your astonishment, Doyle. Please do not boggle your eyes at me and open and close your mouth as if you were a genus of carp. I do not wish to embark upon a metaphysical discussion so early in the morning. I merely point out that I have been making all the running in this. Up to and including having contacts such as Eva. Meanwhile, you have none and rely entirely upon mine. Your clumsily setting fire to the chapel when secrecy, delicacy and subtlety were of the utmost importance, we shall draw a discreet veil over. It is plain to me, therefore, that I must step out from behind your shadow, where you have been at pains to keep me since first we met, and begin to take control. For all our benefit."

Once again I tried to open my mouth and interrupt. Once again he constrained me to hold my peace.

"No, Doyle, whatever you may care to say is no longer of any value. The case is mine and, I daresay, by the end of it you shall be glad that I chose to impose my will on this whole business... brutal and unfair as it may seem to you at this present moment."

He subsided and I, at last, had the opportunity to say something. I duly opened my mouth but discovered, perhaps unsurprisingly, that I was speechless. I therefore simply nodded a curt "good-day" to my tormentor and left the library with as much dignity as I could muster. It did not help my disposition to note that as I turned to leave his presence, he waved me away with a bored air. He then placed the tips of his fingers together and rested them pensively against his lips once again. It was as if, rudely interrupted, he was now at last able to return to his lofty thoughts.

Back in my room, sitting out on my balcony, puffing furiously on my pipe, and clenching the stem firmly between my teeth until it was fit to snap in two, I took stock. It was still my intention, I reasoned, that I should not let this whole affair ruin my rest-cure. I decided, consequently, to return to my earlier resolve. The one I had framed before I had even arrived here – to give Holloway as wide a berth as possible. The whole atmosphere had become oppressive and I was scandalized by Holloway's offensive and thoroughly personal and wholly inappropriate remarks.

Finding myself unable to settle, however, I decided to go for a walk and suck in a few lungfuls of sweet mountain air.

I walked through into the reception area on my way out, and encountered Plantin in his rolling chair. He had come from his room along the ground floor corridor. Despite the excitements of the previous evening, I still detected a distance between us. I nodded a distracted "good morning" and he responded equally coolly. I continued upon my egress and had just reached the front door when Plantin called to me.

I turned to face him. I did not feel very much like another confrontation quite so soon after my interview with Holloway, but I also possessed good manners. When I am addressed, I consider it the height of bad manners not to turn and attend to the addressor.

"Monsieur Plantin..." I nodded a greeting.

He was struggling with some strong emotion. I waited for him to approach and to hear what it was for which he had called me back. He reached me and spoke.

"Doctor, would you care to accompany me for a short while?"

"I was just going to take the air…" I was minded to refuse. However, there was an earnestness in his eyes, so I changed tack in mid sentence. "… so I would be glad to accompany you."

"I am happy to hear it." Although he did not appear happy.

He had had his rolling chair adapted so that he might be able to propel himself at least a little distance, which gave him a degree of independence. I offered, though, to push him, and he was good enough to accept my gesture of reconciliation; for that was what it was.

We left the hotel and turned left onto the main street. We commented on the weather, which again was excellent. I asked after his wife and he told me that following the emotional and physical exertions of last evening, added to which, the lateness of our return from the séance, she had felt it would benefit her best if she were to remain within her chamber for the morning. To rest, to read, to drink coffee in the privacy of their room.

I considered that a sensible and enviable decision, and remarked as such to my companion.

As we walked along, we passed Professor and mevrouw van Engels, in line astern, wearing their by now familiar and apparently habitual tweeds and brogues. Professor van Engels suddenly developed an avid interest in a baker's shop, which he maintained until he was certain we had passed him by. Mevrouw van Engels gave a species of twitch, which could have been interpreted as a greeting, but could also have been seen as an inability to know quite what to do.

"Is it me, or is it both of us?" asked Plantin.

"It is me. But do not ask me why, as I am sure I do not know."

We had reached, by now, a small café with lace curtains and an elegant red and gold painted façade. There were tables set out in the front and, from within, I could smell the rich and inviting aroma of freshly milled and roasted coffee beans. I asked Plantin if he would join me, and he replied that he would be more than happy so to do. The conversation had been general and, while not uncomfortable, still a little strained. Doubtless, we both hoped that the more convivial atmosphere of the café might contribute towards creating an atmosphere in which we might discuss whatever matter was still, evidently, pressing upon my companion's mind.

I moved a chair and brought Plantin up to the table. I then took up residence directly opposite him. We sat there, in the bright morning sunshine, enjoying the relaxed and peaceful hubbub of a mountain village occupying itself with its daily routine. Presently, a waitress came out from within to serve us. I was surprised, but pleasantly so, to discover that she was, in fact, Francesca. She greeted us with a warm smile of recognition and apologized for the previous evening's dramatic finale. We waved aside her apologies professing, truthfully, that we had found it a most diverting experience. None of us made mention, naturally, of Hugo's behaviour.

Francesca took our order and, solicitously brushing a crumb from the crisp, white linen tablecloth by my forearm, left to fill our request.

Again Plantin and I made our small talk, as if neither of us wished to be the first to plunge into the actual meat of the conversation.

Francesca returned and practically leaned over my shoulder to place the coffee jug, cups, saucers, sugar and cream upon the table. Lily of the valley wafted over me. I am ashamed to say, my heart thrilled at her proximity. Her soft, lush, black hair brushed my cheek as she straightened herself up again.

"Will that be all?" She looked down at me in a way that made me feel all at once both protected and protective. Her smile filled my heart with a hope that I had no right to experience. Her smile gave me the impression that I was the only person in the world at that precise moment. It was folly, of course, and I knew it. Yet a sunrise of promise dawned somewhere in the darker recesses of my being. I longed to see her again. Alone. I could not help it.

"No, that is splendid, thank you," I croaked. She turned to leave. I stopped her by touching her arm. "I did not know that you worked here."

"I have to work somewhere. I am afraid I could not say that my séances provide me with a life of luxury." Then, *sotto voce:* "Hugo does not earn enough for the both of us."

"What does Hugo do?"

"He helps in the farms hereabouts; in the mountains, in the valleys, where the work is needed to be done. Today he is making hay in the meadows." She gestured towards the centre of the village. About half a dozen lusty men, stripped to the waist under the hot morning sun, were scything and raking their way rhythmically through the long grasses.

"If you need anything else, just call me."

"A real woman." Plantin observed. It was obvious that Francesca's femininity touched and lifted the spirits of every man that she encountered.

"Indeed."

We sipped our coffees and watched the passing people, barrows and carts. Then Plantin began.

"You are a doctor."

"I am." The opening salvo had a familiar ring to it. Did not his wife and I begin a conversation in a similar way the day before? Or was it the day before that? So much had happened I could no longer keep track of time.

"Then I may talk to you as a doctor?"

"You may. Although I should caution that any practical medical advice should be confirmed with your own physician before you embark upon it."

"Pardon?"

"Consult with your own doctor as well."

"Of course."

"So... how may I assist you?"

"Marie has told you, has she not, how I came to be like this?"

148

He tapped the chair with the fingertips of his right hand.

"Yes."

"So. Well, you should know that while I seem to be on the front of it smiling and also able to manage very well, I am, inside, always finding it difficult to be this way all the time."

"I am sure that you are."

"But I do not want pity."

"I am sure that you do not."

"You must... you must understand that, although I regret my injury, I do not regret my life one little moment. I adore my wife and she adores me. And so I do not ever wish to upset her. Therefore, I keep my secret to myself. She admires me for my strength and my courage. If I were to show her ever a weakness, she would no longer wish to respect me. Do you see?"

I nodded and waited.

"So, it is important for me that you do not explore my difficulties in private with Marie. If she continues to wonder what it is that is the matter with me, she may begin to understand, and then it will all be too late for us."

He had finished. I considered what he had said for a moment and replied, "Marcus, you are a very brave man. I admire you; without pity. I understand your difficulties, but you should understand that we *all* have difficulties with which we have to struggle. Each one of us is different; every difficulty is different for each person. Yet Winwood Reade tells us, in the generality, we are all the same. So your problems are different yet, in having problems at all, you are just the same as me, and I as you." I looked at him; he was watching me talk, but I could not be sure that he was listening. I continued. "As far as your wife is concerned, I think you should trust her more. People are more robust than we think. I believe you can trust her with your secret, as you call it. In my experience, women do not marry the men they see on the outside, although this may be what attracts them. They marry the man they find inside. It is also my experience that they love the soft, confused, vulnerable, struggling man just as much as the big, strong bear."

His eyes had widened during this last homily.

"Do you mean to say that I should reveal my innermost secrets to my wife?"

"I would not just go ahead and say it. But I would allow her in a little closer to your most intimate thoughts. Day by day, you will feel more comfortable to bring her closer and closer in."

"Is this not dangerous? Will it not… rot my marriage?"

"There are always risks in love. But if we did not take them, we would not experience love's joys."

He sat there for a long time, staring into his coffee cup and shaking his head slowly from side to side intermittently.

"All is well?" I asked, after a suitable interval.

"All is well. I will try."

I was profoundly glad that my advice had found a home in his heart. Yet there was still something in his eyes. The way they failed to look directly into my own. He had not given me the whole story. Holmes would have been able to say so directly and, through observation of the person, even identify what it was. If not exactly, then generally, and the object of his studies would have filled in the rest. But I was simply Conan Doyle. An oaf, as Holloway had been so quick to point out this morning. Since I had no means of finding out what was being concealed from me, all I could do was wait. Hopefully, he or Marie, if she knew it herself, might eventually confide in me.

We finished our coffees in idle chatter about the séance last night. Both of us were unconvinced that anything had transpired. Plantin had become very much the sceptic, whereas I continued to insist that there simply was not enough evidence either way to have collected sufficient data upon which to base a reasoned opinion. Besides, even if the evening were a sham, it was an isolated incident. It would take a lifetime, I concluded, to explore the whole phenomenon. I looked into the café, caught Francesca's big, brown, Mediterranean eyes, and asked her for the bill. She arrived presently and I paid, inviting Plantin to be my guest on this occasion. He graciously accepted. I left Francesca a few coins and stood to leave. As I made my way around to take hold of the handles of the rolling chair, Francesca pressed a small folded piece of paper into my hand. I said nothing and slipped the paper into my jacket pocket. I nodded, letting her know that I understood what she had given me as being most important to her, and took Plantin away.

We wandered back to the hotel, content enough in each other's company by now. I could see Francesca's husband, Hugo, toiling in the sun across the village in the meadow. He was working very hard and energetically. It was a wonder to me that he would be able to sustain such effort throughout a full day.

Plantin had expressed a wish to return to the hotel and rejoin his wife. This was perfectly acceptable to me. In fact, it sounded a hopeful note inasmuch as, perhaps, he was already proposing to discuss at least part of that which had been concerning him with his wife.

I brought him to his door and left him to knock, returning to my own sanctuary. I discovered that I had received a new telegram, posted underneath my door. I picked it up and inspected it. Like the previous ones, it had been slit on the underside edge. Just enough to extricate its content and replace it; then sealed with a thin, snail's trail of glue.

I opened the wire and read it. It was from Steen.

ALL CLEAR TO CONTACT SWISS HOSPITAL.

HERR SÄMLICHEN IS YOUR MAN.

GOOD HUNTING.

STEEN

So far so good. There remained, though, the vexed questions of who was opening my wires and why? No doubt someone had established a relationship with one of the telegraph office clerks or delivery boys. Coin usually provided ample incentive in these cases. It would be a simple matter to ensure that the wires took an elliptical route, via the unknown reader, before they reached me. It did not have to be delayed too long. Just long enough for, possibly, a copy to be made and the glue to set. Telegrams to and from England were notoriously leisurely. I imagined that it was most probably one of the messenger boys who, as it were, took the long way round to my hotel room. It would be unlikely to be a receiving clerk. It would be a simple matter for them to read and copy any missive before the envelope was sealed. No slitting would be necessary at that stage. Unless, of course, they wanted me to know my messages were being read.

Whichever it was, if I were to discover the reader of my wires, I had to let him or her think that I had not detected the tampering of the envelopes. That meant that the wires should continue to arrive exactly in the way they had done to date. It was important, above all, that any message should appear as innocent as possible. I toyed with the notion that they might contain misleading information. But that, for me alone, would be too complicated a matter. Many years ago I had realized that I would not make a very good liar. I had an abysmal memory. I would be tripped up every time by others remembering something that I had said or done which I could not remember. This was caused by the simple expedient of my not having actually experienced whatever it was I had just made up. This inability to lie was one of the fundamental reasons why I found all these present shenanigans so unsettling. I had been drawn into intrigues with which I was not comfortable. And now, even worse, I had been set adrift in my lonely coracle or boat to paddle these turbulent waters alone. No, it was best that I did not conceive too many subterfuges, lest I lose count of the phantom facts I would have to assemble – and consequently betray myself.

So, some species of cipher was the recommended course. This could keep the material in the wires open, yet allow me to communicate with someone such as Steen, or Flemyng. It was just patently clear to me that another or others perceived my interest in this business as a threat. I had no doubt, since there was a death involved, that I would be placing myself in an exposed position. Perhaps even my own life might be at risk. Touie would not thank me for this. Were she here, she would have implored me to reconsider; to return home to my sacred duties as a husband and a father. It was indeed irresponsible of me not to consider my family in all of this. I was struck by a great wave of regret. I could only hope that if she and the children, one as yet unborn, suffered in any way as a result of my decision to press on, they would forgive me. I was not morbid enough to compose a will, mindful of my beloved, like some latter-day Nelson before my own Trafalgar. However, I was reminded that I had not written to Touie since I had arrived at the village. Taking pen and paper, I sat at the escritoire and composed a six-sided note of great tenderness and affection to my dear wife. I did not allude to the perils I had recently experienced, nor of those possibly yet to befall me. It was an intimate and private letter between two people who know that the bond between them could overcome all obstacles. I confess, as I completed the demonstrative missive, and signed it with the heartfelt affirmations of my undying love for my beloved, a tear stole into my eye. It lay there, blurring my vision as I sealed the envelope.

I was not so maudlin or melodramatic as to consider that this letter might be the last word Touie would ever receive from me. Yet the thought that she might treasure it beneath her pillow for the rest of her days caused a great depression to enfold me. I had to rise from the escritoire and step out onto the balcony for some fresh air. There, I contemplated the beauty of the created world that was the mountains and the sun and the sky and the trees. As if for the first time.

Silly old fool.

I decided to shake off my solemnity, that I would have a smoke. I fumbled among my pockets for my smoker's implements and realized that they were in my jacket upon the ladder-back chair. I had hung it there to compose my letter. I returned to it and went through the ritual of searching the pockets. As I drew out my tobacco pouch, something small, buff and rectangular fell out with it. I recognized it at once as the note that Francesca had slipped to me at the café.

With a curious mixture of both cool detachment and a thrill of anticipation, I opened it.

> *Please meet me at four o'clock.*
> *Please come to my house. F*

Of course, it was curious. But what was more remarkable, and indeed disturbing, was my reaction to it. My heart leapt and my spirit surged with excitement at the thought of seeing her again. Naturally, it was not a billet-doux. I did not imagine for one moment that it was a tryst. Something much more mundane (and platonic) I was sure lay behind the hastily written note. Yet I was concerned at my reaction. I had barely blotted the letter to my dear, beloved Touie. I had just wandered out upon my balcony to wrestle with my loneliness, painfully separated, as I was, from her. Yet, within an instant, my emotions had been transformed. My excitement at the prospect of seeing Francesca again had carried all other sentiment before it.

I was disgusted with myself and, out loud, I told myself as much. This was unadulterated nonsense. There was absolutely no reason on earth why I should, in any way, seek to alter my life and become more closely associated with this Italian... *siren*. I knew it. Touie, if she were privy to this information, would also know it. Yet here I was, buffoon, as excited as an adolescent at the prospect of meeting this member of the female sex. Had she bewitched me, I conjectured? No. I closed my foolish imagination to all prospect of an encounter with the woman that would be anything other than decorous and appropriate.

But then I wondered whether, perhaps, she had bewitched Brown…?

Had her undoubted exotic and sensual feminine allure captivated the poor fellow? Had he succumbed where I now, I reassured myself, had every intention of resisting?

I had discussed this possibility with Holloway at the fall. It could have been Francesca. Of course, it could also have been her husband, who struck me as a surly and violent cove. Characteristics A plus B, as van Engels would say, leaving us to extrapolate characteristic C: jealousy. *Quod Erat Demonstrandum.* This was perhaps more likely, if the studded boot marks I had found up at the fall were indeed directly related to the tragedy.

However, this train of thought needed to chug readily along in my mind a little further. Brown: lonely, a stranger, susceptible, vulnerable. It did not need to be Francesca, though, did it? Any woman offering her warmth, comfort and companionship would suffice. That is, if he were sufficiently receptive to those particular charms. Should my theory of a tryst hold water.

Who else then?

Marie.

Why?

Because… because… Plantin was very angry with Brown.

Why?

Because… maybe Marie had become attracted to the Englishman.

Why?

Because… because Plantin and his wife's… *understanding*… had been put under severe strain. While the romance was unfulfilled prior to marriage, perhaps it remained unfulfilled, in its entirety, post-nuptials. Or perhaps, despite her belief that Plantin was enough, indeed everything, for her, she was still very young and impressionable. And would she want children? Would Plantin even be able to provide for her in this way? It was distasteful in the extreme that I felt obliged to even begin considering such matters. Not the subject for stories. But this was real life, and I a doctor.

This theory would certainly explain why Plantin was so evidently exercised about my having had, in his view, intimate discussions with his wife about certain aspects of their relationship.

I filed these thoughts and began to explore other possibilities.

Eva?

No. She was someone who would consider using her femininity in quite that way beneath her dignity.

Yet... she and Holloway had found common ground and unity of purpose swiftly enough.

Then again, since she had been the first to find Brown when he was being brought down from the mountain, I could recall no emotion that betrayed any such purported intimacy. Could she have disguised it so well? Did she disguise it even further by immediately setting up a companionship with Holloway? Was she a cool, calculating seductress and murderess...?

Impossible.

Well, then, another tack. Had Brown offended her, perhaps? Had he made unwelcome advances towards her? She knew the countryside. She was a guide. She was positively charming and amenable. She could have – quite easily, I imagined – encouraged a fellow up into the mountains in his town shoes and without his alpenstock. Yet she could do this in all innocence, not realizing the intoxication of her wonderful open charms. Brown could have made advances, she could have fended him off increasingly violently, they could have tottered perilously at the chasm's edge and then... a slip and there he was, gone.

And Anna Pivcevic...?

I did not know enough about her yet. There would be opportunities to explore this avenue further.

And mevrouw van Engels? Who knew what secrets lay suppressed beneath that seemingly respectable and detached Dutch tweed-bound breast?

And then there were the men. Could they all be prone to fits of jealous rage, which might lead to acts of violence? Perhaps it was more than one of them? Perhaps Brown had been manhandled out of the hotel, in his town shoes and without his alpenstock, and forced to walk up the hill to his unique scaffold.

I sat down.

The permutations were virtually endless, and I had not even started considering the other villagers yet, let alone those scores of folk who passed through a district like this on a daily basis. That meant that no scientific benefit could profitably be obtained from the existing evidence. I would have to gather further intimations before I might narrow the field further. That is, I reminded myself, always supposing that there was a murder, that the murderer was still around, and that more evidence was in any position to be gathered.

Which brought me back to the question of Brown's room. How might I gain access to it? Holloway had access to Eva, but he and I were currently experiencing a cooling of relations. Perhaps he might be kind enough to involve me, all the same? I would ask him when I had the opportunity.

My pipe was cold; I had exhausted all the opportunities for exploration in this brumous case for the time being. I had an assignation at four o'clock. How might I usefully pass my time until then?

The answer came in the form of a brisk rap at the door.

Eleven

"Father Vernon, do please come in."

I stood aside and let the priest enter. He shuffled past, the skirts of his plain brown habit rustling. He was calm and reflective. We exchanged greetings and then I gestured to my armchair. He chose the ladder-back, and gestured for me to take the other. I dutifully sat. After all, I was brought up by Jesuits.

"How are you, doctor?"

"I am well. And how are you?"

"Passable. Although with middle-age comes a number of leathery creaks in the limbs and wintry aches to the joints, but I do not complain."

He smiled and waited patiently for me to speak. He seemed entirely content to pass the time in this way. I began to understand that the silence was leading somewhere, which left me with a sense of foreboding. For my part, I found the quiet disquieting. Being direct, I chose neither to humour him, nor to engage him in further pleasantries.

"I am delighted to extend my hospitality to you, Father, and I shall always be glad to do so. Regrettably, I do not have anything by way of a drink to offer you… Unless you would care for a glass of water from the jug over there?"

The priest politely declined, wordlessly.

"In which case, if I am not being too forthright, perhaps you would care to reveal what it is that has brought you to this unexpected but nonetheless pleasing visit?"

He smiled again. "I am glad, doctor, that you are candid, and that says to me that you are a scrupulously honest man. A characteristic I had observed that you possessed in abundance from the moment I met you."

I dipped my head in modest acknowledgment of his kind words. Privately, however, I was struck by the remembrance of how I had chosen not to be entirely frank with him on our first meeting, in the matter of getting in to see Brown's body.

"Of course, you were not entirely straight with me when last we met. But we both knew what it was that you had really come for. So, to all intents and purposes, that does not count."

I looked at him with quiet amusement; he had read my thoughts.

"So, you will not mind me saying, I can be sure, that I was wondering – indeed questioning – why such an honest man should seek, in effect, to prowl around my church and endeavour to set light to it."

I continued looking at him steadily, displaying, I hoped, not a flicker of emotion. He returned the gaze equally steadily. He was darkly serious, but not angry; challenging, but not confrontational. I resolved to offer no response. He had no proof, I was sure of it.

"Come along, doctor, I did not expect silence. You are an honest man and I am not accusing you of anything that I would choose to pursue any further. I am only puzzled and seek enlightenment. It was you. Only you, the decent, upright, English gentleman…"

"Scots–Irish."

"British gentleman… would, after having accidentally set a fire, attempt to put it out and then, before departing, replace the offending oil lamp. Only you, of all the people I might have considered having sought access to Mr Brown, would have had the courtesy to damp down the fire with the sheet. And then neatly place the sheet back on Brown's body. Only you, doctor. Only you."

"Only me? Father Vernon… I…"

"No actual harm was done. Plus, I have had worse in my time. I was a priest in the Rio shanties. This is merely for my own information. It is something also, I might say, I should care to commit to prayer."

I continued looking at him. He was in earnest, as far as I could ascertain. I relented and decided to tell him everything.

Perhaps unwisely, I did not know. However, in my silence I had been thinking rapidly. I suppose Holloway might have styled it a "How do you mean?" moment. Now, my thoughts marshalled, I realized that, in fact, I had an ace up my sleeve. To my shame, I deployed it.

"Father?"

"Yes?"

"You should be aware that my family are staunch Catholics."

"They are? I am pleased to hear it."

"And that I was schooled by Jesuits."

"Not always the best way to bring up a child, if you will permit me my personal opinion? I have met many fine young men who have benefited greatly, of course, but it is not for everybody. We are all different and cannot always conform to either the discipline or the doctrine, or both, if you understand my meaning…? Nevertheless, commendable."

"I have never renounced the faith, but I must admit that through my adolescent and young adult years, other thoughts and considerations crowded in upon me."

"You illustrate my last point admirably."

"This, coupled with a scientific career and observance of great suffering, has led me to a certain amount of… how shall I say…? Falling away."

"Neither unusual nor reprehensible. We are put upon this earth to use our minds and explore creation. The Lord knows what is deep in our hearts, even if we do not."

"So," I refused to be diverted by his extempore homilies, "would it be fair to say that I am still under the authority of Holy Mother Church?"

"There would need to be a period of re-evaluating one's relationship with her," he replied, with due solemnity. "And then there is the question of an act of reconciliation. But provided you have not renounced all that you once committed to in confirmation, in my opinion, yes, you may still call Mother Church your own."

"Then forgive me, Father, for this trick I am about to play on you…"

"Forgiveness? Now there is a long evening's discussion. But yes, I forgive you unreservedly, even if you are about to deceive me. However…" He had been sitting forward with his forearms resting on his thighs and his hands clasped lightly together. Now he sat back and folded his arms, as a kindly uncle about to receive a request of tuppence for sweets from a favourite nephew. "… I daresay that you are about to ask me if what you are about to tell me could be revealed as though it were under the conventions of the confessional? In which case, you would like your comments to be sealed between us and us alone, through the spirit of confidentiality and trust that exists between priest and confessor?"

I reverted to my original policy of silence. This time, however, it was not voluntary. He had anticipated and consequently nonplussed me.

"My son, I am afraid that I have sufficient respect for the holy institution of the confessional not to abuse it, nor to allow others to do so in such a manner. Further, if I were to take your confession, it would be with the intention of hearing all of your hopes and fears. We would also touch upon at least some of your behaviour, both good and ill, since last you confessed which, I surmise, is quite some substantial time ago. No. I will not allow this to be heard in that spirit."

My bearing was, I am sure, registering both perplexity and dismay. I was unsure how to proceed. Father Vernon resolved my confusion for me.

"However, I will, of course, treat our conversation as entirely confidential; between you and me. No others shall hear of it, unless you give me permission to speak of it. I should say, though, that if I thought you had committed a serious crime, I could not, in all conscience, give you such an assurance. Before we proceed, may I have your word that nothing more serious has occurred than the matter to which I alluded when first I arrived?"

"You have my word."

He chewed his lower lip for a moment and surveyed me from beneath a furrowed brow. Then he spoke. "I am pleased that you gave me your word without need to refer to anyone or anything else. You did not give your word on God, the Scripture, anyone's life, nor on your standing as a gentleman. You gave it purely and simply as if, indeed, your word alone was sufficient. As such, I accept it. So," he unfolded his arms and, arms rigid, splayed his fingers on his knees, "we understand one another. When you are ready, pray, proceed."

I told him of our encountering the body as it was being brought down from the slopes; of my theory of the pipe knife and the alpenstock and the town shoes. I told him of the scent of anise-seed and the inspection of the cliff top by the waterfall. I did not tell him of the stray bullet, nor did I tell him about the slits in my telegrams. The former I believed to be immaterial, the latter needed, as I had reasoned earlier, to remain entirely secret. I also did not tell him of my proposed rendezvous with Francesca, since its purpose was as yet unclear.

"And now, tell me about your friend."

"Holloway?"

"Holloway."

"He is not my friend." This elicited no reaction from the priest. "I appear to have... collected... him at Zürich station. He has clung to me like goose grease ever since. It was he who encouraged me into pursuing this investigation in the first place." I felt disloyal. Like a schoolboy snitching on a fellow pupil to our house master. Although astounded at how guilty I felt, I was also relieved to get that weight off my shoulders. A burden that I had not realized I was bearing.

"It is quite understandable that you should speak of Holloway like this if he has imposed his personality upon you without recognizing your inalienable right to privacy. But I would also say that you do have responsibilities in your own right and, despite whatever moral pressures you felt that you were under, you also had the moral right to refuse and ask him to leave you alone. Your breeding and your kindness, perhaps, were your downfall in this respect. Admirable qualities that they are, they must not dominate your every action."

I nodded and tried to look as though I was absorbing this well-meant advice.

"Which brings us to the matter of the séance…"

I was not surprised that he knew of this event. In fact, where this apparently omniscient, some might say meddlesome, man was concerned, nothing seemed to be surprising about him. I told him of the manner in which the séance was decided upon, the reasons for its creation and the subsequent violent outcome of the evening. Again, it was good to be able to talk to someone, anyone, in this way about it. Even if he was a priest and a stranger; or, perhaps, *because* he was.

"I cannot, of course, condone such behaviour. You know that the village is crackling with gossip and rumour about all of this…?"

I did not know.

"I do not believe that you are quite aware of the implications of undertaking such a provocative practice in a place like this." He was calm, quiet, but the underlying tone was of disappointment. "Superstitions long buried are reignited and the flames fanned by idle chatter. Already the event has grown from a simple gathering of a few worthies around a table, through claims of witchcraft and the invocation of unsettled spirits, to suspicions of full-blown devil worship and animal sacrifice."

If his litany had been designed to make me feel uncomfortable, it had worked. However, it did not convince me that, morally, he was in the right. The church had long condemned such practices as a matter of course.

"However, doctor, despite what you may think of the church, my objections are not scriptural. Scripture, it is true, plainly tells us that we should have nothing to do with such matters. Nothing." He chopped a thin cold hand down through the air like a cleaver and went on. "Neither are my objections based on a blind observance of my church's policy on such matters. Though I would appreciate it," he said, in a low-voiced pantomime of a person afraid of being overheard, "if we could keep that among ourselves. The Curia has been known to take a very dim view of fellows who choose to flout their carefully constructed and argued formulae in so cavalier a fashion. No, my objections are purely practical and based upon what meagre understanding I have of the psychology of the individual. It is not how innocent and harmless such a meeting may be, or seem to be. The consequences of such behaviour upon the vulnerable and the susceptible are incalculable. People do not understand. They are not well educated and able to observe such phenomena with the scientific detachment that you and I are able to deploy. People, as a whole, are highly suggestible when the mood takes them. It is all I can do to help guide my flock through the perilous difficulties of superstition and folly, when it comes to simple religious and folk practices. So you may well understand how much more difficult it is to ensure such practices as yours are received with equilibrium. Especially if they are delivered to the flock undiluted and unsupervised."

"I am sorry. I did not realize. But…"

"Yes?"

"But is not Francesca local? Do they not know of her customs and beliefs?"

"They do. And, it is true, a number of people have come to her for private readings. Mostly divination and general advice about the future. People are always so eager to know what will become of them. I believe it takes their minds off how they should live in the present moment. Francesca and her husband, you should know, regularly attend Mass. It is very difficult for me to accept what she does outside her devotions. But that is a matter between her, her husband and their conscience…" His voice tailed off and his gaze drifted away into the distance for a moment, then he brought himself back to the issue at hand. "The simple fact of the matter is that we have had a dead body brought, in tragic circumstances, down from the mountain, and the very next evening a number of strangers are gathered for some sort of occult ritual. That is, as far as the village is concerned. They are making assumptions that are hard to contend with, as you may imagine."

I could imagine only too well.

"I am only glad that Mr Brown's body was removed at the earliest opportunity, or speculation as to his own beliefs would have been taken to extremes, too. A pagan? Lying in a house of God? Well, you might easily imagine what further difficulties that would have presented me, you and the whole community. But it is also why I was particularly concerned about the fire in his chapel of rest. You may very well imagine what connections you alone might make out of all these events, doctor. And, whatever connections you do make, you can be sure the community will have made them also. And a dozen more besides."

"Father, I am so sorry…"

"Oh, do not worry, my son. I am sure that it will all blow over in due course. Naturally, it will enter the annals of the village folklore and be exaggerated out of all proportion as each generation tells the next, on stormy nights around the stoves. Nevertheless, your concerns, as opposed to mine, are that your name has been inextricably linked with all these events. In fact, you have been identified as the chief occult instigator and pagan ringleader. Not a healthy reputation, I would imagine, for any visitor; let alone a doctor."

"No, indeed." Any objections I might have wished to raise with the priest during his lengthy exposition were wiped from my mind. I sat for some moments considering the rumours and gossip that must, even now, be spreading like a bush fire through the village. Conan Doyle the warlock. Conan Doyle the wizard. Conan Doyle the messenger of Satan. I shuddered to think of it.

"Scripture is often filled with great wisdom. Practical advice, albeit wrapped up in religious language. Often, also, tainted with the misconception that it is entirely designed to quash any notions of enjoyment people may entertain. Yet if we were to take many, though by no means all, of its precepts at face value, we would soon come to understand a God who is interested solely in our welfare. Someone whose only concern is in protecting us from ourselves. So, Scripture tells us unequivocally that we should have nothing to do with the sort of matters upon which you and your acquaintances were engaged last night. Practitioners and adherents cry 'Foul!' and claim that this is just repressive, orchestrated religious cant. In truth, just as I have demonstrated to you now, it appears that it might just be sound, practical advice after all. It is not the things we do that matter most of the time, it is how they may be perceived by people who do not understand that is the problem."

He finished and draped an arm over the back of his chair in a manner that suggested he was now leaving the debating floor to me, should I choose to step upon it.

I did not. I had the overwhelming sensation that I had just been preached to in a thoroughly organized and premeditated manner. Ordinarily, I would have met such a lecture with good grace. In such cases, a deferential nod and a "thanks for your advice, must be getting along now" species of shuffled but swift departure usually sufficed. Instead I fumed inwardly. He spoke great good sense – that I could not deny. He was neither patronizing nor offensive in his delivery. That, too, was a given. Yet I was incensed that he might suggest that neither I nor his "flock", as he styled them, were not capable of logical, rational thought when it came to such matters. Yes, I was interested in these things and yes, I even pursued them to a certain degree when I had the time, but it was as a scientific observer. Naturally, one or two people find themselves tripped up by these things, but folk are equally tripped up by church doctrine like as not. To consider that we were incapable of looking after ourselves and restoring our own equilibrium when these affairs turned turtle was beyond the pale. I forbore to give vent to my resentment, however. I realized it would serve no purpose to become engaged in a debate with this man. The only thing preventing me from bidding him good-day was the knowledge that despite all of my indignation, there was no doubt I was culpable. Of course, I still believed he had no actual proof that it was me in the church. Though, I must say, his rationale was compelling. Importantly, I was not about to supply him with a confession. Nonetheless, there was no gainsaying it; I had inadvertently caused the man no little inconvenience in this affair.

"So, what can I do?"

"What can *we* do? Well… I have been giving the matter no little consideration…"

I did not doubt that he had, for one moment.

"It seems to me that the best plan would be for you to do absolutely nothing."

"Nothing?" I said.

"Nothing."

"This seems to me to be the most inept and – may I suggest? – indecisive course of action. Or rather, inaction."

"I quite see how it must look to you. I do not doubt that it is an entirely valid position to adopt. I am sure that there are a number of other courses we could take from this position, all of them possibly fruitful in the end. But I fear that this particular option commends itself as the most useful in our present circumstances." He looked at me as if he were waiting for permission to expand upon his preliminary hypothesis. I nodded for him to continue. Whether or not I liked his tone, his manner, the way in which he had subtly sought to assert his authority over me, his church's authority over me, I could not gainsay the fact that he had spoken good sense so far. For the most part. Besides, I was interested to hear what he had to say. I had to admit I was, myself, temporarily flummoxed by the turns of events he had enumerated. I was consequently at a loss as to what precisely to do next, should I remain unconvinced that doing nothing was the appropriate course. It would be very helpful indeed to hear his perspective; I did not have to follow his advice, after all.

"I have often found that doing nothing frequently ends up being the most valuable and effective course. Let us look at the facts. The village suspects – I will not say believes – that you are involved in some serious and disturbing occult practices. While they might not think it at present, the connection between you and the sudden death of your compatriot remains one that may well be made at some stage in the future. The more you seek to disabuse them of any of these notions, the more likely it is that they are going to suspect that you do protest too much."

I conceded the point, but reserved the right to withdraw from that position, depending upon the outcome of our conversation.

"So, to go about the village as if you do not have a stain on your conscience appears to me to be the most acceptable and positive option. To leave now would be tantamount to an admission of guilt; to restrict your movements to the barest minimum, remaining immured here, for example, equally so. To spend any time lobbying individuals would also raise eyebrows. So, what are we left with? Simply to get on with your holiday and refuse to allow rumour to spoil it."

"This is precisely the thought I myself have had. I will not allow these, by turns tragic and curious, events to upset my plans."

"Bravo for you. That's the spirit."

We looked appreciatively at one another for the first time since he had arrived. He continued outlining his thinking. "So, you go about your lawful business. There are some exquisite and stimulating walks I can recommend, and these would get you out of the village for long periods, on logical and incontestable reasons." He barely hesitated before he asked me his next question, yet I could have sworn the intensity in the way he looked at me changed; as if he had been working all along up to this point. "Have you visited the Reichenbach yet, for example?"

Did he really not remember that this was the place where Brown died? Was he trying to trick me into an admission of some kind? I hesitated. But only for the merest instant. I was momentarily unsure how to answer. I decided that the honest truth would be better than a lie. Although a lie might place me some way from the tragic scene, it would also, nevertheless, be difficult to sustain. Holloway for one, Eva for another, and Anton for yet another, knew that I had been there.

"Yes. I have." I returned his even gaze with equanimity.

"Pity. I always like to be the person to introduce visitors to that phenomenal act of God. Oh well, it always rewards a second, third and fourth visit."

"I am sure that it does. And, I suspect, I shall indeed return one day."

"Be that as it may, while you go about exactly what it is that you came here for, I shall concern myself with removing the blot upon your escutcheon."

"My name does not need clearing," I reminded him.

"Forgive me. By that I meant that I shall spend the next few hours restoring the community's confidence in you."

I was not at all sure how he might manage this or, indeed, whether it was actually possible.

"I am a priest. I have good standing in the village and the surrounding district. It may surprise you, but the people take what I have to say seriously. By and large. And there is another thing…"

"Which is?"

"When it boils right down to it, it is I who could claim to have the greatest grievance in all of this. It was my church that was set alight. It was my parishioners who were the greatest offended by the incursions of visitors onto the consecrated ground at dead of night."

"May I remind you that my discussion with you this afternoon is in strictest confidence?"

And so it shall remain. I will not say it was you that performed the acts mentioned. I will merely say that you and I had a conversation, and that I am satisfied that I can trust you implicitly, and that you are an honourable and decent man. It will be enough."

169

"It will be enough? I should like to believe you."

"I should like you to, too. And then there is the matter of the séance. This, again, is a subject of the greatest concern to Holy Mother Church, is it not?"

"I suppose that it is."

"So, if the representative of that church announces, again, that he is satisfied as to your credentials, and that you had attended, reluctantly, merely as an observer and a scientist because you care to investigate such phenomena – possibly even for a future story – then will that not be both a true and an acceptable exoneration?"

"It will indeed. It is in fact very much the exact case, just as you state it."

"I suspected as much." He leaned back comfortably, like a man who had dined well and was now replete. "You may rest assured that I know just the right people with whom to have a quiet word. Respected and upstanding pillars of the community. Once they are convinced of your innocence, it will take no time at all for these people to convince their peers."

I was relieved beyond expression. Almost from the outset, my visit here had become one long and expanding nightmare. To think that restitution might, after all, be the eventual conclusion filled me with hope. Yet there was still one cloud upon the otherwise sunny horizon. I remembered that in my jacket pocket there lay a square of folded notepaper, upon which had been hurriedly written the request for an assignation. An assignation with the central figure in the séance that Father Vernon was seeking to help me disown. The urge to make a clean breast of this information burned within me. Yet, like an errant schoolboy who knew that whatever prank he contemplated would be thoroughly frowned upon, I was loath to offer up the details for inspection. I knew, however, that he should know at least something of this, and that his views would be most helpful to me in determining my own perspective on the issue. So I strove to find a roundabout way to elicit his opinion.

"Father, I am nevertheless associated with people directly responsible for the séance. How do you advise I treat them if, say, I encounter them in the street, and so on?"

"Ah well, yes… this is a good question. We should take a moment to consider it…" He fixed me with a questioning look. "You refer, in particular I expect, to Francesca and, to a lesser extent, Hugo?"

"I do." I was again astonished that he could be so perceptive. Yet, of course, who else would be so directly connected to the séance? Was this just my guilt unmanning me?

"It is quite understandable that you should not wish to lose the… refreshing… society of this young woman." I felt my earlobes grow warm with embarrassment. This was not what I meant at all. Yet it was also perfectly true. Again, I felt as if he could see right through into my most intimate thoughts and feelings. "When God created her, he gave her more than her fair share not only of femininity, but of kindliness and grace. It is a powerful and heady mixture, and it has led her frequently into difficulties. Not, I should hasten to add, of her own devising. For the most part, she is entirely innocent of the magnetic effect she has upon the opposite sex, and the envy she generates among her own. Oh yes, she knows how to turn on her allure when she needs it – as a daughter may wrap her loving father around her little finger. Girls, I believe, learn these techniques from birth. They practise turning heads when they enter rooms, emitting a captivating aura at will. But Francesca is neither manipulative nor malicious. I do not apportion any negative elements in her personality to her experimentation in her 'gift', as she might describe it. I believe, in her case, that this ability is one per cent intuition and ninety-nine per cent personality."

"She is a fraud, you mean?"

"Far from it. A fraud, to my mind, is someone who deliberately seeks to manipulate or even have power over another by cynically exploiting the other's susceptibility. She does not do this. She believes that she is special. No doubt someone has told her this. Over the years, with some scarcely substantiated results, she has been led along an avenue of self-delusion until she has reached a point whereby she is no longer objectively able to rise above how others perceive her to be. She is playing a role that has been laid upon her to the fullest extent of her personality."

I considered his hypothesis and resolved to spend some time in the very near future reflecting upon it and analysing it from every angle. I was more than aware that he, coming from the doctrine of the church, might well hold a sceptical view of such phenomena. I was, however, unwilling to enter into debate quite at that moment.

"This highly attractive personality of hers," he continued, "naturally leads to a fair degree of… friction… in her relationship with her husband."

"Does he beat her?"

"It is curious how Francesca brings out the protective nature in the male of the species. She unwittingly encourages all manner of men to champion her, to ride like a shining knight out of the mist to slay dragons on her behalf. To rescue her from what appears to them to be a cruel and oppressive marriage."

I looked away, ashamed at such a precise definition of my intentions; motives I did not have the courage to admit to myself.

"I am not revealing any secrets. Hugo himself is entirely open and honest about this. Despite his very public faults, he also comes to Mass every Sunday to seek absolution for his volatile and dangerous constitution. He admits this freely to all his associates. His temper is something with which he struggles on a daily, perchance hourly, basis and I admire him for this heroic labour. But as to whether Francesca needs rescuing from him?" He paused and looked out of the window, as if the answer lay out there somewhere among the mountains. "I cannot say. All I will say is that she attends Mass with her husband, she contributes to the life of both the church and her village, and she seeks only to live peaceably with both her husband and her neighbours. Which is why I do not believe she is as much of a medium as she thinks she is. Not to say that mediums do not go to church, nor do they love their neighbours any less. No, it is simply that her fundamental instinct, the urge that drives her further than any superficial interest in such things as séances, is to be a good daughter of the church. Naturally, I hear you thinking, I would say that, since I am a priest. But I earnestly hope that this is true. She is lost, doctor. And it is my calling to be a shepherd to the lost."

We sat in silence.

"And your advice?" I prompted.

His reply was both quiet and firm. "I fear that you should have nothing whatsoever to do with them."

"By which you mean cut them in the street? But surely that is hardly polite?"

"No, I do not propose that you should treat anyone with anything less than the utmost courtesy and dignity. I merely suggest that a degree of distance should be maintained between you and that couple."

"I see."

"You will do me the honour, I trust, of coming to tea at the house at some point in your stay, doctor?" He was suddenly formal and distant. I looked at him. Was this the real purpose of his visit, to draw me back into the fold? "Not only would I deem it a particular honour, but also it would reconfirm to watching eyes that we are reconciled."

"Is it not, Father, another form of reconciliation that you are proposing? I apologize if I sound overly suspicious. I merely conjecture. I am, as you are aware, familiar with the methods of Holy Mother Church and her children."

"My son, everybody is always welcome back into the flock. And who knows, some day that may very well be your response. But no, I feel we have dug here some excellent foundations for a lasting friendship, and I only seek to build upon that."

"Then it would be an honour for me to accept your kind invitation."

We stood, bowed, exchanged a polite handshake and the priest left.

My first act, once I had closed the door behind my guest, was to cross to my jacket, take out the square of paper, tear it in half and cast it into the wastepaper bin beside the escritoire. My second act was to realize that despite the disposing of the item, I would be unable to forget the time and the venue of the appointment. Nor would I be able to forget the person who had entreated me to keep it. I understood, at that moment, that in this respect, regrettable though it may be, I would be unable to observe Father Vernon's sound advice in this particular matter.

Twelve

Just to get on and enjoy my visit, however, was more easily said than done. Despite the qualified relief I felt at having had some of my burden lifted from my shoulders by Father Vernon, there were still a number of matters to be resolved. Not least the problem of who was reading my wires and why.

I would have to create a cipher. One that was reasonably simple to execute, easily managed by myself, with only the basic everyday elements around me to use. But also easily taught to Flemyng in England, whom I had identified as the fellow most likely to give me the answers I believed I was looking for. Despite Flemyng's initial dismissal of the case, I needed to reopen the dialogue. I considered returning to the library and the English books downstairs. Books always made good keys. Good basic common denominators from which to build a confidential code. Of course, if they can be transported between the two participants in the subterfuge, all well and good. But shipping one book backwards and forwards would be impractical. It would take weeks and I only had hours; days at best. So, everything would have to be conducted through telegram.

But what key would Flemyng have in or near his office in Whitehall that I would also have an equivalent of in a remote village up a distant brae in Switzerland? I tried to imagine the shelves downstairs and settled very swiftly upon the Bible which I had noted there. A common book, and one that Flemyng would be able to access perfectly easily.

I removed myself to the library immediately and returned a short while later with the dog-eared, faded, black leather-bound volume with the flaking, gold-leaf lettering. The pages were flimsy, almost transparent, and crackled when you turned them over. Their edges had been coloured by faint, red printer's staining ink. Sitting at the escritoire, I prepared to create my cipher.

I needed something that would not arouse suspicion. Some titbit of news that anyone intercepting my wires might think that dull old Conan Doyle would naturally be interested in. Yet it would appear of no particular consequence to any other reader. It was with me the work of a moment to realize that the most likely candidate was that most misunderstood of sporting traditions. The cricket test match scorecard. It was beloved by devotees and spurned or treated with consummate indifference by the uninitiated. For a moment, my spirits rose at the thought of using my treasured sport as a Trojan horse for my messages. But then they fell again when I realized that there were no visiting Test teams to England that summer. The Australians were the next scheduled combatants, but they were not due until the following year. However, I consequently surmised that it would not be unreasonable to be interested in the county scores as well. I began, therefore, to work out a scheme.

Undoubtedly, trivia is all very well, but my reader or readers would be aware that I was already in touch with Flemyng. He therefore needed to send me information that in the event was banal but, to my reader, would seem to be possessed of the utmost significance for me. Thus Flemyng would have to be charged with coming up with facts that could not be proven. Facts all the same that would seem to the reader to be of value to the both of us. I did not know if this new contact of mine at Whitehall was up to the task. Steen was a canny old bird, though, and I was hopeful that he would not have fastened the young fellow on to me unless he felt the chap was capable of fulfilling this role proficiently. Unless, of course, I had misjudged Steen and he had completely misinterpreted my recent wires as the arrant twittering of a buffoon; in which case, he may have merely slipped the task of handling my excessive missives to some minion. But I could not dwell too long on that possibility. I had to press on and hope for the best.

With spurious cricket statistics established as my system, I then resolved to ask Flemyng for the close of play scores for the county matches. This would be the easy part. It may well cause the reader to immediately cast the illicitly obtained wire from them with expressions of impatience, or even disgust. What could be more boring for people who were uninterested than a turgid litany of county cricket scores? That is to say, for people who did not realize what rich information such seemingly bland statistics are able to impart. Of course, my plan was that they would impart a whole lot more than even the dedicated observer might realize. But that was another matter entirely.

Sitting at the writing leaf of the escritoire, I asked myself what, exactly, was this splendid and cunning cipher I had imagined I would devise?

A regular browser of scorecards in the daily newspapers would know that their main feature is numbers. Single figures, double figures, even treble figures. There would be the names of the players on the batting side and the names of the players on the bowling side; and vice versa, when the teams swapped round. It would be simple enough, I felt, to substitute the figures in the scorecard for page numbers. But to give my esteemed reader such a simple key would lay our cipher open to access in a very short space of time. Besides, what would be on these pages that the numbers referred to? In effect, therefore, we would have to ensure that there was an inconsistency built into this reference. If the code changed consistency at random, then a reader might light upon one or two identifiable elements. But... the very next time they tried to interpret the next set of figures in this way, the code would apparently switch and there would seem to the reader to be no rhyme nor reason to them. Incongruity and anomaly would force them to start again at the beginning. All the time, the hours and even the days might be rolling past while they wrestled with the conundrum; buying me time.

The notion that whomever it was that had the audacity to open my wires might find themselves put to quite some considerable inconvenience and frustration warmed my heart considerably.

Perhaps, then, the cipher should work only where it concerned itself with occasional batsmen. Not all of them. Perhaps where they were bowled, or caught or stumped, then the cipher would be activated. Where they were run out or ended the day not out, the cipher would not apply. And the inconsistency would be effected. But since there were only eleven players in the team, this could leave me with six or seven scores, sometimes, with which Flemyng might construct his sentences. Time, however, was of the essence so I decided to press on with this theory until it proved thoroughly unworkable. All the same I hoped that it was entirely possible to construct answers in just a few words, provided the questions which prompted them were explicit enough.

If I proposed to use the Bible, I would need sufficient numerals, not only to bring chapter and verse into the equation, but also the number of the word within the verse, I realized. Like a good skipper, I therefore brought my bowlers into play. The bowlers' figures would identify the chapter of the Bible and the verse. The place where the word came within it, the batsmen's scores would make clear. Since batting figures were printed first and bowling second, this was a further variation in the flow of the code, which would take any potential interpreter even more time to unlock. But there was a further complication. How would Flemyng and I communicate which book of the Bible we were using at any given time?

I took out my pipe, cleaned it, filled it and lit it. I went out onto the balcony to ponder. The idea came quite quickly thereafter. Of course, we should use exactly the same book of the Bible on every occasion. There was only one book that could provide us with a broad enough vocabulary in that case: the book of Psalms.

So there, albeit just sketched out very roughly on a sheet of hotel notepaper, was my cipher. I would be careful to set light to it in my fire later to ensure no record of it remained before Flemyng and I had put it into operation. I spent the next twenty minutes practising my theories, refining the system and making adjustments where necessary until, in my humble opinion, it manifested itself as a creditable effort. One, I opined to myself, eminently workable.

Now, of course, came the problem of how to communicate this to my co-conspirator. Not just in theoretical terms, in respect of how to tell him the sequences, but also in very practical terms. How might I let him know by wire without running the risk of having the whole affair exposed by a telegraph operator in the pay of my furtive reader?

It was clear, I reasoned, that I needed to go for a stroll down the brae into the valley and use a distant telegraph office. There, I could only hope, would be a minimal likelihood of my message being relayed to my watcher. To use that office on a regular basis was a thought that occurred to me. I dismissed it on the grounds that it was something of an expedition. An impracticable use of time.

I donned my jacket, boots and puttees, collected my stick and hat, and left with the substance of my cipher in my head. The notepaper, with my workings-out, resided in the grate as a little pile of feathery ashes; burnt and stirred.

Anton was in the lobby and, again, I noted his disposition did not reflect his usual ebullience. This moved me, and I was very much minded to stay and discuss this with him. However, I did not know him well enough, I felt, just to engage him in a conversation of an intimate nature. So I passed through, offering him only a well-meant "hello, how are you?". He responded dutifully and congenially enough. But then he returned straight away to the paperwork in which he was currently engaged at the reception desk.

I had just reached the door when another thought occurred to me, and I turned and retraced my steps as far as the hotelier.

"Anton?"

He looked up from his paperwork. "Doctor?"

"I wonder if I might ask you for a piece of information."

"Naturally – if I am able to help."

"Are you aware of any… conversations in the village, instigated by our little visit to the medium?"

"Do you mean, are people talking about you?" He sounded very much as though all he cared to do was assist me in my enquiry as efficiently as possible.

"Yes. It has come to my attention that the event was possibly not approved of by some of your friends and neighbours."

"No," he shrugged, and looked genuinely blank. "I have not heard anything."

I could not understand it. Anton and his family were surely central to this community. "I was under the impression that the whole village was talking about it?"

"Not that I know of. Although, doctor, if they were, I might not come to hear of it. People do not talk to me at the moment."

"Why not?"

Anton simply gazed at me bleakly, though I felt that if good manners and good hotel management training had not prevented him, he would have as lief glowered. I was taken aback. Noting this curious revelation accompanied by the change of mood, I decided that there was no better opportunity than now to try to elicit from the young man what it was that was apparently unsettling him.

"Anton, I cannot but notice that you have not been so bright and breezy of late. Even now, I sense that you have some pressing matter and that, in some way, I am responsible for it. The way you look at me. If there is anything that I have committed or omitted, I would rather that you spoke to me frankly than have me dwell under a mysterious cloud for the duration of my stay."

My intention was, with my manly honesty, to lighten the whole mood and, perhaps, obtain a nominal explanation of his concerns. I had contrived rather to drive him to greater distraction.

"You English! You live in your comfortable, cosmopolitan world, blowing this way and then that as the wind changes. Gathering up this fad and that fashion and dropping it again once you have grown bored with it. You have no idea what it is to have to struggle day in and day out in a village like this."

I stared at him, startled by his outburst and even more confused and concerned for his welfare than before. "Whatever is the matter,

Anton? I know, for some reason, you have reached a point where you seem to despise me. Yet I cannot help thinking that I have done no wrong. At least, if I have done something, it was committed in all innocence. Will you not talk to me about what it is that grieves you?"

"No."

"Well then, I do not doubt that you have your reasons and every justification for them. I would just like you to know that despite this conversation, I remain your friend and a willing, listening ear – should ever you decide that you need one."

Anton returned to his paperwork without a word. I turned again to leave but felt cross and dismayed that I should have been so summarily dismissed from his presence. I found it impossible to leave without having just one more assay.

"Anton?"

He did not look up from his work.

"Anton, have you seen Holloway?" I don't know why I decided to introduce that gentleman into the equation. Perhaps, intuitively, I felt that he might have as much to do with Anton's disquiet as myself. It seemed to me that the two of them, along with Eva, had become congruent since my supposed companion's arrival. I wondered if it was Holloway's bourgeois relationship with his sister that had so piqued him.

"No." This mumbled, still without looking up.

"And Eva?"

"I have not seen her since this morning. She was supposed to have come here for lunch but she did not."

"Thank you," I responded, and doffed my hat at the crown of his head. It was clear that he had lowered the portcullis and raised the drawbridge. There would be no further progress made on this front for the time being, I reasoned, and departed.

The walking route down into the valley cut a zigzag beaten track into the brae. I was glad of my boots and my stick as the ground underfoot had not entirely dried after the recent rains, sheltered as it was from the warming sun by the tree canopy. Here and there, streams flogged down in heaving tresses of silver, olive and white. My admonition to myself of continuing with my holiday regardless of events seemed, at times on this walk, a little more attainable. It was a beautiful country and an inspiring environment in which to throw off life's cares and simply exist for existence's sake, in sympathy with one's surroundings.

How I regretted, therefore, the thought processes that insisted upon returning me, again and again, to the most pressing considerations. One of my main concerns on this downward trek was Father Vernon. An estimable gentleman, no doubt, and in different circumstances, possibly someone with whom I would have been content to associate. I recognized his temperament as questing and open to argument. It would have been a great pleasure to cross swords with him intellectually but for one small matter.

I did not trust him.

Everything that he said was true; everything had value and everything had purpose. I could not gainsay any of that. The difficulty lay in the question why? It was absolutely true that he had come to me in order to prevent the situation getting out of hand. But why he should do so was another matter. I knew why he said that he was doing so. Again, this rang completely sound. To protect me and to reinstate me in the eyes of the community. But why? Did he owe me anything? No. There were pastoral and spiritual duties related to his behaviour, too, of course. But might there be a deeper underlying reason why? Why, also, was I obliged to amble about the place as if nothing had happened, and keep my mouth shut? It benefited me. Yet if he had an ulterior motive, would it not benefit him equally, if not more so?

I disliked my present, unwelcome suspicious nature. I did not feel that it was at all healthy. I wished earnestly that I might return to the innocence of my younger days. But one cannot unlearn something. I had learned to mistrust, to test, to question and explore. And to suspect. So much so that it had become second nature.

Perhaps Father Vernon's solicitude was out of admiration for my work? I did not think so; he had not mentioned any of my writing, and I could see in his demeanour none of the telltale signs that spoke volumes of a stranger's hidden knowledge that I was who I was. Meanwhile, was there a benefit to him if I did not meet with Francesca or Hugo again? I did not know why, and I could only surmise, but it was nevertheless the case. The reasons he gave, again, made sense and were accurate and fair. So why should I not take them at face value? Because Anton had told me that he had heard no rumours concerning the séance? Admittedly, he had said that he did not hear much at all; but the fact remained. This gossip, which was spreading like wildfire and, it would seem, had the whole village up in arms, may not therefore be as prevalent as I had been led to expect. Why was it that Father Vernon had been the only one so far to apprise me of the situation? Was, perhaps, the whole noble plan to retain my good name just an excuse to keep me quiet and nervous? Out of the way and beyond the reach of others, my relationship with whom might otherwise be an obstacle or a threat to other plans?

And why was he so sure of my innocence?

These baffling conundrums kicked around with my mind as if it were a football as I traipsed down through the forest.

Upon reaching the pretty little town in the valley, though, I thankfully found that I had quite enough to occupy my attention to set my rambling reflections back into the further reaches of my brain.

After a period of scouting around, I managed to locate the telegraph office and found a stall, upon whose table was a pad of telegram forms and some pencils. I tore off the topmost turquoise form and laid it upon the table. I did not intend for anyone to be able to pick up the underlying sheet. I did not care for them to use some technique such as pencil lead shavings, by which they might read off the impression, left thereon, of my handwriting. And so I wrote my message.

Dear Flemyng. Being watched.

Need code. Key Psalms. County Scores.

Bowling Figures. Overs Psalms.

Maidens means verse.

Runs NA. Wickets NA. Batsmen

runs means word number.

B C C&B only. RO NO St N/A.

Regards ACD

Having completed and presented it to the clerk, I paid for the service and withdrew. A task, I felt, satisfactorily completed.

I continued feeling this for approximately twenty seconds. This is the time it took for me to step out onto the main street and stumble straight into Tomas and Anna Pivcevic. They were standing by the window of the office and beaming at me.

"What are you doing here?"

They looked hurt.

"We came down this morning to explore," Anna said. "There is a very fine private museum here. Natural history, botany, insects. Some collector and eccentric left it to the municipality about fifty years ago."

"Ah... I am sorry if what I said just then sounded rude. I did not mean it to be. I was just surprised to see anyone I knew so far away from the village. And these past few hours have been most trying."

"Why?" asked Pivcevic, solicitously. "What is the matter, doctor? Is there something wrong? How may we help?"

"You are too kind. But I mean, what with the death of Brown and the séance and... and, I wonder... have you heard whether the village has been talking about the séance? About us? About my rôle in all of this in particular?"

"The séance?" Anna looked at me curiously. "Well, no. I have not heard anything. Have you, Tomas?"

"I have not. Although I would not blame anyone if they thought we were the laughing stock."

"I see. So... are you about to make your way back up to the village?"

"We were planning to stop first for lunch," said Anna. "Would you care to join us?"

"I should be glad of your company."

We passed a wide, sweeping drive enclosed by high walls and bordered by laurel. The sign at the entrance proclaimed that it was a private sanatorium and that the management offered a wide range of services catering for both physical and mental needs. The thought of taking up residence there for the remainder of my stay, a long walk down a pleasant, welcoming drive to a sanctuary, shut in by gates and a tall wall, was very appealing.

I did not want to run. I did not want to hide. I had come for peace of mind and, instead, I was sinking deeper and deeper into the mire.

We sat at a hotel café window and looked out upon the passers-by who came and went with a steady frequency. It was a quaint little establishment with clean, crisp white linen tablecloths and acres of red velvet curtains. There were newspapers available to read for the clientele. Anna went across to take one and peruse the latest news. It was not terribly exciting; these were just the local weekly journals and one or two of the Interlaken daily presses. Nothing with a wider, international perspective.

I surveyed my companions over the rim of my coffee cup. They were delightful people, short and round like gnomes. Anna had deep brown eyes, the black pupils indistinguishable from the iris. The black ringlets of her hair fell gaily around her apple cheeks. Pivcevic was equally jolly, with a near-shaven head and little round wire spectacles that mimicked his round, merry cheeks. When at leisure like this they laughed and giggled a great deal. Pivcevic continually spread and reclasped his chubby hands, with their Wienerwurst fingers, in continual delight. That I could have snapped at them like a fractious Pekingese upon seeing them at the telegraph office was to pay them a great disservice.

And yet now I trusted no one. Not even, I realized, these Pivcevics. Most of this mistrust, active distrust even, was sponsored by my personal disquiet at my situation. I felt entirely out of my depth. Holloway's arrogant and demeaning assault upon me had done nothing to help. If I were confused and dismayed before by the twists and turns of events, I was even more so after that. Encounters such as those with Father Vernon, Anton and even these two had only served to entangle my thoughts further. Not that the Pivcevics and I discussed such matters at first. We spoke of the edelweiss, which they had visited yesterday up in the lush alpine meadow. They had been as entranced as I had and had resolved to transport some seeds or cuttings home to Bosnia when they returned.

Upon the subject of their homeland, they were most expansive and became markedly agitated. Their generally cheerful aspect was swiftly dulled by the patina of fear and uncertainty. The Serbo-Bulgarian war some half a dozen years earlier had settled nothing and had left the whole region in a more than usual state of ferment. Being both Croats, this left them at even more of a disadvantage. In many ways they were stateless, since they were absorbed in another nation and felt trapped by the confusion of national boundaries. They lived constantly under the shadow of being barely tolerated rather than assimilated. Despite having lived in that part of the world for generations, their family was constantly under tacit suspicion of being the enemy within.

The whole region was in turmoil. Germany, Austria and Italy had not helped matters with their schemes and machinations and brittle alliances. And then there was the growing interdependence of Russia and France. The Pivcevics had grave misgivings over foreign influence in their homeland and the surrounding region. They were convinced that sooner or later the region would be drawn into a dreadful conflict. The consequences of which were unimaginable.

I had long ago understood the unfathomable difficulties that swamped the region. Or perhaps that would be better put as failed to understand. But I had noted carefully, for it was a particular interest of mine, my own country's rôle in all of this. As the senior player in Europe – a fact the other great nations such as Russia, Austro-Hungary, Germany and France refused to accept – it was our calling to act as head prefect. One of the boys, but with palpable extra responsibilities.

It was a revelation to me, therefore, to note how my country's policies actually affected ordinary people in ordinary homes in other parts of the world. Not that I developed a guilty conscience as a result. I believed that whatever methods were employed to maintain the stability of the nations, not least those employed in the Balkans, were justified in the interests of both national and international security. The ends justifying the means? Probably.

And yet it was a shame to see these happy, intelligent people reduced to sombre and nervous introspection, and I told them so. They were grateful for my kind words, and Pivcevic told me that I had not to worry unduly. He and his race were a tough, fearless people who had managed over countless generations to uphold their rights in the most grievous of situations. Doubtless they would continue so to do.

Anna laughed and nervously suggested that Tomas's patriotism would one day land him in some very great difficulty. She rather wished he wasn't quite so headstrong when it came to his partisanship. At this Pivcevic went bright red and countered with a sharp jibe at his wife, telling her to stop harking back to her hobby horse where his wishes were concerned. This was presumably a serious topic of discussion between them, and a sadly recurring, possibly insoluble one. All at once, I found myself in the middle of a long-standing husband and wife dispute, where I seemed to be expected to act as judge and jury on the issue, they both putting their cases to me in rapid succession.

In effect, Anna wanted to cut their losses, leave the past behind and go to join her cousin, who had left for America under similar circumstances seven years ago. Pivcevic was defiant and stubborn and made it clear that he would never leave the land of his birth, nor would he forsake his kinsfolk. He could not countenance leaving people behind, suffering, while he went gallivanting across the Atlantic to live a life of ease in Kentucky or wherever it was.

I was, understandably, unable to pronounce on the matter without offending one or other of the parties in this dispute. Wisely, as far as possible, I therefore kept my own counsel. My taciturn demeanour meant that, ultimately, the storm had nowhere to go and blew itself out. A little of the couple's natural cheerfulness soon returned thereafter and provided the semblance of equilibrium in their relationship.

We paid our bill and set off to commence the arduous climb back up to our village. Downhill, the walk had taken just over the half-hour. The return journey could take twice as long. I suggested, for Anna's sake, that we might consider availing ourselves of a cart back up the hill. But she was as hardy as any highland Scot and refused even to entertain the notion. So we climbed.

Along the way, we returned to other, more recent, concerns. I asked them if they had been in any way dismayed by the séance. They had not. Not that I would have expected them to have been so; their consistent objectivity and healthy scepticism had continued undiminished. They remained unconvinced regarding Francesca's *performance*, as they described it. Their only concerns were for the other attendees, and whether such obvious cant and claptrap might affect those more suggestible folk.

"Did you have anyone particular in mind?" I asked, puffing a little from my exertions.

"Mr Holloway," Anna pronounced instantly, and her husband nodded.

"Why?"

"Have you not noticed the difference in him?" Pivcevic responded. There was in his voice something beyond concern, however. It was distaste. At what, I could not discern immediately.

"Is he different? I have managed only the one interview with him subsequent to that meeting. Although I detected a certain arrogance – and boorishness – I did not feel that his behaviour was out of character." I did not mean to sound disloyal but, then again, ever since my arrival I had made it patently clear that he and I were not in the least friends.

"Well, you know," Anna said, "he came to see us in our room." There was suppressed indignation in her voice, as if there were matters she was prepared to discuss, and some that she was not.

"What did he come to see you about?"

"He said he was conducting his own investigation into the tragic death of Peter Brown. He said that you were incapable of showing any initiative in this respect and that he had, perforce, to venture upon his own, independent course of action."

"Did he, by Jove! And exactly what form did these enquiries of his take?"

"He asked a lot of very personal questions about our background and circumstances," said Pivcevic, speaking, I surmised, in order that Anna did not have to. "He even asked us if we were involved in any way with trade from the Far East, perhaps China."

"What kind of trade?"

"He would not say. Once we had pointed out that we were teachers, nothing more and nothing less, he lost interest."

"He did not, Tomas. He asked us what our recreational habits were like. Whether we enjoyed alcohol or anything else. We thought that he was suggesting that we had been inhospitable, even though we had offered to order him a coffee when first he arrived, which he declined – and so we offered him a glass of ouzo."

"Ouzo?"

"It is a Greek schnapps – some think it is Russian in origin," Pivcevic explained. Although I was already acquainted with the name.

"Yes," I said, "a distilled liquor flavoured by anise-seed."

"Have you tasted it?" Anna looked pleased and proprietorial. "It is a beautiful, delicate taste. I take it with fresh water. I am sure it has medicinal properties. We have a bottle in our room. For our private use."

"Of course," I replied, not caring at all whether they imbibed in the privacy of their own room or in the middle of the street. I keep a tantalus containing whisky and brandy at home. It is of no significance. What was of significance was the simple fact of the ouzo's existence in the same district as Brown's anise-seed-scented demise. I was sure that Holloway had made the connection.

"Did he ask to see the bottle?"

"Yes," returned Pivcevic. "Why do you ask?"

"Why did Holloway ask?"

"He was just interested, I suppose. He had heard of such a liquor, but had never seen or tasted any."

"So you showed him, and he smelled it and then tasted it?"

"Yes... How did you know?"

"I guessed. Was there anything else unusual about Holloway's visit or interest in the ouzo?"

"No."

"There was one thing," corrected Anna.

"And what was that?"

"The stopper for the ouzo bottle was missing. I noticed it as I brought it out of the bedside cabinet, and Holloway remarked upon it immediately."

"Where was the stopper?"

"That is just it, doctor," Anna looked across at her husband as we strove three abreast to surmount the interminable slope. "We do not know. We searched the room high and low and we could not find it. Eventually I closed it with a cloth."

"And did Holloway say anything else about this?"

"No," said Pivcevic. "He was very supercilious and swept out of our room with barely a thank you or goodbye."

"He was very agitated about something," confirmed Anna.

"Very," echoed her husband.

"We do not like Mr Holloway, do we, Tomas?"

"No, Anna, we do not."

Thirteen

I left the Pivcevics to go to their room, and remained in the hotel reception area to talk to Anton. He was civil, but no more.

"Is Mr Holloway returned? I should like to talk to him most urgently."

"He is not, I regret, doctor."

"Is he with Eva, do you know?"

"I do not know. I have not seen Eva since this morning, as I believe I informed you earlier today."

"Thank you, Anton. And if there is anything you ever wish to discuss, you should know that I am a friend, not an enemy."

I made my way upstairs.

I had just sufficient time to wash and change before my visit to Francesca, which I was now even more determined to make. Slipped under the door to my bedroom was a telegram. The envelope was slit and resealed in the usual way. However, it contained little information for anyone interested in reading my private correspondence.

DEAR CONAN DOYLE.

MESSAGE RECEIVED AND UNDERSTOOD.

EVENTUALLY.

EXCELLENT GAME IN PROSPECT.

WILL FORWARD SCORECARD WHEN REQUESTED.

FLEMYNG.

This was encouraging, and Flemyng, if he maintained this positive opening, would very likely prove an intelligent and able ally. I folded the wire back into its envelope and laid it on my escritoire.

Ready to leave for my assignation with Francesca, I was almost out of my door when I had second thoughts. Why leave any message in my room? Of course, people had already read it. I did not know who these people were, but there was no reason why I should expose even the slightest clue that I had something up my sleeve to unnecessary further scrutiny, all the same. I committed the envelope to the grate and set light to it. I watched it burn alongside the remains of the pyre from my previous cipher calculations, gave the ashes a stir with my poker, and departed.

On the way to Francesca's house, I concerned myself with exploring what it was, exactly, that drove me to meet her. I refused to admit that it was any form of attraction, and neither was I going there to receive more psychic insights. Curiosity, then. Pure and simple.

Although I could not conceive what it was that she was so eager to talk to me about, I resolved to put my case first. I wanted her to know how I viewed her practices, so that we both understood where we were in this particular business. I had decided that her *performance*, as the Pivcevics had put it, was flawed. It was my resolve to be honest about this at the outset.

There were further motivations which I barely ventured to investigate. Deeper, darker stirrings, which spoke of frustration, dismay and the overall unfairness of life. That I should have met such a woman and that we could never be more than mere acquaintances. I have heard of happily married gentlemen who have beautiful women as their best friends; however, I have always suspected their protestations of absolute innocence as being deficient. If one is not fulfilled in most aspects of human life by one's soulmate, then there is something wrong with the relationship.

I could have kicked myself. So, it was attraction, too, then, after all?

My knock at her door was followed by a stage wait. When she appeared, she was warm and welcoming. A rich scent of coffee and baking – and mystery – flowed out from her home and drew me in. As I entered, she could not help but look briefly beyond my shoulder, to ensure that I was alone, or that we were not being observed. I could not be certain which. There was a hubbub from the bustle of the village. I had noted a number of passers-by as I arrived at the door, but I dared not risk looking around myself for fear of appearing furtive and thereby exciting further suspicion. She closed the door, took me gently by my forearm and brought me along the hall. The fragrance I remembered so well attended her as she preceded me into the living room. We sat and she offered me some freshly pressed, iced and sweetened lemonade. She promised coffee with Umbrian almond and honey cake later.

"Hugo is drinking with friends. He will not be back this evening."

She released a smile and it embraced me.

I swallowed hard, resisting all that was within me. I was afraid I might succumb to the pleasantness and gentleness that was assaulting me. I drove myself to address her. Quickly, before things were said that might be regretted later.

"Francesca, may I speak first, and may I speak frankly?"

"Of course."

She wore a loose-fitting robe. Her rich black hair framed her face; one twist of fringe fell over her left eye. Her golden earrings danced and glittered whenever she moved her head. She sat with her legs tucked up beneath her in the armchair in a most Bohemian manner. She looked small and vulnerable… and embraceable. I felt that awful ache again. A need to clasp, to protect. To own. Father Vernon had said all those who succumbed to this intoxicating woman had believed they were her knight in shining armour… I became all too aware of such beliefs. The effort to raise myself above this, to refuse to allow any thoughts such as those I had begun to entertain to gain dominion over me, was almost physical

194

and close to unbearable. I knew I had to speak immediately, or fall and be lost for ever.

"Francesca…" I was astounded at how even and calm my voice was, especially since the feel of her name upon my lips enveloped me with that all-too-alluring warmth again, "I do not mean to be rude, and what I propose to say you must believe is for your own good."

She smiled pleasantly and unsuspectingly and swept the lock of black hair from her eye with a gentle hand. "Do you wish to discuss Hugo?"

"Yes and no. It is most particularly about you. And your mediumship."

"My mediumship?" She did not recognize the word.

"Your gift, as people like you describe it."

"Ah, my gift." She was teasing me for my earnestness. I grew somewhat cross with the thought that she might not be taking this quite as seriously as she should. Especially considering I was about to deliver her a dreadfully hurtful blow. So I became firm and direct.

"In private and never to be repeated by me beyond these four walls… I do not believe that act you and your husband gave us last night." I looked at her. Her eyes were still shining at me, though she had the courtesy to replace the smile on her full, red lips to something thinner and straighter. Far more appropriate for the views that I had begun to impart. "Let me tell you what I believe. I believe that the row between you and Hugo was staged and has been much-practised over the years. The idea is to create in your clients a sense of disquiet and disorientation, thereby rendering them more suggestible. This would also serve to remove a degree of objectivity and rational thought. It also enables you to give the impression that at that precise moment, you and your husband could not possibly be in collusion. It also gives a reason for Hugo to sit in the room and yet, to all intents and purposes, not be part of the event. In fact, to appear actively opposed to the event. He is there only, we are led to believe, in order to keep an eye on his wife. She is, judging by the late witnessed arguments, wild, wilful and unorthodox. This all lends an authenticity to your psychic persona. Having established this, it is a simple matter once the lights are out for your husband, who is your accomplice, to physically move objects unobserved and unsuspected. Such as, for example, an old table."

Her eyes were not shining now, but she remained composed and comfortable in her armchair. She did not speak, so I proceeded.

"I am sure that, in terms of giving the public what they want, or think they want, your work performs a certain function. In this, I do not accuse you of anything. However, I hope that you will take this as simple well-meant advice. Your act is transparent. It does neither you nor the psychic world any justice, and my recommendation to you is to desist immediately."

Still she remained silent.

"Francesca…" Despite myself and my lecture, I was still enjoying rolling her name around in my mouth. Although its initial sweetness was beginning to turn bitter. "I am afraid that I do not worry if I hurt you, or hurt whatever slight friendship we may have established between us in the short time we have known one another. I wonder if, perhaps, it is Hugo's influence over you? Perhaps you are obliged, even forced, to re-enact this pantomime on every conceivable occasion…?" I stopped. Here was the knight in shining armour, I realized. Failing to accuse such a beautiful woman of anything, and laying all the blame squarely at the feet of her husband. Someone I had now, conveniently, cast in the role of her oppressor.

Still, I told myself, it had to be said.

"… If there are difficulties between you and your husband of this nature, then I suppose you would be best advised to bring them to the attention of your priest. I am sure that he would be most considerate in assisting you and Hugo to shake off these practices for the benefit of all concerned, not least yourselves."

I had finished my address. I sat back in my chair and looked steadily at the young woman sitting, feline, curled up in her armchair.

"Have you finished?" she said at length, her voice soft and low and thick. She neither scowled nor smiled.

"I have."

"Then I would ask you to leave, please." She unfolded herself from her chair and walked to the door. She held it open, indicating that I should precede her along the hallway and out through the front door.

I stood up. "I am neither concerned nor surprised that you wish me to remain in your home not a moment longer." It was a feeble attempt at dignity when in truth, I was scarcely able to think at all. My emotions were howling like an autumn gale beneath my upright exterior. "I do not doubt that as you reflect upon what I have said to you, you will become increasingly indignant, if not, indeed, outraged. Nevertheless, I trust that one day, some day, you might understand why I felt I had to say what I did. While you may never thank me for it, you may at least grant that I spoke from the highest motives. I would hope that some day you might even grow to have sympathy with me and the position I was in."

"You may go now."

I stepped into the hallway. The silence was as burdensome as the attraction I had experienced towards her just a few minutes earlier. I broke it. "Did you not have something to say to me?"

"I did."

"At the risk of causing further offence..." I stopped and turned. She looked beautiful and tearful and my heart burst with remorse for the pain that I had inflicted. I began again, more uncertainly. "At the risk of causing further offence, may I ask what it was that you had wished to say to me?"

We stood there in the hallway: she unbearably sad and a suddenly lonely, vulnerable figure; I an abject creature who was only just at that point realizing the immensity of what I had done.

I had stormed in without any thought or care, and had launched into my ill-conceived tirade, simply as an act of self-preservation. Coward and bully. How dare I accuse her husband of such things when I was guilty of more insidious crimes? I had been afraid; driven to pre-empt anything that she might have to say for fear that I might like whatever it was. I had ignorantly chosen attack as the best form of defence, just so that Father Vernon, for one, could not claim that I was just another foolish male swept away on a wave of desire. I had clumsily and cruelly trampled all over her feelings so that she could not begin to play with mine. What sort of a gentleman was I? And here we were, standing facing one another, and I could only wish that I were just coming in for the first time, rather than being ushered unceremoniously out into the cold night air.

"You want to know what it was that I wished to tell you?"

"Yes."

"It does not seem to me that you are at all interested in what I have to tell you. It seems to me that you are only ever interested in what you have to say on any subject. And this that you have to tell me is saying how much you despise me and my life. So, if I am so terrible, why should you be interested in what I have to say? I am a foolish, deceitful, nasty woman whom you do not like and you do not care that you hurt me. And yet, even so, you pretend that you are interested in what I have to say."

How could I blame her? Everything she said was true and born of the pain and disappointment I had brought. She had invited me into her home, probably at great risk to herself – not least where her husband was concerned – and her reputation. She had made me welcome. There was no indication in her manner that suggested that she was proposing anything improper or untoward. Yet here I was, accusing her of deception and folly. No, I could not blame her. I had behaved abominably towards her.

"I will tell you because even if you do not care for me, I care for you. That is to say, I know something about you that you must

198

know about, and if I do not tell you it will go very bad for you."

"What is it?"

"You are in very much danger. You will fall. Another will push you."

"Who told you this?"

Was this the village gossip machine running again? Or was it some more sinister connection to which she was privy? Perhaps she knew whoever it was that had pushed Brown until he fell, flailing, over the precipice.

"Nobody tells me this." She fixed me with those deep brown eyes. "At least, nobody in this life. It is my gift that you so despise."

"Your gift? A premonition? You have seen this?"

"No, I have not seen this." She paused, seeking a way to describe whatever it was that had happened. "I just… understand. It comes, and suddenly I know it. And it is true."

"True?"

"Yes, but you do not have to believe this, because you say all I do is cheat, so you cannot believe it."

"Francesca…" I began, hoping that perhaps here I had an opportunity to expand upon my previous clumsiness, explain myself and maybe even soften that blow a little.

"What?" Her eyes gleamed with suppressed tears. Was it an act?

"If you will spare me just five more minutes, we should try and talk some more."

"I would like you to go."

"Five more minutes. That is all I ask."

She shifted her weight from one foot to the other.

"Five minutes." She led me back into her room.

We sat down again. This time, though, she sat upright, with her hands resting lightly on her knees, as if she were a princess hearing an unwelcome suitor's inept petition. Attentive, yet distant.

"Francesca," I began, carefully, "I do not claim that you have a gift. I do not consider that you do not. I do not know."

"Yes. You do not know."

"But if you are true to your heart, if you are honest with yourself, then you *know* if what you are doing in your séances is false, or if they are true." She opened her mouth to speak, but I continued before she could interject. "I do not know. I do not care if they are true or false. That is for you to know. It is for you to decide what to do about it. I would only say this. Sometimes, I understand people who *believe* they have a gift convince themselves that it is true and, whether it is or not, live their lives *as if* it were true. They tell themselves that they hear and understand things. And maybe they do, maybe they don't. I have only started exploring these things for myself. I cannot say either way. I *will not* say either way. But whether it is real or not, to create a situation where a person pretends it is real for others, to make money from other people by it, to lead people into areas and end up having control over those lives by such tricks... this cannot be right."

She chose not to respond.

I stood up. "Now, as I said, you may not thank me. You may never wish to speak to me again, but I would never forgive myself if I had not told you this. For your sake, not for mine."

I left the room and let myself out. I did not hear whether she had followed me into the hallway; I do not think that she did.

I was disgusted with myself; with my prejudices, my presumption, my insensitivity, my cruelty and my weakness. It was unwarranted and boorish behaviour and I felt ashamed. I walked along through the streets immersed in shadow by the setting sun. I chose to skulk sullenly behind the buildings. I half wanted to run back to her, fling myself at her feet and beg forgiveness. The other half longed to hear her footfall behind me. To feel her gentle hand slip into mine. To hear her whisper that it was all right and that she understood.

But above and beyond and beneath and beside and behind it all was a stronger desire. The desire to do absolutely the right thing. To behave properly and correctly. Despite the hideous way I had behaved, the *fons et origo* of my motivation was to slay the dragon.

Temptation.

I could not pretend that what I had done was in any wise noble, but the intention had been to kill any possibility of me falling in love with that woman. I had achieved, at least, that ambition.

I was alone and lonely. I was a thousand miles away from Touie. Through all the recent events, I had been worn down and rendered vulnerable. I should have wanted nothing better than a warm embrace, a soft caress and the sense of security a woman brings. I did not know what it was that Francesca was going to say to me, I told myself. I was only most afraid that it was going to be tender; persuasive. I simply could not allow that to happen. Why I had gone at all, contrary to Father Vernon's wise counsel, I would never know. But once there, I had known that it was wrong. So I had lashed out. It was ugly. It was unforgivable. But I knew it was better than any alternative. Even if all she truly had to say to me was whatever her… what might I call it?… intuition had told her. I only hoped Touie would be grateful for what I did. Not that I could ever possibly tell her. Not that she would ever be proud of the manner in which I did it.

Having thrashed myself to a bloody rag with all that remorse, recrimination and self-pity, I took note of my surroundings again. I realized that I was approaching my hotel. I was just a few steps away from the front door when a figure, dark, wild and burly, leapt out from the alley alongside the building. It grabbed me in a frenzy and hauled me, before I could understand what was happening, bodily back down into that dark, dank, foetid place.

I was still writhing and struggling to break free from the bear-like embrace of the man when the first blow landed. It was on the side of my head and it was as shocking as it was painful. I opened my mouth to cry out for help, but a further severe blow lashed across my lower face and I was spun sideways by its force and down onto my knees. Here I remained, gasping with the speed and shock of it all. Again I raised my head to yell for help, but before I could draw breath, the toe of a boot landed right in the centre of my stomach.

It expelled every last gill of breath that I had in me. I pitched onto my forehead, clasping my midriff, fighting for air. Two blows in quick succession hammered onto my back. Then my assailant, aware that apart from producing a few bruises there was little to be gained from beating me, shuffled sideways and landed a mighty kick into my right kidney.

I let loose a howl and rolled over onto my back on the verge of collapse. Absurdly, as I lay there for that brief instant, moaning and clutching the small of my back, I noticed that I was viewing this whole event objectively. It was as if I were standing to one side and observing the beating I was taking from a purely analytical point of view. The pain was real and my immersion in it complete. Yet there was another part of me that found the whole sequence thoroughly fascinating. I realized that this was not the beating of a calculating and clever person. This was the frenzied attack of someone bent purely on vengeance. I had no time to speculate whom because another kick was launched in my direction.

My eyes, despite the reeling and gasping I was doing, were becoming more accustomed to my murky surroundings. This time, therefore, I could see the foot being drawn back and the lower leg being cocked ready to deliver the excruciating blow. I instantly hugged my own knees to myself, and the toe of my assailant's boot landed on my left shin with a thud. The pain shot through me like a bolt of lightning. However, the action and the unexpected resistance the blow had met with caused my attacker to lose balance for a moment. He had to put both feet firmly on the ground in order to stabilize himself. I knew that if I were to stand any chance of coming out of this assault without further grievous injury, I would have to get to my own two feet as swiftly as I could. I also knew that the moment I made a move from this foetal position I would receive a further debilitating clout to my kidneys.

I therefore did the only thing I could think of to buy time. I lunged with my legs, shooting them out from their tucked position as if they had sprung from a trap. I aimed them straight at the legs of my antagonist. I ensured that both feet landed on the shins, one just above the ankles and the other just below the knees. Whoever it was was jolted backwards a few steps by the violence of it. Already suspecting it was a man, I could now be sure from the roar of surprise and the curses he emitted. Not that I had had any real doubts that my assailant was male. The weight of the blows told their own story.

During that brief moment he took in order to recover, I hauled myself groggily and painfully to my feet and staggered quickly backwards two, three paces.

Now there was no-man's-land between us. Now, if he were to lunge, he would put himself more at risk than heretofore. This realization seemed to hold him. For a brief moment that uncertainty gave me a further breathing space, which was worth its weight in gold.

I sucked in two lungfuls of air, drew myself into an aggressive, challenging stance and assumed the "ready" position. I stood sideways, to present as narrow a target as possible, then set my feet apart; one for'ard, one aft. This gave me balance, a lower centre of gravity, and options to spring backwards or launch forwards as circumstances demanded. I then raised my right fist to guard my jaw and crooked my left arm so that I could present my left fist, now clenched and ready to strike, towards my opponent.

My "ready" position took him aback. There is a difference between a pedestrian making his unsuspecting way back to his hotel and a man who is plainly trained to some considerable degree in the art and craft of boxing; someone who, moreover, has not chosen to fly at the first opportunity, but chooses instead to stay, to square up to his assailant, and to offer battle.

My opponent, having weighed up the odds and possibly deciding it would be difficult if not impossible to circumnavigate me in order to gain the exit to the alley, made himself ready also. Although his readiness consisted in lowering his chin, hunching his shoulders and presenting his hands, fingers extended. He looked like a rugby full-back waiting to tackle a twenty-stone forward who in turn was intent upon trampling him underfoot on his regal process to the try line. However, if he considered me to be a bumbling British doctor interested only in edelweiss and alpine strolls, then he was about to be sadly mistaken.

A further moment passed as we eyed each other in the gloom. This calm before the storm was broken by his decision to chance his arm. He growled like a grizzly bear and leapt at me with fingers which clutched towards my throat. I stepped lightly to one side and applied a clout to his left temple as he passed.

First points on the score sheet to me.

He staggered to a halt, turned, and foolishly, having not learned his lesson, committed himself to quite the same manoeuvre again. To paraphrase His Grace, the late, lamented Duke of Wellington, he came at me in the same old way and so I repelled him in the same old way. I delivered a pretty reminder of my presence, this time to his right temple.

Infuriated, and no doubt by now increasingly aggravated to the point of impulsive rage, he no longer paused even to think. Instead, he spun on his heel and lunged with flailing arms hoping to hit something that resembled flesh and blood rather than thin air. For a third time – was he never going to learn? – I stepped thoughtfully aside to let him pass. Once more, I assisted his passage, with a right fist driven into his ribcage and following through. This augmented his momentum and drove him with a most gratifying thudding noise against the obstinate wall at the side of the hotel.

He let loose a yell of frustration. Finally, having learned his lesson, he decided upon an entirely different plan of attack. He rumbled towards me, head down and both fists clenched just beneath his chin. I waited patiently for his approach. I watched as he drew back his right hand, like an archer with his bowstring, prior to delivering a hammer blow. Before he had the opportunity to deliver it, however, I threw four punches, rapid fire, straight into his solar plexus. Right, left, right, left. Almost military precision. He just stood there, clutching himself and gulping in air like a beached trout.

His head lowered and he began swaying slightly like a birch sapling in a summer breeze. I could, of course, have delivered any number of further blows at will, to almost any point of the man's anatomy of my choosing. But I had always made it a rule never to hit an opponent when he was not looking. Not only did I consider it unsporting, but I also wanted my victim to see the blows being launched. He needed to realize that he was powerless to protect himself from them. Boxing is all about power. Superiority. Arrogance. It is a sport which suits the male of the species very well.

So I waited courteously for him to regain at least some equilibrium.

Eventually, the great brute, who had found it so easy and necessary to catch me off-guard in order to bully me in that violent and cowardly way, raised his head to look at me. He tried a feeble left jab to my jaw. A strike which to evade was simplicity itself. He drew his right hand back again to follow his first shot with a huge haymaker. His intention, I assumed, was to entirely, and without mercy, separate my head from my shoulders. The left jab was plainly designed to encourage me to evade it. In doing so, this would put me in the line of fire of his right fist. This, in turn, would place my head in exactly the correct position to receive the incoming, and for his part hopefully unseen, right fist.

However, it was an old trick and one I had no difficulty in recognizing. Before he had even embarked on the second phase of his strategy, viz: the right hook, I had not only evaded the left jab but had leaned back and danced two quick steps to the right. I had avoided the now redundant left arm. In order to reach me with his haymaker now, he would have to shift his balance and practically lean across, and over, his own left arm to land any sort of shot at all. That is, if he were agile enough. I had seen sufficient of him by now to know that agility was by no means his strongest suit.

All of this took place in an instant. I found that time always did slow down to an extraordinary extent when I boxed. For me, I had always found when in such bouts that I began to think more quickly, more lucidly and more accurately than when I was just lumbering along on my daily round. Having seen and evaded his dull plan, I therefore decided that it was time to finish the business.

With decision came icy resolve, immediately followed by action.

I landed two sharp, stinging jabs straight into my opponent's ribcage just under the heart. He buckled and dropped his hands, tipping forward in the explosion of pain he was experiencing. I brought my right up from around my waist. With a most satisfactory and percussive "crack" I made point-blank contact with the dimple in the centre of his chin. This blow, for I have experienced it myself in my younger, greener days, snaps the upper and lower teeth together with unforgiving velocity. It has been known to loosen, crack or even dislodge the occasional molar. It also serves to drive the jawbone straight back into the skull. There is a sensation not unlike being hit on the cranium by a falling log. This is accompanied by a bright flash, or a succession of lights. Meanwhile, the tang of something similar to iodine instantly pervades the nasal cavity. Usually the recipient of such a collection of sensations ends up in a crumpled heap upon the canvas.

The recipient of this particular sequence of sensations did not disappoint. His knees crumbled like crushed chalk and he expelled a deep sigh that turned into a moan. And then he collapsed.

I stood over him and allowed him a few seconds' respite, after which I jangled his ribs with the point of my boot toe.

"Hey!" I called, loudly enough to cause him to stir. "Hey!"

He groaned and rolled over onto his back.

"Hugo. Can you hear me?"

He groaned in affirmation and clutched his head, his jaw and his belly in that order. I spoke German. Apart from fisticuffs, it was the only language we both understood.

"I do not know why you attacked me and I don't particularly care, but you should know that I have no intention towards your wife and never shall have. You should also know that I was boxing

206

champion at both school and college. If you forget either of these facts, I shall be more than pleased to remind you of them at any time. Just ask."

With that, I retrieved my hat, which had fallen off in the initial mêlée, dusted it with a few swift passes of my hand, and replaced it upon my head. I rather suspect it sat there at an immodestly jaunty angle.

I left the alley to the accompaniment of Hugo's soft moans.

I did not know why, as I told him, I had been attacked. I surmised that a drinking companion of Hugo's, on his way to the bar, had seen me paying Francesca a private visit and had told him. He, returning in a rage, had perhaps seen me approaching my hotel and had decided there and then to ambush me. It could be, though, that there was a more sinister reason, and he had been either ordered or paid to set upon me. And then a further possible explanation occurred to me. Perhaps Francesca and Hugo had planned the whole escapade. Perhaps they merely disguised it as an *affaire d'honneur* or *d'amour*. Perhaps Francesca had deliberately lured me to her home.

With these confusing and unnerving considerations, I stepped into the hotel and made my way to my room to bathe my bruises.

On arrival I studied my appearance in the mirror. It seemed I had escaped lightly. I really had no wish to discuss my recent bout with my fellow guests. It would not do to have to reveal why Hugo had attacked me. My body, certainly, was mottled from his blows. I resolved to wear light trousers and to cover my arms until the bruising subsided. Thankfully, though, he had hardly touched my face; the reason one keeps one's hands up when boxing. Any red marks, I felt sure, would fade quickly. In the meantime, they could be passed off as how a British complexion can sometimes look after too much exposure to the Alpine sun.

Fourteen

Back in my room, regaining my equilibrium and contemplating an early supper, I became aware of raised voices in the room next to mine. They continued for a short while. Then there was a slammed door, followed by the sound of voices in conversation. Having restrained myself thus far, I found it impossible to resist looking out at this point. I opened my door tentatively and peered around the frame. Werner was standing by the bedroom door next to mine, looking awkward and seemingly not knowing quite where to put his hands. Sobbing fitfully on his ample left pectoral muscle was mevrouw van Engels. I approached them and asked what the matter was. She turned watery eyes towards me.

"Don't hurt him. He does not mean it." She buried her face into Werner's ample breast again. For a moment, I thought that she was talking about the Bavarian. However, the latter's bearing did not suggest either that he was being indiscreet nor that, at that particular moment, he bore anyone sufficient malice to require physical restraint. I therefore concluded that the subject under discussion was someone else, and that someone was most likely the professor himself. Bavarian with characteristics A, B plus C; Dutchman with characteristics X, Y plus Z – so to speak.

"Is it your husband, madam?"

She turned to look at me and then nodded. She nestled back into her hiding place, as if she were playing peek-a-boo or hide-and-seek.

"I can assist in nothing if you will not explain what it is that is distressing you." I was hoping to jolt her out of her hysteria. It was to no avail. Like a bear in deepest winter, she refused to emerge from her cave. So I suggested to Werner that he take care of the lady while I went to see if I might track her husband down and extract, perhaps, a little more clarity from him.

As I left to go downstairs, I suggested that they repaired to the lady's room. They withdrew as suggested and I heaved a great sigh. Domestic incidents on top of my current pursuits of investigating murders, falling off cliffs, being shot at, and ambushed by thugs were the last things I required at the moment. However, the problem needed resolving, as van Engels might say, so resolve it I must.

I did not know why I was always so eager to be the person who takes up the reins on any runaway carriages. It was perhaps due to my childhood. My father was a drunk and a spendthrift, and eventually needed clinical care for his mental disarray. Perhaps I subsequently grew unable to endure any such disturbance between two people. I always felt the need to repair emotional damage between people as quickly as possible. I remembered the dark nights lying under my bedclothes with my coverlet hauled tightly over my head, trying to make the sound of my father's unmanageable outbursts and my mother's corresponding rages go away. Night after night I wanted desperately to leap from my room, clatter downstairs, box both parents about the ears and order them to desist. Undoubtedly, it was this deep-rooted urge that drove me to seek out Professor van Engels and try to effect a reconciliation.

I found the gentleman in the library. It was he, I assumed, who had closed the shutters. He sat on a hard oak chair in the darkest corner, leaning forward so that his forearms rested along his thighs, his hands clasped together. The room was musty with last evening's tobacco smoke, as it always was, but there was a further fug – the reek of both stale and fresh alcohol on exhaled breath. Brandy, I should have thought. All at once, I was transported twenty years back to one of many interviews with my father. All the emotions of those terrible, confusing, disconcerting times washed over me like a rip tide. That unbearable concoction of fear, disgust, hate, compassion, incomprehension and an overwhelming desire to weep, mixed with a powerful refusal not to. These emotions sallied forth from the depths of my memory, where I thought I had sealed them away permanently, and laid clamorous siege to my soul once again.

I approached van Engels, as I had approached, on many occasions, my father. I pushed open one of the shutters to allow in a little light and air. I then drew up a chair close to the Dutchman, and sat down. He did not look up. Oftentimes my mother, who had just contributed to a ferocious row with my father, would despatch me as the peacemaker and the bridge-builder. It was pride, perhaps. It was also weakness. I was very young, not even an adolescent yet, and still I was obliged to take on the mantle of mature adulthood; to display the negotiating skills of a seasoned diplomat.

I now realized how intensely unfair, cruel even, they had been to use me in such a way. I also realized how when people are broken down, they are no longer able to consider matters objectively. They are unable even to seek help in their extreme, unremitting incapacity. It occurred to me that what some folk need, even in advanced adulthood, is the security, authority and wisdom of their parents. Yet with parents like mine, I suppose that I rarely experienced those particular qualities.

"Van Engels?" To my shame, I did not know his first name. "Van Engels, it is I, Conan Doyle." He did not look up, so I persisted. "Is there anything that I can do?"

"Nothing."

I had elicited a reaction, at least.

"We should talk."

"Why? What for? It is useless."

"What is useless?"

"Everything. It is all useless. When it all comes down to it, we are all alone. People always let you down. People you trust."

"We are never alone unless we choose to cut ourselves off from other people."

"I choose this."

"Why?"

"Because I do."

"Yes, but why do you?"

210

He looked up and across at me. His eyes were still capable of focusing, I noted; so he was not too inebriated. He was slurring his words and much of what he said was pronounced in the deep, greasy manner of the drunkard. But he was, I believed, capable of conducting an intelligible conversation, at least. I repeated my question.

"Why do you choose to be alone?"

"Because it is best."

"Running away?"

He became agitated and stiffened. "I am not running away. You cannot say I am running away. How dare you suggest this? Who are you to talk to me like this? You do not know. You are not my keeper."

"I know… I know… I was only saying…" I crooned; nothing worse than an angry drunk.

"Well, don't say this."

"I won't."

"Well, don't."

"I won't."

It seemed he was settling, but then he erupted again.

"Who are you, anyway? You have no right. How dare you! This is your fault. You. I blame you!"

"Me?"

"Of course, or are you so stupid you cannot see it? Yes. You are stupid. I always thought you were stupid. You disgust me. Stupid, disgusting man."

"I do not understand."

"No. You do not. This is because you are disgusting, stupid."

"I am not stupid and, I should add, I do not think that the personal abuse you are addressing to me is really helping very much. It is also not polite."

"Tchah!" he said. But he abated, my firm tone holding him for a while. He resorted to hanging his head and resting his arms along his legs as before. Occasionally his head bobbed, as if he were

211

nodding off. This was the alcohol seeping across his consciousness like the Thames mist and taking control. At length, he forced his head to jerk up and to look at me again. "Why are you here? I do not want you here. Go away. Leave me!"

"I am not going away."

"Why not? I insist you go away."

"I am not going away."

"Why not?"

"Because you say you are always alone and people always let you down. I am not going to leave you."

"This is because you are stupid. And a fool."

"Then the world needs more fools. I am happy to be a fool."

"Then you are a fool to be thus happy."

"Perhaps."

He licked his lips and ran his sleeve across his mouth. He looked about him, as if coming to terms with his environment for the first time that evening.

"Fool," he said again, throatily.

He then began to talk.

It was a meandering monologue that for such a structuralist was completely out of character. It was as if he wanted to drain himself of all the impurities and detritus that had built up within him over the years. Nearly all of it made absolutely no sense whatsoever. Oftentimes he would come out with whole sentences in Dutch and these also, I believed, contained many expressions of disgust; with himself, with me, with others – it made no difference. I allowed him to ramble on for about fifteen minutes, pouring out his anguish – which is what it was – to me, and yet I need not have been present at all. I was also aware that whatever it was that he was trying to exorcise from himself, whatever evil memories and past hurts there were contained in that lengthy rant, it was probably only a hundred thousandth of the pain and anger that lay so deeply – probably ultimately immovably – embedded within his bosom. His was a tormented soul, and my own wept for it.

When he finally allowed me the opportunity to speak, I let him know that I did not think any the less of him. I also told him that not everything that he had told me would be resolved in one conversation nor, indeed, in one day. There was much that he had told me of his anger that I did not understand and resolved privately to see if his wife might enlighten me.

His whole soliloquy had consisted mainly of invective against his colleagues at Utrecht and among his peers in academia throughout the world. Paris and Cambridge particularly featured as some kind of latter-day Sodom and Gomorrah in his book. He was not clear on why exactly he viewed all these people with distaste. Neither, when I asked, would he elucidate. Superficially, therefore, it seemed that he was just a bitter, disaffected human being who could see neither virtue nor value among his fellows. In my experience, however, to look only upon the surface is to take an unhelpfully simplistic approach. There were depths here that needed exploring, and I intended to start exploring them – if not through him, then through his wife – at the earliest opportunity.

The main task at that moment, however, was to reunite them and if not actually effect a reconciliation, then at least engineer a workable truce. Undoubtedly, some intense ill-feeling existed between them also. No one escaped the all-pervading displeasure of van Engels. I suspected, by what sense I could make from his tirade, that nevertheless she cared for him, his health, his safety. He may profess not to care for her, which he was frequently doing in our interview, and with venom, yet I rather imagined that it was not in fact the case.

I encouraged him to accompany me back upstairs to his room.

"I will not go."

"Nevertheless, old fellow... this is the best course for you at this moment."

"I will not go..."

I sensed this time it was more reluctance than obstinacy, so I persisted.

"You will have to see your wife again sooner or later. So it might as well be sooner. What you need most of all is a few minutes' lie-down on your own warm and welcoming bed."

"Why? Do you think I am drunk?"

"Yes. I do think that you are drunk."

He laughed bitterly. "Yes, you are right. I am indeed drunk. And I don't care this much —" at which point he snapped his fingers greasily "— for what people think about me and my being drunk."

"You are quite right. It doesn't matter what people think about you. Drunk or sober. What you need is a little lie-down to collect yourself. And then you will be able to discuss matters with your wife."

"I do not care two figs for my wife."

"Nevertheless…"

I took him gently by the arm. He did not resist, but rose from his seat like a lamb. He allowed himself to be led upstairs from the library, professing all the time that he really was rather tired after all, that a little lie-down would be really quite a good idea at the moment, and that I couldn't make him do anything he did not care to do. I replied that naturally I would not expect him to do anything he did not care to do, and that I would not dream of forcing him to do it.

Mevrouw van Engels met us at the door of the bedroom. She said nothing to me or to her husband, recognizing immediately the situation and taking control, probably through force of habit. She sat her husband upon the bed, removed his tweed jacket, knitted tie and brogues, and folded him in among the bedclothes in the most practised way.

I left immediately afterwards. She did not look up to see me go. I repaired to my room for no other reason than that I wished to be alone with my own thoughts for a short while. Intense emotion, my own or others', I found quite draining.

I arrived for supper in a very sombre and reflective mood. I was by now late, and hoping that I might have missed the other

214

guests and would therefore be able to dine alone and in peace. My wish was partly fulfilled inasmuch as there was no sign of the van Engelses, for obvious reasons, Werner, Holloway, or Marcus Plantin. The latter two had presumably dined and left earlier. Marie was there, as usual, just finishing her coffee, while the Pivcevics had embarked upon the consumption of some species of syllabub.

I immersed myself in a venison steak that my dining companions informed me had been shot the day before. Not by Werner. The topic of conversation was the séance and, depending on one's point of view, how exciting or risible it had been. Unfortunately I was not very good company and contributed little to the discussion. Other than, that is, to refute entirely the suggestion of Marie's that the spirit of Holmes had indeed been vested in Holloway. She challenged my view by asking whether I had seen him recently and whether I had noticed a distinct change in his manner. I confessed that I had not noticed any difference. He was still, in my opinion, the same boorish fellow that I had first encountered on my train from Zürich. I confess that my dining companions were somewhat taken aback by the directness with which I expressed my opinions, and the very personal way in which I spoke of someone who was not even present to answer my criticisms. But it had been a very long and tiring day and, besides, I did not feel that I owed the fellow anything. Nevertheless, I was ashamed that I had allowed my personal sentiments to encroach upon what was, after all, simply polite conversation. I therefore apologized immediately for any offence I had caused. I vowed silently to refrain from such outbursts in future. It was not becoming to a gentleman, no matter what difficulties may have brought him to such impropriety, to discuss others in such a manner. Furthermore, it served no useful purpose.

Concerning displays of personal opinion, I could not help but notice that the hotel proprietor, Georg, Anton's father, was serving at table. He was doing so, I further noticed, with very bad grace indeed. Every dish that I ordered was brought to my place and hurled onto the table from such a height that it clattered noisily and appeared at risk of shattering into tiny fragments.

I perceived that the other guests were not being served in this combative manner. Such behaviour was therefore for my benefit alone. Having considered the possible causes for this gentleman's disaffection with me, I could only relate it to two possibilities. Either it was somehow connected to the scene Holloway and I had encountered on leaving the hotel for our walk up to the waterfall the previous day, or it was relating to the séance, the body and the rumours circulating about me that Father Vernon had said he would take steps to quash. The first I could do nothing about until I had gathered further evidence as to the exact nature of Anton's unhappiness. The second, I was under instructions not to address at all.

My only option in the face of such plate throwing, therefore, was to accept it with dignity. I ate whatever it was that was flung peremptorily down before me, without comment. Although the consideration that I, a complete innocent, seemed to have found my name a hissing and a by-word in so short a space of time left both the venison and subsequent syllabub next to tasteless.

The other guests had all left by the time I had completed my meal. Georg, having cast the last of his pearls before me in the form of a cup of coffee and a coarse cognac, had departed. Having completed my meal, it remained for me to dab my lips with a napkin and stand up. No one had made mention of a session in the library, so I resigned myself to the not unattractive proposition of a quiet pipe upon my balcony and an early night.

As I left the dining room to cross the reception area towards the stairs, I was surprised to see standing in the doorway a figure wrapped in a cloak and a hood. The pervasive scent of lily of the valley hung heavy in the air.

"Francesca...?"

I was at first delighted and then, directly afterwards, perturbed. After all, I had only too recently trounced her husband and unambiguously called her integrity into question. My initial smile dropped from my face like a cataract. Francesca, on the other hand, did not appear to be the bearer of recrimination. She seemed concerned and nervous, but I could not detect anger, hatred or even admonishment upon those charming features.

"Doctor."

She had whispered and approached me cautiously. I took this to mean that she was not comfortable to be seen in public with me, or perhaps, to be with me at all.

"Would you care to come to my room?" I asked.

She couldn't help smiling. Then I realized what I had said and felt flustered.

"No, thank you." She spoke hurriedly and passionately. "Doctor, you cannot stay here. My husband is in a furious rage and people are saying that the near fire at the church, the séance, my husband's injuries, even the sad death upon the mountain was your fault. Though you may not have done this yourself, you have visited it upon us."

"A very superstitious people, country folk."

"Perhaps, but also difficult if you do not know how to handle them. I know very well, this."

"Well, I cannot just up anchor and leave. To me, that would be an admission of guilt, wouldn't it?" I spoke as a man of the world, from the perspective of experience. My sangfroid appeared to reassure her.

"No, I can understand this. But you should, perhaps, leave anyway. Perhaps you could start to say that you have had an urgent telegram. Or maybe a friend has invited you to stay somewhere else? Some simple reason that people can believe."

"Lie?"

"Yes, if it will save you. I do not like how the people are talking about you. Also... what you did to my husband. They will never forgive you."

"And you...?"

217

She hesitated.

"That is not the point. Go. Please."

She turned to leave and, despite myself, I touched her on the arm and caused her to turn back. I wanted her to stay close to me for just a moment longer. She looked at me with questions haunting her eyes. Questions that she felt had to remain unasked.

"Do you know Father Vernon?" I asked instead.

"Of course."

"He is talking to people. Telling them the truth about me. It will be all right. You shall see. All shall be well…"

She gave me one last look as she moved off down the hall and out into the night. "No, doctor. It will not."

I made my way to my room greatly disturbed. Undoubtedly I was becoming enmeshed in any number of difficulties and distractions, and reality seemed to be slipping further and further away from me. I was growing unable to grasp what was happening, and where, precisely, my role lay in all of these events. There seemed to be no touchstone, no pole star, no truth in all of this. I had followed a path, one pace at a time, through everything. I believed that to the best of my ability I had been patient, thoughtful and rational. Yet with every step I felt I was being coaxed further into a mire. A mire upon which a thick fog was descending. Was I losing my mind? The sheer uncanniness of this whole district and its people would have brought anyone to question their sanity.

Napoleon once said that the greatest failing on a battlefield was not to make the wrong decision, but to make no decision at all. I knew that without forward momentum of some description, circumstances were exceedingly likely to collapse in on me. I would then be consumed by an even worse situation than the one that I was presently enduring. I decided, therefore, first to reopen negotiations with Holloway. Despite our differences and our late falling out, he was the closest to these problems. Two minds working in harness on this would be the most likely arrangement to bring palpable results.

I disliked intensely, naturally, the notion that I had actually become reliant on this wayward and contrary individual, but needs must when the devil...

That is to say... needs must...

Holloway had not been present at dinner. I reasoned he may well still not be at the hotel. It was for me the work of a moment to establish this by trotting up to his room and knocking. Receiving no response, and this time refusing to speculate on the meaning of the silence, I collected my hat and stepped out to scout the village and try to locate him.

I found him at Francesca's café. As I approached from the street, I could hear from within people either drunk or intent on becoming so. The noise billowed out from the depths of the building in squalls. It was now a livelier and differing place from the establishment I had visited with Plantin for coffee. It seemed more, not to put too fine a point on it, disreputable. A fog of tobacco smoke diffused the already dim gaslight. This, combined with the thick embroidered wall-hangings, gave the whole room the aspect of a bordello. The result was an atmosphere of enhanced intimacy and exotica. I could see Holloway sitting near the window. I made a move towards the café with the intention of drawing him aside for an earnest conference. However, the thought of facing so many villagers and there potential acusations gave me to something occurred as I approached the entrance that gave me pause. I withdrew sharply into the shadow made by an adjacent building.

Francesca, now out of her cloak and back serving at her place of work, approached my acquaintance, beaming. He looked up from his beer and returned the smile with warmth. She reached out a hand and tousled his hair. He, sitting, while she remained standing, curled his arm around her waist and pulled her to him. She stood there, her hip nestling against his ribcage and gave no impression that she found such behaviour in any way brazen.

I became aware of my emotions. Jealousy, outrage and disgust at Francesca. Hatred and righteous indignation at Holloway. This allied with complete incomprehension as to what it all meant. All these reactions and more fought a bitter battle for supremacy within me. The more none of them was able to establish supremacy, the more they clutched and tore at my soul; a storm-tossed sea crashing against a crumbling chalk cliff on a foul winter night.

What right did I have? I asked myself. I had no claim upon Francesca, nor did I ever wish to have one. Holloway, for his part, had not behaved so abominably towards me as to warrant such a boiling hate as I was experiencing at that moment. Yet here was I, fiercely opposed to all that I was witnessing. It was as though I were the one being cuckolded, made a fool of; it was my back behind which such displays of intimacy were being enacted. And then there was the confusion. How could this scene make any sense? For sure, they had met at the séance. For sure, Holloway was one of the significant reasons that the meeting had taken place. But Francesca was… more intelligent than that. At least, I would have thought so. And Holloway? Well, where did Eva come into all of this? At the thought of that kind, innocent child being hurt in any way, the fury within redoubled in its intensity.

Francesca did not remain long at his side. She collected a glass that stood empty upon his table – a feeble excuse for a liaison, I thought – and returned to her duties within the bowels of that scandalous place. Holloway leered around the room. He suddenly appeared transfixed by something. I, for my part, had by now decided to continue upon my chosen course to discuss matters with him. So I was once again on my way in through the entrance of the café when I saw what it was that had attracted his attention. He had risen from his seat and had become engaged in conversation with a fiddler beside the piano, which stood against one sordid wall. I found a spare seat at Holloway's vacated table and tried to ignore the numerous heads that turned my way. None of them, it would seem, were doing so in a spirit of welcome. I watched in growing amazement as the fiddler relinquished the instrument into his hands. Holloway deftly placed it beneath his chin and took up the proffered bow. He drew the fibres with great dexterity across the strings. In a very short space of time, he stilled the clamour in that place. It was a most moving and lyrical bittersweet melody. As he played, his eyes closed, rapt in his art. He swayed and persuaded the music out of the instrument with an uplifting sensitivity. If I had not seen it with my own eyes, I would not have believed it possible. He had become a different person. Thus transformed, he gave a beautiful virtuoso performance; not of the highest degree, perhaps, yet compelling. Man and violin were one, and the absorbing air veritable soul-food for those of us privileged to hear it.

At length, Holloway completed the piece and stood there, as silent and still as high cloud in a summer sky. He appeared as if he were savouring the lingering notes, now falling from the air like dew. His stillness was reflected in his audience. Then someone – I rather suspect that it was I – began to clap. The applause was taken up around the room. The cries of "Bravo!" echoed to the rafters.

As if waking from a dream, and surprised to discover that he was not alone, Holloway opened his eyes. He gazed about him. He returned the violin sheepishly to its owner and weaved his way through the congratulating crowd back to his table.

"Ah, Doyle," he said, slightly abashed, as if I had caught him out doing something shameful. This, naturally, was far from the case.

"That was simply wonderful!" Despite all my faults, I always give credit where it is due. I begrudged him nothing for his technical ability and musicianship. Even if I did begrudge him much in many other areas.

He looked longingly across at the fiddler, who had embarked upon a brisk, scratchy air of his own.

"It is quite astonishing, Doyle."

"What is?"

"Well, I daresay, like me, you learned an instrument as a nipper as a matter of course."

"I did." I forbore to expand upon which instrument, for fear he would accordingly encourage me to perform upon it; something I was not in the least interested in doing.

My concerns were not his, however, as he had something far more mystifying to expound at that moment. "I could never play like that, though."

"But you did."

"I know I did. But I did not know that I could play quite like that. I have never played so lucidly, sympathetically, fulsomely in my life before."

"Never?"

"Never."

"So… what came over you?"

"Exactly. What… or indeed … who?"

We surveyed one another with a wild surmise.

Slowly, despite the context of our discussion, Holloway returned to something of his former self. He dipped into his pockets and produced what I assumed were some very recent purchases. A briar and a creaking leather tobacco pouch. Presumably he had been smoking the pipe earlier and had let it go out, for there was still some tobacco in there. He topped the contents up with more from the pouch. I refrained from telling him never to relight old ash. How disgusting that is liable to taste. He tamped down the pipe bowl with the steel stub end of his smart new ivory-inlaid smoker's tool. Then, with a stainless steel Vesta case of his very own, he lit it. He sucked on the stem like a beginner. Rapid little pecks that showed the tobacco was not drawing at all well. But he stubbornly persisted. I recognized the rub as predominantly Virginia from the light, sweet fragrance. I also noticed, however, a slightly thicker smell, like burning resin.

Eventually, he gave voice to his thoughts.

"You, Doyle, were the catalyst, the alchemist trying to extract gold from base metal. You are Doctor Frankenstein."

"And you have become his creature?"

"You gave Holmes life. You brought him to us."

222

This was foolishness in the first degree, this tortuous speculation. Yet there was something in Holloway that fascinated me. There was no doubt something immensely familiar in his bearing. I had imagined it all a thousand times over the last three years or so as I composed my stories: the mannerisms, the attitudes he struck, the tone of voice and the way in which he persisted in addressing me.

Had Holmes obtained human form?

Fifteen

Francesca returned to our table and, while acknowledging my presence as far as the unwritten laws of civility required, she paid me scant further attention. Holloway ordered for both of us. Bestowing on him her most womanly smile, she departed to fulfil our request. She brought us two beers and floated off soon afterwards.

Watching them flirting, for that was the only word which could possibly describe their syrupy behaviour, the dormant jealousy was once again awakened within my breast. All consideration of a possibly substantiated Holmes dissolved like will-o'-the-wisp. I once again confronted merely a dissolute Holloway, and conflicting emotions. Holmes would never have flirted.

Never.

Then again... if whatever was supposed to have happened were true, there would be two spirits contending for the one tortured soul within the frame that was the human form known as Holloway. My mind reeled as I tried to grapple with this concept. Stevenson had written masterfully about it. I realized it was futile to struggle and resolved to simply address the person who was speaking to me, in whatever form he took, upon whatever terms he employed at any given moment. At that instant, it was my understanding that I was relating to Holloway. I addressed him as such.

"I need to discuss with you again the contents of Brown's room."

He laughed. Rather, he emitted a giggle. This then, like an Icelandic geyser, developed from an initial bubbling rumble into a full-blown gush. I was instantly offended. Our conversation of late – if not, indeed, all our conversations – had left me defensive and sensitive. Any reaction of this nature was certain to set me off like a taper touching gunpowder.

"I fail to see what is so hilarious, Holloway."

"No… no… you do not." The laughter subsided. He became strangely fierce; icy. "You do not see. Anything. That is why I have had to be doing all the seeing for you." He sucked on his pipe, like an infant on a rusk. "My dear old Doyle, the whole business has moved on substantially since we last spoke. Sub-stan-tially."

"How do you mean?" The expression escaped my lips before I remembered how that familiar phrase would be received. He released peal upon peal of laughter. This was sufficiently strident to attract the attention of clients on tables within a ten-foot radius, despite the ambient noise.

"How do you mean! How do you mean!" he squawked. Having indulged himself, he rallied. Taking his pipe from his mouth, he proceeded to jab me on the sternum for emphasis. "How do I mean… is that Brown's effects are immaterial to the case now."

Well, I was not so sure of that myself. However, it was futile to pursue the matter with him in such a state. It had become evident that rather than seek his help, I should explore other avenues. Anton, perhaps? I could try to get back onto some sort of even keel with him. Concerning Holloway, therefore, I adopted the taciturn tactic, waiting simply for him to expand further. This he did not. Instead, he occupied himself with inserting his pipe into his mouth and looked around him with a mixture of arrogance and diffidence. He really was a most appalling fellow. I recalled my previous meditation upon any possible relationship I would have were Holmes real. If this encounter with Holloway had any positive outcome at all, it was this. That were Holmes and I ever to meet, we would never get on.

At length, whoever Holloway was at that moment deigned to speak. What he had to say was germane, although how he broached this appeared initially to have little bearing upon our foregoing conversation.

"Let us examine the facts. According to your hypothesis, the person who murdered Brown managed so to do by rendering him insensible on a liquor containing anise-seed. He – or she – then brought him to the top of the fall. Here he – or she – contrived to cast him into the abyss. However, bringing the victim to the scene of the crime insensible is, you have to admit, highly unlikely. It would have resulted in the need for carrying him. Who alone in this village is strong enough? Unless there were – what? – four people? A secret society afraid of discovery? I doubt it. Eva would know and would have told me."

How Holloway, if it were indeed he, could mention that delightful creature's name in such circumstances I did not know, but I refused to be drawn into that discussion. "I do not believe that your conclusions fairly represent –"

"No, Doyle! You will listen to me."

I seethed.

"You appear wholly unable to appreciate, Doyle, how your facts lead us to the conjecture I have just presented to you. You say that he was in everyday shoes and with no alpenstock. Then he could only have been dragged up there against his will, or encouraged there in some other manner. Either way, to be frank, it is immaterial. He was up there. I am more concerned with your question in respect of the anise-seed. I have been making enquiries. It is clear that Brown did not ordinarily indulge in excesses related to alcohol. In effect, he was a dry old stick in every sense of the word – a fellow who found a cup of tea was more than strong enough to slake his thirsts. Could he have been forced to drink the alcohol? Perhaps. But I favour the theory that he supped it willingly, either at the hotel or upon the cliff. Now, as we have discovered, ouzo contains anise-seed. The Pivcevics have admitted possessing such a liquor. They are Croats who, by all accounts, are an unstable people at the best of times. The top of their bottle was missing. I discovered this during the course of my investigation. This item was discovered – by myself, I repeat – at the location of the fall. It is merely a step further to conjoin those two facts and establish the identity of the murderers. How they inveigled or coerced him to the cliff top, or carried him up there, is merely detail. A matter for them to elucidate upon when they are confronted by their heinous and unforgivable deed. No doubt, being thus confronted, the immensity of their action will drive them to confession in due course."

"Do you propose to confront them with their alleged guilt?" I surprised myself to find that despite my prejudices, I was to a limited extent giving him some credit for his reasoning.

"No. I have sent word to the valley and have been assured that the authorities there will send a policeman with due despatch at the earliest opportunity. Though I've been told responses are generally slow in these parts. Our duty therefore is to remain nonchalant and calm, observing while not being observed. Startle them and they will fly. Soothe them with normality and they shall suspect nothing until it is too late."

I could not, of course, eliminate the Pivcevics from my own suspicions. Whatever "proof" Holloway had was possibly flimsy. His logic, though, was entirely reasonable. Just as Holmes's would have been. Holmes, however, often got things wrong as well as right, I reminded myself. The couple's guilt was by no means established beyond reasonable doubt. If it were true, to be confronted by friable facts might only serve to alert them. Once dismissed for lack of hard evidence, they would be able to bolt, or take other drastic action. I suggested as much to my haughty companion. He nodded and accepted the point, but then asked another, more disturbing question.

"But why are you always so eager to defend them? Perhaps you are in league with them?"

I did not believe that he was being serious, so I did not offer a reply. This served only to pique his curiosity.

"Silence is your answer? Now – why would that be?"

Again, I refrained from responding to his insinuations. But his eyes were now drilling down, like a gimlet, into my innermost being. I began to feel a growing discomfort. He had clearly decided, among other things, to set himself upon my trail. Thus focused, it would perhaps only be a matter of time before he would turn his unwarranted attention fully upon me. I shook off this speculation as I sought to shake off all others. This was not Holmes, I reminded myself. This was just Holloway.

He had been considering matters meanwhile. Still staring directly into my own eyes, he spoke in what he obviously considered to be a measured manner.

"All right, Doyle, if it were not the Pivcevics, how would you explain the ouzo and the bottle-top?"

"If I were to try to explain it, I would suggest that someone… else… is seeking to leave 'clues'. Clues which point away from them and at other innocents. Whatever you may make of the matter, however, Holloway, I cannot and will not deem it as evidence against the two of them. I consider the premise unprofitable to our enquiries. Not least because, with all due respect to Anna, she is not the seductress that you would have her to be."

"She is a woman. All women are seductresses if they turn their minds to it. It really rather depends on the person being seduced and the purpose of seduction, don't you think?"

It was true; any woman can resort to powerful feminine wiles if they so choose. Attraction is not merely physical. It is metaphysical and chemical, too. "Well, then, let us take Tomas instead. He is hardly the excellent physical specimen that you would that he were. Even together they could have neither enticed Brown against his will, nor carried him up onto the mountains."

"He is a fervent patriot."

"And what has that to do with anything?"

"Patriotism drives ordinary people to extraordinary things."

"But still does not equip them, in cold blood, with the strength of four in order to manhandle a dozen stone of supposed deadweight up perpendicular paths."

Holloway, I could see, was beginning to become irritated by what Holmes would describe as my gratuitous impertinence. I observed increased myofibril activity in the region of his jaw muscles, causing them to contract and relax in his growing agitation.

"I very much doubt that you are correct, Doyle." His tone approached the sinister. "However, your case, as I recall, rests solely on surmise and a pipe knife…" Then just as suddenly as he had tensed, he relaxed. He had plainly remembered something to his advantage in this weird tennis match of words.

"As you say, Holloway, the pipe knife may prove of no value, but until it is found we may not dismiss it as a possible factor."

Ignoring my contribution to the conversation, I could see that he was intent upon manoeuvring himself into a position from which he proposed to triumphantly reveal something of great significance.

"But it is retrieved," said Holloway suavely, clearly imagining he had checkmated me.

"Found? Where?"

"Where one might have expected to find it." He rummaged in the pocket of his jacket. Eventually he extricated a ragged sheaf of paper, dog-eared and folded. It was much abused by having spent, I should imagine, some considerable time being thrust and rethrust into that same pocket. He tossed it flapping limply across to me. He then sat back to suck upon his pipe and contemplate infinity, which, it would seem, commenced at some point just over my left shoulder.

I unwrapped the paper as I would unwrap a parcel. I folded this leaf over to the left and the leaf underneath to the right, until the whole was revealed to be a broadsheet newspaper. It was this morning's edition of one of the Interlaken journals. I perused it for a moment. The length of time it took me to review the page irked Holloway, whose *coup de maître*, he could see, was being delayed by my fumbling.

"In the middle. At the bottom," he rasped, still not deigning to look at me.

My eyes fell to the spot described and almost immediately focused upon a couple of column inches dedicated, it would seem, almost exclusively to me. It was written in German; roughly translated it read:

DETECTIVE WRITER FOILED

Well-known English fictionalist, Dr Arthur Conan Doyle, creator of the apparently increasingly popular Sherlock Holmes, consulting detective stories, has not managed to live up to the ideals of his creation in a real-life drama that has been unfolding upon our own doorstep.

The article went on to relate the Brown mystery in some detail and, rather unflatteringly, described my attempts to unravel it as "naïve but well intentioned". It outlined the key elements of my case and pointed out that my theories stood or fell upon the discovery of the pipe knife. It continued:

That pipe knife, your newspaper can now reliably report, has been found. It was handed in to our offices yesterday by a bright young fellow, a Master Jens Heckert, who had spotted it at the foot of the Reichenbach Falls, near Meiringen, while on a ramble with his school friends yesterday. It is undoubtedly the missing smoker's implement as it has the initials P. B. (Peter Brown) engraved upon it. Prosaically, it was simply discovered lying at the base of the gorge into which that unhappy walker so tragically fell last Saturday evening.

The article concluded by questioning what steps I would propose taking, now that the spine of my investigation had been so swiftly and simply removed. It suggested, coarsely, that perhaps my best move would be to catch the next train home, in order to continue my fictitious fantasies, at which I was evidently more adept than I was at investigating real-life mysteries.

I fought hard to refrain from offering any expression that may encourage Holloway in his evidently growing delight. I could see his eyes glinting in triumph as they sought to remain focused and ostensibly uninterested upon that infinite point beyond my shoulder.

I lost the struggle. "Why would you…?" I did not complete the sentence. Accusation was futile. The whole business rankled immensely – only Holloway knew of my theory about the pipe knife. That he had gone as far as to seek out a reporter in order to discredit me confirmed all I had suspected about his character. But the fact remained that the pipe knife had been found. My only solace was that as of that moment I need have absolutely nothing to do with that fellow sitting opposite me ever again. As far as he was concerned, my contribution to this business was concluded. Moreover, he had so distanced himself from me of his own accord that I was no longer obliged to pursue our flimsy acquaintance further.

However, I had not reckoned on the extent of his tenacity. I was on the verge of standing in order to take my leave when his eyes languorously swivelled like an armoured cruiser's guns to engage mine.

"Of course, if your case has fallen apart while mine remains intact, we are left with a very pretty conundrum indeed. The question of the ouzo bottle-top."

"What of it?"

"Even more likely, it would seem, an indictment of the Pivcevics, now, wouldn't you say?"

"Hang your Pivcevic theory."

"Have you any other notion to offer?"

"Plenty."

"Yes, you would have."

I drew myself up to my full height in the chair. "And what, pray, do you mean by that remark?" I was to repent bitterly my choice to be thus aggressively defensive. I was understandably hurt and offended. Yet I should have retired in good order and prepared a more robust defence at leisure. *Il faut reculer pour mieux sauter.* Nevertheless, I pressed on. "It is a very clumsy way to murder someone – push them off a mountain…"

"But if it is necessary? What would have brought it to such a crisis? Find the reason for that and you will find the motive. Find the motive and you are on your way to finding the murderer."

231

"Yes, but… I believe the liquor we are seeking is absinthe. Not only is it a very potent alcohol, but it also contains wormwood, a powerful narcotic. I am sure the hospital report will confirm the presence of this. So, whoever it was plied Brown with absinthe at some point. They then took him up the hill and sweated him on the trails until he became thirsty. Then Brown drank from a mountain stream. Absinthe, if water is added soon enough after ingestion, is understood to inebriate again. It would therefore be far easier to topple him from a cliff, while making it look like he was drunk."

"Perhaps. But why? And who knew him well enough to ply him with alcohol? Where did he get the absinthe from?"

"Are you sure it was not on the inventory Anton made of Brown's room?"

"Positive."

"Absinthe is a particularly French drink. The Swiss like it, too, but it is most fashionable in France. I have a friend, Oscar, who started with the same publishers, Lippincott's, as I. He is particularly partial to it."

"So you are saying you are looking for someone who, perhaps, came via France to Switzerland?"

"I don't know. I cannot narrow it down like that."

He paused and fixed me with a look. "Holmes can."

I winced. "Holmes is a fictional character. He does what I want him to do."

"Be that as it may… your theory rules out all the Italians, Germans and, according to this, Croats…"

"Holloway, I must admit I never suspected the Pivcevics anyway. I still cannot subscribe to your theory."

"Oh, you cannot subscribe, eh? Do you know what I think? I think that you cannot subscribe to my theory simply because it is mine."

"No, Holloway."

"Do you know, I am beginning to wonder… Did you come via France?"

232

"As it happens, yes, I did."

"And you are English like Brown."

"Irish. Whereas you are English, if you insist on pursuing this tack."

"Yes – but I did not become obsessed with some half-baked story about pipe tools."

"We have discussed this…"

"You may think you have discussed it. However, it is curious, is it not, doctor, that the one thing upon which your whole theory hinges appears, as if by magic? And yet the only person that searched the pockets and made the inventory of his personal effects in the church was you."

"You saw them…"

"I saw nothing, Doyle. You pulled them out like a magician in the dim light from oil lamps, called them out to me and replaced them immediately, before I had the chance to confirm them with you by sight. What would it involve to palm the tool and slip it into your own pocket? What would it involve to take this mysterious and, frankly, convoluted theory to extremes? I tell you what it would involve… someone who wanted to throw the real detectives off the scent."

"Now, Holloway…"

"I put it to you, doctor, that you are more involved in all of this than you make out. Although I cannot prove it yet, I will. Yes… it all makes sense, now. Absinthe, my eye! No wonder you have been so keen on not wishing suspicion to fall upon the Croat couple. The couple, you may remember, with the albatross of the ouzo stopper hanging around their necks. You do not want them suspected because, somehow or other, you are involved. If they are dragged down, you will be dragged down with them." He leaned towards me over the table and his eyes glinted ominously. "Just what exactly, doctor, is your game?"

I began to wonder whether I should have pushed him off the mountain when I had the chance.

He sat back again. "Let me list a second string of evidence that has, little by little, been accumulating as I have been observing your work." He settled in his seat, thrust his legs out before him and drew, once again, upon his by now slobbery pipe. He inspected the ceiling as he did so and, with no urgency, commenced to enumerate.

"One. You do not wish to examine the body. At least when I am present. Two. You overset an oil lamp, which ran the risk of cremating any evidence. Of course, you could blame me for this. I do not doubt my insistence on your continuing meant that I reacted in an unfortunate manner. However, it would have taken very little for you to use my frustration to turn the whole business to your advantage and tip the lamp over. Three. You are deliberately obstructive towards any theories that I propose and, indeed, have repeatedly refuted my concerns over the Croats. Four. You offer obscure and ultimately insupportable ideas regarding certain artefacts such as pipe knives. Five. You search the hotel's office, without permission, for goodness only knows what... Yes, do not bother to goggle at me and bluster, Doyle, Eva noticed you had been in there, too. She's told the village. What else is there? Oh yes. Five..."

"Six."

"Six... you become lost in a fog and claim you were shot at – or perhaps you had another assignation as yet undisclosed? Did you deliberately engineer a falling out with me upon the cliff top just so that you could cast the pipe knife down the abyss? Did you, in fact, Doyle, meet up with Brown yourself and kill him, and somehow acquire that tool as part of the process of deflecting any suspicion from you?"

"This is patently absurd."

"No, Doyle, elementary."

"You were with me throughout the day that Brown died..."

"Not after we had all retired for the evening."

"But he was surely dead by then?"

"How do you know?"

"I don't. But the post-mortem report should confirm it."

"Should…?" He barked a short sharp dismissive laugh. "Of course, I have no proof, no absolute evidence, Doyle, but you should know that I am on your trail. And if you had even an ounce of decency in you, you would do best to confess it all and allow me to hand you over to the Swiss police when they arrive."

"Outrageous. You have now entirely taken leave of your senses."

"A shame. I had rather hoped that you would make matters easy for all of us. You shall be brought to book either way – and this way would have been so much more dignified."

I stood and jostled my chair aside. The action caused the others around us to turn and stare. "Acquire your evidence if there is any. Of which, I can assure you, there is none."

I looked around me. It felt as if the entire village were watching me. It would not be putting too fine a point upon it to say that there was perhaps suspicion in their eyes. There appeared also to be resentment… dislike… even menace. I had dismissed Francesca's earlier warnings, being confident that Father Vernon would quickly be able to rebuild the villagers' trust in me. Now I was not so sure, a sense of deep unease fell over me.

I hastened out of the café and stood on the street gulping in crisp night air. I felt dizzy, betrayed, baffled.

How on earth was I going to weather this storm? For weather it I would have to try. Whatever had been said, had been said. The thoughts had been thought. The connections made.

Absurd, preposterous.

Yet although I could argue every point, the popular mind is prone to fantasies and misconceptions. These rapidly become fact and are almost impossible to dislodge once they have set in the collective conscious, hard as igneous rock.

I made for my hotel. In the reception area I encountered Eva, returned at last. She glanced up with a hunted look. My presence did not offer her any comfort. It was plain that she too viewed me with distrust, even distaste.

"Eva…"

"Do not speak to me, please, doctor."

She had been crying.

"I thought you should know Holloway has been…"

"Do not talk to me about Mr Holloway. Now… if you will excuse me…" She rushed off into the office and closed the door firmly.

I stood there for some moments, finally utterly overwhelmed.

Eventually I retreated to my room. I stepped out onto my balcony.

Night had long fallen. The mountains could be distinguished as Prussian blue against a navy blue sky. The stars looked like the living room lights of a million hillside cottages, reaching back across an infinitely expanding landscape. The actual living room lights of the remote cottages, speckled across the opposite side of the valley, looked like stars. An alpenhorn began its mournful mellifluous moan. It sang a forlorn tune that wandered the lonely valleys in search of a home.

Sixteen

The next morning, moving rather stiffly after my bout with Hugo, I arose, washed, dressed and then sought consolation in the view: the gleaming mountains, the wide blue skies, the constant sun. However, I was still angry. I unwisely called to mind my interview with Holloway the previous evening. I ran through the conversation again and again. I inspected the whole interview from every angle. This naturally served to provoke me more. I finished my ablutions and dressed. In doing so, I sought to distance myself from all that might have vexed me. This enabled me to slip into a far more positive and determined frame of mind, and to clarify things, rather than wallow in self-pity and resentment.

My thoughts now ran thus. If Holloway had felt it was important he take over the case, what else had he done? That is to say, what else might he have done to engineer a situation whereby he was in the position to take the case over? This led to a second question. If he were capable of such behaviour, was he capable of murder? I got no further than that. For, I reasoned, if I had been in his company most of that fateful day, then he, too, had also been in my company. It would be a relatively simple matter at some point to address the issue and bring my innocence out into the open. Although I confess I was presently at a loss to know when that precise point would come.

A further aid to my release from doleful thoughts was that a telegram, slit, had been pushed under my door during the night. It was from the hospital and confirmed that the injuries sustained by Brown were consistent with a fall of the kind that he had experienced. It went on to state that the injuries had been sustained while he was still alive, and that they had brought about his demise. There were no other injuries of note. Also confirmed was the fact that he had ingested a significant amount of anise-seed and alcohol. The report did not speculate whether the two were possibly linked. Most revealingly, a trace of wormwood was also found. This confirmed, as far as I was concerned, that what I had smelt on his lips that night in the chapel of rest was absinthe and not ouzo. Unless, of course, there was a brand of ouzo which also used wormwood as an ingredient.

The most interesting thing about all this information, however, was that it no longer meant as much to me as it might once have done. I was at war with Holloway, and whatever conclusions he was reaching, rightly or wrongly, I would henceforward stubbornly plough my own furrow. I noticed that I did not even feel any sense of self-righteousness at this evident exoneration of at least part of my theories. It was just an item of fact that I could store away and put together with other evidence gathered as I continued my own investigation.

I was just reaching for my smoking things, when the door received a light knock. With a sigh, I called for whomever it was to enter. Mevrouw van Engels joined me on the balcony. She sat in my little wicker armchair across from my little wicker table. She had a weal on her left cheekbone. It was livid and fresh.

"What happened to your face?"

"It is nothing. An accident. Really, an accident."

That second insistence that it was an accident caused my suspicious faculties to prick into life. "Was it your husband?"

"No."

"Then who? Werner, after I saw the two of you last night?"

Her eyes flickered off down to her left and then returned to engage mine. "It was an accident. Say no more about it. It is not important."

"How did it happen?"

"An accident, I tell you."

"Mevrouw van Engels, I do not know what is going on and I am sure that you do. You should be aware that whether you know it or not, you wish to tell me. If you did not, you would not have come here. Not with your face marked with the obvious product of some sort of violence. You need sympathy, help, and some way out of the morass in which you find yourself. I can offer all three. Perhaps not a solution, but a path. But I cannot begin to put what I can do into your hands unless we are perfectly frank with one another." I looked at her. She was meeting my gaze on equal terms. "So, what is it to be?"

"I do need your help, it is true. But this accident," she touched her face lightly with her fingers, "this is not to do with it. So, I will tell you about my husband."

I considered for a moment and realized that half the truth was at least better than none for the time being. I also reasoned that the other half would most likely follow as a matter of course, by explicit or implicit references.

"Please, proceed."

She nodded gratefully and commenced her tale.

"My husband is a very intelligent, hard-working and kind man. A decent man. Ever since he was a young boy he has studied very diligently and passed all of his examinations with flying colours. He learned from his youth how to work, and work well. This made him, you will understand, a very solitary person – but not inhuman." She paused in order that I might indicate my understanding of this important point, which I did gladly. "We met at university – while I was living with my father, a professor of English – he was a student of mathematics. I sometimes wondered if he married me because marriage was something to add to his things that he felt he needed to achieve in his lifetime. But that is another story."

Or was it the whole story? I thought, but said nothing.

"So, we went on in life. After his graduation, I gave up my work in the library to help him with his research. He would toil away into the early hours. He would not speak a word to me. I would run the family home and call him when I thought it was time he took a little more sustenance. Every day, without fail, he would get up and go straight into his study at about seven o'clock in the morning. He would appear at around midday to spend twenty minutes with me for our lunch, and then he would return to his work. At about six o'clock, he would appear and I would have a cup of fresh coffee and cake ready for him. He would drink and eat and we would exchange the day's news. Or, rather, I would inform him of everything that was going on in the world. Then he would return to his work for another two hours, after which time we would have our supper. He would then either read an academic or mind–improving book, or he would play the piano. He was a very accomplished musician, doctor."

"Was?"

"He has stopped these last two years – and you should know why."

"Pray, continue."

"You see, he is, as I have explained, a very clever man. A terribly clever man. All his life he has been told this; his work and its results have confirmed this. Although on the outside he was very humble, hard–working and placid, inside I believe his achievements were eating away at him. Gnawing at his very soul. I mean to say... how could anyone so successful not feel a sense of pride and a growing self–belief?"

I agreed.

"And yet, he was a solitary man. Oh yes, we would talk, but we would never talk about his work, his achievements. I thought that he was a remarkably modest human being and admired him. I did not know that inside he was brooding. Lusting after greatness. Striving for more and more achievements. Can you understand? He was driven by vanity. Everybody believes they have a unique part to play in this world. Everybody. But if that means you will destroy everything else in your life to do this one unique thing, well, it can be a good thing – or it can be very bad."

I understood. An introspective fellow driven by success to greater and greater heights – and no one to provide a balancing, objective perspective because he did not rub up against anyone else to any significant degree except his wife, who was totally compliant. No one, then, to keep him rooted in reality, normality.

"And then it happened." Her voice was thick with emotion.

"What happened?"

"The news came through from Sweden. The project that he had been working towards, for seemingly his whole adult life; the project upon which he had built his every waking moment, for which he had received every encouragement, plaudit and help from the university; the project that he was, perhaps, just a few weeks away from completing... it was announced that a French mathematician had had a breakthrough as a result of a mathematical competition. Everything that my husband had incarcerated himself in his study for over those many long years, had worked his fingers to the bone and his brain to a standstill over – all gone. Ashes. Wasted. Pointless."

"He believed his life had no further value?"

"It was not to do with feeling anything, doctor. He was too numb to feel or think. It was fact and it destroyed him. All his work had been directed towards this one target. Apart from a few scraps of philosophical argument and an item or two of inspired calculus, there was nothing salvageable from the wreck of his life's work."

"Did he know that this... Frenchman... was approaching the same conclusions as he?"

"Of course. All these people were constantly in communication with one another. Each group had different orbits: Paris, Heidelberg, Cambridge, Leiden, Utrecht, Yale, Oxford, Berlin. Each had their own little communities, and occasionally information was even slipped between the groups and this advanced the work for everybody. But you do not understand academic rivalry. It becomes a matter of honour to be the first and bring tribute – and funds – into your university."

"An honour or an obsession?"

"When you spend your life on one task, do you want it all to go to waste?"

It was a terrible tale. No one who engages upon a life's work like this starts out wishing to be famous. But as time goes on, and one battles away in one's ivory tower, the only true motivation must be to either simply complete the task and be grateful that the work is done, or to set your name in stone in the history books. The danger comes when you contain both within yourself and do not seek a perspective from those around you – especially your loved ones. Van Engels's relationship with his wife was very probably secure and loving in its own way. Yet he had devoted himself so much more fully to his mistress, academic achievement, that they were unable to share the most personal matters with each other. Holmes swore he would never marry, as it would distract him from his life's work. I began to wonder: no matter how laudable – how wise or sustainable was that position in practical terms?

"When did this happen?"

"Two years ago. The eruption came in the form of the results of a mathematical competition announced a year before by the king of Sweden and Norway to celebrate his sixtieth birthday. My husband entered it with a will, as did many others from various universities – some helping others, some attempting it alone."

"This is the competition the Frenchman won?"

She nodded. "At first the shock was so great it was as if our lives had exploded. Desolation lay all around us for weeks, months. Despair, depression, tantrums, arguments. I hated it. You know, even now I am not allowed to mention that Frenchman's name, or discuss what it was that he did. Even with people like you, out of my husband's hearing."

"It really is desperate. I suspect that it was a matter of either proving or disproving a classic mathematical proposition. Euclid's. A long-established anomaly that had not been resolved over many years."

"No. It was not this achievement that so destroyed my husband. Others had shown that Euclid's fifth proposition was impossible to prove some years ago. This was a revelation in itself and set many academics on the particular path my husband, among others, set out upon. No, the significant development was the Frenchman's winning memoir on the three body problem in celestial mechanics. It included the first description of homoclinic points, chaotic motion and the utilization of the idea of invariant integrals…"

I must have looked blank. She pitied me. I was an intellectual disappointment. Imagine anyone not knowing about homoclinic points, chaotic motion, and invariant integrals!

"It is not important."

Though clearly it was.

"What is important is that it has meant that nothing could therefore be as constant as we once thought." She explained in as simple terms as she could. She had been a librarian at the university. She was intelligent and she was interested in this work, I could see. There were plans for women to claim a hall of learning of their own at Oxford. She would be an ideal candidate.

"What was the more sensational matter was to begin to show how, therefore, mathematics was not a perfect science after all. For hundreds of years, since the Enlightenment, people had held that scientific truth was beyond the possibility of doubt. That the logic of science was infallible. If scientists were sometimes mistaken, this was assumed to be only from their mistaking the rules. Because of the proposition that mathematics is, in fact, imperfect, the cornerstone of scientific certainty was now uncertain. Where could we turn if a perfect science like mathematics had logical, demonstrable contradictions?"

"And this Frenchman has built upon all of this and begun to reach the conclusions your husband was racing towards?"

"Yes, coming to the conclusion that those things once held scientifically true and unalterable are only choices among many choices. Geometry, for example, is therefore not true, merely advantageous. One applies certain principles, depending on one's perspective and how convenient it is to one's particular scientific pursuits. So, too, the conventional understanding of space and time. They will have many ways of being measured and none is necessarily more true than another. This… man… is proving, step by inexorable step, that there can be any number of facts, each of which, within reason, may account equally well for observations in experiments. The more general a fact is, the theory goes, the more useful it is. Those which can be applied many times are more useful than those which have little chance of being used again."

I confess, I was a little confused by this explanation. I determined to sit myself down at some time, set out for myself what the arguments were, and study them. Nevertheless, what she seemed to be describing was a mortar shell among the massed ranks of scientific thought. All science depended on there being certain constants. If we could not depend on them, then everything we had based scientific thought upon to date had to be utterly rethought. Astounding.

"And your husband was as close to this explosion in ideas as this Frenchman was?"

"And others. Either in his camp or in other camps. To cap it all, the memoir with which that man won the prize had an error in it. But that error only served to help him advance his other theories further. My husband did not make such an error. Because of that, he did not reach the other conclusions as quickly." All at once, she flushed. "And I should not be discussing this with you."

I waved her concerns away. "I will not tell anyone. But surely, there is some use to which he could put all that he has done?"

"As I said, we looked at that and discovered only a few scraps were fit for the purpose. You will understand that to reach this conclusion meant going over exactly the same ground. Once that work is published, what use is it for another to have identical material?"

"Then he must advance from this point. You say what has been unleashed is a whole new way of thinking. He has a head start in this?"

"You do not understand, doctor. His morale is non-existent. He does not care. He cannot be bothered to even consider the prospect.

We heard of some work going on here and there: looking into the nature of time and space, celestial mechanics and further work into chaotic motion – wonderful, fascinating, pioneering work – but my husband discounted it immediately. He did not wish to get his hopes up, he said; to dedicate himself to some future 'pie in the sky', as you might call it, only to have it all crushed again at some later date." She became urgent. "I am afraid, doctor. For him, for me, for us. A Dutch friend working in England told us of this place; you English hold Switzerland close to your hearts as a retreat, a place to come for one's health. We liked the idea – far away from anywhere. We could forget everything and try to mend our wounds. Try to put some distance between us and all of the past. But I believe, when we get back, the university will no longer require his services. Oh yes, he could carry on teaching. But research was his life. He has barely put pen to paper since that awful day last year when we discovered that we had lost the race."

"And he has grown increasingly angry and bitter since then?"

"It has taken root and proliferated like some form of ground elder."

"What about his literary ambitions?" I scraped around to expose at least some chink of light in this woeful tale.

She regarded me in the way someone who conceals a guilty secret might look. "He is very angry with you."

"Me?"

"Because he gave you his work and you have not read it."

"Not read it? I have not had the time!"

"I should think it a courtesy when someone gives you something they value highly to show them at least a little respect and respond as quickly as you can."

"Madam, I have had other matters with which to contend; not all of them frivolous. In fact, I might even venture to say that none of them are frivolous."

She stood up, informed me that I had made her feel as though she were entirely incorrect to hold her husband's interests so close to her heart, and bade me good morning. I saw her to the door and closed it behind her. It was madness, of course, that she should so readily leap to her husband's defence after having spent the greater part of our interview explaining how insecure he was. Yet that insecurity was the reason why she was also so protective of her mate. It was, from her perspective, yet another assault on the sensitivities of an already fragile human being. How was she to know what it was that might simply tip the poor, beleaguered fellow over the edge and down into the abyss of self-destruction? Alcoholism, vagrancy, insanity or suicide lay just at the bottom of that particular descent.

In my experience, such foul and ravenous beasts are stalking just the other side of any door seeking to devour whomever they may.

Despite my indignation at being expected to jump the very moment anyone chooses to snap their fingers, I could not in all conscience blame her. She was terrified for her husband whom she loved, despite his ill-use of her. Probably beyond all words and all reason. Who could have borne such a burden as she had otherwise?

My breakfast arrived, courtesy of Anton. I offered him a "Good morning". He endeavoured half-heartedly to return it before exiting. Or perhaps, more accurately, quarter-heartedly, or even eighth-heartedly.

For my part, I fell to my wicker table with its lusty rustic contents with a relish. As I commenced my breakfast, I believe I may even have hummed.

Having eaten well and savoured the view, I tripped lightly down to the breakfast room. My intention was to establish who was present and enjoy a cup of coffee with them. As I made my way, my subconscious lobbed a further question into my head. Having cleared it of unhelpful thoughts, my mind was now a vessel brimming with new, challenging and vigorous ideas.

I reached the breakfast room door. I could hear voices. They were speaking in that low, melancholy tone one encounters when breakfasting at a hotel. All of a sudden, I realized that I simply could not face my fellow-guests after all. I was far too chipper and eager to press on with my affairs for all of that nonsense. So, veering away at the last moment, I set my course towards the hotel lobby and the main street beyond.

At the telegraph office, I composed my telegram. I told Flemyng that I was interested in knowing the current cricket score and then I asked (a) is Richard Holloway an Old Alleynian; that is to say, an old boy of Dulwich College? And (b) is Richard Holloway a member of Blackheath Rugby Club? I then made my way back to the hotel.

As I returned along the main street, I happened to glance up. I glimpsed Frau von Denecker. She was standing stiff and still upon her balcony, leaning upon her cane. The breeze caught the folds in her black silk gown and ruffled them like wavelets on a lake. It was as though she had been waiting for me; as if I had been meant to be drawn to her. She turned her head slowly and, from her elevated position, looked down at me. She lifted her thin white hand and, in a simple, efficient gesture, beckoned me to her. I nodded and entered the hotel while she stepped back inside her room.

"The door is open."

I was received with her customary exemplary courtesy, although this time there was no tea party.

"Would you care for something to drink?"

"No, thank you."

"Well, doctor," she betrayed in her eyes a glint of the mischievous but spirited young woman she would once have been, "you have become the talk of the village."

"So I understand. It is all false, of course."

"What is?" She cocked her head like a hawk surveying a coney.

I considered for a moment and decided that in the present urgent circumstances the bold approach would bring the swiftest results. "I realize, Frau von Denecker, that you may know more than I, or that I may know more than you. I am happy to tell you

247

much, but probably not everything. I am aware, in a situation where I am at liberty to trust no one implicitly, that discretion must perforce prevail."

"You may rest assured, doctor, that everything you choose to tell me will remain in the strictest confidence. I should warn you, however, that I may or may not elect to use any information you do choose to present to me, at least the material substance of it, as I see fit."

"How you may use what I tell you, why you may feel constrained so to do, and why even you may feel you have an opportunity to use it, I could not begin to guess. However, I will entrust the information I shall impart to you within those clear terms."

If we were on opposing sides, which in the grand scheme of things we probably were, I believed that these particular circumstances put us on the same side. I took her, therefore, at her word – and she at mine.

I proceeded to tell her much of what had occurred over the past few extraordinary days. Brown, the séance, Holloway, my investigation, our falling out. I did not tell her about our raid on the church, the wires, my encounters with Francesca and Hugo. I did not even tell her about whom I or Holloway suspected and the clues that we had found. Nor did I expound upon my theories – for fear of ridicule, mostly.

I concluded by saying that Father Vernon was supposed to be attempting to re-establish my good name. That he had advised me to continue about my business as if nothing were amiss. However, there was no doubt that the village had nonetheless implicated me in the whole Brown affair. I was concerned that matters had gone too far to warrant such an approach any longer, not least because the police could make their appearance any time now. Consequently, I ran the risk, no matter how slight, of arrest by that very same implication.

She had studied me carefully throughout my deposition.

"Hmm," she said. "It is unfortunate, doctor, that you did not feel comfortable enough with me to tell the whole story, but...

no, doctor, there is no need to protest, nor is there any need to explain… it is quite understandable. You have been subsumed by the most trying of circumstances. It must be hard for you to know how far you may reveal anything without prejudicing your own well-being. There are times, doctor…" she continued playfully, and tapped me upon the knee, "… when circumstances outstrip one's ability to prove one's integrity. At which point it is more important to *not* react than to react. Father Vernon is correct. You should do nothing. That is…" she looked at me with sudden seriousness, "… nothing except retreat."

"Retreat? Do you mean leave? Return to England?"

"Doctor, I have no doubt whatsoever that you are completely innocent in all of this. I trust you as, indeed, I hope you trust me."

"I do."

"And thank you for that. However, I can tell you that all the great disasters of history have been brought about by pride and stubbornness. That you have no intention of 'running away' as you probably would describe it, is an entirely laudable, even gallant, outlook. However, what is speaking to you, and in you, is pride. Pride that you refuse to be defeated. Pride that you believe yourself capable of resolving these complex matters. Pride that you are a well-known novelist and, assuredly, will become even more well known in time. If you are innocent — and I say again that you are — then to leave and return to your country, your home, your family may leave a whiff of scandal in Switzerland, but it will remain in Switzerland. Get clear of all this nonsense. Put your life back to its rightful degree of normality. End fitful and futile speculation and make a stand."

"A stand? I thought that you were advocating retreat?"

"A stand in the sense that you are saying to everyone here: I do not care for your petty intrigues and your small-town preoccupations and misconceptions. I am free and I assert my right to continue so to be."

I had to admit, put like that, it seemed to be quite an easy and comprehensive solution. Just walk away, wash my hands of the village. To make the bold statement that I am not interested in what

249

people think. I know who I am and that person is taking control of his own destiny.

"But is that not pride also? Or, at the very least, arrogance and effrontery towards this gentle people? To say to them, 'I do not care for you – I am above all of this'?"

She considered this. "You are quite right. Yet it is not to be executed as a demonstration of pride. It is to be undertaken with humility. You are asserting your right to be free and reject any constraints forced upon you by society's arcane practices and mores."

"Yet *you* do…"

"When it suits me, it is true. And when it does not, I do not." She unleashed a dazzling smile that spoke of years of apparent conformity hiding a lifetime of rebellion. Perfect behaviour offset by flashes of contrariness. "Believe me, stubbornness is when one refuses to assess the reality of the moment and thus choose the appropriate times at which to exercise one's unorthodoxy."

"I must admit it has all become rather tiresome."

"I am sure that it has. My sympathies."

I stood up, took her hand and kissed it, as warmly as anyone would kiss such a hand in such circumstances. "I am grateful to you for your counsel, Frau von Denecker. If I may, I shall spend the rest of the day considering my position." I turned to leave.

"Doctor."

I turned back; she was sitting there, elegant, correct, unfathomable.

"I am glad to have met you."

"And I you," I responded, gratified. "Whatever I decide, I trust that it shall not circumscribe our relationship."

"Whatever you decide – it shall not."

SEVENTEEN

I made for my hotel and my quarters. I had a great deal to think about, and yet I was unable to apply myself to those pressing thoughts. I had barely entered my third-floor sanctuary when there came a meaty thudding upon my door. I opened it and there, framed as if he were a full-length portrait of *The Master of the Hunt*, was Werner. He had come complete with shotgun, broken and pivoted upon his right arm. He had what appeared to be a ream of paper clutched in his left hand.

"Herr Doctor," he squeezed himself into my flimsy wicker balcony chair, "I have come so that you will read my play. I was just about to go out hunting, when I thought I would see if you were in. I will go hunting after you have read this."

"I am awfully sorry, Günther, my dear fellow…" As I ventured to complete my refusal, he slapped the manuscript upon the table. He then jabbed a thick finger down onto it, as if intent upon driving the sheaf of paper right through the surface and onto the balcony floor.

"*Nein*. I have heard how you refused to read the professor's work. This you will not do with me, please. You will read it now. I will watch."

I sank slowly into the opposite chair, only too aware of the sulky gleam of devoutly polished gunmetal nestling still in the crook of the Bavarian's right arm. It was eyeing me slyly from its break, like a wolf. It was waiting, no doubt, for any excuse to snap together and explode in my face.

I took up the manuscript and began to read, turning the pages and soaking up the dialogue. It was, as he had intimated earlier that week, written in German. Although I was not fluent in the language, I was thankfully reasonably proficient.

It was not as ham-fisted as I had imagined. Surprisingly, it was a tale of great charm and sensitivity. By turns thoughtful and inventive, it spoke lyrically of a young hunter (naturally), a serving girl, a remote hunting lodge and unrequited love. The piece was written in the flowing poetic style currently out of fashion, but was all the more engaging for all that. The piece ended in tragedy, with the servant girl being accidentally shot by the young hunter who, subsequently, overcome with grief and remorse, terminates his own existence.

I did not read every last word and stopped often either to compliment the author upon a well-constructed scene, or to offer advice as to how best to approach a technically difficult structural point. We sat there for over an hour and a half – I engrossed in my reading, he solemn, earnest and visibly encouraged when I occasioned to commend him upon his craft.

At the end of it all, I felt that I had begun to understand Werner better. I always find this when I read another's work. Often I can evaluate a writer's personality, proclivities and preconceptions through the words they write. I can tell whether I would like them if I met them. Werner was complex. There were dark recesses in his life, as with us all. But he was also, at times, sensitive and very humane. Most of all, I could see he cared about people passionately. His boorish predilection for violence against woodland fauna did not override all other considerations. Whether he could haul anyone up a brae and cast them callously into an abyss, on the evidence of his manuscript, was another question. It was seemingly beyond him. Having said that, what we all may do in momentary fury is something else entirely. Murder trials throughout the world turn on fixing the precise moment that the act of murder occurred. Counsel argue this question among themselves, and before judge and jury. Is the act of murder, no matter by whom it is perpetrated, an instance of a moment's insanity? No matter how cold-bloodedly one plots, the actual event of terminating a human life means that the perpetrator must, necessarily, have taken leave of their senses. So the argument runs.

Stevenson believes this to be the case. In Jekyll and Hyde, he explores this hidden potential in us all. We all seek to become superhuman. We all believe we have a destiny. But in our pursuit of determining our calling, do we run the risk of following the wrong path and end up unlocking the monster in us all? On the other hand, there are many academics who nowadays believe that evil is inherent. We are either born with the propensity for wrongdoing or we are not. They believe that this inclination is evident in our facial features, and even the length and characteristics of our limbs. There has been much extensive research in this area.

And then, of course, we are different people in different relationships. We can appear a fool to one person and a hero to others. Like a consummate actor, we are able to adjust our personality to accommodate the person we are talking to; to conform to their image of us. This alchemy could easily unlock whatever evil may or may not be lying dormant inside any individual.

I looked across briefly at Werner. Yes, he could slip, just as easily as may any of us.

Having achieved a degree of intimacy with the Bavarian, through discussing something as precious and painstaking as a manuscript born of his spiritual, creative soul, I felt emboldened enough to address another matter that had been occupying my thoughts.

"Günther."

"Yes, Herr Doctor?"

"May I speak frankly?"

"You may."

"Mevrouw van Engels. When I left her with you to go and track down her husband, she was unmarked. When I next saw her, she had collected an abrasion on her face. Do you know anything about this?"

His face assumed an expressionless aspect. His eyes became as flat, dark and emotionless as an ancient furnace pond deep in the Sussex Weald. I recognized this emptying. It was the face of contumacy. The eyes betrayed a lie. That is to say, liars do not realize that this studied "innocence" is the strongest evidence of the exact reverse.

"*Nein.*" He stood abruptly, gathered his masterpiece, bid me good-day and left. This was all done, it seemed, in one simple, flowing movement that left me barely able to raise myself from my seat as a courtesy towards a departing guest.

"Well," I said to myself out loud. "Well, well, well," I continued as I pottered around my room, tidying this and that for no apparent reason. I was trying to gather my thoughts in order that I may make either head or tail, or perhaps both, of Werner's curious, precipitous departure. It occurred to me a moment later that he had been looking over my shoulder during the course of his lie. Looking over my shoulder would mean looking at the balcony next to mine. A balcony attached to the van Engelses' room. I stepped outside and noted that there was nobody there; in evidence, at least. That there might have been someone there was, naturally, a possibility. That they had heard me ask my question would therefore also be a possibility. Although there could also be another reason why Werner had felt it necessary to leave as quickly as possible. On the one hand, I had been reading, and commenting on, his manuscript. On the other, I had not yet begun to peruse van Engels' red ribbon-wrapped stories. My Bavarian friend might conceivably have felt, if he had glimpsed a van Engel on their balcony, that he had jumped the queue.

I made my way downstairs to order lunch in my room. I did not feel like facing anyone over the dining room table. I needed time and space to think things through. I hoped, as I went down and came back up, that I would not encounter anyone, either. In the event, I did not. Anton, in the meantime, had been as distant but as diligent as ever.

My lunch was a surly, solitary affair. I could enjoy neither the good, Swiss mountain food nor the good, Swiss mountain scenery. Preoccupied, I found that I had returned to a fretful state and was unable to make sense of anything again. I wished, most earnestly, that I could receive some sudden "dog that barked in the night" revelation. I longed for an event that would explain all or, at the very least, show me the clear path ahead. Alas, to no avail. As I worked and reworked the details of the past few days over and over again in my mind, I found that they were growing more and more tangled. By the end of my lunch I was exhausted, frustrated and furious both with myself and with the entire situation. Frau van Denecker was right. I would be best advised to simply chuck it all. Throw the whole affair into the air like a deck of cards and walk away, liberated.

I sat and smoked a pipe briefly and then wandered back into my room. Presently I noted a scratching sound, like a mouse behind the skirting. I realized that something was being pushed under my door. I crossed to it and picked it up.

Another telegram.

I inspected it. It had been slit and resealed in the traditional manner. The paper along the bottom was still damp with glue. My fingers trembled slightly as I opened it. I knew that it was from Flemyng and that it would give me at least a start along some of the avenues I was exploring. Once open, the wire confirmed the sender.

The cricket scores. *Now we are getting somewhere*, I thought. *Good for you, Flemyng*.

But my eager expectation was short-lived.

What I had in my hands was simply a stream of ticker-tape, set out on a telegram form, but not broken up. Despite myself, I noted with some amusement that the Swiss clerk had been unable to make head nor tail of them, being English cricket scores, a code in themselves. I consequently had to spend the first fifteen minutes transposing the strips into a recognizable scorecard at my escritoire.

Once I had set out the initial batting scores and bowling analysis in some sort of order, I bent to the task of analysing the first few names and figures. Unusually, they seemed to be the details of an obscure tour match, the visit of a Netherlands team to Yorkshire. The batting order consisted of a list of names such as Eyken, de Haas, de Groot, van den Bosch and van Oosterzee.

I took up my Bible, turned to the Psalms and dallied a little with the figures attached to the names. I quickly found, to my exasperation, that they had no secrets to reveal to me at all.

It was evident, as far as I could tell, that Flemyng had missed the point entirely.

Or he had not come to terms with my cipher at all.

Either way, I felt suddenly very much at a loss as to what to do next. With a creeping desperation, I returned to the figures and wrestled with them, trying to apply my format every which way. None of them produced any fruit.

I cast my pen down upon the blotter and let out a whoosh of air in bitter frustration.

I stood up from my seat and, I confess, in a fit of petulance, flung myself backwards onto my bed. I felt, embarrassing though it is to admit, close to tears. I turned my head to one side and stared unseeingly at the wall for quite some considerable time.

Had Flemyng missed the point entirely? Was he inept? Could I trust him? If I could not trust him… was he implicated in all of this in some way? Were there dark and mysterious forces at work beyond my own superficial understanding of events? Was, perhaps, Whitehall infiltrated by some secret organization bent upon the destruction of the British government? Perhaps even Steen was involved? It would explain much. Brown, possibly, was their agent. He had been discovered and killed. Conceivably Frau von Denecker knew more about this than I understood also. Was she trying to get me out of the way, to avoid having to have me disposed of, just as she had done with Brown? If indeed he had been disposed of on her orders… Was this why Francesca was so keen for me to leave? Had she, as I had had occasion to speculate before, used the subterfuge of a "psychic" message that I was in danger to frighten me into such a course of action?

Had cruel and wilful chance, having thrown me into this cauldron, caused me to contact the very man in Whitehall who needed to know, for the worst reasons, what was going on in Switzerland?

It explained a lot.

I sat up on my bed with a lurch. My heart surged with anxiety. My breath was shallow and I became intensely fearful. I tried to calm myself and retain some sense of perspective. But to no avail. I tried to tell myself that my imagination was running away with me. The mind that had conceived Sherlock Holmes had started to see shadows and hobgoblins where, most probably, there were none. I forced myself to think. To rationalize. But then I slipped back into irrationality and took the last absurd step of my current fixation. Perhaps Sherlock Holmes's spirit had indeed been manifested in this place. Perhaps all the weird and convoluted conspiracies I had conjured up over the past two or three years had been manifested with him. I emitted a whimper of dismay and flopped upon my back again.

It is to the credit of the mind, rather than its owner, that despite my personal alarm and paranoia, it chose to carry on mulling the matter over somewhere down in its deeper recesses while I fiddled away inanely up top. As the time passed, it started to send messages of encouragement and insight up onto the surface of my consciousness. Little signals that said: *Hold hard, old man. Think I've got something. Bear with me, there's a good fellow.* Eventually, my subconscious mind's assiduousness and downright doggedness paid off. Soon after, my superficial self began to listen to the signals being sent repeatedly from below.

Flemyng was no fool. Not according to all the admittedly limited evidence so far. He had said in his last message that he had, eventually, understood what was being asked of him. Therefore, my mind told me, he would have sent what was required. Just in a different form. It was I who was the sluggard when it came to unlocking my own cipher.

So, armed with that logic, I decided to return to the scores and work out exactly what my contact had done.

Sitting at the desk, I gazed at the wire again. What had I called these scores? Obscure. One might also have called them dull and uninteresting. The Dutch do not excel at cricket. This is why they come on tours to play Yorkshire club sides, rather than full-blown national teams. No doubt, one day, being the determined and proud race that they are, they will eventually come up with a side that can compete at the highest level.

Nevertheless, these scores appeared of very little general interest. I began to wonder whether, far from being addled, Flemyng had added an extra dimension to my cipher, so he could cover the tracks and protect me. In short, if the Dutch cricketers would forgive me, he had made the information uninteresting; at least, to the casual reader. Certainly, it was unremarkable. This was definitely the effect that it had on me. Would it have had the same effect upon the person or persons unknown who had decided to read my messages? They would have received this one, begun to unpick it, and then rapidly tired of the task. Or they may have felt it so insurmountable as to be beyond them. Perhaps this was why the glue was still wet? Perhaps it had been passed on to me much more quickly than usual because it had been deemed of no consequence.

It fell to me, therefore, to persevere, and set out every last statistic that Flemyng had forwarded.

After a few more minutes of painstaking endeavour, I found lying before me in scorecard form the remainder of the Dutch match and, much more hopefully, the entire first innings of a Surrey versus Nottinghamshire match at the Kennington Oval. This was more like it, I thought. Steen may well have told Flemyng that I was a Surrey man. This may have been why he had chosen this particular match, and a further clue that I may, at last, be into the substance of the thing.

Surrey vs Nottinghamshire at the Kennington Oval
SURREY 1st Innings

1	R. Abel	b. Shacklock	1
2	Mr W. W. Read	c. Robinson b. Shacklock	16
3	G. A. Lohmann	b. Shacklock	10
4	J. M. Read	run out	45
5	*Mr J. Shuter	c. and b. Shacklock	2
6	R. Henderson	c. Dixon b.Attewell	7
7	W. H. Lockwood	st. Dunn b. Shacklock	0
8	Mr E. C.Streatfeild	b. Barnes	22
9	W. Brockwell	b. Shacklock	5
10	J. W. Sharpe	c. Dunn b. Flowers	17
11	†Mr A. F. Clarke	not out	0
	Extras	Byes	4
Total			129

NOTTINGHAMSHIRE 1st Innings

1	A. Shrewsbury	b. Lockwood	6
2	*Mr J. A. Dunn	run out	12
3	W. Gunn	b. Lockwood	58
4	W. Barnes	c. Lohmann b. Abel	6
5	W. Flowers	b. Lockwood	27
6	F. J. Shacklock	c. Clarke b. Lockwood	3
7	W. Attewell	b. Lockwood	6
8	Mr J. S. Robinson	c. Abel b. Lockwood	10
9	Mr A. O. Jones	b. Lockwood	6
10	H. B. Daft	not out	2
11	†M. Sherwin	c. Brockwell b. Lockwood	0
	Extras	Byes	9
Total			145

Nottinghamshire Bowling

	Overs	Maidens	Runs	Wickets
Attewell	15	2	42	1
Shacklock	16	3	59	6
Barnes	10	4	12	1
Flowers	7	2	12	1

Surrey Bowling

	Overs	Maidens	Runs	Wickets
Lohmann	8	1	20	0
Lockwood	21	7	37	8
Abel	21	6	18	1
Sharpe	17	1	40	0

I took up my Psalms again and began to write out the numbers in the sequence I had put forward to Flemyng, bowlers first. First bowler: Attewell of Nottinghamshire. Good man, as it happened. Number of overs bowled, 15. Number of maidens bowled (overs bowled from which there resulted no score), 2. So that was Psalm 15 verse 2. I then turned to the batting figures. Batsman Abel (Abel by name, able by nature), one run (though not so able on this occasion). I turned to the fifteenth psalm and looked at the first word of the second verse. It was "he".

"Promising, very promising," I muttered under my breath. I continued working through the procedure and found that the scores were producing words that displayed a certain structure and logic; nouns and verbs. It was most encouraging. Moreover, Flemyng had added a wonderful little finesse of his own. I had suggested, to break the cipher up and give it a further irregularity, that Run Outs and Not Outs should not be counted. He, the bright young fellow in Whitehall, had turned that to his advantage and was using those elements as punctuation.

I sat back in my chair and looked at the words I had extracted from the mass of names and figures before me, and which the Psalms had graciously yielded up as fruit of my labours.

He is not/he is/trusteth him not.

The first phrase answered the question *Is Richard Holloway an Old Alleynian?* The second, *Is Richard Holloway a member of Blackheath?* The third was entirely Flemyng's own work and sent a shiver down my spine when I read it. What did Flemyng know? What else had he found out? Or was he merely expressing an opinion from the evidence so far presented to me?

My heart warmed to such a successful, if unnerving, outcome to the whole process. I felt an intense sense of achievement. I sat there, silently thanking that bright fellow over in England, who had so studiously and effectively put my ideas into practice.

My only hope was that whoever was reading these scores did not know enough to realize how false some of the figures were. I also hoped that the Surrey and Nottinghamshire players never got to see the material in front of me. Abel out for a single run, forsooth!

And then I wondered what the true score was.

Unquestionably, there was something amiss about Holloway. Whatever it was, and my cipher did not allow sufficient latitude for that degree of elaboration, it was clear that I was up against a redoubtable adversary. He was plainly unstable. But he had also, it would seem, been invested, or had invested himself, with the skill, ingenuity and lethal guile of Sherlock Holmes. A more volatile mix in a human being I could scarce imagine. Moreover, and perhaps even more dangerously, he was in possession of a number of facts and hypotheses that placed me at the very centre of his murder investigation.

My imagination leapt once more. For a fleeting moment, despite myself, I even began to wonder about my own creation. Did his spirit actually exist? If so, had he been aware during these past few days and weeks that I was discontented with him, to the extent that I was considering plotting his demise? If so, had he taken it upon himself to hunt me down? I shuddered, and shook my head. I tried to cast off such nonsense. Yet somewhere, buried deep within my psyche, the wild fancy clung on. It resisted any effort on my part to dislodge it.

I took out my watch. It was the middle of the afternoon. I closed the shutters and lay down in the darkened room to think. It had been confirmed to me by a hopefully uninterested Flemyng that I should beware my antagonist. This was now my primary consideration. I needed to construct a plan to deal with this information.

However, lying down in a shuttered room in the middle of the afternoon was possibly the least helpful thing I could have done. I often thought through conundrums of work or writing in this manner. On this occasion, though, the hour at which I had chosen to embark upon this particular exercise was also the very hour in which I customarily took my forty winks.

I dozed off.

My awakening was as shocking as it was sudden.

In the blackness of the shuttered room a hand clamped itself over my mouth. At the same time, my chest was crushed, as though somebody was kneeling upon it. Terrified, I found myself unable to breathe.

Panic, which was the next emotion I experienced, has interesting and sudden effects upon the individual. Essentially, adrenaline is created by the body in such volumes that it courses immediately around the system like an electrical charge. This energizes the nerves and muscles which enable one to either fight or flee, according to one's circumstances and needs. It also causes the cardiovascular and pulmonary systems to increase their work rate to an astonishing level. In short, the more my chest was crushed and my breathing passages were obstructed, the more urgently I wanted to breathe. Consequently, in my need to breathe, the more I struggled like a fellow possessed. I began writhing and twisting and emitting yells of distress. Yells which were muffled by the powerful hand that was resolutely fastened across my mouth. The more I felt I was being suffocated, the more I panicked. The more I panicked, the more pressure was borne down upon me. The more pressure, the greater I thrashed about.

Suddenly, in the midst of this tumult, whoever it was spoke.

"Shhh, shhh, shhh, doctor. Be quiet! Be still!"

I realized that had my assailant been of a mind to murder me, he could have easily done so while I dozed. He had no reason to wake me. It followed, therefore, that he was restricting me in this way in order that I would not raise an alarm. It further followed that if I were to survive asphyxiation long enough to discover what it was for which he had awoken me, I had better give him some indication that I did not intend to make a noise, if only he would take his hand from my face. I summoned up every last reserve, suppressed my pressing need to struggle for breath, and compelled myself to lie inert.

The scheme worked. Within a couple of seconds, the pressure upon my mouth relaxed. A couple more seconds and it drew back sufficiently to offer me the chance to inhale. I took a great heaving gulp of air, as if I had just surfaced from twenty thousand leagues beneath the sea. Presently, the pressure upon my chest was also withdrawn. It was indeed a knee. Thankful, I began to feel just a little more comfortable than heretofore. A few moments later and I had recovered sufficient oxygen in my bloodstream to venture a word or two. Or seven.

"You dashed fool! You nearly smothered me!"

"Sorry, doctor. I had to make sure you didn't call out."

The voice came from the region of the shutters. I heard a click as the fastening was turned, and a creak as the panel was swung open. It was still daylight, but the sun was low and colour had already begun to empty from the scenery.

I had been endeavouring to place the voice ever since he had first spoken. Now, framed by the open window, I added the voice pattern to the silhouette.

"Father Vernon?"

"Yes, doctor."

"What in heaven's name are you doing? And why did you have to be so violent about it?"

"Shhh. I will explain all…" He completed opening the windows, and returned to my bedside. I was, by now, sitting up. He drew the ladder-back chair from the escritoire. As he did so, I realized that my workings-out concerning the cricket scores lay higgledy-piggledy beside me on the bed. I gathered them up and shovelled them into my trouser pocket. He brought the chair closer to where I lay, as a visitor beside a patient.

"You have not much time. So you had better listen carefully. They are after you. The Swiss here. I do not trust them. They are likely to take matters into their own hands, if the mood takes them."

"Like they did with Brown?"

"No. I do not believe that was the affair of any villager. In your case, however, I am just certain that here alone, among these remote mountains, where nothing untoward happens, folk come to their own conclusions very quickly. With tragic consequences."

"You cannot believe that this is likely, surely?"

"I have heard about such things occurring once before. Maybe forty years or so ago. But nevertheless… It was an unmarried mother. They did not intend any harm. But the village advanced en masse late at night and, fuelled by beer and preposterous speculation, fell upon the unfortunate woman's house. It became a witch-hunt. Flaming torches lit, they came for her in order to evict her from her home. She took fright, ran, fell down a ravine. She survived, but she lost her child. Such a pitiful tale."

"I would not run."

"On the contrary, that is precisely my point. It is best you leave, or you will aggravate an already volatile situation. Get out of the way; let everyone come to their senses. By all means, return in a week or so. You can give notice that you propose to return. You may then come back with embassy officials so that everything can be done calmly and above board."

I considered the matter. Before I had time to reach any conclusion, Father Vernon spoke again, urgency now creeping into his voice.

"I beg you. Take your money and your travel documents. In Bern you will find powerful friends and lawyers to help you. Here, you are alone."

"Not completely." I looked at him; he smiled. "But where would I go? I cannot go down into the valley for fear of meeting the authorities coming up. And anyway, it is more inhabited, the nearer I get to Interlaken. Word may already be out for me."

"I agree, which is why I brought this." He lifted, from the floor, a satchel.

"Which is…?"

"I have brought a couple of loaves and a flagon of Fendant wine. Don't ask where I got it from. Some cheese, an oilcloth and a thick blanket. Enough provisions for a whole day's walk, rain or shine."

I eyed the leather pack with its shoulder straps. "Won't running away be some kind of admission of guilt?"

"You will not be running away. You will be continuing your holiday elsewhere. They do not know that you know all of this. The only thing they will know for sure is that they did not see you leave. That is all."

"Are you sure that you are not simply trying to escort me off the premises?"

He let out a deep sigh. "The longer we discuss this, the more time we waste… Tell me, my dear fellow, why would I want to get rid of you?"

"I do not know. And I am not likely to know, if that is your purpose."

"Then, if it helps, I shall come with you."

"You?"

"I."

I surveyed him, in his sandals and brown habit. "You are not dressed for a ramble over the mountains."

"All the better. If I were looking like I was going a-wandering, then my own part in this would come under scrutiny. Besides, the habit is useful for all manner of purposes; in this I rejoice that I follow my brother Francis."

His words brought to my mind's eye the founder of his Order. I remember being introduced to St Francis of Assisi at Stonyhurst. He had been named Giovanni – John – by his mother. His father, a wealthy cloth merchant, newly returned from his favourite country, France, renamed him "Francesco", the little Frenchman. Despite his upbringing, *Il Poverello*, the Little Poor One, eventually renounced everything. Inheritance, wealth, comfortable life. He spent the rest of his days wandering the hills and mountains of Umbria in his ragged brown habit and grubby, worn sandals. I looked at the man sitting by my bed. The mendicant life would certainly suit him far better than the one he was currently leading, in my view.

"But won't you be missed in the village?"

"There is a retired priest; I use him as my locum. I have been known occasionally to just suddenly set off for a couple of days. I am something of an enigma in these parts." He smiled ruefully at some memory, the tale of which I suspected would probably never be told. I wondered, though, if it were in any way similar to that of St Francis. Born privileged, well-to-do. Renouncing all to follow God, to follow *Il Poverello*…

I considered all he had told me.

"Thank you so much for your solicitude, Father Vernon. I have to admit, your arguments are most convincing. However, I regret to say I remain unconvinced. Arthur Conan Doyle does not run. He stands and fights. Right is on my side."

"You will not go?"

"I will not go."

He heaved a sigh. "Then, as I see it, you have two further options."

"Which are?"

"Stay and be judged by those not able to judge you fairly. Right may be on your side. But *they* aren't."

"Or…?"

"Lay low, while we think of a better policy."

"Lay low?"

"There are plenty of places around here where you would be safe. Get yourself a little breathing space. This would in turn allow me to create the right conditions into which you may emerge and plead your case in safety. I could perhaps go to the police in the valley on your behalf. If I can engineer it so that your interview is with the police and the police alone, well, then you may be able to convince them of your innocence. Without any excitable rabble-rousers confusing the issue."

It took me no time at all to assess this latest proposition.

"Admirable. Where should I go…?"

Father Vernon described to me a circuitous route right into the centre of the village. He then set off, carrying the satchel he had prepared for me, as if it were his. I followed about a minute later to ensure we were not connected. I stepped out brazenly, as if I hadn't a care in the world. As if I had merely wandered out from my hotel to take the air and would presently return there for my evening meal. Walking as I did in full view of the village, I could not believe that he was genuinely directing me to somewhere safe to hide. Until, that is, I emerged from among the houses into the open space at the centre of the village. Here was common land. I strolled across the sward as one taking a Sunday stroll over South Norwood park. Suddenly, the friar appeared from behind the village hayloft and beckoned me. I made as if to continue, and then sprang to one side, into the shadow of the hut. He thrust me inside with the satchel. Promising to return first thing the following morning, he set off for his church.

I secured the door and climbed up the rough inner ladder to the upper, boarded level. Here was piled bale upon bale of hay and some loose sacking. A short while after, I made my supper and ate it. I was surprised how hungry I was. Having dined informally but well, I arranged for myself a temporary bed with the hay bales and lay down to rest.

I slept the sleep of the just.

Father Vernon returned in the cool light of a grey dawn. The air was misty. But experience told me that the sun would burn that off by mid-morning. Then it would be another kiln-hot day. Were I here for my health, I would have exulted in the notion. As it was, the thought of being choked up in a close, dusty and constricting casserole of a hayloft, my thoughts were less than bright.

He had brought coffee, bread and cheese, and watched me with evident satisfaction as I fell to my breakfast with relish. The coffee was sweet and bitter, and lifted my spirits considerably.

We talked about Holloway. About my belief that the young man probably indulged in opium, in the form of resin chipped and mixed with tobacco and smoked in a pipe. I had thought, in some way, to stimulate my companion with this information. Inform him of certain habits with which he and his community up here in the middle of nowhere were unfamiliar. However, he appeared unperturbed. I realized that he had lived a dozen lives prior to his present incumbency. He would no doubt have encountered such practices elsewhere.

Offering his apologies, he then left again to take care of his parish. He promised a swift return. We needed to explore more fully my options beyond this interim position in which I now found myself.

Having nothing better to do, it was but a short step for me to fall to pondering the nature of Brown's demise itself. If it *were* murder, I wondered, what would have brought it to such a crisis? Find that and one would find the motive. Find the motive and one would be on the way to finding the criminal.

Was there a sexual motive, perhaps? Holloway was right: there was a general innocence to my Holmes stories; asexual. Some, I don't doubt, especially considering my central character's confirmed bachelorhood and need for Watson's manly company, may even have suspected him of homosexuality. This was neither the case nor my intention; although I have no antipathy towards the orientation itself, despite society's prevailing attitude.

Having reached that stage in my train of thought, I was brought up short by another, completely astounding and wholly unbidden, insight.

Anton.

Of course. His particular care and attention upon my and Holloway's arrival was because he thought that he recognized kindred spirits. This was why he had made the unusual suggestion of sharing a room. Why he looked oddly at me when I denied any relationship with my erstwhile companion.

Was that why there had been family tears? Had he, encouraged by my apparently bohemian behaviour, decided to reveal all to his parents? To the detriment of family harmony? Eva would have taken his side.

It was possible, I thought. In fact, it was more than possible. Surely, that was why he had so taken against me ever since? To all intents and purposes I had encouraged him and, in his view, subsequently betrayed him. Betrayed, as he saw it, "our kind"; that is to say, his kind. I determined to broach this subject with him the very next opportunity I had.

I returned to my consideration of Holmes's character as I had contrived it. He was not unlike Father Vernon. A celibate. Someone who put all his psychic and physical energies into his work, his calling. He simply had no time and no desire to apportion any of his life to women on a social basis. Judging by the van Engelses imbroglio, that was perhaps a wise decision.

Before I had come away, I had been reading in my medical journals of the beginnings of exploration into sexuality as a motivator of who we are and why we do things. Aristotle tells us that character is defined by what we do. Could there be a sexual motive for the murderer still waiting around? It was a thin thread, but it was at least a thread.

And, I argued with myself, was there more than just the miscreant's motive to consider? It was important that one should explore the mind of the perpetrator. But one may also be well served by examining the motive of the victim. Why should he put himself in a position whereby he is liable to get himself murdered?

Because he wants to? Because he trusts?

When we explore a person's illness, sometimes in the medical profession we do not always first look for the cause, we look at the symptoms. Then we delve into the root of the problem. After which, we consider how they may have actually acquired that problem. Only by following this process may we discover the actual cause of the illness. Especially if we are not acquainted with that particular illness in the first place.

So then, concerning the anise-seed – absinthe, ouzo, or whatever it turned out to be. How would someone manage to make another person drunk? A person who is unaware that this is the purpose of such drinking?

A man who is, perhaps, captivated by a woman.

This brought me right back to the matter of sexuality. I realized that I needed to know *exactly* who Brown was. Married, single? Confirmed bachelor? Roué? I knew that he had been described as a dry old stick. But that did not mean his private life was not rich with sensuality.

Turning to the murderer, whoever it was might have come with the express purpose of killing him. Whoever it was, if this was the purpose, might not have remained. They might have left immediately, to return to wherever they had come from. Far away. Another country? Another continent, even.

It was too frustrating. All detective fiction relies on a conceit. A conceit that the murderer waits around long enough to get themselves caught. How I hated my bonny, neat stories. All constructs and lies, sleights of hand and *trompe l'oeils*. All designed to misdirect the reader.

Around and around the mulberry bush I went: Why would a murderer wait around to be caught? Examine the motive, I told myself. Why would a victim allow himself to be killed? The murderer either was no longer around or was capable of going to ground. Why would they need to carry on planting clues, as if they were a protagonist in one of my stories? For I believed that was what was happening. It seemed to me that if Brown had been despatched, it had been done perfectly neatly. No loose ends to be tied up. And yet... Here a lost and found ouzo stopper. There a pipe knife in a gully. Here slits in telegrams. There rumours and gossip seeking to have me excised from the equation. Real life just was not like that. Therefore there had to be another reason altogether why I was stumbling on these things. Either I was being given anise-seed rags for a serious purpose, or someone was intent upon making a fool of me.

If it was for a serious purpose, why the anise-seed rags? To put the hounds off the scent, perhaps? What scent? The thing was, I was not on any scent. Perhaps whoever it was did not know this?

On the other hand, what if all this was in order to ridicule me? Why? Because they didn't like me? Reason enough, I supposed. Because they didn't like Sherlock Holmes? Also reasonable. Because they hated both me and my Holmes stories? My success? A stronger reason; starting to get strong enough to amount to a motive. But then, if people don't like someone or something, they simply avoid them or it. Or make it clear that they don't like them.

However, if they hate them, that is different.

Hate has a habit of hiding itself.

A poem of Blake's came to me; about hate. About how hate can be nurtured behind false smiles and a pretence at friendship.

Hate is a very powerful motive. Hate if sunned with smiles and watered with tears can move someone to action. Dislike is generally passive or, if active, motivates a person away from the object of dislike. Hate can become obsessive and verge on mania, or at least overbalance into it.

I sat down on my hay bales and began to compose a list in my mind of all the people who would have hated me for Holmes. Hated me enough to bait me and goad me with these parodies of clues. And then I desisted. The list was simply too long and impossible to compile because of all the anonymous people who may have read my stories and resented me for them.

I tried another tack. I returned to the question: If there were a murderer, why were they still here? Because they lived here? Because they had to be here? Because they wanted to be here?

Round and round... and round... and round the dashed mulberry bush.

I peered out again from my hide. The sun was busy baking the high land. I became aware, in the distance, of the sounds of the hay harvest recommencing. They had finished in my immediate vicinity in the last day or so, and were now working the meadows further up towards the mountains. The swish swish swish of scythes was soothing, rhythmic. They were collecting winter fodder. They had to keep the animals fed through the long, dark, snowed-in months. Otherwise there would be no milk, no meat for the community. It was seemingly unimportant to make hay while the sun shone, and yet it was vital to the whole food chain.

I thought of Hugo. And then of Francesca.

And so the long morning wore on.

I listened to the church clocks striking the quarters, halves and hours. I peered through the crack between the wooden walls, and watched the cats in pursuit of mice and voles in the recently shorn meadow.

In the distance, along the main street, I believed I could see Marie pushing Plantin in his rolling chair. I imagined them smiling in the clean, warm, alpine summer's day. How I longed to be just strolling along with them, taking the air.

I thought of my clean, comfortable, welcoming room, with its breakfasts on the balcony overlooking the shining mountains.

It was too much for me.

I felt lonely, desperate, lost and exiled.

I wanted Touie. I wanted my family. I wanted to be home.

For the first time in years, I wept.

Father Vernon returned. He noticed my sombre, subdued appearance, but I did not apprise him of my current melancholy. Instead, I told him of some of my thoughts about motive and asked if he could do a little investigating, since I was hamstrung by this hayloft. I did not know what he may find, or how he may begin to go about such enquiries.

"That is, if you do not mind making such enquiries?"

"You need to know."

"And what if they discover you have been helping me, and throw you into jail?"

Father Vernon shrugged and smiled gently. "I am a friar. A cell is a cell, be it institutional or monastic. I can pray anywhere. And in the end I will be found innocent."

"Surely you would be charged with helping me evade justice, as they would perceive it…?"

"I would be found innocent, because you are. God will provide. And even if he does not, he is still God."

With those reassuring words, and leaving me with some bread, cheese and water – prison fare – he left.

I was still not certain that he would not return with a policeman or two. But I refused to allow myself to think those thoughts. I ate my lunch and drank the water. It was growing, as I suspected it would, unbearably hot.

I had finished the water. The inside of my mouth started to taste like chalk. Shortly my lips would crack as a riverbed in drought. Worst of all, considering my need for secrecy, I couldn't smoke my pipe. Although that was just as well, bearing in mind the fire hazard a few dry hay bales and a desiccated wooden structure represented.

I looked out through one of the cracks again.

Eva was heading towards the hotel. In my confinement, I began to remember the first day. Those few, precious moments of happiness, that sense of freedom and friendship before the world turned sour and I was left blundering about in this present fog and turmoil. I remembered the alpine meadows, sweet with fragrance, and tried to recall the honey smell of the edelweiss...

"I need to get into the village," I said.

Father Vernon had returned, thankfully, with some more water. "Why?"

"To stretch my legs, to smoke, to feel human and not a prisoner..."

I also knew I needed to telegraph Flemyng and ask him to establish for me who exactly Brown was. But since I had told no one of my Whitehall contact or my wires, and had determined to keep it a secret, I did not mention this. Should anyone ever let slip Flemyng's name or cricket scores or some such privy information, I would know immediately that it was they who had read my wires.

Father Vernon surveyed me. He had uncovered nothing of note with his own recent prowling around. I do not doubt he thought I was completely mad to consider venturing back into the village. I, a wanted man. But he also understood that I may be more able to discover things than he. He also realized, I am sure, my burning need to engage in some activity. I would simply go mad, cooped up as I was.

His eyes lit up and his mouth shaped into a crescent smile. "I will see what I can do... I will be back shortly."

I sat on the hay and peered again through a crack between the wooden planks of the loft. I watched Father Vernon leave, framed by the backdrop of clouds bubbling up around the mountains. Then I moved back across the floor and looked out through another of my spy holes, down into the village main street. My gaze was met almost immediately by the sight of Hugo returning from the meadow with a scythe. His shirt was off his back and draped across his shoulders. I felt a pang of remorse that I could have treated him so cruelly. Then

I remembered that it was he who had started the fight, and those feelings evaporated swiftly. It was only a day or so ago that he had been cutting the hay right beneath where now I sat. Most probably, I was sitting upon the hay he had scythed. It gave me a sense of irony to dwell upon this trivial point.

Having nothing better to do, boredom carried me off to sleep.

When I awoke, it was still hot and stuffy. But the reason I had woken was because, only lightly asleep, my ears had heard someone approaching the building. I shuffled across as quietly as possible to look out through a crack at whoever it was. My beady eye spied a returning Father Vernon carrying a box, and with a capacious bag slung over one shoulder.

Upon entering, he proffered the box. "I have a disguise for you in here…"

"A disguise?"

"You shall have to shave off your walrus moustache and take off your spectacles, of course. They are quite part of you."

"My moustache?"

"If you want to get out there…"

"But… without my spectacles… I shall be blind as a bat."

He reached into the box and produced a selection of eyewear.

"Try these. It is a hotel lost property box. I take it you do not want any umbrellas, snuff boxes or false teeth?" he continued, producing the items one after the other like a magician.

"No, I do not."

"I often collect these boxes from the hotels around here. Since they have not been claimed, I reserve the right to send them on to the city where the poor may benefit from them. These will all go there, too. Except, perhaps, one pair of spectacles, hopefully. So – try these on…"

I found a pair that did not give me a headache and allowed me to see with a degree of clarity. Satisfied with my new appearance, the priest then produced a friar's brown habit from his bag.

"I am to wear this?"

"Of course. Folk may wish you good-day at a distance, but other than that they tend to give Franciscan friars a wide berth. I trust it is out of respect and deference to our holy calling. Moreover, I am always having brother priests up here; one more won't make any difference. They come here for a rest. To think, to sit, to pray. To refresh themselves before returning to the fray. The only danger is if they spot your mountain tan. Or if someone thinks to talk to you, to perhaps enquire politely how you got here. But it is nearly dusk. Besides, I doubt they would get that close or be that suspicious. Nothing happens here. More, even if something does happen, it is assumed it is nothing. Now, come along and shave off that moustache…" He produced shaving implements, a bowl and a bottle of water from his pack. "And, when you are done, I shall give you a tonsure." A large, threatening pair of scissors emerged after the shaving materials.

"I will not have you shave my head. I am thin enough up top as it is."

"Then you may borrow my wide-brimmed straw hat." He said this quickly enough to make me suspect that there had never been any real intention of providing me with the monk's pride and joy.

The hat was followed almost immediately by a lady's handbag.

"And this?"

"Contains rouge. One of my parishioners left it behind last week. I have been meaning to return it to her. Now I know why I was not meant to, quite yet. She did not need it in a hurry."

"Yes, but… why rouge?"

"Once you have shaved your moustache off, the lip underneath will be pale and white in contrast to the rest of your ruddy face. It should be enough to fool the casual observer. As I said, no one looks closely at a friar. I can vouch for that."

We set about my transformation.

"Would you like to act, doctor?" He was smiling broadly as he applied the finishing touches to the rouge upon my newly shaven upper lip.

"I should like that very much. But I would not act in anything where I had to pretend to be something I am not."

"But this is what all acting is, surely?"

"No – one acts by *being* something one is not. No pretence."

My first deed upon being released from my jail was to light my pipe and luxuriate in every moment of it. I moved about the village cautiously at first. Huddled and shuffling. However, I noticed that people were turning to glance at me as I passed. So I decided to behave more boldly. I stood more upright and lengthened my step. Now people weren't giving me a second thought. Father Vernon was right. People simply pass the religious by without a second glance. It was as if I did not exist. I was of no interest to them. So I made my way along to the telegraph office. I wanted to compose my request for information about Brown's personal history from Flemyng. Late in the afternoon, as it was, I hoped that the office had not yet closed.

It was good to be out in the fresh air. Good to be among people again – albeit people who could at any moment betray me to the police and seal my fate for ever.

To my great relief, the telegraph office was not yet closed. I composed my message.

URGENT. NO CRICKET.

WHO IS PETER BROWN?

PERSONAL HISTORY PLEASE.

There was no need to use the cipher; I was not asking for anything that needed to be kept from any unknown reader. Besides, I needed a response as quickly as possible. Turning the information into a scorecard would only delay matters. I did not sign it, for fear of revealing my identity to the telegraph clerk.

Then I tore the message up.

Departing from our usual pattern would alert Flemyng to something amiss. Reading my message from his perspective, it could have been written by anyone. It could have been written by someone trying to get information out of him. Without his knowing that it was indeed me, Flemyng may reason that someone could have realized that the cricket was a code. They could have given up trying to decipher it, and had simply tried the direct approach in order to get some plain text, and facts, from England. Flemyng would reasonably assume it to be foolhardy to respond to such a blatant request. It would run the risk of revealing something detrimental to my personal safety. I clearly had to sign it with my own name. But that would mean giving away the fact that I was still in the village. I went out and sat upon the steps of the office. I smoked a pipe. Presently, I went back inside and rewrote my message, signing it with the words:

REGARDS, IGNATIUS

ASK STEEN

Ignatius was my second given name. A name I shared with my old college friend Robert I. Steen. It was a link to enable him to certify for Flemyng that it was indeed me sending this curious missive.

Then I sent it.

Leaving the office, I was aware that I had finally gone beyond the point of no return. Of course, sending such a message was a huge risk. But, as I had reasoned, if anyone was reading telegrams on my behalf, then they probably already knew who Brown was. So Flemyng could tell them nothing new. If the reply never came, it would only mean again what I already knew. That someone was intercepting my wires. The only other risk was letting people know I was still in the village. But they would have to find me first. In the meantime, there was a chance that the grouse would be disturbed by all of this. It could drive my quarry straight into my waiting guns.

I found myself wandering the village deep in these kinds of thoughts. I was still lost in this reverie when I almost banged right into the one person I most needed to avoid.

"Hello, padre." Holloway continued past, without pause. He was weaving slightly. Whatever he had just been indulging in had doubtless made him generally less inhibited with everyone he came across. Even Franciscan strangers. But I could see that he was also walking around in a fug. I wanted to chase after him. Shake him until his brain rattled. But, I supposed, it wouldn't have rattled. It was clearly, at present, mush. I let him go. Which was a shame, because I might just have sought to make him agree he was my alibi. To know that my disguise was so effective was small consolation.

I walked on towards my hotel. No particular reason, other than I was not ready to return to my stifling eyrie quite yet. I passed Plantin and Marie, returning I assumed from an afternoon perambulation. They also did not give me a second glance.

Unrecognized, unacknowledged, an extraordinary emotion then engulfed me. I wanted to be part of society again. I wanted my existence affirmed. I vowed there and then that if ever I got out of this whole catastrophe alive, I would never again scorn the company of members of the human race. Even members of the general public; no matter how gauche or satirical their approach to me may be. I would indeed welcome their attention and stop when they spoke to me, and give them the time of day when they asked for it.

I reached the steps of my hotel. Despite any reservations I may have had, I realized I needs must go inside. I had sent a telegram to Flemyng. He was most likely going to reply to the customary address. Care of the hotel. I needed to let someone know that messages for someone called Ignatius should be held at the reception desk until collection.

With a wry smile to myself, I assumed the name Brother Ignatius, the Franciscan friar, and stepped over the threshold into the hotel hallway. How I proposed to disguise my voice, I had yet to work out.

Anton was there, diligently going over his books. He was an able and assiduous hotelier. His parents should have been proud of him. He looked up as I entered. I suppose my previous encounters had made me overconfident of my disguise. I watched as his eyes registered in turn welcome, curiosity, sudden recognition and then intense concern. To my dismay, I could see that he was about to raise the alarm. I had to act quickly.

"Anton. Let me speak. Please."

He hesitated.

"Anton, I know your secret." I was taking a risk. I did not *know* his secret; I had only guessed. But this was a desperate moment, and it was all that I could think of in so short a space of time.

"What secret?"

"I know that you were interested when Holloway and I arrived. That you thought that we were more than simply friends. That this encouraged you, I believe, to reveal your innermost feelings to your close family. They have not, I suspect, reacted in quite the way you had hoped. My relationship with Holloway is not at all how you thought it, though. I nevertheless wish to apologize for being inadvertently the creator of the circumstances in which you find yourself."

He was perhaps considering denying that anything at all had taken place. But he was also an honest fellow and such untruths were simply beyond him. Moreover, I suspect that my own honesty perhaps offered him the chance to unburden something of the great troubles through which he had struggled these many years and, most particularly, these past few days. Who knows? Perhaps the fact that I was wearing a Franciscan habit had something to do with it also. For all he knew, this was my customary clothing and I had merely spent the past week in mufti for my own reasons.

"It has not been… too 'charming' these recent days. But I love my parents and my parents love me. We shall get along. Eva has been wonderful."

"I do not doubt that she has. But would you consider leaving here, perhaps? Living somewhere where you are less… exposed, I suppose is the word?"

"At risk of word getting out? I long ago realized that I can never escape this place. And anyway, it is my home and I like my work. If people find out – and maybe they already have, which is why I am not included in the gossip and rumour circle – they shall have to concern themselves with their own worries. I belong here."

"If you want, I can see what I can do. Perhaps we may find a passage for you to England? That is all I am saying."

"I do not want charity."

He was a very stubborn, very human young man. And brave. I did not know whether it was the case here in Switzerland, but in Britain to practise as a homosexual was a criminal offence, as my friend and Lippincott colleague Oscar Wilde knew only too well.

"But you have not come here to talk about me, surely, doctor? The last I heard you had left to explore further afield for a day or two. Which was why your cases are still in your room. I assumed you would return shortly. And, of course, pay your bill."

"I thought nobody talked to you in the village?"

"I take it that you are innocent of all that they are saying about you?"

"Of course."

"I did not doubt it." For the first time for quite a while, he smiled. I was grateful for that.

I told him that I had been hounded and that someone was intent on driving me out of the area. This had led me to suspect that I was closer to the truth than I knew. I told him how I had decided to unravel the mystery; that the Franciscan habit was a disguise, and that he should hold on to any telegrams addressed to someone called Ignatius.

He readily agreed to assist and promised me that my secret would be safe with him.

"I am sure it will be. It would seem that you are very good at keeping secrets."

I thanked Anton for his help; we smiled and shook hands.

Outside, I saw the boy from the telegram office. My initial thought was that he was bearing Flemyng's response to my wire. However, it was far too soon for that to have arrived. This was confirmed when he passed the hotel and continued along the main street. I do not know what came over me, but I purposed to follow him and discover where that particular missive was headed.

He approached and went into the café.

I took a seat upon a low wall along the street a short way. I began filling my pipe.

The boy departed a minute or so later and disappeared back towards the telegraph office.

I began to light my pipe. After a few puffs, Francesca appeared. This was something of a surprise, as I had assumed the wire had been for Holloway. Why I had thought that he had taken up residence at the café, I do not know. Nevertheless, Francesca was an interesting enough development, for all that.

Sitting upon that low wall and puffing, seemingly absent-mindedly, I followed her out of the corner of my eye. I was about to drop off my perch and follow when, to my surprise, I noted she entered the Hotel Eiger. As there was no need to move, my position affording me the greatest advantage in terms of surveillance, I remained where I was, puffing away.

After a short while, Francesca appeared upon Frau von Denecker's balcony, talking animatedly. She remained there only for an instant, however. Presumably called, she looked startled and moved back inside quickly. Was she afraid of being seen by someone?

If so, it was too late: I was that someone.

It was only then that it occurred to me. I had been in disguise and had sent my telegram under the pseudonym of Ignatius. However, the recipient's name, Flemyng, would be well known to whomever it was intercepting my messages. The wire delivered by the telegraph boy into Francesca's hand at the café was most probably a note of the message I had sent to London. If that were the case, at the very least it proved to them that someone, if not myself, was still in the village. Someone who was still asking questions of Whitehall.

I made a strategic withdrawal to my hayloft.

What I had just seen on the balcony, and what I had concluded concerning the wire, told me that I could not wait a moment longer. Plans were very likely being made. Plans that required that these two otherwise unconnected and up until now unconnectable people had to take necessary risks. Risks such as talking together, being seen together. Why did I think that? Because possibly, up until now, they had felt safe. They had not had any urgency in their transactions. But I had disappeared, and with my disappearance came their loss of control over me. Then came the wire asking about Brown. Further possibilities began to present themselves to my mind. They forced themselves more and more firmly into the shape of a realization. A conclusion, even. Of sorts.

I felt sure that if I were to deliberate on all of this for a little longer, this would be my "dog that barked in the night" moment.

I climbed out of my disguise and back into my own clothes, thinking all the while.

Why were these two people connected?

The aristocratic Austro-German and the Italian waitress?

They had to be connected.

They were connected, for I had seen Francesca on Frau von Denecker's balcony. Frau von Denecker would never have concerned herself with petty matters. Matters of state were her stock-in-trade; they were her *raison d'être*.

But why here, the middle of nowhere? What were matters of great moment doing tucked away in a tiny unconsidered corner of Europe?

Precisely because it was the middle of nowhere; like a doctor in a haystack.

Here, in the middle of nowhere, where there weren't even policemen permanently stationed, anything could happen. Because everyone *knew* that *nothing* happened. Peace had reigned supreme in this backwater for centuries. People falling down mountains may be remarkable, but since it was well known that nothing happened here, the locals would just shrug, turn their backs and declare it was an accident. Since only accidents happened around here. And then they would get on with their daily round, quickly forgetting all about it.

It occurred to me at that moment that the whole village was the dog that did not bark in the night.

EIGHTEEN

Father Vernon returned a while later. He was quite agitated. Absorbed in my own thoughts, I failed initially to note that he was carrying my own knapsack plus my hat, gloves and ice axe. Before he could speak, I began to air my own concerns.

"Father, what do you know of Francesca?"

"What do you mean?"

"The man alone in a foreign country is sadly prone to many temptations. There is, as it were, a valve inside his head, which the hormones that trigger the sexual drive pass through. They consequently swill around, increasing the sexual urge until their victim either conquers them, or succumbs. People as dry as a stick, like Brown, for example, I believe, are no less prone to this irresistible drive within them than anyone else."

"I have often believed this myself. Why, for example, did Samson, despite all the evidence, repeatedly allow Delilah to trick him?"

"As anyone who has been in a railway accident would confirm, even if one is only travelling at twenty miles an hour, when the impact comes, one cannot prevent oneself lurching forward."

"This temptation we Franciscans learn to struggle with on a daily basis… hourly. Minute by minute sometimes."

"And do you win?"

"I have to."

"A man who is not called like you does not have such strength of purpose. If a woman is giving off signals that she is interested in him, and he does not suspect her motives, then he is unable to resist her."

"Someone seduced him? It is all right, my son, there is no need to be shy. I am a man of the world. When we Franciscans take the habit, we do it because we are realistic about the world and all its fallenness. Our novitiate is all about finding out whether we live in a make-believe world or a real one. If it is make-believe we may not enter the Order. A friar who existed on make-believe would slowly but surely be driven mad, or worse, to violence."

"Then you understand perfectly."

"I understand perhaps more perfectly than you may give me credit for. It is Francesca of whom we speak, yes?"

I barely dared admit it to myself, but yes, it was that lady I was accusing. Much to my regret and torment. I nodded. "She possibly plied him with absinthe. She works in a café, after all. Then took him up the hill. Even if she had no more absinthe to hand, she might wear him out upon the high trails until he became thirsty. Then he might drink from a mountain stream. Absinthe, if water is added quickly enough, inebriates a man again. With an unusually high alcohol content, it is possible. Especially since it also contains wormwood."

"Is that not a poison? He was poisoned and thrown over the cliff?"

"Possibly. This is what I believe we are on the verge of finding out."

"But why? I mean... sexual attraction I understand, but I cannot see Francesca... No... I cannot see her, or even her husband Hugo, reaching as far as murder. For whatever motive."

"You do not see the real person. Just suppose that Brown was an intelligence agent, pursuing her for some reason..."

"What reason?"

"Imagine, if you will, Francesca's 'gift' in the wrong hands. Her allure and her skill in divination. Or rather, her ability to convince others that she can divine things. She befriends young men with connections to the governments of their countries, and she seduces them. Not physically, necessarily, but with her supposedly supernatural powers. In the course of these interviews, perhaps she does a reading for them? The more she intuitively tells them about themselves, the more they fall in love with her, the more they believe she really can see through into their deepest secrets. The more they believe this, the more they might reveal the true secrets of themselves, and with these reveal whatever work they are undertaking for their governments. For an enemy power, she would be a very potent weapon indeed, do you not agree?"

"Well, yes, but… this is so far-fetched, my son. I cannot imagine for one moment…"

"Neither can I. But look at the facts. I have just recently seen her in interview with Frau von Denecker. Have you ever noticed any such association?"

"No, I confess that I have not."

"Just imagine, therefore, if Frau von Denecker were actually her contact. Perhaps they are both working for the Austrian government. They are preparing for another war, maybe. For some reason, they have had to lie low here in Switzerland for a time. Take cover and regroup. But in due course, Francesca could be brought back out of storage and encouraged to continue operations in some European capital city or other."

"Francesca!" Father Vernon exclaimed.

"Yes, that is who…" I began, but he interrupted me.

"No – don't you see? Like Francesco. St Francis, the little French man? Francesca: 'The French girl'. Frau von Denecker is a Catholic, is she not? It is her little Franciscan joke."

"You mean Francesca is a false name? An assumed identity?"

"Why not? Perhaps she is French really. I always thought she had an unusual Italian accent. This would explain it. She maybe had a role, as you described, in Paris. Not the Franco-Prussian war perhaps. She would have been too young. But in the military, diplomatic, political intrigues that have gone on ever since. Maybe something went wrong, she had to be taken out of there… found somewhere else to go for safety. For the time being."

"Yes, Switzerland."

"No – Italy. She came here with her husband from Italy."

"Which is why she was given the name. French girl living in Italy."

"Which is why she was given a husband."

"You suggest that even her marriage was arranged to conceal her true identity and purpose?"

"I do not know what I mean any more. The enormity of it. I cannot take it all in."

"But perhaps Hugo, rather than a convenience, became a liability. There was talk that he violently assaulted a fellow in Italy who was making unseemly advances towards Francesca, which is why they had to move here."

"Somewhere quiet and out of the way?"

"Switzerland. Its very peacefulness and isolation is perfect for hiding peoples' money… and people themselves."

"And now they bide their time, waiting for whatever new development on the world stage will require their secret weapon to be brought back into active service in some enemy city somewhere…"

We sat in silence for a long while, awash with many a thought. The extraordinary implications of what we had discussed grew larger and ever more monstrous by the second.

"With her Italian background as the perfect disguise, she did not just act the part. She lived it," I said, at length.

"But why did she kill Brown?"

"I don't know. Was he on the trail of Frau von Denecker? Or maybe on her trail? Or maybe they fell in love and she found out who he was? Or maybe they fell in love and he got too close to her, became a risk, and had to be excised. She was a woman whose whole life was service to her masters, so much so that she would marry in order to conceal her identity. Someone who would think nothing of moving countries to escape justice? This is what we need to smoke out. Their cosy nest has been disturbed, and we need to keep prodding them now, until they make a mistake."

"The thing is, if they killed Brown because he came too close, why would they not want to kill you, too?"

My eyes widened. He continued.

"Surely they would reason that the mind that could come up with the sort of plots it comes up with would begin working these sorts of things out eventually."

I put that alarming thought out of my mind. "Something still puzzles me, though. Why would she set about planting clues? No matter how hard I try, if she *were* a professional, someone who would even marry a boor and a bully to protect her identity, I cannot believe she would expose herself in such a way. So then, they must have been planted by someone else."

It was clear that I was becoming befuddled once more. I would be misleading myself again over these two women, if I wasn't careful. Time to review matters. I related to the friar my deliberations, some days previously, when I had first properly tried to wrestle with this whole affair. I related to him the simple equation I had put before myself in order to try to make sense of the business. I told him that I had put the basic elements to myself as propositions, like van Engels's Euclid:

A man is killed.
There seems to be evidence that it was no accident.
A person or persons unknown have connected my presence with it.
Their behaviour implies that they are afraid of something being discovered.
I, for some reason, am in a position to solve the case.

It all still appeared a perfectly sound hypothesis upon which to base my enquiries. However, reviewing it all with Father Vernon in the light of my current situation, I now realized that the last postulate was faulty. I had used the expression "the case" and had foundered upon that false principle ever since. There was no such thing as a "case". Singular. Were there perhaps two cases? At the very least. On the one hand, there was Brown's demise, and on the other there was… what…? Matters related to the sad death of the man. Possibly some elements directly connected with it. But most importantly, not everything that had occurred in these past few days could necessarily be ascribed exclusively to it. There was other mischief going on. And it was that realization which now exercised me. Someone had used the occasion of the tragedy in order to play their own sordid games with me.

"Well, all of this is, I am afraid, now academic," Father Vernon suddenly declared, remembering the true purpose of his visit.

"Why?"

"I was talking to one of the influential folk in the village after lunch, as I said I would, to settle the rumours about you. He told me something that has disturbed me a great deal."

"What?"

"Essentially, my friend, it is too late. The village worthies sent word to the police in the valley. They are already on their way and may well arrest you on arrival."

"So be it. I am sure that I can justify everything I have done to their satisfaction."

"No, you do not understand. It is beyond your justifying yourself to them now. They are coming for you on suspicion of Brown's murder."

"But why?" I had already begun to suspect the answer.

"It appears that your Mr Holloway has approached one or two folk here with some fairly substantial theories. These make it clear that, at the very least, you need to be detained."

"Well, the village worthies might care to check Holloway's 'facts' with me before they go chasing wild geese and unnecessarily involving the law. Holloway is my alibi. Certainly at the time of Brown's death."

"Not according to Holloway. It appears that while he could vouch for your presence at certain times of the day, he could not vouch that you had been inseparable the whole day and night. The fact remains, doctor, that you are at very real risk of being arrested for murder."

I opened my mouth to utter a protestation at the injustice of it all. He made an impatient gesture. He did not have the time for the luxury of a debate. "I know that you did not do it. But it would seem to me that at this delicate moment, you now have two options."

"Which are?"

"Stay where sooner or later you will be discovered."

"Why? You deemed it secure enough up until now."

"That was before the alarm was raised."

"What alarm?"

"That you may not have left the district temporarily after all."

"Who raised this alarm?"

"I do not know."

"Anton?"

"We have no time to discuss who did or did not raise the alarm, doctor. You must either stay here and be caught, or…"

"Or…?"

"Or, as I suggested before, make your way to the British Consulate in Bern, where you might seek both sanctuary and legal representation."

I rose from my nest of hay, and started putting my walking boots and puttees on. In the final analysis, I needed to remain at liberty for as long as necessary. For as long as it took me to untangle everything.

"Won't they be watching all the tracks?"

"This is a possibility. It is your only hope, though." He counted off my options upon his fingers, and waved an airy arm in various general directions. "You could go south and round through the valley or go by the Trummelbach towards Stechelberg. You might even go west over the Sefinenfurgge, or even south-west over to Kandersteg…"

I sighed; the names might as well have been Chinese to me. "Which direction would they be least expecting me to take?"

"Well, I suppose directly up. Into the mountains."

"Up, then."

"Up it is. You should leave first. I shall amble nonchalantly around the village for quarter of an hour, let my locum know I shall be away for a short while, gather up my own things and so on. Then I shall follow. I can show you the route you must take."

I did not care for the sound of that. He might never follow. I hesitated again. Then I sat down once more. "Why help me?" I asked.

He winced, but courteously tried to hide his exasperation from me. "Because I believe in your innocence and do not trust, under the present circumstances, that you shall receive an entirely fair hearing. I may not, of course, journey with you the whole distance. I have other responsibilities. But I may accompany you this evening, as long as I am back in the parish at some stage tomorrow."

It was, of course, an absolutely impossible choice. Everything I had heard about the difficulties I was currently in was all total hearsay. In effect, it had come almost exclusively from this Franciscan eccentric before me. He seemed genuine enough, but who could tell? I could not confirm it by asking any other person. If the situation was indeed as he had described it, asking such questions may very well arouse suspicions. People might take it upon themselves to detain me until the police arrived.

And then I remembered the wire in my pocket from Flemyng regarding his warning with reference to Holloway. That too had to be an indication that all was not well. With Holloway, at the very least. And he was a dangerous opponent. Then it struck me. Holloway's glib "Hello, padre". I thought he had not noticed me. But it may well be that he had. It may well be that he was the *fons et origo* of this latest untimely development. That finally decided it for me. I simply had to leave, if only in order to take stock. Here in this hut, I was a sitting target. I did not put it beyond Holloway to suggest to these so-called village worthies that a search of the village might produce results. I had to get out. At least until I could come up with a better plan.

I stood up again, and took hold of the hat, gloves and ice axe that Father Vernon had so wisely brought.

"Splendid!" He clapped his hands together briskly, indicating that he considered the matter finally decided. He would brook no further prevarication. He proffered me my knapsack. He also gave me the satchel he had brought previously; doubtless now re-stocked with further victuals, and other items necessary for flight. "Come along. I shall arrange for your other effects to be packed and sent on to you, when you wire from a position of safety. In the meantime, you merely need to take what has been here provided…"

So I left my hide. Avoiding contact with anyone as best I could, I clambered over the little knoll that stood beyond the village, and scuttled away up into the woods. There I was to wait at an agreed rendezvous.

The grass upon which I sat and waited was crisp and short. Sheep had grazed here recently, and the stubble had been hardened by the sun; clay fired in a kiln. There was a large rock beside me upon which, popular legend had it, Mendelssohn had once sat and composed. He had used the breathtaking view of the village and the mountains and the valley beyond for his muse. I surveyed the view myself, now stretching away beneath me in the evening light that rendered everything into pastels. I consulted my watch and observed that it had been at least forty minutes since I had halted. Moths were beginning to awaken in the pit of my stomach. They produced that dusty fluttering that comes to one who, at first content and settled, begins to doubt the wisdom of that disposition. I took a sip from the flask of fresh mountain water Father Vernon had supplied me. I tore off another chunk of his rustic seeded bread and took some cheese. It was hungry and thirsty work, escaping.

Where could he be?

This was, as it happened, not the first time that exact phrase had borne in upon my reflections, there on the mountainside. Now I noticed, however, that the tone of the question was becoming harsher. More strident. More anxious. Mendelssohn may have noted that it had risen from B minor to F minor. Had the friar, after all, succeeded in some plan yet undisclosed? A plan whereby, despite his protestations to the contrary, I had been surgically removed from the affairs of the village below? The thought of having been thus inveigled rankled. It spoiled the taste of the otherwise wholesome bread and creamy cheese.

A moment later, I became aware of a rustling in the undergrowth. My recent brush with a spent hunter's bullet had made me more sensitive to such incidents than usual. I scanned the vicinity.

There… in the trees below… a wild animal, perhaps?

A hunter?

Werner with his rifle? This time he might not miss. *I'm devastated! An accident! I am mortified!* He would tell the village worthies at the peremptory inquest. They would just shrug and reply, *Well, he did have it coming to him. No matter. Would you care for a beer?*

I looked at Mendelssohn's rock and calculated how much time I would need to scurry behind it. It is not usually possible to evade a high-powered hunter's rifle for ever. One only had to consider the silent witness of the venison upon one's supper plate to know that. Perhaps I should just break cover and bolt? The venison in me counselled caution.

As stealthily as possible, I gathered up my things and repacked them. I kept one eye on the trees and the path in the surrounding area from which I had recently come. The rustling, shuffling sound drew closer. I took up my ice axe. I was tensed and ready to spring like a roebuck surprised at its watering hole. Anger, fear, animal aggression rose in me in equal measures. Whoever it was, was about to receive the full fury of the pent-up frustration and emotion of the past few days. Conan Doyle the author people knew. Conan Doyle the doting father and caring doctor they knew also. Conan Doyle the whirling dervish they had yet to be acquainted with. But acquainted with him they most surely would be. And in a very short space of time.

Then I caught a fleeting glimpse of brown habit. It was flickering briefly in the light through the trees, occasionally turning bronze by the setting sun.

A moment later and the figure of Father Vernon revealed itself in its entirety. He was striding noisily among the trees, making a bee-line towards me. Ever the suspicious one, I peered beyond him to see if he was accompanied, or had been followed. He was alone. He had taken a short cut straight across where the path made an elaborate hairpin, in order, presumably, to make up for lost time. He caught sight of me and waved a cheery hand.

Soon, he had bustled up alongside me, upon his back he bore a substantial rucksack. We shook hands, I with no little relief. With barely a word between us, save the friar's apology for his tardiness, we set off on our upward journey.

I glanced across at him as we walked. His strides were rhythmic and natural; he was in his element. However, he looked grave.

"What is the matter?"

"I encountered your Mr Holloway as I was leaving to join you. What has come over the man?"

"In what way?"

"Well, once I would have considered him a rather pasty-faced, sedentary city clerk. But he has been revitalized. Such energy in one ordinarily so dissolute I have never seen. Word has got out, and it was not I, that no one has seen you for some time. You have not been to your hotel; nor have you come for your meals. This has concerned some people greatly."

"Which people? Holloway?"

Father Vernon shrugged. "Possibly. But there are more than he now concerning themselves with your whereabouts. I am not saying it is a hue and cry just yet. But it is coming to the boil, I would say. They wonder perhaps if you have made good your escape. There was a meeting in the centre of the village to discuss what to do. They are thinking about sending out search parties. Holloway seems to have taken charge of matters. When I left he was clicking fingers and issuing orders as though he were Wellington at Waterloo."

"Did you tell him where you were headed?"

"Of course not. I let the whole commotion swirl off in whatever direction it chose to take itself. And then, when absolutely sure I would be neither seen nor followed, I set off to join you. Which is why I was so late."

"So, they are after me?"

"Not necessarily. As I said, they don't know where you are, but are concerned you have departed. The commotion is more to do with your prolonged absence."

"Have the police from the valley arrived?"

"Not by the time I left. You still have the advantage of them. They may well soon decide you have gone, however. Though they will not know where. Neither will they know why."

"Then we had better keep moving; stay one step ahead of them – literally."

We fell to conversation as we walked. At first we discussed lighter matters, to take our minds off the situation in which I was now immersed. My companion gave me a potted history of himself. It was Francis of Assisi whose story had inspired him to follow suit: to forsake worldly things and serve only God, the disenfranchized, those on the margins of society. One thing led to another and he found himself in the priesthood. He still could not quite understand how. Finally, after serving his God and his Order in South America, he ended up in this tiny little Swiss backwater. Here, after all his idealism and passion for the underprivileged, he had grown slowly disillusioned. Why had his Order sent him here? To this comfortable, sleepy little village that spends its days minding its own business? He didn't know. He knew that the Order often chose to move its friars away from the places they had felt called to – in Father Vernon's case, the slums of South America – to places where they might experience a whole new way of life. A different culture. A place where they might develop new skills, new ministries. The only new skills Father Vernon had learned, he confided ruefully, was how to drink good Swiss wine without losing his grip on his parish or his work.

It struck me that our tramp up into the hills was to some extent rekindling the passion he had once had for the life of a friar.

Sooner or later, however, our discussions perforce moved on to other topics.

"You know, of course, doctor, that there is no smoke without fire?"

Here it is, I thought; *the real reason why he encouraged me all the way up here*. Now I am alone. Now he may dispose of me as he sees fit. How foolish I had been. How gullible. I stopped and turned to face whatever fate he had in store for me. This had all gone on too long; it was good that it was being brought to an end like this. "Do you suspect me of being implicated in some way with Brown's death all along?"

His reply, however, surprised me. Perhaps it was meant to.

"No. I do not suspect you. However, the fact that someone does is the problem. Someone has put it abroad that you really were the one in with Brown's body. That it was you who set light to the church. In short, the conclusions the village worthies have reached, they may not have reached on their own. Someone may well have put you and your supposed guilt into their minds at some time. Find that person and we will find the real suspect. That is what I intend to do, once we have spirited you away safely."

I begrudged him the pursuit of this person in my absence, but said nothing.

The craggy moss-stained rocks that stuck out from the slopes among the trees reminded me of the tors of Dartmoor. Sprinkled among them was an enormous variety of pretty little alpine flowers such as gentian. They were stubbornly refusing to be uprooted, either by the wilderness that surrounded them or anything the weather could throw at them. We passed a track leading to a remote farmhouse where, Father Vernon told me, they made some splendid local cheese. We deemed it impracticable if not downright irresponsible to pay them a call and make a purchase. However, I regretted not having the opportunity to do so.

"What are you thinking, doctor?"

I laughed gently, and shrugged. "I was just remembering. It is interesting that you spoke of spiriting me away when spiritualism seems to be very much one of the reasons I am now tramping uphill with you."

"Do you believe in the supernatural, doctor?"

"Yes. But I have only just begun to explore it. In this thinking, I am still down in the valley. You are probably, with your faith, already high up here somewhere."

"I am in the valley, too, doctor. I do not have a faith. I always get cross when people talk about *their* faith as if it were a possession, something you can own or even earn. It is *the* faith. We simply explore it. And not at all well."

"Is spiritualism a faith?"

"It involves a suspension of disbelief. This makes it look like faith. Rational human argument will say it is faith, but it is something else. Impossible to detect the difference. However, unlike a belief in God – which incidentally, some may still possess while practising spiritualism – this is not faith because it demands proof. Faith, by definition, needs no proof. It is experiential and it is subjective. No one else can know what it is that you feel or believe in the fundament of your being. Spiritualism is just humankind's demand for tangible evidence that there is something out there. So it cannot be faith. Although you can use faith as a tool to achieve this ambition for evidence."

"But surely there is nonetheless something in the concept of getting in touch with other spiritual planes?"

"Most definitely. However, the general processes that the practitioners go through leave much room for doubt."

"Are you suggesting that they are all self-deceivers, or worse, charlatans?"

"No – I am suggesting that until peer review can test their methods of exploration of their beliefs, then their belief system will perforce always be diminished in the world's eyes."

"Peer review?"

"It is possible for one academic to thoroughly disagree with another's conclusions, yet respect that person's methodology and research. Are you familiar with the Bible, doctor?"

"No longer, although I have recently renewed my acquaintance with the Psalms."

"Religion has tested itself by using all the great academic thought down the centuries and has not been found wanting. I am not talking about research like your Mr Galton's statistical enquiries into such matters as the efficacy of prayer. One cannot test prayer any more than one can test spiritualism. By definition, the answer to prayer is a gift from God; it cannot be summoned. It most surely cannot be demanded, just because humankind wishes to make a statistical survey of its efficacy. However, the only way to assess anything is by conducting one's research using an accredited system or methodology. If the process can be acknowledged, then the conclusions, while disagreed with, must be at least respected. How many professors of spiritualism or mediumship are there in the world? Oh, I know well-meaning people can fund a chair and try and give it academic status, but how many bona fide universities have set up a paranormal department from choice? Yet they all have theology and philosophy departments."

I understood what he was saying. But was it not also true that as a practising Christian, he was bound to say that? His notion of peer review was interesting to me, however. Just suppose a thoroughgoing scientific, empirical and assessable approach was taken to spiritualist phenomena? Now that would be something worth exploring. Of course, one does not have to be a believer to be a theologian, does one? Therefore one does not have to have psychic powers in order to explore the supernatural realms.

"Theology is just the study of God; you don't have to believe to explore the phenomena associated with the Unknowable."

"Are you a theologian as well as a Franciscan and a priest?"

"As it happens, yes. But I am afraid my theology does not necessarily sit kindly with the Holy See. So I keep it under my hat." He grinned and scratched his tonsured head. "But we are not here to talk about me. As far as you are concerned, you would be best advised to go to ground for a few days. Let the hue and cry die down, then we'll see about spiriting you away to Interlaken and home. The whole valley will be alerted for the moment." At that precise moment, he stopped. He stood stock still, almost as if he were smelling the air like a pointer. He was listening.

"Doctor, did you hear that?" His voice had sunk to a whisper. We both stood and listened intently. In the dusk, everything had taken on a sepia wash from the last of the copper light cast against the western skies by a sinking sun. "Do you hear it?"

I could not be sure. If anything, it was a very indistinct cry. Perhaps someone hailing another over a distance. But it could just as easily have been my imagination.

Father Vernon had retraced his steps to the last turn in the path. There he was more able to look back and down the slope. I joined him. He was standing very still and alert.

Somewhere, far below us, a dog barked.

"Just a dog barking," I said. "One should not see the sinister in every rustle and snap."

"Dogs live in the valleys. They are in the village. There is no call for dogs to remain in the mountains at night."

With that, I too became still and alert. We remained in that position for a few moments.

"There…" whispered the priest. "Did you hear that?"

"Dogs!"

"And Arthur…. look…"

I barely noticed that he had used my first name. I stood at his shoulder. Loomed over by the mountain above, and shrouded in tree shadow, the forest had fallen into dusk a good half an hour before it reached us. I peered at where he was pointing.

"There, and there… do you see?" His voice betrayed his disquiet.

"Yes."

300

About a thousand yards away and directly below us on the lower slopes of our climb, I could make out little orange flickers. Three or four of them.

Lanterns.

They were moving, for they were, by turns, being hidden and revealed through the intervening trees. As if to confirm our fears, we heard another bark from a dog and then someone calling out. An answering call came from another direction. There was no doubt that the sounds had come from the vicinity of the little intermittent specks of amber.

"They are tracking us," said Father Vernon.

Nineteen

Clutching our accoutrements, I followed Father Vernon as he scuttled back up the track. Soon, as apprehension laid its cold grip on our hearts, we found ourselves jogging steadily up the slope. With every hail and halloo behind us, our pace increased. So did our pulses. I had never wondered how it felt to be a hunted stag among the glens; now, unfortunately, I knew only too well.

I tried to work out how they had managed to find our trail. It was not beyond the realms of possibility for someone to have gained access to my hotel room. They may have taken an item of clothing and they may have subsequently given it to some hunting dogs, in order that they might learn my scent and begin following it.

We blundered on along the track in the gathering gloom. The twilight would not last long at this latitude.

Father Vernon tugged at my sleeve and pulled me off into the trees which still lined the last of the lower reaches of the mountain.

"Up," he urged, breathing heavily.

We began to stumble and clamber off the track and up the steeper slopes. There were roots here, fallen rocks, boughs and other impediments. They hammered at my toes, bruised my ankles, slashed at my shins and calves, and wrenched at my knees.

Still we clambered in the deepening darkness.

I understood fully Father Vernon's intention: to get over the top of this ridge and scramble down into the neighbouring valley as quickly as possible. This would hopefully take us away from our pursuers. We had no idea whether we would succeed in throwing them off our scent. But it would have been only a matter of time before whoever was tracking us had caught up with us, should we have stayed on the path.

It took us about twenty minutes to scale the slope above the trail. We arrived at the top of the ridge, which was now clearing the main timberline. Here the landscape began to turn itself into tundra. Heaving and gasping for breath, battered and bruised, we gave ourselves the luxury of a temporary rest. I slumped onto the ground, dug out the water bottle from the satchel and drank deep. We by no means felt secure. But at least we had achieved our primary objective. One thing to be grateful for. Our self-approbation did not last long. It came like a blow to the midriff.

This time, I saw it first.

"Look…" I pointed down the slope that led into the neighbouring valley.

Tiny crocus flames of distant lanterns were weaving their way up the corresponding path through the darkness on that side of the ridge.

"Someone," said Father Vernon through clenched teeth, "has been very clever. They have sent word to these other villagers that the game is afoot. They could only have started barely half an hour after our initial pursuers had set off. They have second-guessed the direction in which we have been travelling."

I had begun a while ago to have my suspicions as to who that someone was.

"Come on." The friar hauled me to my feet and we set off along the ridge as it rose towards the great mountains ahead of us. Below, behind and either side of us like some other-worldly wake straggled the light from a score of lanterns. They were becoming more evident now, as the evening deepened. And as they drew ever closer to their prey.

I couldn't help thinking that we were being beaten towards waiting guns like grouse. I shook off that melancholy consideration and set my face to concentrate upon my continued ascent.

By the time evening had fully fallen, we found we had been pursued up into the height known as Kleine Scheidegg. The trees had all but disappeared. All we had as cover were folds in the stark uplands or the occasional rocky outcrop. The wind was keener here and the snowline barely a thousand feet further up. It was a spare, cold wilderness. The mountains were suddenly haughty, heartless and cruel. Mad, bad Byron had come this way in 1816. He had called the great Aletsch glacier, lying beyond the mountain ridge ahead of us, "a frozen hurricane".

Father Vernon was anxious that we continue directly up the couloir and onto the snowfield. Here it would be thick enough to dig a snow hole in which we could spend the night. But we needed to gather what was left of our strength before that desperate assault. We flung ourselves gratefully behind a Neolithic-looking slab of rock. It would have done very well should it have been needed by the ancients intent upon some species of human sacrifice. We peered back the way we had just come. Everywhere in the shadows, beating across the ground we had only recently covered ourselves, could be seen those unrelenting lanterns. Anger crept into my heart and lay there in sullen reproach. Why had I come all this distance just to be caught anyway?

"We are surrounded," Father Vernon noted. "We might just manage to hide away from them for a few hours. At the moment it is probably just villagers armed with pitchforks and axes. Maybe one or two shotguns," he added, obligingly. "By morning the garrison at Interlaken will have been alerted, along with the canton police. They will come. In the morning, they will bring up the mountain guides and…"

"And…?"

"Hunters with rifles."

"They can't shoot me," I protested, then added preposterously, "I'm a famous novelist." Slightly more practically I continued, "They have no evidence."

"That's not what I heard," the priest said, unhelpfully.

I grimaced. What I needed most at that point was reassurance, not gloom. "You do not now believe that deluded fellow Holloway's rubbish, do you?" My voice had risen about an octave higher.

He did not get the chance to answer. Before he could open his mouth, a voice spoke out of the deep purple gloaming studded with torchlight below us.

"Doyle!" I recognized that supercilious slur to the voice. It carried perfectly clearly across the quarter of a mile of silent tundra that separated us. "You might as well give yourself up. We've just about done for you."

I remained silent. I did not wish to give Holloway the satisfaction.

"You may have felt you were being clever coming this way, old chap. But it was easy to deduce in which direction you had gone. Your walking boots and ice axe were missing from your room. As was your knapsack. Wouldn't have needed it if you were going to go down into the valley. Anyway, you might have been spotted going down. No, you were always going to go up. The least obvious escape route and consequently the most obvious. Which is what I told the people here. You really are most predictable, old man. At my suggestion, they wired the villages on the other side of the ridge and set them off too."

It was a fair piece of deduction, I had to admit. Up away from people. Despite the desperate situation, I wondered idly whether I would have reached the same conclusion had our roles been reversed.

"So, why don't you just be a good fellow, save us all the trouble and come back with us? We won't bite."

I was not so sure of that. I was not sure of anything any more. I turned to Father Vernon to see how he was feeling. He laid a hand on my forearm. It was at once comforting and resolute. Interestingly, no mention had been made of my companion yet. Hopefully, he might still get away from all of this undetected. I owed him that at least.

"Should I go? Not that I want to."

"No."

"But if I went with them, they would leave and you could make your way back down later. No one would know of your involvement."

"It is not over yet. We may still get you safely away from here. We just need a little time to think of a plan. They have not caught you yet. And why are they now calling out to you? Are they afraid that you are armed? Are they exhausted like us? We should wait a little while longer, at least."

"Good man."

We took a turn each at the flagon of fine Swiss wine and lay back for a moment.

"What's that?" The friar sat up. His breathing increased. I got onto my haunches to listen more attentively.

The once-distant barking was very much nearer now. I fancied I could hear the dogs' paws rustling through the undergrowth as they bounded up the slope in our direction. Along with barking we could now hear yelping. The sound of excited dogs, hunting dogs, dogs closing in on their prey.

"It appears as though we have a little more climbing to do, doctor."

"It appears so."

Crouching there on a cold and blustery high alpine brae, listening to the approaching creatures, I had visions of a huge hellish hound. I imagined it pounding out of the darkness towards me. With a huge blood-curdling howl I could picture it clamping its great slavering jaws around my throat, then shaking me to and fro as if I were a cornered fox. I shivered and shook off the idea as best I might. Now was no time to quail.

"Come along, Doyle!"

Suddenly that languid voice again rolled up towards us like a mist.

"This really is getting rather tiresome. Let's be having you, or we shall have to let the dogs off their leashes." This comment was reinforced by a sudden and far more violent barking from the creatures. Someone had most likely stirred up the animals in order to emphasize the point, in order to send terror winging its way up towards us like some species of mystical black crow.

I could not help but think as I crouched there, a hunted creature, that Holloway's voice had taken on a different timbre. A more curt, slightly cynical, world-weary intonation. Moreover, it sounded as if he were playing a part. A part, it began to concern me, I had written for him. It was as if he were *playing the part of Sherlock Holmes*. Indeed, as if he believed *he were Sherlock Holmes*.

I tried to chase such thoughts from my mind. But, even as I sought to do so, another thought seized hold of me, not without a grimace of pawky humour: these were dogs I earnestly wished had not barked in the night.

Then, finally, I thought that if I ever got out of this, I would definitely kill him... *Holmes*, that is...

"We cannot stay here," I said, shaking myself out of my morbid reverie. "I do not intend being torn apart by a pack of hunting dogs. Let us get on. I will not be prevented from solving this mystery. Whomever it was, was concerned enough to drive me from the village in this way. It is why they want me caught and put away."

"At least for a period of time. It could be weeks before you were brought to trial and found innocent, if you are..."

"*If* I am innocent? Not very encouraging!" Despite the circumstances, I found I was able to grin. "Then, if I am not allowed to go down, there is only one other way I can go."

"Up?"

"Up." I started to collect my things together. "One thing is for certain, we have no time left to discuss matters. I feel sure they will do what they said and let those hounds go at any moment. Holloway has no intention of waiting for reinforcements tomorrow. We shall have to climb like cats up a tree if we are to throw those hounds of his off our scent."

"Up." The priest repeated. He then said, with a wisp of irony in his voice, "You do know where we are, don't you?"

"Where?"

"We are crouching at the foot of a little masterpiece of God's called the Eiger."

307

"I've heard of that…" I tried to remember in what context. Then it came to me. On the first day, Eva had referred to that great grey slab of a mountain as the widowmaker.

"However," Father Vernon thought out loud, "there will be no watch at the north face immediately behind us. They would not have had time to send anyone round that far. And besides, no one has ever climbed it, so why should they need to cut us off from it?"

"Which is why we have been deliberately driven in this direction. Up against the wall. Clever – really very clever." I marvelled at my nemesis's ingenuity and foresight. We had been outmanoeuvred. He had pressed us back and back until we had found ourselves against this sheer wall. Calling it to mind as I had marvelled at it that first day, I recalled that it was a concave and hooded blade, like the inside of a vast pen nib. He didn't have to follow us any further; he could afford to wait, I realized. All night, if necessary. As far as he was concerned, we were not going anywhere. I looked again at the task looming out of the bowels of the earth and rising into the vast blackness above me. "Why has no one ever climbed it?"

"It is sheer and bitter. If it rains, the rock face streams with a thousand pounding waterfalls. And when it has finished raining, the water forms verglas which glazes the rock and covers the surface with iron-hard ice. If it doesn't rain, then you are at risk from falling rocks. If your fingers do not grow numb and lose their grip within the first hour, then the ice on the rock face will throw you from it; and, if that does not succeed, then the higher you get, the stronger the wind. You will be pulled and tugged at until you are hauled off it and hurled onto the scree a thousand feet below."

I stared at him through the gloom.

"Thanks." I paused to swallow hard. "Nevertheless… climb it we must."

"At night? How? By feel?"

I did not need to see his expression; the tone of the voice said everything. Was I entirely insane?

"Well…" Having stepped off over into the abyss of foolishness, I was loath to try to scramble back now, "… it is our only chance. If we cannot go under it, and we can't go back, we have to go over it."

"Arthur! This is madness. We cannot possibly do this." The wind tore the words from his lips and scattered them across the cliff face like spindrift.

"I know, Father, I know. But I am desperate and bereft of ideas."

"But…" he considered, "if we cannot go over, perhaps we might be able to go around…"

"Around? How do you mean?"

Holloway would have sneered had he witnessed those words. He would have sneered all the harder had he heard what the priest then said.

"I have attempted this other climb before, in my time." His words were whirling, curling and fading in the mirk. "If memory serves, since we have not yet reached the true base of the crag, we might be able to work ourselves laterally and eventually over the Eiger's shoulder. This would take us towards the trade route that wends its way over on the eastern flank…"

I tried to picture the peaks of the Berner Oberland in my mind's eye. They rose and fell, like shark's teeth. At the junction of one peak with the next, like the shoulder of a twin-headed giant, we might find better, and less sheer, purchase for our fingers and feet.

"I have managed it once before. In daylight. It is far more accessible for we duffers. We are not trying to break any records or place our names in the history books, after all, are we, my friend? Doctor…? Are you still undecided…?"

"No. I just wondered why we had not thought of this before."

"Because if we had set off directly for that route, we would have been cut off by Holloway's troops. By taking this route we have, by chance, drawn the net in tighter on us. Or rather it has drawn itself tighter upon us…"

"So now we have entered a new dimension? The vertical rather than the horizontal plane."

"Precisely. Now we can reconsider our options…"

Now, up above and beyond the apex of our pursuit, we would be able to elude them by working our way around outside the perimeters of the net and traverse onto our new route. It could not have worked out more hopefully than if we had planned it.

"As it happens, in my rucksack I have an ice axe, rope and pitons and other climbing gear." The friar produced the items as he spoke, and then revealed woollen socks and a burly pair of studded climbing boots. He started to pull them on in place of his sandals. He looked at me, and through the night, I could see his grin. "I thought we might have to go 'up' at some stage. I just did not imagine for one moment precisely which 'up' we would have to take."

"Then, my dear fellow, lead on. Lead on."

"As you say, my son. And let us commend our souls to God as we do so…"

Which was hardly encouraging.

Accompanied by the occasional yelp and wail of the dogs below us, we turned our backs on the lanterns, whose lights were becoming increasingly larger by the minute. We scrambled somewhat irresolutely across towards the starting point for our insane attempt.

We managed the early stages of the ascent clinging on to the rocks and cracks through the ice and snow fairly easily. It was a difficult climb, but we were ambitious. It was as if the great monster was keen to draw us in towards it in our folly and ambition. As we climbed higher, though, the problems presented to us became more pronounced, and our weariness began to tell. We approached a particularly difficult crevasse but, before we reached it, we were faced with an almost vertical wall. Of course, it was preposterous. We had managed only a short amount of puffing and panting and wheezing, scaling the widowmaker, before we realized exactly what it was that we had undertaken.

Were it one of my stories, I do not doubt I would have left my heroes hanging perilously from a cliff by their fingernails at the completion of one week's story. My readers would have gasped at such bravery mixed with folly, and would have flocked to purchase the next instalment to see, precisely, how the two dashing fellows might overcome their desperate predicament. In a tale of success in the face of grave danger, mastered by sheer courage and derring-do, my fictional heroes would have – bloodied but unbowed – achieved the summit of the mountain. They would have stood there, proud and tall, laughing at the puny attempts of their pursuers to emulate their impossible feat.

But this was no fiction. This was harsh, cold, pitiless reality. Two unprepared and under-equipped gentlemen of indeterminate age, fitness and stamina were simply not able to achieve such a gargantuan task.

Father Vernon encouraged me from somewhere in the darkness a few feet above my head. It was curious. Just his voice. A human voice full of both endeavour and frailty. Yet it was enough. I gritted my teeth and set my face to press on.

We worked our way diagonally for a short while longer. Then, little by little, I began to feel that we were now high enough and far enough away from the dogs and their handlers that they would not be able to follow us further that night.

It was indeed now fully night. I had been driven by indignation ever since we had left the village. But having ascended this last half-mile up ice and snow on pure adrenaline, and thoroughly out of condition for this type of exertion, I knew I was now almost completely spent. After a little longer, aware of how desperately dangerous it would be to try to proceed by feel alone, I called to my guide.

"Father, we should rest. We are safe enough for the moment. Let us find a shelf to lie upon and start again at first light."

"My dear boy, those were my sentiments precisely. I have just reached such a ledge. I am just up and to your left. It is an easy climb, if you follow the traverse. I'll secure your rope at my end and bring you up."

He was as good as his word. I soon find myself scrambling, knees first, onto the ledge. Father Vernon had enlarged the space by chopping more room out of the ice and snow. It was broad enough for us both to lie down upon. We wrapped ourselves in our blankets and oilcloth. We then secured ourselves with ropes, which were in turn secured to boulders. The whole effort we tied off on pitons, driven into the flank of the granite beast.

It was bitterly cold. We were exhausted and only had water, bread and cheese with which to nourish ourselves. The wine had been drained long ago. I looked out over the edge down into the blackness below. I could see the lanterns, but they were concentrated off to the left. Holloway had missed us and, by our climbing, his dogs were no longer able to pick up our scent. Further, by traversing as we did, we had moved away from our initial point of contact with the peak. We were, indeed, some dozens of feet beyond a point below around which the lanterns were congregating. Shortly, I imagine, Holloway would work out what we had done. I would have given anything to see his face at that moment. But then the question would be: What would he do next?

Now that it was night, I suspected he would understand that further pursuit for the time being would be futile. He would know that we would not be able to get very much further in the dark. And we were all dreadfully weary. He would doubtless, therefore, set out his pickets. They would keep watch all night and prevent us slipping through his lines in the darkness, if that were our intention.

Sure enough, about half an hour later, I could make out bivouac fires beginning to sprout up all around in a crescent beneath us. In the darkness, they looked for all the world like Napoleon's *Grande Armée* camped out upon the far ridge, the night before Waterloo.

The friar and I scraped some pure snow into our water bottles to provide us with vital drinking water in due course. We settled ourselves down for sleep.

It was a cold, comfortless and disturbing night. But at least we rested. The first streaks of grey had not even begun to silver the distant horizon before Father Vernon shook my shoulder and we began dismantling our camp.

Presently, we roped up and set off up the traverse over towards the ridge itself, working the stiffness out of our fingers and joints. We paused at one point to look briefly across at the awesome north face, after which Father Vernon indicated that it was time to commence a more direct ascent. He chipped away with his ice axe at the layer of hard snow that encased the precipitous rock, and we nosed back towards our target ridge. One that lay tantalizingly beyond an immense buttress.

We had to climb and to rest and then to climb again. It was tortuous, slow and infinitely painful; to the limbs, the extremities and the lungs. My ribs felt as though they would separate and the intercostals twang off like so many strips of India rubber with the exertion. But, as the iron grey sky started to grow gold, as the sun dragged itself wearily into a pale blue sky, we found hope rising equally within our breasts. I began to trust implicitly my companion's balanced progress. Soon, soon enough, we discovered ourselves atop the snow-crusted scar that lay like a craggy ligament between two great peaks. The Eigerjoch.

We flung ourselves down in the icy whiteness and lay there for many minutes, heaving and moaning with the pain and the lack of air. At that great altitude, the particular quantities of oxygen and nitrogen necessary for efficient respiration were very hard to come by. At length, we sat up and looked at each other. Our faces were pale and already weathered. Our eyes were clammy and red-rimmed. Our lips were chapped and peeling. As we caught sight of one another, we recognized both the absurdity of our situation and the quality of our achievement. We shook hands. It was a silent and surprisingly sombre gesture, considering our extraordinary feat. An understated act that nevertheless spoke more profoundly of what had occurred than any amount of rejoicing.

The friar told me of an account he had read of the 1886 ascent of the south ridge, and he wondered aloud how hard it was. It would, we reasoned, depend on the conditions, but that the only way to find out was to attempt it. The snow had been good, however, on our way up. So it was possible we would find similar conditions on the ridge.

We broke out what was left of the bread, cheese and snow-water, there at the blustery shoulder of one of the most challenging peaks in Europe. Consuming our meagre rations, we watched the sun rise higher in the sky.

I heard the bark of a dog come whipping up from the stark uplands a thousand feet below us. I peered down and could see specks. By now, Holloway had discovered our flight, and was at something of a loss as to what to do next. Father Vernon tapped my arm and pointed. There were folk scaling the face of the Eiger. But we knew, and they probably knew also, that we were a good two and a half, maybe three hours' climb ahead of them. We could sit and gloat abaft our splendid saddle for a while, without risking capture. It was a fine feeling. A very fine feeling. I lit my pipe and smoked the best smoke of my life. If there were a God in heaven, I felt very much closer to him up here than anywhere else in the world.

"Come on," said Father Vernon, struggling to his feet, "it is all downhill from here."

After the first hundred yards, which we climbed in pitches, we realized that the snow was ideal and the ridge benefited from it. There was no cornice to complicate matters. Nevertheless, we avoided overconfidence, which had led – and doubtless would continue to lead – inexperienced alpinists to tragedy.

After the Eigerjoch, we found that the underlying conditions were easing and we were presently able to swing a little faster across the snowfield at the top of the great glacier called the Fieschergletscher. Our aim was to join the north-east ridge of the Mönch. It was a complete expanse of white, like the arctic landscapes I had experienced in my younger days, on this side of the ridge.

"It is an example of not thinking the problem through that they leave this flank exposed." The priest laughed immodestly as we pressed on.

I tut-tutted and agreed. "Such short-sightedness, indeed!" The words had barely left my lips, though, when my companion, not for the first time, stood stock still. I looked in the direction he was staring. I noticed, a considerable distance across the snowy expanse, two specks. Then four. Then ten. These specks were working their way steadily across the clean white brae and around towards the Eiger. There, they would be behind us. Holloway had not taken the Eiger for granted after all. He had rightly assumed it was possible for us to scale part of it, at least. If so, then we might slip away around the side and over. Which is just what we had done. These pursuers must have been allotted this task sometime the evening before. It would have been impossible for them to have made so much ground otherwise, had they done so the moment they had noticed we had slipped their net. Those men must have been toiling up to their present position since dawn.

Anger once again caught me up and squeezed me in its dread grip. Exhausted and not thinking clearly, I began to accept that the spirit of Holmes had taken that Englishman over. *He knows I want to kill him*, I thought, *and he simply cannot allow it. So it is kill or be killed*.

"But they might still be too late." Father Vernon gave voice to his inner debate. "We have already stolen a march on them."

"How far away are they? An hour?"

He nodded. "They may already have seen us, though." He was already beginning to get out of breath after the exertions of the night coupled with the high altitude, its thin air and now the searing sunshine. "But we still have time."

"Exactly; while there is time, there is time enough."

He instinctively looked behind us. I knew what he was thinking. Somewhere there, currently hidden from view, were further pursuers. And then, doubtless, with such foresight as he possessed, Holloway

315

would have despatched another section of hunters from the Kleine Scheidegg district up along our side of the glacier. Albeit that they, too, were still some significant distance beneath us.

Holloway's relentless pursuit was a weapon he was wielding with consummate skill. But I was dashed if I was going to let the fellow best me. Not now, not after everything I had endured.

"The Lord will take care of us," was the priest's heartfelt contribution.

We were, as it happened, now standing in the Valais, out of Bernese jurisdiction. But it would not have taken the authorities in one district long to convince another to hand us over, should the evidence be compelling. So where could we go? It was past noon and to remain on the hill for much longer would be further folly. The nearest Valaisian village was more than fifteen miles away. That would be a stumbling progress over snow and ice. That left setting a course back towards the way we had come. Not directly back, but down towards the more readily accessible lower snow- and ice-free slopes and civilization beyond.

We pressed on. We had to zigzag round the crevasses in the steeper part of the glacier above the rock rib. If we moved fast enough, the men trying to cut us off would not be able to intercept us before we could be through, between their rapidly closing pincers, and away. But the geometry did not look too promising. Those across the glacier from us, the only pursuers currently in view, most probably had field glasses and were observing our trajectory. Every time we altered course, they also adjusted theirs. It was a race, and the more the minutes ticked by the less likely it became that we might squeeze past them.

Especially if they had rifles.

This latest morbid thought had only recently occurred to me. After all, they were no doubt equipped and experienced mountain folk. We were, who…? A city doctor and a friar in boots. Our toes were probably already developing frostbite.

It was after we had adjusted our course for a fourth time that I noticed something on the slopes in the lee of the ridge. It was a hut.

A little rickety, wooden construction sitting incongruously among that expanse of white icing. I tapped Father Vernon on the shoulder and pointed it out to him. He nodded and set course for it.

We did not know why we were heading for it. It brought us on a more direct route to meet up with the people assigned to cut us off, and further away from our escape route. Nevertheless, both I and my companion sensed that this was the only option in the present circumstances. In effect, our last option. So we struck out for it as fast as our weary legs would carry us.

A moment later and it felt as though something had slapped into the white iciness beside us. A little ledge of snow on a rise to the north collapsed as if someone had stepped on it. A moment later and we heard an unmistakable snapping noise which then echoed around the icy peaks. They did have rifles. They were shooting at us. If they were not careful, they would have nobody left to ask questions of later.

"Come on!" I cried. Two more shots flew past us and I felt the familiar disturbance in air pressure, the slight raising of temperature and the lazy hum of the bullets as they thankfully missed their marks. The shots plunged recklessly into the snows behind us. In a few seconds they would have worked out our exact range and direction of travel, I thought.

Another shot buzzed past my ear. Then, all at once, we were at the door. Father Vernon grabbed the latch and hauled at it as though he were intent on wrenching his shoulder out of its socket.

"Frozen!"

A bullet thudded into the wood above our heads. It sent splinters and dust in all directions. In an instant I had grabbed my ice axe. I began hefting it like a Viking berserker at the lock. With a satisfying rupturing noise, all resistance gave way and we were through. We tumbled in, one after the other; the door behaved as if it had been flung open in welcome.

Inside, if we were hoping to find guns or dynamite or a direct telegraph line through to the British embassy in Bern, we were sadly mistaken.

Urgently, we began searching around for something – we did not know what – *anything* that might help us.

There were old blankets and some rusty tins of food. Useful if we were staying the night – but that was impossible for us. In fact, I realized, if those men outside with their rifles had any say in the matter, we may not even see the next morning.

Father Vernon was muttering. He held up what appeared to be some very basic weather-monitoring equipment. "Useless," he pronounced, and flung the items over his shoulder to land with a clatter on the hut's wooden floor.

I found some geological experimentation apparatus; that went the same way as Father Vernon's weather-monitoring instruments.

"Ah!" cried the friar, and held up a box.

"What have you found?"

"Flares"

"Flares?"

"Yes – you light them like fireworks and they shoot into the air and show people you need rescuing…"

"Excellent," I replied, and then it came to me: "What people?"

"The people from the village."

"Which village?"

As if in answer, another bullet thudded into the hut wall.

"Ah yes, I see… they already know we are here, don't they?"

"Yes. Unfortunately."

I could hear shouting.

"What are they saying?"

Father Vernon listened for a moment. "They are asking us to surrender to them. No – *telling* us."

"Surrender? Or simply step outside so they can get a clear shot at us…?"

We continued our increasingly frenzied search. We found a few tools for either cutting or gathering material such as glacier ice or granite. "What on earth are these doing here?" I asked.

"I have no idea. I know that they are surveying this whole district because there is an intention to raise a railway up into the mountains. Perhaps these have been left here to support the mission."

I cast them aside. All of it was utterly useless to us in our predicament.

The men outside were even closer now. Their voices carried to us across the silence of the bowl created by the great peaks of the Berner Oberland.

I moved some sacking from a few items stacked over in a corner and revealed dark-goggles. These were to keep out the painfully bright white light of the sun reflecting on the snow.

And then I found them…

Skis with ski poles.

"Skis!?" the priest exclaimed. He looked at me as if I had finally taken leave of my senses. "What purpose might they have, pray? A Sunday morning outing? Or perhaps you feel they will send us flying into our pursuers' arms more quickly. That at least would mean it would all be over and done with swiftly. Perhaps the judge will be asked to be more lenient as a result. *'Oh yes, they were guilty of seeking to evade justice – but they were the quickest people ever to surrender themselves, M'lud…'* *'Fair enough, ten years commuted to nine and a half. Take them away!'*"

I understood his frustration and looked at my companion kindly. The exertions had finally unmanned him and he was at a loss as to what to do next. The burden of having effected my escape and helping me evade the pursuers – this, for him, was the proverbial last straw.

"Father Vernon, I have read of a Norwegian's experiments with sliding downhill on these things. Do you not consider the prospect of such an escapade diverting? It may even be exhilarating."

"You left out the adjectives 'dangerous' and 'foolhardy'."

"Of course. But there is no gainsaying it. They would be swift."

"Swift."

"Swift."

As if to hurry us up in our deliberations, we were hailed once more from outside. They clearly believed they had trapped us. Although they were undoubtedly stumbling with difficulty through the deep drifted snows to reach us, there was no question of them being soon upon us. It was now or never.

"Well," said the friar turning a ski in his hands, "I have had a little experience with these…"

"And I have no alternative…" We looked at each other.

Now it was, then.

Father Vernon kilted the skirts of his habit so that he looked as if he were wearing pantaloons. He donned a coat that was hanging on the door, left by some previous visitor, and placed a pair of goggles onto his face. He strapped on the skis and I followed suit.

"Three… two… one… Go!"

We burst out of the door with two eight-foot strips of elm strapped to our feet.

The movement took our hunters by surprise. They were still not close enough for us to make them out clearly. I hoped, similarly, that they would not be able to make us out, either. Father Vernon's anonymity was vital.

But they could still raise a rifle to their shoulders if they so chose.

As we slid down the great snow-fast glacier away from the hut and the Eiger, I looked over my shoulder. I caught a glimpse of one of the men raising his rifle. The sun glinted dully off the metal. I shut my eyes and huddled as low as I could. For a moment I waited to hear, above the sound of the wind in my ears, the winging of a bullet passing me. Or worse: feel it driving into me like a red-hot poker. Neither happened. A few moments later, I heard the crack of the gunshot. He had missed by a mile. Or, at least, he had missed by enough for me not to have heard the bullet itself. While the glacier was mercifully smooth and not too sheer, allowing me to maintain a semblance of balance, with every second that passed, our velocity and trajectory was taking us further and further away from them. Unless we were most unfortunate, it was now even more unlikely that they would be able to get a sufficient bearing upon us to let off another shot.

My calculation proved correct and we never heard another thing; nothing except the sound of the rushing wind in our ears as we raced down the long sweeping expanse of the gleaming glacier. We directed our trajectory towards the lower slopes with their bright skies opening their welcoming arms before us.

We made an absurd sight: an increasingly bewildered middle-class doctor/author and an unhinged priest careering down a mountainside at gathering speed on lengths of wood.

I started to laugh uncontrollably. I think it was hysteria.

Twenty

We left the skis, poles, goggles and jackets at the village where we had landed up later that afternoon. We sent them back to the hut on the mountain with a thank-you note and sufficient francs to pay for the hire of them. I signed it "Conan Doyle".

I was free. Free to do whatever I chose, free to make my way to the embassy in Bern, or just catch the night train to Paris and the ferry home the following day. Home. Home where Touie and my two children, one yet unborn, waited for me and would hug me and enfold me in their love.

But something inside me said something else.

Go back. It is the last thing that they would expect.

When I told Father Vernon of this urge, he gaped at me as if I were now beyond redemption.

I explored my own reasons for going back and tried to explain them to my companion and, I hoped by now, friend. I wanted to clear my name. I was aggrieved that anyone should have considered me worth pursuing. I did not wish to leave under a cloud. Moreover, if I were guilty, would I not make good my escape by leaving the country now? What guilty person in their right mind would consider returning to the people he had just evaded? And, despite everything, I did consider myself to be in my right mind. Unlike one fellow I could mention.

In the event, it did not take much arguing from my side to convince the friar. Perhaps he understood more than I knew. Perhaps he felt exactly the same, but for different reasons. He, after all, was more innocent even than I. His only condition was that I should return to the hayloft in the first instance, until the ground could be properly prepared for my being restored into the village society.

I agreed.

Meanwhile, I almost dared not admit it to myself, but I had become thoroughly possessed of a dark, brooding, seething hatred – of Sherlock Holmes. I did want to kill him. I had already begun plotting his murder. This second part I did not explain to the Franciscan.

"Perhaps when we return you might elicit further help…" I mused, hating the thought that we should continue this enterprise entirely alone.

"From whom?"

"Pivcevic," I announced in a flash of inspiration.

"Who?"

"At the hotel. A Croat. He is a jolly, rotund fellow with a wife. Of all the guests, I have found him the most sympathetic and rational. He will respond to our needs, I feel sure."

"If you say so…"

We returned via carriage and packhorse and then came back up along the valley on the last train before the line closed down for the night.

The toil up that, by now, familiar tortuous track in the chill, misty night was almost unbearable, considering our recent exertions. But it was dark and that meant we might not be seen. As we approached the village, we could hear the public clocks chiming midnight.

I had barely, once again, been ensconced in my hide in the middle of the village, when, through my familiar crack in the wooden wall, I saw my persecutor. My erstwhile pursuers had undoubtedly straggled back into the village long before. But some of them were still up and about with their lanterns, and their dogs. I could just about discern Holloway in their lamplight. He was talking with someone in uniform judging by the glint of his buttons: a policeman who had been summoned from the valley. I began to grow concerned again. Had they given up the search, or were they yet going to work their way through the night, from house to house… hayloft to hayloft…?

To my relief, after a brief discussion, the gathering finally dispersed and my nemesis made his way back to the hotel.

My hotel. Wherein lay my bed; still denied me.

I rolled over and made the hay as comfortable as possible, which wasn't very comfortable, it should be said. However, exhausted and drained of all emotion, I fell straightaway asleep.

The subconscious mind is an extraordinary instrument. While one sleeps it can continue making its calculations. It turns data over and over and produces results that one might never have come up with, had one been left to one's own super-conscious devices. So it was with me. I had fallen asleep disturbed with turbulent thoughts. I had spun and writhed upon my hay bales, never fully believing all the time I was lying there that I had fallen properly asleep at all. Yet now I had found myself in that half-sleeping, half-waking state which so often leads to the most particular and invigorating suppositions.

Once again I found that, as in the case of the alpenstock moment, I had apprehended something I had not hitherto appreciated that I understood. Shaking my head to try to get a grip upon what, exactly, my mind was trying to impress upon me, I realized that it was something to do with Holloway and that violin. Slowly I began to understand that my subconscious mind had raised an important fact. The fellow had played it with a deftness and technique that was simply impossible to acquire through the dour lessons we were all obliged to endure in our youth.

One conclusion was that the spirit of Holmes had been vested in him, and that my creation was an accomplished violinist.

But that was impossible. Holmes could not actually play the violin. He was a work of fiction. Spirit or no spirit, even in metaphysical or supernatural terms, it would be impossible, surely?

And then, as I slowly shook off the remaining sullen shackles of sleep constraining the agility of my mind, it became clear to me. As clear as the Jungfrau and just as obvious. A violinist wears his flower in the right buttonhole. Holloway had picked an edelweiss and put it in his right buttonhole, with his left hand. This could only mean one thing. He was an expert violinist in his own right. He could already play the violin. It wasn't Holmes guiding his hands at all.

His intention with that night's display at the café was to indicate to anyone who may have been interested that he had indeed been vested with the spirit of Holmes. I still did not believe that anything supernatural had occurred in that séance. In truth, what had occurred, it was now abundantly clear to me, was very, very natural indeed. Natural, yet by its nature greatly misunderstood. We have not yet charted the personality to any significant degree in science. Holloway, in short, had a propensity to mania. In his case it was an obsession that was in the main unhealthy. His continued attachment to me, or rather to my creation, Holmes, supported my diagnosis. His dependence on artificial stimuli, his wild accusations when he felt his deductions to be superior to mine, reinforced it.

That was not to say that his psychological relationship with "the spirit of Holmes" was not real. At least in his own imagination. It was not beyond anybody, whatever their emotional state, to adopt a different persona, if it so suited them. Anybody was more than capable of "becoming" someone else. Living, eating, sleeping, breathing a new personality, a person may even lose track of their true selves. Holloway had just such a mania.

If it were not the ethereal and supernatural Holmes vested in Holloway assisting him in his virtuoso performance upon the violin, then the young man's talents were of an entirely different, and far more prosaic, provenance. I lay on the musty, dusty hay, observing the morning bustle of a village getting about its legitimate business. Holloway was a talented musician. I supposed that he had even earned his living at some time with a concert or chamber orchestra, if he did not still do so. And now I had my purchase upon his real character, I was in a position to make of him and his pretences what I chose.

He must have, for some reason, attached himself to me at Zürich. So he came to the Berner Oberland by chance. Hence his inappropriate clothing and his purchase of that outrageous costume.

To unmask him now was my first instinct. I wanted to rush into town and hammer on his door and call him out in front of the other guests, and Eva; I wanted to denounce him with relish. But there was much that I still did not understand, and to allow him to think I was still far away was my greatest weapon at that present time. Unquestionably, if he had made one such slip, he would make others. It was my duty to observe, remark and make notes as appropriate. Build my case carefully, rationally and stealthily.

I heard discreet voices.

Shuffling to one of my spy holes, I looked down. It was Father Vernon. But my heart stood still at the sight. He was accompanied by the policeman I had seen with Holloway upon his return. Had the priest decided that now, at last, it was time to hand me in to the authorities? He was at the very least more than incidentally acquainted with Frau von Denecker and Francesca. Had the Franciscan finally broken from cover and revealed himself for what he was – a major component in this intricate puzzle? But on the wrong side from me.

I spun round and searched in panic for somewhere to hide, or an opening through which I might escape. However, it was to no avail. I was trapped.

I pressed myself into the furthest corner of the hayloft and awaited my fate.

I continued to listen to the voices of Father Vernon and the policeman. They sounded curiously relaxed for people who were about to effect what was on the friar's part a betrayal, and on the policeman's part an arrest.

And then they were upon me. Or rather, they had reached the hayloft. I pressed myself even harder into my corner and fixed my gaze on the door.

I tensed.

There was one last hope.

If I sprang at the two of them as they opened the door, I might just catch them by surprise, bundle them backwards and make my escape. It was all I could think of…

And then they were gone.

I could hear them wandering past. The gentle lilt of the conversation passing casually backwards and forwards between them gave the impression that they were sauntering along; out for a pleasant stroll.

Tentatively, I left my position in the corner of the hayloft and moved as silently as I could to peer out at the two men.

They were definitely passing me by. I almost felt offended. It was as though I wasn't worth their time and trouble.

It was about half an hour later that there came a gentle tap on the door. This time, I hadn't heard anyone approaching – which unnerved me.

"Arthur…? Arthur, it is all right. It's me, Father Vernon."

I let him in. Behind him, I noticed, was Pivcevic, who had the most puzzled look on his face.

"He understands why you are here and is happy to help. I have convinced him of your innocence."

"How?"

Father Vernon shrugged and tapped the side of his nose. "I am a priest," was all he said.

Somewhere among the mountains there was a flash of summer lightning.

"And the policeman?"

"What policeman?"

"The one I saw you walking and talking with a short while ago…"

"Oh. You saw us?"

"Yes, I thought you were bringing him to arrest me."

"Doctor… how could you?" the friar smiled. "Do you still not trust me?"

"I do not know who to trust. I dare not trust anyone."

"Not even me?" asked Pivcevic.

"Only so far," I admitted. "You cannot blame me…"

There was a rumble of thunder, which echoed around the slopes and down into the valley.

"No indeed, we cannot blame you," agreed Father Vernon. "However, as to the matter of the policeman: he had come up from the valley expecting simply to find you and take you back with him for an interview. I explained how you had gone missing, how the village had decided to try to find you – but had failed. When you saw us, we were going to find some of the village worthies so he could talk with them about the next step."

"Which is…?"

"A house-to-house search. I thought it – expedient – to walk with him and hold him in conversation as we passed your hide. Just in case he got it into his head to search here, as well."

"Thank you, Father."

The friar grinned. "I must admit a little guilty *frisson* of enjoyment as we passed – knowing who was inside… But I didn't lie. He never asked me a direct question. Never assumed I knew anything about anything."

"You seem to know a lot about all this, though, don't you?" Pivcevic smiled at the priest.

"I know that the good doctor is completely innocent."

"Of course," Pivcevic replied. "Which is why you are absolutely right to protect him."

"But now, we must decide what to do next," Father Vernon said.

"Well, I've been thinking about that," said I. "Something you said has struck me as being really quite useful."

"What did I say?"

"Well, in my view, enough is enough. We need a catalyst. Something that would flush Holloway, Francesca, or whomever out into the open once and for all. And I think you have just mentioned it."

328

There was another distant flash of lightning.

"The catalyst? What?"

"The policeman's house-to-house search. Perhaps we can use this to our advantage. How would it be rather than letting the policeman surprise residents, if we let it be known abroad that he is making his house-to-house search for me?"

"To what purpose?" asked Pivcevic.

"Well, essentially, we can observe the whole of the main street from here. It is possible that guilty parties may make some kind of move during the day, once the word has got around that their homes may be subjected to a search. There is a risk, of course, that absolutely nothing will happen. Alternatively, the whole village might take it into their heads to dispose of illicit possessions, and the main street will eventually be teeming with folk. But at least it is something. If it means, ultimately, catching Holloway disposing of some hitherto unforeseen evidence, or returning Francesca to the same room as Frau von Denecker, then so be it. We could then descend from our observation point and confront them with the facts of the case as I have so far assembled them."

I heard thunder again, a tympany roll, resounding around the slopes as if it were answering its own call.

"You mean us to stay here with you?" Pivcevic asked.

"If you are willing."

"Possibly…"

"Are you perhaps concerned that your wife does not know where you are?"

"No, she knows I have gone off with the priest here. She's on our balcony, reading; she won't worry for a while yet."

"Then all is well."

"But what about this other evidence you have assembled?" Pivcevic asked.

"No time to go through it all with you at present, my dear fellow. However, I assure you, there are many facts, and they all fit the case…"

Father Vernon moved to the door.

"Where are you going?" I asked.

"To start to tell people that the policeman is conducting his search… I know just who to tell. I have not been a priest in this village for all these years without knowing who the most efficient gossips are. I have to say, though, it is not much of a plan. However, if anything is to come of it at all, surely my getting word out is of the utmost necessity?"

"Agreed."

The friar departed, leaving Pivcevic and me to settle down to our surveillance of the village. We took a crack in the wooden walls apiece and waited.

While we had been talking the skies had turned solemn, grey as granite. A gloom had descended upon the village, as if we had bypassed day and gone directly from morning to dusk. The air, whilst still warm and humid, was heavy and sullen as if nature itself had received some melancholy news.

Father Vernon returned a short while later. "Well, the pebble is in the pond. I have started the rumour mill and it is grinding its way through the village; though not so much a rumour, and not so hard to get started. The policeman's search is a reality and had already started to ruffle feathers even before I began helping the news to spread."

"Thank you," I said.

"Oh, by the way," continued the priest, "here is your telegram." He handed it over to me. "Anton gave it to me when I went to the hotel to find Mr Pivcevic here. He seemed to know all about your Franciscan disguise and had connected it to me." He settled down to look out of a spyhole.

"A bright fellow." I opened my wire and squinted at it in the dim light. It was from Flemyng. It ran through a short list detailing Brown and his background. It was only when I got to two words, juxtaposed, that a great thrill of excitement coursed through me.

They were the words: MATHEMATICIAN and CAMBRIDGE.

"What does it say?" enquired Pivcevic.

Before I could answer, there was another flash of distant lightning and a rumble of thunder. And then Father Vernon summoned me to his spy hole.

"Also a guest at your hotel I believe?" he asked.

Looking out at who he had indicated, I knew that someone had indeed been flushed out by my ruse. But, I noted, it was none of the ones I had suspected initially – that is to say, Holloway, Francesca or Frau von Denecker.

It was mevrouw van Engels.

Dressed in her changeless tweeds and brogues, I realised I was not surprised to see her. Indeed, subsequent to my reading the telegram, I confess I had from that moment begun to expect it.

"Tomas and I will go after her," I said to Father Vernon. "You had better keep an eye on Holloway, Frau von Denecker and Francesca. If they move, follow them and try to ascertain what it is they are up to. If they appear liable to quit the village, delay them."

"How?"

"I am sure you will think of something. And… telegraph this person." I handed Flemyng's wire back to him. "Use my name… no, sign it Ignatius… ask him about the two women."

"We need to find out what she is about," I advised Pivcevic. "So let us not catch her up. Let us endeavour to follow her without being seen."

"Agreed."

We set off across the meadow as quickly as we dare.

I couldn't help thinking I should not have left the wire with Father Vernon. What if, ultimately, he was involved in all of this? Yet he had proved solid and true until now, despite all my previous misgivings. Was it not about time I trusted someone?

Taking care not to be seen, we left the village and struck out after mevrouw van Engels into the deepening darkness of the wooded mountainside, made gloomier still by the approaching storm. There was another lightning strike and the thunder now followed shortly after. As we climbed, growing hot with the effort and with the closeness of the air, we tried very hard to make as little noise as possible. I dreaded the outcome and would rather not bring it about any sooner than necessary by being rounded on before we reached that point.

However, she did not turn around. She pressed on. I could hear her taking ever shorter and shallower breaths.

And then the rain came. A great white burst of electricity lit up the clouds over our heads. This was followed instantly by thunder cannoning around the mountains, sounding for all the world like the opening salvoes at the start of Waterloo. This was followed by thick drops of rain, heavy like blood – a patter at first but very quickly turning to a steady downpour; this, soon afterwards, becoming very quickly a storm, driving across the mountains in huge swathes, submerging Pivcevic and me, and I don't doubt mevrouw van Engels, in its torrents.

Then, all of a sudden, we were there. We had arrived where, if truth be told, I always knew we were going the moment I saw the Dutchwoman head off out of the village. I soon recognized the lush vegetation, the distant din that had grown into a powerful roar to be heard above the rainstorm, and the lank mist that rose up from the abyss like a spectre.

I could see her through the rain. She was standing some yards from the edge of the uppermost Reichenbach fall as Pivcevic and I arrived upon the scene. I held out a hand to prevent my companion advancing further for the moment. We stood there, breathing heavily, and drenched.

She was taking it all in, as if for the last time. Fear grew within me; a surmise of foreboding. Was she about to pitch herself headlong into the black, bellowing abyss for a reason, or reasons, unknown? I could not tell, but I knew that if she did, the whole sorry tale may go down with her. Like her life, it would be extinguished somewhere far below in the chasm. This exercised me and I was ashamed that this was my first and main reaction to the tableau being played out before me. My first reaction should have been that I did not wish any human life to be concluded in such a manner. Or, indeed, at all. However, before I had time to dwell upon this further revealed flaw in my already deeply imperfect character, mevrouw van Engels began to move.

I could see her take one, two, three steps closer to the edge… and then she hesitated. Pivcevic and I exchanged looks as best we might, given the conditions, and simultaneously took a long pace towards her.

She inclined her head, as if trying to hear something. And we, all three, waited. Despite the downpour and the roaring of the fall, there was also a silence. Deeper than the quietest moment and heavy with possibilities. Pervading even the tumult of the storm and the pounding of the force over its lip and down into the jaws of the ravine.

I understood finally, then, that she was remembering.

At length, she stepped right up to the edge of the cliff.

I could bear it no longer.

As though I had been propelled from behind by a powerful hand driving me hard in the small of my back, I surged forward. As I did so, I could see her raising her right hand into the night sky, like a farewell salute. She drew it back, as if holding an invisible javelin, which she intended to hurl into the heart of the gorge.

At the same moment, and most probably as a result of my sudden forward movement, I was assailed from the side and dashed off my feet by a violent assault. A man was howling in fury and frenziedly grabbing at me. It would seem that in order to prevent my reaching the woman he had intercepted my trajectory and sent me flying sideways.

We went crashing down upon the dank, rugged ground at the same time and fell to struggling furiously with one another, he in his frenzy, I in shock and terror.

I did not know at that precise moment what had become of the Dutchwoman or the Croatian. I was, suffice it to say, otherwise engaged and was presently concentrating all my efforts upon resisting this ferocious ambush.

Preserving my own life.

Unlike when I had been accosted by Hugo in the alley beside the hotel, this assault was not designed to deliver me some species of lesson or beating. It was aimed specifically at restraining me and subduing me. To that end, my aggressor kept me locked in his embrace and pinned down in the mud and the rain-soaked grass.

Even so, I managed at one point to struggle free. But the other fellow contrived to re-engage me in our wrestling match. I was not sure whether he had any particular outcome in mind other than to restrict me and prevent me from breaking free of the engagement. To that end, we found ourselves unfortunately and involuntarily struggling our way closer and closer to the edge of the precipice.

As I became aware of this increasingly inevitable threat, I tried valiantly to land one or two telling blows upon this determined adversary, but in vain. He in turn, unaware, I suspected, of the looming peril, tried to separate my ribs one from another. He did this through the simple expedient of driving sharp, powerful punches into my thorax.

I felt my feet skitter on the crumbling wet rocks right at the edge of the abyss. The tumult beneath them pummelled my senses, just as my ribcage was being pummelled by my tormentor. Realizing where I was, and terror bringing reserves of energy and power, I managed to wrest myself clear and throw the other man away from me.

"Oh no you don't, Doyle!"

Before I had time to collect my thoughts and gather myself sufficiently to resist the next onslaught, he lunged at me once more.

I did not know whether it was his intention to thrust me over the precipice and down into the force. To be sure, however, that was precisely what was likely to happen as we engaged again at the top of the fall, like two great stags clattering antlers. I was driven back on out into space. Suspended perilously above the sucking torrent and the glistening maw below, waiting to receive its latest victim, I cried out in horror.

For a brief instant I believed that my end had come.

I could not possibly escape this doom a second time.

But that is precisely what happened. The Reichenbach fall, at its summit, is bestrewn with vegetation. In my last desperate act, my legs flailed out beneath me. As they did so, my left foot caught against the springy roots of a sturdy bush. It had been quietly growing there, minding its own business since, I imagine, prehistory. Using that tough, flexible base, I locked my leg straight and gained myself enough purchase to thrust myself back towards the cliff top. In doing so, I drove hard against Holloway's equal and opposite force. I clung on to him for dear life.

Surprised by the sudden impetus of my resurgence, his own effort subsided sufficiently for me to change my angle of attack. I twisted myself until I was more firmly onto solid ground. In doing so, of course, I had skewed around. This guided Holloway himself towards the edge of the precipice.

Indeed, over it. His feet slipped on the mud made impossibly oily by the rain. Now it was his turn to yell in horror.

We had not let go of one another during all of this. We both had a strong grip upon each other's forearms. Now, though, in his justifiable panic, he released his right-handed grip of my left arm and swung around uncontrollably.

He was at my mercy.

But not for long.

I clutched more urgently with my right hand and reached with my left to grasp a sinewy shrub. For a moment he dangled there, swinging like a weathercock. He was suspended out over the void, flailing his free arm and kicking his legs in terror. The shrub started to tear out of the soil by the roots. The storm continued beating down on him, as if its sole intention was to drive him off the cliff and into the turbulent, rock-strewn waters below.

"For pity's sake!" I cried, close to bursting with the effort of maintaining my tenuous grip upon the poor unfortunate. I was barely able to keep him or myself from plummeting into eternity. "Help us!"

Pivcevic was the first to move; mevrouw van Engels followed, in a daze.

They took hold of me. They hauled me upright and then backwards. Then, as if I were a human hawser, they proceeded to take it in turns to heave on the arm which held Holloway. Once they had contact with the terror-stricken fellow, we all three tugged and dragged at his arm. His torso followed, until he had been pulled, inboard as it were, like a drowning sailor into a storm-tossed lifeboat.

I sat upon the ground, my hair plastered, no doubt, about my head, and my clothes sodden, and spattered with mud. Blowing hard, I tried to restore my equilibrium after this latest encounter with these appalling falls. Holloway lay face down in the puddles beside me. I could hear him sobbing quietly to himself.

Looking up, I could see mevrouw van Engels, sitting upon a moss-covered rock. The one upon which I had taken refuge during my previous visit to this place. She sat leaning forward and staring into infinity. The faint phosphor of the force caught her face, causing her eyes to gleam like gunmetal. She, too, was crying.

At that moment, I heard a metallic click beside my left ear and felt something cold and ominously hard nudge itself against my temple.

"Do not make any sudden moves, doctor. Nobody needs to get hurt."

"Tomas…" I said, wearily. I was at the end of my tether and in no mood for any more nasty surprises. However, since what was being held to my head was presumably a revolver, I did not see fit to make any sudden moves. As requested. "What is all this about, now?"

"You know very well, doctor. Not content with murdering poor Mr Brown, you have now made an attempt upon two further lives…"

336

"Two further…?" I felt sick. I was not sure if it was the recent exertions and perilous predicaments, or as a result of this latest accusation. "I made no such attempts, Tomas. You saw what happened."

"Yes, I saw what happened. Even in this light it was possible to see what happened. You planned all of this, to have me accompany you as witness. In the darkness, you most probably expected that I would see what you wanted me to see. A woman in distress, planning to take her own life. You purportedly racing forward to save her, like a knight in shining armour. But then 'accidentally' you would instead precipitate her over the cliff."

"That is not…"

But he was in a declamatory mood and trampled all over my sprouting protests. "If it were not for the foolhardy but noble action of Mr Holloway here… and I am sorry, Mr Holloway, that my wife and I so misjudged you… you, doctor, would have succeeded in your devilish plan."

"But this is outrageous!" I attempted to climb to my feet to confront the fellow. But my footing was far too slippery. In any case, the muzzle just jabbed more firmly into the bony part of my cranium. I recalled that I was in no position to become outraged.

"I have heard the rumours concerning you, doctor. I have also noted the fact that rather than face justice like a man, an innocent man, you chose to abscond at the first opportunity. I also noticed that you had half the village in pursuit of you. Half the village, sir," he prodded me recklessly in the head with his pistol, "cannot be wrong. In my country, the rule of law is either too slow or too stupid to act. In my country, sometimes decent people have to take the law into their own hands. In my country, sometimes natural justice is the best."

I heard the hammer being cocked back.

"Holloway – for goodness' sake, man, tell him."

Holloway groaned but made no further contribution to the debate.

"What is there to tell? Mr Holloway made clear his suspicions to us last afternoon, while trying to gain support for his pursuit of you. He made his case very clearly and concisely and I, for one, had no further doubt. Imagine my surprise, therefore, when I was summoned to assist you in your spurious vigil."

"Imagine!"

"I could, of course, say nothing as the priest was also present – whose loyalty, at that precise moment and place, was questionable. I knew immediately that I needed to bide my time. If this was a conspiracy, to show my hand so early and in such dangerous company would have been sheer folly."

"He was there because he had seen reason. As I wish you now would."

"And what reason is that, doctor?"

"That all of this has absolutely nothing to do with me. I am a complete innocent, and have been since the moment I arrived in this woebegone place. I have been inextricably fouled by the most vexatious and extraordinary circumstances. My only crime is that I had the overweening presumption to believe that I could make a difference and assist in some small part in the solution to the whole sorry affair."

The pressure of the muzzle against my temple had eased slightly during this exchange. But now it pressed back firmly into its customary place. I was painfully conscious that the weapon was still cocked.

One slight move, one tremor, and...

"Well, if you did not kill Brown, doctor, who, pray, would you suggest did?"

I did not care for his tone but I could not deny the fact that upon this one point he had me. Following mevrouw van Engels, I had become increasinglyconvinced, or had convinced myself, that it was she. But now, her desperate and forlorn attitude had given me pause. Faced with the stark reality of having almost been killed in a second encounter with the fall, added to the imminent possibility of being shot, all my clever deductions had been swept from my mind. And then there was the precipitous and violent reappearance of Holloway. He must have seen us following the Dutchwoman.

There was another possibility, of course. Could Pivcevic himself be the murderer? Shoot me and he could walk free.

A further flash of lightning lit up the landscape. Out of the corner of my eye I could see the barrel of Pivcevic's revolver. It gleamed with menace.

"I am afraid, Tomas, I once thought that I knew who it was that had caused Mr Brown's untimely demise, but now I am not so sure."

"Oh, come along, doctor. Indulge me."

"Perhaps we might return to the village and discuss the whole affair?"

The revolver was jabbed fiercely into my temple. I yelped.

As if to concur with Pivcevic, some thunder rumbled.

"Very well, then," I gabbled, "if you cannot wait, I believe it was mevrouw van Engels who caused Mr Brown's untimely death."

There was a stage wait, and then Pivcevic burst into laughter. I felt the barrel waver and shake involuntarily. I could only hope that his finger was not currently curled around the trigger. I tensed to spring. Perhaps I could wrest the weapon out of his grasp while he was thus distracted. But he quickly regained his composure.

"Van Engels? That poor benighted creature? Now I know that you are lying, doctor. And I do not like being thought a fool."

The revolver steadied and the muzzle pressed so hard now against my head that I was almost overbalanced. Was this it? Was this the end?

"But, Mr Pivcevic…" A voice, thin and unhappy, floated across the cliff top from the direction of the rock and above the noise of the rushing water. "Dr Conan Doyle is absolutely correct. It was indeed I who killed Peter Brown."

TWENTY-ONE

Having spoken the truth out loud for the first time, mevrouw van Engels dissolved into an anguished howl that echoed around the rocks high up under the stormy sky. It was as if she had finally allowed open a fissure she had been holding pressed tightly closed. Now that the pressure had been relaxed, the magma of despair and dereliction, like the rain, poured forth in huge, unmanageable volumes.

Pivcevic paused for a moment longer. He was disorientated by the storm that was blowing pitifully from the woman just a few feet from him. He seemed uncertain now quite what to make of anything. Then, at long last, the gun barrel's pressure eased and presently fell away entirely. I took the opportunity to stand. Since I could sense no further resistance or potential objection from my erstwhile captor, I moved swiftly to the lamenting lady's side. I put my arms around her. Her whole body shook uncontrollably as if in a convulsion. She howled once more at my touch. Then, eventually, slowly, her agony subsided and the storm, although not stilled, at least relented.

Lightning flashed some distance away.

"Come along," I suggested, in due course. "Let us return to the village where we might talk about everything in more sympathetic surroundings."

"I am sorry, doctor..." Pivcevic began.

"Quite understandable, old man," I replied. Although I confess I did not feel in a particularly forgiving frame of mind.

"Should we not bind the lady?"

"Certainly not."

There was a further rumble of now departing thunder.

Pivcevic did not ask how I might be so certain she would give us no trouble. And I did not volunteer the information. How I knew she would indeed give us no trouble was another matter entirely. It was intuition, mostly. A person thus overcome by grief and remorse, and goodness knows what other dispiriting emotion, is hardly likely to suddenly acquire a criminal disposition. They have to be watched, of course, for any signs of rallying. But I believed that she would not make life any more difficult for us than it had been of late. There were further reasons, though. A logical sequence of events had begun forming themselves in my mind ever since I saw the lady departing the village in such haste and in such a direction. They were linked to my receipt of Flemyng's telegram. Undoubtedly, a great and piteous tragedy had occurred and, equally undoubtedly, the lady who presently leaned, grieving, in my arms was the person responsible. But there was much that remained unasked and unanswered. My primary concern, though, was that we all get back down to the village where much, if not all, might at least begin to be explained.

There remained the question of Holloway. I was still unclear as to precisely what part he had to play in all of this. And, in terms of being concerned about how he might react at any given moment, unlike the woman, there was much still to be cautious about.

I let go of mevrouw van Engels and stepped across to Tomas Pivcevic. I tapped him on his gun arm and asked him quietly to accompany me. We walked across to where the inert form of Holloway, darkness within darkness, lay upon the cliff top.

"Holloway?" There was no answer. I assumed that I had not spoken loudly enough above the roar of the force, so I spoke again, more firmly. "Holloway?"

He stirred and moaned. He had sobbed himself into incapacity.

"Will you come with us? You will not give us any trouble, will you? My companion here is armed. We do not intend to threaten you. We do not wish you any harm. But you will understand our caution in the circumstances, and will respond as a gentleman. On your honour."

There was a pause. The longer it persisted, the more concerned I became. At length, mournfully and in a voice slurred by exhaustion, dissolution and dismay, he replied: "What have I done?"

At long last, the rain began to ease off.

We meandered our way back to the village, up hill and down dale. It was a wearisome trudge and we were a melancholy and motley group. To top it all, although the rain had by now stopped all together, we were all still soaked to the skin and shivering. Our diverse thoughts, guilts and anxieties assailed each of us as we trod the muddy path that led inexorably towards whatever fate still held in store for us.

Of course, some of us had less to fear than others. I had been exonerated. Nevertheless, as Pivcevic had shown, popular opinion might not necessarily conform with the facts of a case. I did not know how I would be received in the village by the inhabitants. I would be wise, I told myself, to prepare for the worst.

Pivcevic was, clearly, wracked with guilt, from which no assurances from me seemed capable of absolving him.

Holloway battled with private demons and mevrouw van Engels walked as though to the scaffold.

We entered the village in silence. The last thing I wanted was to be confronted by a hostile welcoming committee of villagers, still probably intent on my capture. In the event, while people still wandered the area in restless knots of twos and threes, we managed by ducking down side streets and plotting a course along the rear of houses to evade everyone.

Somewhere a dog barked and was answered by the bleat of a sheep.

We eventually found ourselves at the hayloft, where we rejoined Father Vernon. Outside we could hear the steady drip of the remnants of the rainstorm as it dropped from the eaves into the mud below. Father Vernon confirmed that there had been no untoward to-ings and fro-ings to report. It would seem that I had received the lion's share of the adventure. Would that I had not.

Holloway and mevrouw van Engels sat on the hay while we others convened a swift council of war.

"Well, what to do now?" asked Pivcevic.

"We must surely persist until we have attained a satisfactory outcome to this entire problem," I said.

Avoiding again, as best we could, encounters with any villagers, we picked our way through the chalets and houses to the hotel. Father Vernon, for his part, had gone to find the policeman. He had promised that he would not return with the custodian of the law, nor even tell him where we were, until he had gained that gentleman's complete confidence. To accomplish this, he would relate the events at the fall and thus assure him of my innocence.

Diverting a barely comprehending Anton from his paperwork, we occupied the library for our interview session. Pivcevic had gone to report his safe return to his wife. She was now in the room with the rest of us. Pivcevic stood over Holloway and mevrouw van Engels. I could see the shape of his revolver in his still-damp jacket pocket. I was certain there would be no need for it, at least where the Dutchwoman was concerned. The lady was in no fit state to challenge anyone, nor to suddenly take to her heels and flee. Holloway, on the other hand, did cause me some concern. But it would seem even he had resolved to remain compliant. This was, no doubt, related to his cry of dismay up at the fall. What *had* he done? I wondered. In any case, he had had his fill of adventure and seemed content to drift along with the flow like so much flotsam. Or was it jetsam?

Anton, having supplied us with strong coffee and biscuits, had left us to our deliberations.

Father Vernon arrived shortly afterwards, having found the policeman. I discovered later from Father Vernon that the young man had been enjoying a meal at the mayor's home. This had followed an exhaustive, earnest, but ultimately fruitless search of a number of homes. Father Vernon had managed to extricate the fellow by saying he had something private to discuss with him. Something the mayor would get to hear about in due course, no doubt; but something in which he would be unable to involve the mayor at that particular moment. In this way, Father Vernon managed to get the policeman to himself and explain as best he might why he had come to fetch him.

The policeman entered our room with the priest, seemingly somewhat dazed by the developments with which he had been confronted by the Franciscan.

"So," said the upholder of the law in the Canton, "we have a little story to tell, yes…?" He surveyed the room.

Since no one else took it upon themselves to respond, I spoke. "Yes, and we would be very glad if you helped us make sense of it all."

"This is why I am here." As if to indicate that the interview had commenced, he sat down on a chair in the middle of the room with his notebook at the ready. From this central position, he was able to observe each one of us and ask his questions; which he did while taking notes and occasionally licking the point of his pencil.

Mevrouw van Engels sat with her fists clenched and her knees clasped firmly together. She sniffled from time to time into a small linen handkerchief, lovingly embroidered by someone; perhaps herself in younger days.

"Mevrouw van Engels?" The policeman spoke good English, and had obviously decided that the whole interview would be conducted in this language, as it was common to all of us. "I understand from Father Vernon here that you said, at the Reichenbach Falls, that it was you who had killed Peter Brown?"

She nodded, slowly.

"Would it be possible to explain what, exactly, you meant by that?"

"It is easy to understand what she meant by that," Pivcevic interjected. He was shushed by Father Vernon, and his contribution subsided.

"We are not a court of law, and we are not here to prosecute nor persecute you, mevrouw. We are merely interested at this point in getting to the facts," the policeman continued, gently.

"I did kill him."

The policeman looked across at Father Vernon and then back at the woman. "Mevrouw van Engels, I need to be certain of what you mean. Are you perhaps taking the blame for something that was, when all is said and done, an accident?"

"I did kill him," she repeated. Now in her voice was a different tone. An attempt to convince herself, perhaps. Or perhaps an attempt to convince us.

"Did you? Or did your husband kill Peter Brown? Are you protecting him?" Pivcevic chipped in again.

"No!" she cried.

"But it was because of your husband that Peter Brown died," I said.

Concern entered the woman's eyes, and then she looked down at her hands. She knew I knew. At least, she knew I knew something and had guessed much else besides. For the first time I noticed that her fists were not clenched entirely closed. One held her handkerchief, but the other…?

The policeman had clearly also noticed the Dutchwoman looking at her hands.

"What are you holding, mevrouw? May we see?" he asked.

She looked up at him, her eyes jewelled with tears. Keeping them fixed steadfastly upon him, she turned her hand over. Like setting free a sparrow, she unfurled her fingers. In the palm of her hand lay a pipe knife, glinting innocuously as if unaware of all the trouble it had caused me this past wretched week. The policeman took charge of it.

"Does it have the initials P. B. on it?" I asked him.

"It does."

"This is what she was going to throw off the cliff!" Pivcevic cried. "When she knew there was going to be a house-to-house search…"

"A memento?" queried Father Vernon.

I understood his question. The thought of a murderer keeping an item that had once belonged to his or her victim was a macabre one. Yet it was not unlikely. "A memento, if you like," I said, "but I daresay it was an accidental memento, in the same way that it was an accidental death. Am I not right?" I looked at the lady. She continued to return my gaze. What was she thinking? She knew I knew something. But how much, she could not ascertain.

I wondered why she was so keen upon remaining taciturn. Perhaps because it was a very private matter. To be dealt with privately. Like Monsieur and Madame Plantin, she simply did not speak of such things publicly. Or indeed at all. Yet she needed to speak of them. For me, this was the whole purpose of the interview. The police might want justice, Father Vernon might want truth, Tomas might want retribution. I simply wanted to help. If she were purged of at least a few of her demons, she might just stand a chance of redeeming what remained of her life. Not now, not tomorrow, but sometime. To do this, I knew that she had to unburden herself of the whole tale. It was too easy to say "I did it" and take whatever punishment was meted out without needing to expand further. She thought it was the better way, no doubt. We needed to convince her otherwise.

She had lapsed again into silence. It seemed to me that it would be a very long time indeed before we arrived at all the facts.

"Perhaps it would help if I explained a little of what happened?" I looked towards the policeman, and then over at mevrouw van Engels. "You can stop me and elaborate if I am uncertain on any detail?" I received no response, verbally or physically, even from her eyes. So I looked again at the policeman. He gave a shrug as if to say, "By all means try if you like, but I am not sure where it will get us…" So I began.

"You were up at the fall with Peter Brown. The gentleman was an eminent mathematician from Cambridge. I could not tell you your relationship or the direct cause for your both being up there.

But I suspect it was mutual attraction, was it not?"

I paused to allow her to reply. She chose not to. I looked towards the policeman. He gestured for me to continue and licked the end of his pencil again.

"… he was lonely. You, although you were married, were also lonely, yes? And sad. And vulnerable. And in need of comfort. The comfort of a friendship. A true friendship, do you agree?"

Still she did not respond.

"So… Peter Brown, although a bit of a dry stick, somehow fulfilled that need in you. Your husband, whom you loved, had completely disintegrated, hadn't he? He was no longer the man you had come to know. It had been hard enough supporting him while he was intent upon, or indeed obsessed by, his work. Once the world had caved in around your ears last year, he had become – well, if not impossible to live with, then it was becoming very difficult so to do. He was a complete stranger to you by now, wasn't he?"

She gave an almost imperceptible nod.

"It was not just *his* hopes and dreams that had shattered the day his research project crashed, was it? And you couldn't cry, because you had learned how not to and, anyway, you needed to be strong. For him."

Her eyes had closed. I knew that she was urging me on, but couldn't watch, so to speak.

"Peter Brown was attractive to you. You did not know why, I suspect. The perverse alchemy of humanity. You most probably did not discuss his work at first…" I paused, again to give her the chance to respond. Still she did not.

"Of course you did not discuss it. This was why things went wrong up at the fall, wasn't it?" I looked at her. "Wasn't it?"

Once more, she offered the faintest of nods.

"Yes, this is clear. Perhaps I might venture to suggest then, that although innocent – at least, that is how you viewed it – you arranged to undertake an afternoon's walk with Mr Brown. An excursion to the fall, of which you had both heard but had not seen…"

"He told me about it," she said, her eyes still closed.

"It was he who suggested it? Yes, I can understand that." I waited to see if she would elaborate further. She did not. So I proceeded, all the time making my tale sound like just half of a conversation, which she might enter at any time. "There was a kindred spirit which included, among other things, intelligence and loneliness. To this he responded, and wished to explore further with you, am I right? A walk would be innocent enough and yet allow you two to spend long hours together. Your husband spent so little time with you anyway. I suspect that you often had to find ways of passing interminably empty days while your husband occupied himself with his work or, latterly, with his grief. Is that not so? To go off for a few hours would not have seemed unusual to either of you. So you walked for some considerable period of time, growing to like one another. Trusting one another. Responding to one another. Perhaps you even began to wonder why you had not married Mr Brown rather than your husband…?"

"No. It was not like this." She opened her eyes suddenly.

"What was it like, then?" asked the policeman.

"We became deep friends, yes. But I never doubted my husband. Even in the difficult times."

"It occurs to me," said Father Vernon quietly, "that they have always been difficult times for you, mevrouw."

"We had been for one of our secret walks. Out of sight of the villagers. We always left separately and met somewhere beyond view of prying eyes. He produced a bottle; it was half full," she continued, slowly, turning her eyes to the priest as if she had seen him for the first time. And then she subsided into silence.

"Absinthe?" Father Vernon asked.

She considered for a moment longer and then recommenced, "Yes, absinthe. I do not always drink alcohol."

"I am sure that you do not," the friar replied.

"It was foolishness because we threw away our inhibitions. This is always dangerous. He told me about them, the Reichenbach Falls, and I was very excited to see them. We thought we could be there and back before supper. We took the absinthe with us. We

348

had thought to lay a trail to put off the hunting dogs so that they would not track down the poor wild creatures. It was why he had the bottle. Peter was very angry about things like that. The way we kill, kill, kill for fun. But… we stupidly drank the absinthe instead. He threw the empty bottle away before we got there. Probably cut the paw of one of those creatures he wished to protect…" She fell silent, lost again in thought.

"What happened next?" the policeman prompted.

"We walked. We talked. We reached the crest of the fall. We sat and ate the few items of food we had brought with us. We drank some water; we had had enough absinthe. And yes, because of all of that, foolishly, we kissed. And I was warmed and comforted. Then he took out his pipe and smoked and we talked some more. About the world, the mountains, hope, life, dreams. As he put his things away, like a little girl I asked to see the knife he had used."

"Why like a little girl?" the policeman asked.

"I felt silly. Giggly. Flirtatious. I knew once he had smoked his pipe we would have to go back. I did not want to leave yet. So I pretended to be terribly interested in the pipe knife. So he gave it to me. I knew that once it was all over, we would not be able to see each other again. I kept it and put it in my knapsack."

"And you went back to the fall tonight, once you thought it might be discovered, to cast it down, like a lover casting a rose in their beloved's grave?" I suggested.

"Something like that." What I suspected was shame crept into her voice. "When he had finished his pipe and given me his knife, I still did not want to leave. I felt light-headed… unusual… but happy. Terribly, terribly happy. The happiest I had ever felt. So, to stop us having to leave straightaway, I tried to think of something else we could talk about."

"That was when you asked him about his work?" I prompted.

"Yes." She was barely audible.

"You found out that he was working at Cambridge on the same project your husband had been working on. But his work had been crucial to helping the Frenchman you told me about reach his conclusions and destroy your husband's spirit?"

"I did not know what really happened after that. On top of everything else, especially on top of my happiness just then, it was more than I was able to bear. You understand?"

I understood. A lifetime of repression and frustration and corked emotions emerging at this cruel slap in the face at the very moment when she had begun, for once in her life, to hope that there might be, after all, more to her existence.

"I screamed. I told him that he and his mathematics colleagues had destroyed my husband and his life's work. And then he could not stop me screaming. I wanted to hit out. To smash something. He was terrified. I picked up his alpenstock. I just wanted to crash it into something, the ground, a tree, but he thought that I had gone berserk and was going to kill him. He backed away from me. He was right at the edge of the fall but so scared he did not notice. I was screaming still. But this time I was terrified because I thought he was going to topple over. Yet I was in such a frenzy, I could not control myself enough to calm down and bring him back from his peril. Instead, I swung the alpenstock around and pointed it towards him. I was afraid to go too close to the edge myself. I wanted him to take hold of the end so I could pull him back from the precipice. I was afraid he might panic if I approached him, and we would both fall to our destruction. Afraid. Afraid. Afraid."

She began to sob. Wracking, unbearably agonized sobs. Anna Pivcevic went to her and held her. We waited for a while, allowing her storm to blow over and the tears to subside. And then, still in Anna's arms like a little girl who had been scared by monsters of her own making, she finished her story.

"He thought I was attacking him. He saw the alpenstock pointed towards him. We were still yelling at each other, neither making any sense. I wanted him to grab it. That's all. I just wanted him to grab it. Which is why I pressed it towards him. But... in his fearfulness...

he took a step backwards. It was too far. He slipped, he tried to regain his balance. He fell. I screamed again."

We all stood or sat in silence. Sombre. Feeling the poor woman's pain. The policeman licked the tip of his pencil and made another note.

Eventually, I spoke. "It was an accident."

"I killed him."

"That is for the enquiry to decide," declared the young policeman, closing his notebook. "But if it is as you say, then I think that it will be seen as an accident there, also."

She did not look up, but I could feel stillness enfolding her.

In due course, Father Vernon spoke. "But I do not understand about Mr Brown's shoes. Did you not say that he was an experienced walker? Did we not hear that they had agreed to walk? It was not the spur of the moment. Would he not have prepared himself properly?"

"He did," she volunteered. "My husband and I had not come for the walking; it was not an interest of ours. We had come for the peace and the rest. We had heard that it was a very tranquil district, up here among the mountains. So when Mr Brown suggested I might make that visit with him to the falls, and I so dearly wished to accompany him, we arrived at an obstacle. I had none of the equipment that he possessed to take the paths we wished responsibly. I could not buy any walking boots because my husband controlled all our money. It would have been an extraordinary request of mine to seek funds for such an item as a pair of walking boots. Mr Brown offered to pay, but I would hear none of it. So we found another solution."

"Which was…?" I asked. Despite the solemnity of the occasion, I could not wait to hear the solution to the riddle that had vexed me from the moment I had laid eyes upon the poor fellow's body.

"I would wear his studded boots and he would wear his town shoes. He would use his alpenstock for stability and, on rougher sections of the route, I would take his arm. Together, across relatively undemanding terrain, we felt that we could make the distance in reasonable safety. I had always been cursed, I had felt, with big feet. But on this occasion, I felt them to be a blessing. At first, anyway. The boots were still a size or two too big, but two pairs of Mr Brown's thick woollen socks compensated. They would also prevent blisters, he told me. I returned the socks to his room. His key hung in the office behind the reception desk. I collected it and returned it when everybody was busy preparing the evening meal."

"Along with the boots and the alpenstock?" I offered.

"I could not return home alone without the security of the alpenstock."

"But you did not raise the alarm?" asked the policeman.

"I went down to look at him, in case he was still alive. He was not. I did not know what to do. I had killed him. He was dead. It was not as if I could bring him medical help. I panicked."

"And the pipe knife," I mused out loud. "You forgot that you had it and only discovered it when you had unpacked, after you had replaced the other items and the key…?"

"Yes."

"So, what about the pipe knife with the initials P. B. that was discovered at the foot of the falls and mentioned in the newspaper?"

She looked at me blankly. "I do not know anything of such a knife or such a newspaper story."

The policeman had not heard of this either, and reopened his notebook. Everything was not quite as cut-and-dried as clearly he had begun to suppose it was.

"I put it there."

A voice, hoarse and subdued, drifted across to us from the corner of the room.

"I put it there," repeated Holloway, now that he had attracted our attention. "I had one engraved. I had taken a copy of the hotel skeleton key Eva had lent me. She found out later and was disgusted." He looked around the room and found little sympathy in the faces of anyone there, either. "I had a case to solve…" he pleaded.

This at least put the incident in the café that I had witnessed into perspective. Holloway, having offended and been admonished by the woman to whom he had been desperately and instantly attracted, sought solace in further female company. Francesca, on the other hand, was… well… her naturally solicitous self.

The young man continued, "I took one of your visiting cards from your room, doctor. I had a pipe knife engraved P. B. I bought myself some smoking implements of my own in the process. I took the knife down into the valley and found my way round to the bottom of the Reichenbach gorge. There I tossed it into the rough where it looked as though it had fallen, but where it was nonetheless visible. I then went and introduced myself to the editor of the newspaper as you, doctor. I told him I was investigating a case. The case of the missing pipe knife, if you like. This knife." He delved into a pocket and produced the counterfeit object. "It was returned to me by the newspaper office when they had no further use for it."

"Why did you do it?" Father Vernon asked.

"I could not bear the good doctor's arrogance and pomposity. I had become certain, through my association with him, that his theories were all bunkum. Despite his 'wonderful and much-admired' consulting detective stories, he had found nothing of real value, or so I had thought; he had blundered and pontificated with no hard facts. I believed it to be the Pivcevics. It was only a matter of time before something to prove my theory would turn up. I just believed I was helping matters along, that's all. I had found the ouzo, hadn't I? That was proof, wasn't it? Proof enough."

"You went into our room and took the bottle-top?" asked Pivcevic, incredulously. For my part, I wondered briefly if he had not taken against the Pivcevics specifically because they had had no opium, although coming from that particular crossroads between East and West, he had unfairly assumed otherwise.

"I went into everybody's room. Just to see." Holloway shrugged. "I found the ouzo and reached my conclusions…" He shook his head mournfully. "They were wrong. I was wrong. And I nearly ended up causing – what? Two more deaths up there at the falls? How could I have been so stupid? I was idiotic. I'm sorry. I am so sorry."

I did not know what to say. None of us knew. So we stood and stared at our shoes for a while, contemplating the complexities of humankind.

The policeman closed his notebook once more. "Perhaps I shall need to have a further conversation about your behaviour, sir." He directed this at Holloway. "You are not purposing to leave in the next day or so?"

Holloway shook his head.

"Come," said Anna Pivcevic at length, and took mevrouw van Engels by the hands to raise her off the chair. "We must get you back to your husband – he needs to know." She looked across to the policeman who nodded his permission.

"No! I could not possibly." She backed away against the wall in dismay.

"There is no need. I am here." A further voice came from the doorway.

"How long have you been there?" demanded the policeman.

"I came to look for my wife," said Professor van Engels. "Or is that a crime now, too? I was going to look out on the street. Sometimes I find her wandering out there alone, during the day or late at night. I never thought to ask why."

"What did you hear?" asked Father Vernon, joining Anna Pivcevic beside the lady in a gesture of protection and support.

"I heard that I have been a blind, selfish, self-centred, brutish bully to my wife. I heard that, as a result, my dear wife understandably turned to another for companionship, human society, a gentle response to her honest needs. I heard that, because of how I have behaved towards my wife over these past years, and especially these past months, she has been driven to distraction. I heard that, as a result, a terrible and infinitely regrettable accident has occurred. I heard that if there is anyone ultimately to blame

354

for all of this, if there is anyone who really needs the forgiveness of others, it is I."

He had walked into the middle of the room and had addressed each one of us in turn.

We could see that he had been crying.

Twenty-Two

I was on the way to Meiringen, the town which lent its name to the whisked egg and sugar dessert invented by Gasparini. Father Vernon had a friend who ran a hotel there and who had wired to say that he would be delighted to put me up for the second part of my stay in Switzerland. We had discussed options. I was now clear of any blame. There was in any event no substantive case to answer, except, perhaps, that of wasting police time by fleeing from justice and hiding up in the hayloft. But no one, not least the policeman, had felt the need to pursue that matter. Nonetheless, I did not feel I could remain there any longer. It had been a very unpleasant experience: séances; being hounded over mountains in the middle of the night; being shot at; and nearly meeting my end not once but twice at the Reichenbach Falls. I had therefore resolved to complete my stay somewhere else. Where they did not know me. Should I ever return to this country, with my family, I would find another district altogether. Stevenson tells me Davos is particularly fine.

Father Vernon had joined me in my room to help me pack and to accompany me at least part of the way. I had decided to spend the afternoon walking to my next destination. Blow the cobwebs away, so to speak. Clear my mind and make a new start. I was pleased to see that in honour of our little adventure upon the Eiger, he wore his friar's habit but studded walking boots. Having arranged for my baggage to be taken ahead in a cart, I hitched my knapsack onto my shoulders, put on my hat, took up my ice axe, bade one last farewell to the mountains out of my balcony window and set off with him downstairs.

We had said our goodbyes to the Pivcevics earlier, very much earlier, that morning. We had walked with them to their room following the interview with van Engels. We had talked for an hour about the events, and then the priest and I had bid them farewell at that point. They would be sleeping long into today.

In the lobby, Anton, Holloway and Eva were waiting. I was somewhat surprised to see the latter two together. Holloway had been making his peace with her. An uneasy peace, it would appear. He continually cast timid, if admiring, glances in the young woman's direction. Eva was all sunshine and light again. Goodness, health and joy exuded from every pore. A superb advertisement for her sex, her country and her people. Tall and gangling, fit and vital, her eyes smiled and her spirit thrived in the fresh mountain air. I remember thinking to myself, as I had thought when I first met her – could it only have been at the beginning of this week? – if only I were a few years younger. But then I was married, and thoroughly happily, too. So enough of that.

We stopped and talked for a short while.

"I suppose you, too, shall be leaving, now that this is all concluded," I said to Holloway.

"In fact, doctor, I've decided to remain in the village a while longer. Not least because the police still want to discuss my part in this whole affair. Eva has agreed to stand beside me." They exchanged a smile. "Not sure how the villagers will treat me, though; not after everything I put them through…"

"I will look after you," said Eva, and gave his hand a squeeze.

It was clear that he was going to try to fight through his personal battles. He had no one really to go back to, and he had everything here that he needed to help him; in other words – Eva. He had a mania, of that there was no doubt, and this had driven him to further, nearly disastrous, excesses. I imagine that, too, would have been Holmes's fate had I left him alone with his cocaine habit and his boredom. But he intended to make a new start, get a grip, make some changes. Holloway, that is.

"Did you know I asked my friend in England about you?"

His eyes betrayed no sign of this knowledge. "I did not. What did they tell you?"

"That although you told me you had gone to Dulwich, you were not, in truth, an Old Alleynian." I was blunt but spoke without rancour.

His face reddened. "I confess I truly do not know why I said that. I apologize unreservedly."

I accepted his apology. Now was not the time to knock off a scab that had already begun to form. I suspect, for a frustrated young man, such a provenance added a touch of *je ne sais quoi* to his biography. "And what about your claim to have played for Blackheath? I understand that this was the more legitimate claim."

He bowed his head in discomfiture. "It was there at the Rectory Field that I first heard of you and your stories. I had felt an affinity, I suppose one would describe it, and had pursued you through the pages of Lippincott's and The Strand. Eventually I even discovered where you lived. I had taken, in my spare time, to wandering around the streets near your home on the off-chance of catching a glimpse of you." He gave a short, mordant laugh. "In fact, I had plenty of spare time, as it goes. Although I was by trade a concert violinist, I was not, and presently am not, attached to any particular orchestra or string ensemble."

I wondered if that was only half the truth and that in fact his unstable temperament meant that he was unable to keep a steady job. Another trait of Holmes, exaggerated and contorted, perhaps? This unpredictability manifested itself in the actions he took as he proceeded to relate what he did next.

"Passing you casually on the street one day, I overheard your conversation with your driver. You were loading your valise and trunks onto the four-wheeler immediately prior to your departure for Austria and then Switzerland. A moment of madness and I was convinced that it would be fascinating to pursue you. Hoping perhaps to 'bump into you' by chance and…" Now he looked painfully shamefaced. Bringing such matters out into the cold light of day revealed them to be the follies that they were. I noticed, though, that during this speech, observing his awkwardness, Eva had laid her hand on his arm. "…and maybe I would even end up your lifelong friend. So I raced back to my rooms in order that I might collect the wherewithal – money, papers – to embark upon what I now perceive to be a woefully misguided quest and try to catch up with you at Waterloo. I discovered that I had missed you, so I followed on and, eventually, knowing sufficient of your further travel plans… managed to eventually coincide with you at the Zürich terminus."

I was astonished.

"But I insist, doctor, that I am truly a reformed character. I now see where such obsessive behaviour leads: to the top of a fall, and perilously close to going right over it. It will not be a feature of my personal practices again. I swear it."

"I am glad to hear it."

Eva just smiled and gave Holloway's hand another squeeze.

I then handed Anton a package. "Would you see that Professor van Engels gets this, please?"

He took it from me and nodded. It was the Dutchman's story. Unread.

We made our farewells. I reminded Anton that I was at his service at any time, for whatever reason. It was an offer with which he seemed genuinely pleased. I had the effrontery to give Eva a peck on the cheek. I trust we both enjoyed the gesture but, doubtless, for entirely different reasons. Then, with no little relief, I shook Holloway's hand gravely and finally left that mad, bad and dangerous-to-know young fellow behind once and for all. I was leaving him in a welcoming, supportive community, a healthy environment, and Eva's care. If anyone could give a person reason to reform and make the most of themselves, Eva could. It is amazing what the love of a good woman can do.

I turned to go, but suddenly Holloway called after me: "Oh… Doyle?"

"Yes?"

Almost apologetically he held out his hand. I thought for a moment that he was going to shake mine again. But then I saw it was clasped around something. He turned his hand over and opened his fingers. There on the palm lay a thin, metallic object. It was the counterfeit pipe knife he had bought. "I thought you would like this…"

Wordlessly, I took it and left.

Outside Father Vernon and I encountered Monsieur and Madame Plantin taking the air. We began to say our goodbyes, but Marie stopped us.

"I wish to thank you, doctor. For my husband and I have, indeed, begun discussing things. To be honest," she continued in that delightfully insouciant way she had, "Marcus has improved his temperament noticeably as a result."

Plantin gave her a friendly, but nevertheless disconcerted, glance. If it were unseemly to be thus embarrassed in public, however, he allowed himself on this occasion to be overruled by his wife's love and concern. Long might it continue, I thought.

"This new openness will take some getting used to," he remarked, with a rueful smile. "But it is true. It had reached such a situation that I had become furious with poor Mr Brown, who, I understand, you have discovered fell by accident – which to my mind was always the case."

"So it would seem." I did not volunteer any further information. None was sought.

"I am so ashamed of my ill-feeling towards the gentleman. I regret particularly that I had admonished him heartily the day of his tragic demise. I would not wish him dead. But he had been always so morose. He obstinately refused to enjoy the beauty of his surroundings and the opportunities for enjoying them. Opportunities which, in my case, were far more limited." He tapped his legs. "But now I see that this anger was as much a fault in myself as in the gentleman. I regret to say, I similarly admonished the hotel proprietor's young daughter, Eva. Marie, having witnessed that, began to tell me that enough was enough, and it was that event that meant we started talking. Talking properly. Eva, I am pleased to say, has forgiven me my ungracious outburst."

I understood entirely and reminded him that while he had this beautiful landscape to enjoy, he also had other things in which he might justifiably rejoice. At which point I took the liberty of now pecking Marie on the cheek. I shook the Frenchman's outstretched hand and Father Vernon and I took our leave of them.

We stepped out briskly along the main street. As we walked, Father Vernon fumbled through the slit at the hip in his habit into a trouser pocket beneath. He subsequently produced a piece of paper.

"Before I forget, I was asked to give this to you."

I took it and noted that it was another telegram from Flemyng. Doubtless the answer to my questions regarding Francesca and Frau von Denecker. However, I was in no position to read it, as it was simply a ticker-tape stream of cricket scores like before. Another Netherlands match against Hull at Kingston upon Hull, it would seem. Followed by Middlesex vs Surrey at Lord's. I was able to note, at least, that Baldwin, Richardson and Wood were in for Streatfeild, Sharpe and Clarke. None of whom had performed terribly well against Nottinghamshire. Perhaps they were replaced, or injured, or were simply otherwise engaged. I could even establish that the information referred to psalms, verses and words 7:5:11; 9:6:21; 3:2:3; 2:1:8; 4:3:17; 23:4:10; 10:2:11; 7:1:11; 3:1:8 respectively. But I was gallingly unable to extract any further information than that.

"Oh dear," I said aloud, "unfortunately I left the materials needed to best... appreciate... this back at the hotel on the library shelf. Would it be too much of a bind if we returned for a short while?"

"No need." The Franciscan stared playfully ahead as he spoke. "Apparently, I am told it says: *Let Them Be. People Will Shadow Them. Trust Me.*"

I stopped. My lower jaw hung open. "How did you...?"

He said nothing in return. He simply carried on walking and I caught him up. A moment later and he looked up pointedly. My eyes followed the direction in which his were indicating. I could see Frau von Denecker upon her balcony leaning on her silver-topped cane. She nodded her goodbye and smiled as graciously as always. I doffed my hat in return. Two ships of the line rendering passing honours could not have offered a more dignified scene. And then I understood.

My assessment of the relationship between the sensual French/Italian woman and the distinguished Prussian/Austrian woman was perhaps not as misguided as I had begun to believe. And, of course, this priest accompanying me plainly knew more about such matters than he would ever begin to admit to. Or was it simply that he was just their father confessor? Involved, yet not involved? In the world, yet not of the world? It could quite simply be that he had been concerned for me, as it was his duty to be concerned for all humankind. Perhaps Frau von Denecker had advised him, without offering any details, that he needed to be concerned for me; that his best policy, she may have told him, was to encourage me to leave the village as soon as practicable – as soon as it was clear I had not been involved in any shenanigans with regard to Brown's death.

It did explain who was reading my wires and why they had been so keen that I leave. In my investigation, anything might have been uncovered. Things that had nothing to do with the puzzle that needed to be solved but were nonetheless highly sensitive; dangerous, volatile, even. I realized that mine was a simple code, after all. One eminently decipherable with the kind of resources available to a great state and its intelligence machinery. I supposed that they would move on soon, too, Francesca and Frau von Denecker. Find another country. Lay low until the great wheels of history turned and Francesca's "uncanny" powers were needed again. Deep, deep and turbulent waters indeed. It was best a simple doctor and writer stayed clear of them, for fear of slipping over the edge and drowning.

We had, by now, reached the end of the village and were beginning to turn our toes eastward. My way passed along the great ridge above the valley that ran like a giant's spine beneath the austere gaze of the great mountain range south of us. At that moment we were hailed from behind. We stopped and turned. Francesca ran to catch us up. She looked as beautiful as ever in the bright morning sunshine.

"I wanted to say goodbye. I saw you out of my window. I wanted to say goodbye."

We looked at each other for a moment.

"I am sorry about Hugo," I said. "Tell him I apologize."

"I will tell him. And he apologizes also."

"Does he?"

"I will tell him that he apologizes. He is a good man. But he is also very stubborn."

"This much I realized." I could still feel the bruises.

"So."

"So…"

"I am glad that you are going. For you. But I am sad that you are going. For me."

"Thank you. That means a great deal to me."

"And I wanted to thank you…"

"For what?"

"For being honest. When you came to see me."

I looked at her steadily before I replied. "Honesty is the best policy."

"Sometimes it is not possible to be honest."

"I understand." I looked into her deep brown soulful eyes and wished that I could linger there a moment longer. But that too was not possible.

"Well, goodbye then." I held out my hand.

She stepped forward daintily, and rose up onto her toes so that I might kiss her proffered cheek. I leaned forward and, as I did so, she turned her face slightly. As a result, in the act of kissing her cheek, I also caught the corner of her mouth and I tasted her lips. It was electric and I knew, at that moment, though we might never meet again, I would always remember her fondly. She was undoubtedly very good at making men remember her.

Then she turned on her heel and walked quickly back to her home, and her husband; whom, despite everything, it was clear she loved.

We too turned upon our route.

As we walked, we discussed the Bible. Father Vernon talked about the work being done to unpick that which appeared anomalous in Scripture. Why one Gospel might say one thing and another Gospel might contradict it. It was down to how Scripture had come to be put together. The work also involved looking deeply into the beliefs and customs of the people who had written the words down for future generations to cherish. He told me about the quest to unearth the historical Jesus. That extraordinary man who really had lived and breathed and walked upon the earth. The friar told me a little of the extensive research being undertaken by theologians and historians throughout Europe. Work as fascinating and as gripping a detective story as anything any author might come up with. The world had not caught up with this work yet. And it would be a very painful experience when it did. It did not mean that miracles did not happen, nor that Christ did not rise again, he said. But it required many new perspectives and even the church, he noted ruefully, would have difficulty coming to terms with all of it. It could take years, decades, centuries perhaps. Revelation was not static, it was emergent. Otherwise it would be a dead religion. God walked alongside humankind. He did not simply set them adrift in a boat to fend for themselves.

"And your moral?"

"Be flexible. Be flexible like me, otherwise you will break."

We marched on in silence for a while. I could hear the crickets rasping like rubbed straw and the hillsides ringing with cowbells.

"Thank you for restoring my faith," Father Vernon said, at length.

"In God?"

"No, I always have faith in him. Or rather, he always has faith in me. No… my faith in humankind. Although 'kind' may not quite be the appropriate word."

Physician, heal thyself, I thought.

We heard a distant gunshot. The report reached the mountains and made them shout it out among themselves.

"Werner."

Father Vernon nodded. "Possibly. He is a very complicated fellow. But noble, despite his bluff exterior."

"I believe you are right. Mevrouw van Engels had received a violent mark upon her cheekbone. You do not think he could have advanced upon her and she threw him off?"

"Far from it. More likely she advanced upon him for comfort and in confusion. Being despite outward appearances very much the gentleman, he may have tried to extricate himself and she stumbled. Something like that. Despite all his hunting rifles, his is a gentle soul."

"Is it possible that this landscape might eventually make anyone gentle?"

"It is more than a possibility. It is fact. Everyone succumbs eventually."

We reached the Reichenbach Falls a short time later. I was looking forward to my first hearty meal in Meiringen. But there was something I had to do first.

We arrived at the head of the great fall and listened to its thunder for a moment. I then produced Holloway's counterfeit pipe tool.

"What are you doing with that?"

"I am going to throw it down into the waters, where it belongs."

We stood in silence for a moment.

"Did you not tell me how you tried to conjure up the spirit of Holmes? Do you think you managed this?" the priest asked.

I thought long and hard about all that had happened. "I don't know."

"Spirits and phantasms. Murders, victims, criminals. They all have risen out of nowhere. You must ask yourself if this was a trick of the mind or are there, indeed, other forces beyond this, beyond our understanding?"

I looked again at all the events of the past week. From one perspective it was absolutely true. I had conjured something out of nothing. Not wholly my fault, of course, but nevertheless the fact remained. A complete Sherlock Holmes case had risen as a wraith out of the mist and, for a while, had taken a very real shape. It had become painfully tangible. Then, almost as quickly as it had come, it had simply dissolved like the morning dew. Undoubtedly there were issues and concerns. But they belonged to another time and place; the realm of high politics and diplomacy and cloak-and-dagger people. The people who truly belonged to that other, fantasy world were the best equipped to dwell on those planes of existence.

But there was something else. I had enjoyed it. The whole experience had been confusing, frustrating, dismaying, terrifying and outrageous. I had never been so frightened or so scandalized in my entire life. Yet, and this was perhaps the most outrageous thing of all, I would not have missed it for worlds. As far as the investigating was concerned, I had been both a bumbler and an oaf. But I had, it had to be said, bumbled and oafed my way to a reasonably satisfactory and justifiable conclusion. I had not been as prescient as I might have wished throughout the whole affair. But then I was just a rank amateur, after all. What had happened, though, was that I had acquired the taste for detection. Heretofore, it had been a diverting pastime to write my stories. All the adventures through which I had forced my hero had resulted in the experiences being vicarious ones for me. Holmes and Watson enjoyed the thrill of the chase on my behalf, so to speak. Experiencing it for myself, I had found that there was much to relish, much to learn and many techniques to ·quire. That brought out the eternal student and scientist in me. It ·my opinion that plainly, with my reputation as a constructor of detective fiction, I might well find that others may also choose to bring their real-life cases to my attention.

Holmes, I realized, standing there at the top of the Reichenbach Falls, had changed my entire life. Even in these last few days, despite the exasperations and even the terrors I had undergone, there was no doubt that he had acted as something of a restorative. He had reinvigorated me. He had swept away my growing cynicism and world-weariness. He had reintroduced me to my enjoyment of my own humanity and humankind in general. Yes, unlike Father Vernon, I did mean kind. Always kind, as a species, despite the efforts of individuals and groups to sully that reputation. I had much to be grateful to Mr Sherlock Holmes for. But, it was also clear, he must now be put behind me. Just as this whole affair would be. I did not know how I would do it. I was committed to a further sequence of stories, but I resolved there and then, perched at the edge of that great force of water, that I would find some way of finishing the Holmes stories for ever. Something spectacular, perhaps. Noble and courageous and highly moving. Having said that, I told myself, even if I were to dispose of Holmes there was no reason why I might not also bring him back to life again. If the time were right. When the world needed him again. When everything in my life was in better perspective.

Who knows? I thought. *As Father Vernon advised, be flexible.*

I cast the pipe tool down into the chasm. I watched it briefly glint silver, and flash like a leaping salmon in the watery sunlight. It spun and plummeted, skipped off a couple of crags, performed a final exultant cartwheel, and plunged into the milky green froth, to disappear for ever from view.